DARK LAKES: THREE-BOOK COLLECTION

MAGIC EATER | BLOOD STONES | PAST SINS

M.V. STOTT

BECOME AN INSIDER

MAGIC EATER

1

I suppose this all started when I woke up without a single clue as to who I was, where I was, or why I was bleeding from so many different and interesting places.

My name is Joseph Lake, or at least that's what I've decided to call myself. Not the most inspiring of choices, I know, but I couldn't find anything else that felt comfortable, so Joseph Lake it was. The fact that it stuck made me wonder if the name meant something; like maybe it was a family member's name, or a good friend's, or even a good enemy's, but I Googled that thing down to a nub and ended up with nothing. Just one of many deader than dead ends I've chased aimlessly ever since I woke up next to that lake.

That was ten years ago. At the point this story kicks off proper I was stalking the streets of Carlisle in the middle of the night, dressed head-to-toe in black. This was my first time following a stranger at a discreet distance, but I'd seen enough movies to know the best colour outfit to wear for a good stalk. To begin with, I'd even been wearing matching black shades, but it soon became apparent that this was not my brightest idea. What with the whole night-time thing. Yeah, I didn't feel too smart as I shoved those in my back pocket, I can tell you (even less so when I sat on my backside and crushed the things).

The stranger I was following was a homeless woman who looked like a charity shop threw up over a passing Helena Bonham Carter. Or in other words, like Helena Bonham Carter. She'd been tossing up red flags in my head for the last two months, so a bit of following seemed in order.

Anyway, back to my mysterious origin story. I was found by a fisherman named Joseph (hence the forename), face-down, and very, completely naked beside Derwentwater, which is one of several bodies of water that make up an area known as the Lake District in the far north of England. Yup, you got it, from thence derives my surname.

Wait, that's a lie, I wasn't completely naked, I still had one sock on. I still have that sock. It's the only clue I have of my past life and who I really am, though it's difficult to extrapolate much from a sock other than, "I wore socks." Even Sherlock Holmes would need more to go on than that, unless I've skipped over *Sherlock Holmes and the Man Who Wore Socks*.

It was chilly out. I pulled my long coat tight around myself as I did my best to keep a discreet distance from the homeless woman, who seemed to be aimlessly wandering here, there, and nowhere in particular. She'd been showing up a lot recently. Not just hanging out by the cash machine I passed on my way to work, or pushing a trolley full of tin cans past me on the high street. No, she'd been turning up all over the place. I'd look out my bedroom window and she'd be sat across the street. I'd get to work and she'd be lurking in the car park, going through the bins. It felt a lot like she was following me. In the end I thought, well, two can play at that game.

So, there I was. Following a homeless woman around the streets of Carlisle—Cumbria's only city—in the middle of the night. No, *you* have too much time on *your* hands.

I'm sure most would have brushed the woman's arrival as coincidence, but when you have my kind of strange and stunted history, you tend to see the weird shining out from the ordinary and coincidental. No, this wasn't one of those situations where you buy a pair of red trousers and suddenly you start noticing people wearing red trousers everywhere you look. This woman was following me, I was sure of it. Keeping tabs on me for reasons yet to be ascertained.

A little part of me even hoped it was because she recognised me. Maybe I'd been a tramp, too, before... well... before whatever happened happened and I wound up unconscious by a lake wearing nothing but a sock and an all-over bruise. Maybe that's why it had been so difficult to find anything out about my past; perhaps I'd been on the streets for years, away from polite society, living off the grid.

The tramp stopped and turned, so I ducked into the doorway of a betting shop that stank sharply of piss. For a moment it looked as though she was going to walk back the way she came and discover me lurking in my not-too-discreet, urine-scented hidey-hole, but then her head twitched to the left and she darted off down an alley. I counted to five then sprinted after her, coat tails flapping, heart pounding, grinning a lot more than I should have been.

I didn't want to bust out of the alleyway and find myself smacking into the back of my quarry, so I slowed down to a walking pace, one hand trailing along the old, crumbling brickwork that lined the narrow crack between two shops.

And that's when the first strange thing happened.

As my fingers traced the old bricks, a peculiar mood descended upon me. It was... *fear*. No. Not just fear, fear mixed with hunger, mixed with pain, mixed with desire. It felt like it was washing over me again and again, a multitude of disparate emotions and memories, like I was pegged to a beach and the sea's waves were battering against me, over and over, and if I didn't get away quickly I might just drown in all of the intoxicating, terrible feelings of dread and—

A scream.

My hand snapped away from the bricks of the alleyway and my head dropped back into the here and now.

There had been a scream. Not in my head, not in whatever weird thing it was that I'd just experienced, but out there, in the night. Not a fun scream. Not a *playing around and being young and boisterous and drunk* scream. No, this was a real blood-curdler. A proper, *"For God's sake, won't somebody help me?"* scream.

I ran toward the sound.

As I burst out of the dark of the alley and into the comparatively bright square, my foot kicked something heavy, and I found myself sprawling over the obstruction and tumbling to the cobbles, my head bouncing painfully as it connected with the ground.

I lay there for a few seconds, getting my breathing under control and trying to decide whether to throw up or not. I went with *not*. I pushed myself into a sitting position, the world tilting, and gingerly placed a finger on my throbbing temple. I could already feel a lump rising like that of a cartoon cat struck over the head with an oversized frying pan.

Feeling stupid for not looking where I was going, I peered behind me to see what I'd managed to trip over. I was expecting to see a bag of rubbish, or perhaps a tree root pushing up from a crack in the cobbles. What I was not expecting to see was the body of a woman with her throat torn out.

No, I wasn't expecting that at all.

2

The pain in my head forgotten, I shuffled over to the prone body laid out flat on her back. I swallowed, my throat dry, a metallic tang in my mouth that made me want to gag.

'Hey...' I said, my voice emerging as an arid whisper. 'Are you... are you okay...?'

Yes, it was a stupid question, but I think I can be forgiven for it, bearing in mind the circumstances. After all, it's not every day a person happens across the body of a violently murdered woman.

The victim looked to be in her early thirties, her eyes still wide and staring blankly up at nothing. What was the last thing those eyes saw, I wondered. At what point had she realised her life was about to be given a savage and painful full stop? I felt a fist of anger clench in my stomach.

Now that I was closer I could see that not all of the blood on the ground was made up of random splashes and sprays. Some of it looked as though it had been arranged in patterns. Delib-erate shapes. Occult symbols written in an unknown language that made me feel strange to look at. It almost seemed as though the shapes quivered. Like they buzzed with a dark energy. Impossible, though, surely? I concentrated again on the blood and found it static this time. I must have been imagining things. A product of bashing my skull on those cobbles, no doubt.

Had the tramp murdered this woman? She'd come this way, but surely she couldn't have had time to do this. But then where was she? Who carries on running after they stumble across a dead body?

Hands shaking, I reached out and tried for a pulse in case I was wrong about the prone woman's condition. I was not wrong. I shivered; not because of the cold of the night, but because her flesh was already cool to the touch, which was, well, wrong. This had happened recently. The blood was still wet, recently spilled. I looked at the ragged tear in her throat. At the blood pooling out on the ground, mingling with her long, red hair. What could do that? A knife? Or—

Another scream.

Okay, this was too much. This was all much too much. It was dark and scary and dangerous, and it was stupid to even think about going anywhere near that scream. I'm no hero. I should have been getting as far away as possible and calling the police so they could get their arses into gear and sort this mess out. So why were my stupid feet carrying me smack bang into the jaws of danger?

'Stupid, stupid feet...'

I crossed the little square in record-breaking time and raced down another alleyway. This time it didn't open up, but turned left, then right, before finally emerging into a back street behind a parade of shops. As I stepped out, I had the forethought to look at the ground to make sure I didn't go tumbling over another dead body.

No dead body this time. That was a good start.

I looked around, senses straining for any indication of danger, my every nerve ending feeling like it was tingling, achingly alive. There were large, overflowing bins and big metal skips. Gates leading into shop backyards. Another alley in the distance, leading the way out. Plenty of places to hide. To lurk. To coil up and pounce on anyone foolhardy enough to investigate.

Everything was quiet, like the back alley was holding its breath to see what would happen next. I hoped it was something nice and not at all deathy.

Okay, Joe, get a hold of yourself.

Something moved: a shape, a dark patch of the world, something my eyes wanted to ignore. It leapt from the shadows and barged into me, knocking me down. As I headed for the ground I reached out to grab hold of something—clothing, a limb, anything—and my fingers brushed against something wet and cold and—

Hunger, Hunger, Hunger.

So many screams, so much blood, and Christ, the need, the need, it never stops, never ceases, it's just there-there-there, demanding more, and they scream as I approach and I like that, I exist for that moment, and then the feast! The feast! I can gorge on their fear and their... the fox waved, I could see his face smiling back at me. The fox wore a little helmet, and seemed over the moon that I was—

It cut out as quick as it started, the terrible hunger, the taste in my mouth, the overpowering need to gorge on... on awful things, was pulled away and I was on my knees, teeth bared, fingers digging painfully into my chest. Wincing, I pulled my hands away and sagged, panting, glad that whatever had just happened was over.

But of course, it wasn't over. There was more horror to come.

I looked to where the... the thing, the dark shape, had emerged from and saw two feet sticking out. Another woman. Another corpse. What the hell was happening? All I'd been doing was a little light stalking and I'd stepped into a nightmare.

'Help... help...'

She was alive. Holy buggering shit, she was still alive!

I scrambled over on my hands and knees to find her curled up, bloodied, but still breathing. I must have surprised the attacker; spooked them before they finished the job.

'Please... please...'

'Hey, hi. It's okay, don't worry, it's okay.'

I burbled these and other words at the woman, relief washing through me as my hands fluttered over her, trying to make sure she didn't bear any wounds that looked immediately life-threatening, like a cleaver sticking out of her neck.

She flinched away at first, or at least, tried to. 'I'm still in me. I'm still in me,' she croaked.

'What? What do you mean?'

'Don't take it, please, please, it's mine, it's...'

'It's okay, don't panic, you're going to be okay. What's your name?'

But that's all she managed to say before she shuddered and passed out. I yanked out my phone and dialled for an ambulance, praying to God, Buddha, and whatever those alien ghost things are Tom Cruise believes in, that she survived until the paramedics showed up.

3

The chairs in hospital waiting rooms always seem to have been selected with your discomfort in mind. I sat, dog-tired and wide awake, in one such object of torture as the strip lighting overhead coughed and spluttered and did its best to tease out a fresh migraine.

'Chloe will be out in a minute, love,' said Big Marge from behind her reception desk. Big Marge was in her late fifties, with enormous barmaid hair and a neck that, through some optical quirk, appeared to be thicker than the head perched on top of it.

'Thanks, Marge.' I dragged myself up, headed over to the coffee machine, and got myself a disgusting styrofoam cupful.

'What exactly were you doing out there in the middle of the night, anyway?'

'Just, you know... exercise. General walky exercise. Leg stuff. Circulation is important. You don't want to clot. Never want to clot. Clots are killers.'

Big Marge looked me up and down. 'Mm-hmm...' There was a rumour in the hospital that Marge used to earn money travelling around unsavoury pub backrooms and beating all-comers in arm wrestling bouts. Knowing her the way I did, I saw no reason to doubt that.

I was no stranger to Carlisle Hospital, or to Big Marge. I work at the hospital as a caretaker, cleaner, and all-around handyman. It pays terribly, and the canteen lunches do nothing for my figure, but it settles the bills and allows me plenty of freedom. I used to wonder what job I had before I woke up with my life missing, but nothing sparked any sense of recognition, and I couldn't for the life of me find a stand-out aptitude in myself that helped narrow things down. As far as I could make out, I wasn't that great at most things. The idea that perhaps I was a homeless person, a drifter, like my mysterious lady friend, was starting to make a lot of sense

'You Joseph Lake?'

I jumped at the unexpected intrusion, causing piping-hot coffee to spill over my fingers. I swore and waggled my hand around like I was trying to fling off a piece of sticky tape. A woman in a sensible suit and a dark red leather jacket stood before me, screaming "police" from every pore. I should also say that she was black, but only because that's such a rare sight in Cumbria. Around here you're about as likely to stumble across a troll under a bridge as you are an individual not sporting a paste-white face.

'Hi!' I said. 'Sorry, I didn't hear you sneaking up on me.' I held up my burnt fingers, which were already turning a nice shade of rouge. 'Good job we're in a hospital, eh? Efficient.'

'I didn't sneak up on you, I walked up on you.' Her voice was clipped and to the point. She seemed like the kind of person who didn't like to waste ten words when six would do the job just fine.

'Well, that is one light-footed walk you have there. You'd make a great thief, you could walk right into a sleeping person's bedroom and clear the place out without making a peep.'

'I'm not a thief.'

'Glad to hear it.'

'Nor a murderer.'

'Great, me neither,' I replied. 'Messy business. Plus, not a huge fan of blood. I mean, I'm a big fan of it when it stays inside our bodies, in its proper, you know, "venue", but not when it gets out and about. Not when it goes out to party.'

'You Joseph Lake?'

'Of course, I do come across blood quite a lot, as you can probably imagine,' I said, gesturing around my place of work, 'I think that's actually helped me master the distaste a little. Otherwise, stumbling across the kind of thing I did tonight would have sent me into a bit of a puke frenzy.' I mimed puking. 'Which actually is great for another reason as I have a weird phobia about throwing up outdoors.'

'Please answer the question.'

'I am Joseph Lake,' I said quickly. 'Well, not really. Joseph Lake is what I decided to call myself. Sorry, long story.'

'Woke up by a lake, memory loss, I've already heard it.'

'Oh, okay.'

'So, you're Joseph Lake?'

'Yes, ma'am.'

'Great. Glad we've got that established.'

She looked at me with disdain, sniffed, and pulled out her regulation notepad. She had a natural, scary authority to her that was at once terrifying and deeply attractive. I was pretty sure she could beat the crap out of me with little to no effort.

'Are you new? I asked. 'I've not seen you around here before.'

'Been here a couple of months. Transferred from London.'

'Ah, that explains the accent, I was actually going to bring that up.'

'I know I have an accent.' She looked at me as though she were a scientist peering through a microscope at a particularly troubling specimen.

'So, you know my name, and you are...?'

'Detective Maya Myers.'

'Ah, "Detective". A beautiful name for a boy or a girl.'

I gave her my best winning smile. She arched one eyebrow slightly then looked back down at her pad with a dismissive sniff.

'How is she?' I asked. 'The other one, I mean. The not-dead one.'

'Still not dead, but it's touch and go.'

I felt my body begin to relax. I hadn't realised until that moment just how clenched up I'd been since finding the woman laid out in the street, so close to death.

'So she's not dead and everything's great,' I chirped. I did a little twirl and punched the air like I was at the end of a movie, ready for my freeze-frame and end credits.

'Everything's great?' repeated Myers.

'Yup. Great, tip-top, fine and dandy and randy. Not the last one. Nothing about this is randy.'

'One woman is dead, another close to it, and a psychotic murderer is loose on my streets. Everything is not "great".'

I squirmed a little under her glare, went to reply, then thought better of it. She was right. It was stupid of me to react that way, the euphoria had just overtaken me for a second. A woman had lost her life tonight; lost it to someone... to someone not altogether right. I still felt as though the aftertaste of the attacker—well, aura, or whatever it was that I'd experienced when the killer barged past me—was coating the roof of my mouth.

'Mr Lake, what were you doing walking through Carlisle city centre at three a.m.?'

Stalking a woman.

'Me?'

'Yes, you,' replied the detective.

'What was I doing?'

'That was the question.'

'Just, you know... catching the night air. Nothing bad or illegal. You can count on that, one-hundred percent.' I gave her my best *I'm not at all suspicious* smile, and attempted to lean against the coffee machine in a casual manner. The coffee machine turned out to be on my right, not my left, and as I staggered to one side, knocked over a chair, then just about managed to right myself before I crashed to the floor, I began to worry that I was not making the best of first impressions.

'You seem nervous, Mr Lake. Any reason for that?'

'Well, I did just break up a potential double murder, so yeah. I mean, he might come after me. He saw my face. Do I need police protection? Is there a safe house anywhere? Will I be safe in the safe house? Sometimes those things get compromised. I've seen movies.'

Detective Myers closed her notebook and pocketed it. 'You're in shock. I'm going to have a lot of questions for you, so come into the station tomorrow.'

She turned and walked back into the ward. I had the distinct impression that I'd made her "suspicious" list. Which is a bad list to be on when the list belongs to the lead detective of a murder investigation.

'Will do,' I replied. 'I'm actually looking forward to it!' Yeah, bit of a weird thing to say, that.

Big Marge watched Myers exit through the hospital's automatic doors, then turned to me. 'Now, *her* I like.'

4

I was sat on a wall in the hospital car park enjoying a smoke when Chloe finally came to find me.

'As a health professional, I feel it's my duty to point out how bad and stupid that is.'

I smiled and passed it to her.

She leaned against the wall beside me and took a drag. 'Ah, sweet, sweet poison.'

We sat in comfortable silence for a few seconds, watching the sun come up. Chloe Palmer was a doctor at the hospital, and as near to a close friend as I had. She was also very pleasant to look at. Sometimes I got the impression that she was attracted to me, in a holding-hands-and-skipping-through-a-meadow sort of way, but I'm a bit of an idiot when it comes to romance, so I hadn't taken a swing. Better to nurse an unrealised crush for the rest of my life than to take a chance and face thirty seconds of acute embarrassment.

'How is she?' I asked.

'Still alive. She's been knocked around something fierce, though. I had to stitch up a few nasty wounds.'

It suddenly occurred to me that if the assailant had been carrying a knife as they pushed past me, they could easily have sunk it into me on the way past. I'd taken a hell of a risk chasing after that scream. Being brave and doing the right thing were a bloody dangerous way to go about your day.

'What's her name?' I asked.

'Mary. Mary Taylor. I'm pretty sure her mum used to teach me French at school.'

'Est-ce vrai?'

'Oui.'

'Huh, small world.' I watched as Chloe leaned her head back and sent twin plumes of smoke streaming from her nostrils like a... like a.... sexy dragon? A sexy, non-scaly, wingless, person-shaped dragon. Yeah, let's go with that.

'Here,' she said, passing back the ciggie.

I took a pull. 'What about the, uh... the other one? The dead one?'

'A friend of hers, Janet Coyle. She's in a drawer already, ready for an autopsy in the morning.'

Janet Coyle. I hadn't known her, but having a name made her seem somehow more real. Which was stupid, but true. She wasn't just an anonymous slab of meat and bones that someone had tried to turn into confetti, she was a real person.

I closed my eyes and I was back in the square, knelt by the unfortunate Janet Coyle with her torn-out throat and strange symbols scrawled on the ground in her own spilt blood. Maybe if I'd been a few seconds earlier, she'd have been alive too. As the image stayed with me, Miss Coyle began to fade, and the scrawled shapes and squiggles began to sharpen. To glow, almost, in my mind's eye. I felt like I could see energy pouring out from them, trails snaking up into the air. They felt familiar, somehow. Like I should be able to read them, like it was a foreign language I'd once been fluent in, but had been neglected and lost

'Oi,' said Chloe, shoving my arm and making me stumble to the side a little. 'Not putting you to sleep, am I?'

'No! No, absolutely not. Not been to bed yet. Running on fumes, here.'

'You know, it's a good thing you were there, otherwise we'd have two corpses in there rather than the one. You're sort of... well, a hero, I suppose.'

'A hero?'

'Mm-hm.'

'Huh. Yeah, I suppose I am really.' I passed her back the cigarette.

'What were you doing out and about in the middle of the night, anyway?'

'Oh, you know, just stalking a woman.'

Chloe let the smoke seep lazily from between her parted lips. 'Should I be jealous?'

I laughed, though it came out weirdly high-pitched, so I abandoned it as quickly as possible, hoping Chloe wouldn't notice.

'That was a very strange and high-pitched laugh.'

Damn.

And then I did it again by way of reply, turning it into a little cough for some reason at the end. Chloe cocked an eyebrow, then dismissed it.

'So, stalking, eh? Any particular reason?'

'Well, there's a very curious homeless woman who I'm pretty sure is following me and may be the key to unlocking my strange, unknown and very mysterious past.'

'A homeless woman?'

'Very homeless, and I keep seeing her everywhere. Sometimes three or four times a day. I'll be minding my own business—'

'Perhaps indulging in one of your weird, high-pitched laughs.'

'Right, and I'll turn around and there she'll be, standing right next to me.'

'She's probably just a local nutter.'

'Ah, yes, that is a very distinct possibility, but on the other hand...' I opened my arms wide in a, "Who knows?" sort of way. 'This could be it. A clue. A toe in the door.'

Chloe didn't seem so sure. 'If she pulls out an old syringe and jabs you in the eyeball, don't say I didn't warn you.'

'You have my word.'

Chloe raked a hand through her dark bob. 'Did the police-woman talk to you yet?'

I nodded. 'Detective Myers, yes. I don't think she likes me. She definitely gave off a very heavy *I-don't-like-you* sort of vibe. I'm very receptive to vibes.'

'I'm not surprised, you do tend to give off a spectacularly bad first impression.'

'Um, in what way, exactly?'

'The first time we properly met was when you crashed into my car.'

'There was a bee. I've explained all about the bee on numerous occasions.'

Chloe chuckled, took a drag, and handed a quarter-inch of cigarette back to me. Then—rather unexpectedly, I might add—she turned, smiled, and wrapped her arms around me.

'You're hugging me,' I noted.

'I'm just glad you're safe, you big goon.'

'Right. Shall I hug back, or...?' She let go. 'Nope, good. Nice hug. Brilliant hug.' I gave her a thumbs-up.

She smiled and shook her head. 'Okay, I'd better get back to the grindstone. Go home and sleep.'

'Will do.'

'You can put your thumb down now.'

'Yup.' I put my hand in my pocket and watched Chloe disappear back into the hospital. Now, that was almost definitely a signal of some sort, wasn't it? Almost definitely. Unless... friends hug too. I've seen them do it in sitcoms.

I turned and made my way over to my battered little car, my head full of corpses and Chloe; which made for a weird cocktail. For a second, I thought I saw the homeless woman staring at me from the far end of the car park, but in the time it took to blink, she was gone.

5

I woke up around midday from a muddled dream about torn-out throats, mystical symbols, and Chloe hugs, still feeling dog-tired from the previous evening's strange and awful events. I shuffled my way to the shower and let a blast of frigid water smack the fug out of me.

Let me paint you a picture of my home:

I currently reside in a small, three-room flat in a scenic little town called Keswick, a good forty-five-minute drive from Carlisle. I suppose it would make sense to live closer to the city that I actually work in, but something about living within the boundaries of the Lake District just felt right. Spending longer than a couple of days outside of its boundaries makes me feel antsy, like I'm a baby in the womb who's become disconnected from its umbilical cord.

Also, it just looks nice out here. Keswick has all the picture postcard, countryside trappings you associate with this sort of place: dry stone walls, hills, green bits, sheep, lakes, the awful stink of manure after the farmers muck-spray their fields; all that good stuff. There's also a pencil museum within walking distance of my flat, so don't for a second think this place isn't rock and roll.

The flat I live in might be small and losing a protracted battle with an aggressive strain of creeping mould, but I'd come to think of it as home, and couldn't bear the thought of abandoning it to some stranger. Plus, it was really, really, really (really) cheap, and in my world, cheap trumps a funky smell and a bit of lung fungus any day.

Dried off and a bowl of cereal in hand, I slumped on the ratty couch (which I'd liberated from a nearby skip one fateful night) and brought my laptop to life so I could check on my website. It's a simple site: a large pic of my face with the words "Do You Know This Man?" and a little message board to leave comments. I set it up a few months after I woke up by Derwentwater. At the time, I'd been something of a cause célèbre, with the police and journalists doing their utmost to try and figure out just who the hell I was. I even made a few appearances on the radio and telly, but it all came to nothing. A few people came forward, but they were either mistaken or just trying to soak up a little of the limelight for themselves.

No one who really knew anything poked their head above the parapet. Every lead that was thrown up took us nowhere. Eventually, the police told me I'd better get used to things the way they were. For a while, I'd call in several times a day, but eventually they, pretty firmly, told me to stop doing that. Immediately. They would contact me if anything came up, but it was pretty clear I'd slipped to a low, low priority. Unless someone walked into the station and handed them a bunch of information, the investigation was done.

Not great.

I was meant to accept that I was a man without a past. Without history, family, friends, or lovers. Without memories good, bad or instructive. I was just this new, floundering, gangly beast; a newborn with the body of a man in his mid-thirties. I had a few dark weeks after that realisation sunk in, let me tell you.

Now all that's left is my dogged, some might say "heroic"

(well, they might), determination, and this barely-visited website of mine. I clicked the link and my big face popped up.

'Hello, handsome.'

I checked the message board for fresh comments. As usual, there was nothing new to see. Actually, that's a lie; there was a very helpful comment from a bot who wanted to inform me that their friend made $2000 a week working from home, but it seemed unlikely that this would lead me to my mysterious past, even if I could use the extra moolah.

I closed the laptop and tossed it to one side. I was checking it more out of habit than hope these days. I hadn't seen a new lead in over four years. I was beginning to accept that Joseph Lake was who I was: a hospital handyman with nice hair, a great coat, and an unhealthy interest in the strange. I suppose you could call that my second job—not having nice hair, that's a full-time gig—but looking into the weird and wonderful goings-on in my surrounding area. And it's no lie to say this whole area is bubbling with weirdness. Being one of those weird goings-on myself sparked my interest, and I suppose gave me a distant hope that by exploring other strange happenings in the local area, I'd eventually bump into something useful I should know about myself.

Yeah, so far that hasn't really worked out, but I live in hope.

I have a second website dedicated to my, well, occasionally paid hobby. It's for anyone who wants to hire me to look into something freaky going on in the neighbourhood. Such a request would be my first port of call today.

I slurped down the last of my bowl of Rice Krispies and got dressed. After that, I slipped into my beautiful coat, gave my hair an expert hand-ruffle, plopped on my wide-brimmed hat, and headed for the door.

My poor little car coughed and spluttered as I headed at speed out of Keswick and off to my appointment.

Oh!

That was another thing I did know about my old self: I'm a driver. I had to pass my test again, but the moment I got behind the wheel it was obvious I knew my way around a gear stick.

So, for those of you keeping track, I'm a man who wears socks (at least one) and knows how to drive a car. How the police haven't been able to figure out who I am with those hot leads, I'll never know.

The scenic Lake District opened up before me as I left Keswick behind and tootled down the Borrowdale Road, singing a Weezer song to myself (*Buddy Holly*, naturally). I had to make do with singing the lyrics solo as the car radio didn't, and never had in the time I'd owned it, work. I paid three different people money to rectify this situation, but within days of it being fixed, the newly refurbished radio would conk out again. Fed up of throwing good money after bad, I decided to soundtrack further journeys with my own mouth.

As I drove, Derwentwater—the lake I was discovered naked and bloody beside almost ten years back—slid up to join me. The road I was travelling on hugged close to Calfclose Bay, which was where I was prodded into existence by a fisherman's boot. I've spent many evenings sat at the point I was discovered, looking out across the water, waiting for a spark of something to hit me. A memory. Just one. Some fragment of my life, of what had happened to me. Was I a criminal? Was I the victim of some strange and random attack? Was I a Tory, for Chrissakes?

But no memories or revelations ever came; just the silence of nothing. And sometimes ducks quacking, which really took the edge off my solemn brooding.

Shrugging off my morbid thoughts, I sang louder to cheer

myself up (an Elton John number this time, *Saturday Night's Alright (For Fighting)* if you must know). I soon found myself at the pub I'd agreed to meet my prospective client in. I walked into the cosy bar and winced at the smell of stale beer. The ceiling was stained yellow still by the ghosts of smokers past that had huddled beneath it, puffing away for decades.

I scanned the tables and booths. The clientele was thin on the ground and exclusively male. I purchased a glass of lemonade, a packet of crisps (cheese & onion), and settled down in a corner, swiping a copy of the previous day's paper to flick through. By the time I'd finished my fizzy drink, and leafed through the paper for the third time, I was getting the feeling that I'd been stood up. I was just rising to leave when the door opened and a woman in her late-fifties shuffled in, looking around for the person she was supposed to meet. Putting two and two together, I stood up and beckoned her over.

'Hey there. Mrs Coates, is it?'

She looked around, a little embarrassed by my greeting, then rushed over, sliding into the booth to sit opposite me.

'I'll take that as a yes,' I said.

'Mr Lake?'

'In the flesh. Would you like a lemonade? I've finished mine so this would be an opportune moment to get one in for you while I refresh my own.'

She blinked twice. 'You what?'

'Lemonade? To drink?'

I returned a minute later with a glass of pop in each hand and another packet of cheese & onion pinched between my teeth.

'So, Mrs Coates, why don't we get straight down to brass tacks? You know, that may be the first time I've used that phrase. I should Google where it comes from. "Down to brass tacks". Odd one, isn't it?'

Mrs Coates eyed me warily, as though she'd invited the vicar in for afternoon tea, and only upon allowing him into her living room, realised he was actually a wild mongoose with a switchblade.

'Don't worry, I'm not mad, I just make a poor first impression. I have that on good authority from a friend of mine.'

'Your friend is right,' replied Mrs Coates, swigging back a mouthful of lemonade.

I took a look at the woman sat opposite me—her tightly-permed, blue-rinsed hair, her smoker's mouth puckered like a cat's behind, her tired, lived-in body—and wondered what on Earth she was talking to me for. I was hoping for something juicy to distract me from all the recent murder business. It could be anything, anything at all. A haunting in her mews, a suspected vampire bite sighted on the lily-white neck of her favourite niece, the body of a deceased faerie fished out of her ornamental pond, anything! A potential gamut of weirdness stretched out tantalisingly in front of me.

'Mr Lake, my cat Boris has gone missing.'

Or it could be a missing fucking cat.

'Come again? It sounded like you said you dragged me all the way here because of a cat.'

'Yes. My cat Boris is missing.'

'Yup, that's what I thought it sounded like.' I swallowed a mouthful of pop and a crisp or two.

'I'm beside myself with worry, Mr Lake. My Boris is an inside cat. Oh, occasionally he'll take a little stroll around the garden, but he never crossed the garden fence, he doesn't like it out there. So for him to go missing, for days, even... well, I imagine you can understand my distress.'

She placed a couple of MISSING CAT posters down on the table. Boris the cat looked back at me, one ear white, the other black.

'Mm-hm,' I replied, tipping the rest of the crisps into my mouth and having a good chew. 'Mrs Coates,' I said, trying not to spit crisp shards into her saggy face, 'I'm not really in the beloved pet retrieval business. I'm in the weird, unexplained, and hopefully supernatural business. Unless your cat was of the witch's variety, or perhaps resurrected from a pet cemetery, I'm not entirely sure why you decided to look me up.'

'Oh, well you see, Mr Lake, it's not just my Boris. There's Ginger, too.'

'Ginger?'

'Oh, yes. And Cotton, Sooty, Nemo Bananapants, and that's just the cats from my street. All told, as far as I know, a good twenty-seven cats have gone missing, and all on the same night.'

'Twenty-seven?'

'Twenty-seven.'

'In one night?'

'In one night!'

Hm. Okay, maybe there was something to this story after all. It wasn't the village greengrocer levitating off the ground and speaking in ancient Babylonian, I'll grant you, but that many cats going AWOL in a single night definitely strayed on the weird side. Chances were it was just some local nut with a cat compulsion, or maybe the local fox population was getting bolder, but what the hell, it would help take my mind off the events of the previous night.

'Okay, I'll have a poke around, Mrs Coates. See what's what.'

'Thank you. I do worry for Boris, he should be home and safe.'

'My fee is fifty pounds a day, with a minimum of four days payable.'

'Oh, okay. That's a bit steep.'

'A small price to pay for the hope of rescuing poor, lost Boris, is it not?'

'Of course. Of course, yes.'

I held out my hand. 'Those four days are actually payable upfront. In cash. Paper cash, no coinage, if you please.'

Mrs Coates dug into her bag for her purse.

Two-hundred quid.

Even if the whole cat thing turned out to be a whole load of nothing, as very much suspected, two-hundred smackeroos was not to be sniffed at.

I sipped at my second glass of lemonade and had a think about what I'd like to spend my money on.

6

'You were supposed to be here thirty-three minutes ago,' said Big Marge, eyes fixed on the pages of her suburban infidelity and botched tit-jobs magazine.

I strolled up to the hospital reception desk and gave her a wink. 'Aw, that's nice. Have you been counting the minutes until I showed up? It must be love.'

Big Marge raised an eyebrow then jabbed a meaty thumb in the direction of a mop and bucket. 'I'll tell you what you're not going to love: the three inches of shit up the walls of the second floor Men's.'

She was not wrong.

As I mopped up a stranger's abandoned deposits, I found myself musing once more on my recent terminal encounter. Someone had attacked Mary Taylor and Janet Coyle, and I found it highly unlikely that it was the mysterious tramp who was responsible. No, whoever it was—*whatever* it was—had something of the unnatural about them. I'd felt it in that burst of... of whatever it was that washed over me when our skin briefly touched. Something of the night had attacked those women. Something hungry. No, something *starving*. A patch of dark given life. A shadow that sought to kill and feast. Which sounds crazy, I know, and probably wasn't going to fly too well when I was called up to take part in Detective Maya Myers' no doubt thorough investigation.

Whatever it was that had killed that woman, I could only hope that Mary Taylor had something useful to offer the police so they could cage the animal before it struck again.

'You know, you really have a gift for cleaning up other people's shit,' remarked Neil Smith, doctor and all-round wank puffin, as he entered the toilets and made his way to the urinal to relieve himself.

'Doctor Neil—'

'Doctor *Smith*—'

'Doctor Neil, I'm going to take that as a strange yet genuine compliment as, to do otherwise, would make you seem like a tosspot, and I know you don't want to be thought of as a tosspot.'

Neil made to reply, stumbled as he tried to fully take in my reply, then gave in, zipped up, and began to wash his hands. He eyed me evilly in the mirror. 'I don't like you, Lake,' he said.

'Well, you've certainly kept that close to your chest.'

He narrowed his eyes again, unsure whether I was taking the piss or not. For someone so well-educated, he really was quite slow.

'One day, turd boy, something horrible is going to happen to you. Something worse than horrible. Something just, ooh, awful. And when that happens, I'm going to be there, front row and centre.'

'Something worse than this conversation?'

Doctor Neil grimaced, threw the paper towel he'd been drying his hands on in the bin, and stomped out of the room, swishing his white doctor's coat in a way that didn't at all scream *embittered supervillain*.

I finished up, washed my hands three or four times in scalding hot water, then complied with my stomach's grumblings and went off in hunt of a vending machine. Not every man can think of food after such a near-turd experience, but I have a surprisingly strong constitution for a person of such a remarkably svelte build. Besides, this wasn't the first present I'd been given from the bottom shelf.

'There you are,' said Chloe, rounding a corner as I bit down on the second finger of my Twix.

'Were you looking for me?' I asked, desperately hoping that the smell of excrement wasn't clinging to me like some poop wetsuit.

'In your dreams,' Chloe replied, grinning.

'You just missed another classic Joseph and Doctor Neil showdown.'

'You know he doesn't like it when you call him Doctor Neil.'

'Doctor Neil doesn't like it when I call him Doctor Neil? Did Doctor Neil tell you that, because Doctor Neil hasn't said a thing to me about it.'

Chloe grinned and gave me a playful shove.

'So, how's Mary Taylor?' I asked.

'Alive and awake.'

'She's spoken? Does she know what her attacker looks like? Does she know why he was attacking her, or what he was hoping to get?'

'Whoa, whoa,' said Chloe, raising her arms, 'I'm sorry but I haven't interrogated her to within an inch of her just-about-hung-onto life just yet, Columbo.'

'Right, yes, of course. Though perhaps more Sherlock than Columbo. I would never wear such a ratty coat.'

Chloe rolled her eyes and managed to look so adorable doing it that I practically swooned.

"Gis a bit of that then,' she said, snatching the last of my Twix and sliding it into her mouth in a way that may or may not have made my knees wobble a touch.

'Are you okay?' she asked. 'You've gone a bit pale. Well, paler than normal, so really, really pale.'

'I'm fine. All good in—'

'Please don't say "the hood".'

'—The corridor. All good in the corridor.'

Chloe smiled as she turned and headed away. 'Cheers for the choccy. See you later, Columbo.'

'Yes, but not if I, you know, see you first, you won't. Not in a stalkery way.'

'Oh,' said Chloe, turning on her heel and walking backwards, 'I made a crap-load of chilli last night. It's gotta go if you fancy tea at mine tonight.'

I want you to understand how much self-control it took at that moment not to launch myself from the floor and go for another of those freeze-frames.

'It's a date!' I said. 'Well, no, not a date, but another thing. A meal.'

Chloe shook her head and turned to face where she was going again, disappearing around the corner. 'Come round about seven, yeah?'

'Will do!'

Okay, was that a date? It could be. I mean, I said the word "date" twice. But Chloe didn't, she just said she wanted to get rid of some old chilli before it went bad. Then again, she didn't say it wasn't a date after I mentioned the word date. Twice. Maybe it was a date?

No.

Don't be stupid.

Or...?

I know I sound like a man who has never known the touch of a woman, and there's some truth to that. After waking by Derwentwater ten years ago, I was too preoccupied with just who on Earth I was to really be interested in hitting on the ladies. Plus, well, in some respects, it's like I am only ten years of age. I had no experiences stored in my head from my no doubt legendary sexual history. Not a kiss, not a hand-hold. After a few years, I did make some tentative steps into the world of boy-girl stuff, but then Chloe came into my life and, well… I won't say I've exactly been saving myself for her, but I hadn't been actively trying to give my equipment a thorough means-test either.

And now here we were.

With the maybe-could-be-date.

Chloe and me.

Or is it Chloe and I?

As I pondered the conundrum further, I liberated more chocolate from the vending machine. Once I was done with that, I went to pay the surviving member of the previous night's horror show a visit. I wanted to check that she was well, but I had an ulterior motive. I wanted to be close to her, to see if any of that residual weird sensation I felt the night I found her was still there. The strange feelings and sights that had washed over me. See if I could make sense of it. See if she was in any fit state to answer a soft question or two about exactly who she was, why she was in hospital, and who her friend in the morgue was.

I was going to try and put it more delicately than that though. I may be an idiot, but I'm not an *idiot*.

I tapped softly on the door then stepped inside.

'Hi, Mary, are you awake?'

The only response I got came from her heart monitor, *beep-beep-beeping* a faint hello. It was as the door closed behind me and I stepped towards the bed that I began to realise that something wasn't altogether correct. It was a sensation as much as anything I actually saw. My skin itched and I felt gooseflesh rise.

'By the pricking of my thumbs,' I said, voice hushed.

That was the point I saw the markings on the floor. Strange shapes, daubed in what looked like blood, arranged in a circle around Mary's bed. The same sort of occult-looking symbols I'd seen around the first victim.

This was not good.

'Mary?'

Something dripped on my head, stopping me in my tracks. I lifted my hand and touched the spot, bringing my fingers before my eyes to see sticky red.

'Oh…'

I looked up to find a dark, quivering shape attached to the ceiling. Now I had a starker look at the thing, it was less person-shaped than I first thought. It had a torso, legs, and a head, but the rest of it consisted of numerous octopus-like limbs that held the thing on the ceiling by row upon row of suckers.

At this point, I should have been racing from the room, screaming my throat raw as my bladder voided itself, but instead, a strange calmness descended over me. A sense that what I was looking at was not a creature from a lunatic's fever dream, but vermin to be exterminated.

'You're done,' I said. 'You've had your fill, now get the fuck out of here!'

The creature's hairless head twisted sharply to look at me, its eyes giant, wide, and entirely yellow. Its mouth a screaming beak that screeched with fury.

The strange sense of calmness suddenly left me to be replaced with a familiar, all-consuming terror. I staggered backwards, almost falling over the chair behind me. With little time to think about what I was doing, I grabbed the chair and launched it in the beast's direction. The chair struck it squarely on the head, causing it to scream in anger before its octopus limbs sent the thing swiftly towards the window, launching it through the glass and out into the car park beyond.

I gasped for breath, relief coursing through me that the thing had chosen flight over fight, then ran to the broken window to see where the creature was fleeing to.

I saw no sign of the beast, with its huge yellow eyes and numerous gross, sucker-limbs. Instead, I saw the homeless woman, sprinting away from the hospital.

7

Checking on Mary, I was relieved to discover that she was unconscious but otherwise okay. Some fresh wounds, but only superficial. For the second time now, I had been her unwitting saviour from Mr Octopus. Which, no, is not the most fearsome of names to give to the dark, twitching horror I'd witnessed clinging to the ceiling with its thick mollusc limbs, but it was the first thing that sprung to mind.

I pulled out my phone to snap a few pictures of the occult shapes daubed on the floor around her bed. As with last time, I felt a strange sensation teasing at me as I looked at the symbols. A sense that they were imbued with an energy of sorts. With a meaning that my brain insisted I understand, yet couldn't quite be grasped.

Mary moved and moaned in her bed, derailing my train of thought.

'It's okay, Mr Octopus has gone, you're okay.'

I patted her arm like a worried aunt, then darted from the room, intending to tell Big Marge in reception to get the police on the blower. I then screeched to an almost-falling-over halt as I realised I was leaving Mary alone, and that Mr Octopus might well take the opportunity to return and finish the job. Also, I realised that I still had my phone in my hand, and could call the police myself without leaving her side.

So I did that.

An hour later, I was sat in the hospital reception, cradling a styrofoam cup of coffee and chowing down on my third bag of crisps. My diet really was shocking. It was a wonder I cut such a lithe, dashing figure. With great hair.

As police wandered back and forth, I went over what had happened in my head for the hundredth time. The beast, the creature, Mr Octopus; there'd been no sign of it after it launched itself through the window. The only thing I'd seen was the homeless woman who'd been stalking me, legging it out of view. A reverse of what happened the previous night, when I'd chased after the woman, only for her to give me the slip and feel the dark shape barge past me.

Was it possible this woman and Mr Octopus were one and the same? I'd read all sorts of interesting guff about shape-shifters in my trawls through the internet, although they tended to be from person to animal; human to wolf, mainly. I hadn't read anything about people turning into half-person, half-octopus thingies. I was fairly sure I'd remember one of those.

'Deep in thought again, Mr Lake?'

Detective Myers' matter-of-fact tone snapped me out of my thoughts. I looked up from my coffee to see her and a second detective stood before me.

'Ah, Detective Maya Myers, good. Good that you're here.'

'Is it?'

'Well, not good. Tragic, because of the earlier murder. And

the new almost-murder. But now you're here, I'm sure things will settle down.'

'Was that sarcasm?'

'Oh. No. I don't think so.'

Detective Myers raised an eyebrow. It really hadn't been sarcasm, I was glad she was on the case. I like to think I'm an okay judge of character, and something told me that no one as scary and no-nonsense as Myers could be anything other than a first-rate detective. And judging by what I'd seen so far, that's exactly what this case was going to require.

She nodded towards the man stood next to her. He was short, a little pudgy, and almost entirely bald, despite looking to be only in his mid-twenties. God can be cruel.

'This is my partner, Detective Sam Samm.'

'Sam Samm?'

He nodded. 'Two 'M's.'

'Where?'

'The second Samm.'

'Right.'

Detective Myers pulled out her notebook. 'So, the details.'

Ah, yes, those things. Tricky. I could hardly tell her the truth of what I'd seen, or at least what I thought I'd seen. I'd have sounded like a raving loon. People do not have beaks or rows of octopus limbs bursting out of their sides. Not in Cumbria, anyway. Maybe in London.

'Well,' I said, 'as I told the first officer on the scene, I entered the room to find a... a person was—how I would describe it now?—leaning over Mary Taylor's bed. So, I said, "Hey now, you there, what's all this about?" just like that.'

Detective Myers' face slid from neutral into unimpressed. 'Mm-hm, go on.'

'Then, I sort of just ran at the bastard.'

'I'd have been cacking me pants,' said Samm. 'I don't really like confrontation.' He shivered and stuck his tongue out at the same time.

'Detective Samm,' said Myers, 'what made you want to become a police officer?'

'Hm,' he replied. 'I think it was the film *Dragnet*, with Tom Hanks and Dan Aykroyd. My favourite scene, if I had to pick one, would probably be the bit with the massive snake.'

Detective Myers gave him a long, hooded look, then turned back to me. 'Continue.'

'Right, yes, so, I sort of, put my head down, fists up, ready to, you know, box the fiend, and he turned tail and legged it.'

'Through a second-storey window?'

'Yup. Straight through, Superman-style. And off he went.'

'I see,' she said, sounding as though she hadn't swallowed a word of it. 'Tell me, Mr Lake, would you have any reason to be lying to us?'

I sat back, eyes wide, feigning shock like a pro. Believe it or not, I've had no formal acting training. 'Every word is the truth, I swear it on my mother's grave.'

'You don't know who your mother is.'

'No, but I'm sure she's a lovely woman and I wouldn't want to say untruths around her burial plot. Assuming she's dead that is.'

'Can you give us a description of the attacker?' asked Detective Samm.

'Ah, well, no. A bit. Some. Not much.'

'To the best of your recollection.'

'A person. A human person,' I replied.

'A human person,' said Detective Myers.

'Yep, I'm very clear on that point.'

'Great,' said Detective Samm, 'you're being really helpful.'

'Anything beyond "human person", sir?' asked Myers.

'Well, dark. Dark clothing. Dark hair.'

'Dark skin?' asked Detective Samm.

'Pretty dark.' Of course, he was entirely black, but the last thing I wanted was for the police to start harassing the area's very limited stock of non-white people, so I fudged it a bit. 'Let's say they had in-between skin. Average skin. A bit tan.'

Detective Myers sighed and wrote "In-between skin" in her neat, efficient handwriting. Got to appreciate handsome penmanship – my own shaky scrawl makes Guy Fawkes' post-torture confession signature look positively immaculate.

'Did you get a look at their face at all?' asked Detective Samm. 'Because that would be really useful.'

'Ooh, ah, well, only a very quick flash. It was all so fast. Sudden. Speedy. Over in a heartbeat. But I'd say.... beaky. A beaky nose.'

Detective Myers flipped her notebook closed and slid it into the pocket of her red leather jacket. 'Thanks, that's all been very helpful.'

Now *that* was definitely sarcasm.

'Okay, Detective Samm, go grab the surveillance tape. Maybe we'll get lucky and the assailant shows up on one of the security cams.'

'Good thinking. That's London thinking, that is. I'd never have thought of that.'

I turned to Detective Samm. 'The bit at the end of the film where Dan Aykroyd says, "Twice", then raises an eyebrow and Hanks reacts... that's my favourite part of *Dragnet*.'

'Ha! Yes. That is funny. He means sex. Nice to meet you.' Detective Samm waved at me and headed off on his merry way.

'He's nice,' I said.

'Want to tell me why you think you can feed me a bunch of shit, Mr Lake?'

'What? No shit, no shit. All very non-shitty.'

Detective Myers stepped forward and looked down at me. 'I know when I'm being lied to. Normally that's a gift in this job, but in this case the truth is bleeding obvious.'

'I promise you, on my maybe-dead mother's grave, I have told you all that I can.'

I shrank back as her eyes bored into me.

'I'll find out the truth, Mr Lake.'

'I believe it.'

She nodded. 'You still need to come to the station to make this and the previous statement official. Don't make me come and get you.'

'Understood,' I replied, my voice barely audible.

And with that, she turned smartly and headed out the door.

8

As my car headed towards Oldstone, the village from which all the cats I'd been hired to locate had absconded, I felt a mixture of unease and relief. Relief that Mary Taylor now lay safe in her hospital bed, with two burly armed officers stood outside the door, and unease about... well, basically everything else.

A monstrous murderer with octopus limbs and a face only a mother could love was on the loose. A creature that may or may not also be the homeless woman who was stalking me. Occult symbols daubed in blood. My lying to the police about the truth of what I'd witnessed. All in all, it was adding up to the sort of episode that made the whole world feel as though it had been shoved off-kilter.

Whatever was happening, I was unwittingly involved somehow, that much I was sure of. The homeless woman, whether she was the monster or not, was clearly part of this, and she'd been keeping her eye on me for a while. How these things connected, I hadn't a clue, but it certainly made me feel as though I was swimming in less than safe waters.

At some point, confessing everything to Detective Myers might be my only option, but for now, I'd only sound like a lunatic. Which was a real pain because I'd have liked nothing more than to pass this all over to the proper authorities and keep my head down. But then who are the proper authorities where octopus monsters are concerned?

It was all a little unnerving, so I decided to distract myself with thoughts of what might be waiting at Chloe's flat for our maybe-date. Twenty minutes later, as I completed my second full-throttle rendition of *I Wanna Sex You Up* by Color Me Badd (tell no one of this), I pulled to a stop on a leafy, pleasant street in Oldstone and unfolded myself from my little car, locking the door behind me and patting her on the roof.

Yes, I am the sort of person who gives their car a name. Deal with it.

I turned from the Uncanny Wagon and looked around Oldstone's main square. A patch of grass with a single, giant tree sat at the centre of Oldstone, around which were situated the usual village fare: a church with a little steeple and a "Jesus Created Adam & Eve, Not Adam & Steve" poster on the announcement board strapped to the gate. Obviously, a very enlightened vicar ran the place. Then there was the village pub, named The Oldstone Arms, a post office, greengrocers, and lastly a general newsagents. All very normal, all what you'd expect of a small, northern village, right down to the back-wards cleric.

Still, there was something strange about this little town. Something off. Something that made me shiver. I couldn't put my finger on it, but it made me feel uncomfortable. Imagine brushing your teeth, reaching for the water, and swigging down a glass of fresh orange juice. That would taste very weird. This was like that. Sort of.

I found the first MISSING CAT poster shortly after, taped to a lamppost along with seven more. Each of them was the same: a black and white picture of some moggy with a name and contact details underneath, a plaintive request for anyone who might have seen their beloved pet to get in contact.

The posters were everywhere. There wasn't a lamppost, telegraph pole, or car windscreen that hadn't been plastered with one. Whoever owned the photocopier around here was making out like a bandit. Mrs Coates had not been exaggerating when she hired me. Cats were becoming decidedly scarce around here.

'Hi there,' I said in as non-threatening a manner as I could muster to a girl, aged around seven, with a pile of warm-from-the-copier posters pinched under her arm. 'I wonder if I might ask you a question or two?'

'Depends,' she replied, stapling the poster for poor, beloved Nemo Bananapants directly over one asking for information regarding the retrieval of Mittens, who was new to the house, but still very much missed.

'Depends on what?' I asked.

'Whether you're one of them perverts me mam talks about.'

'I can assure you that I'm not. My name is Joseph and I'm a... detective. Of sorts.'

'Detectives can be perverts.'

'True, but not in this case.'

'What do you want? Come near me and I'll scream and gob on you.'

Charming.

'I see you're missing a cat. In fact, judging by the small forest of paper coating this village, it seems a lot of people are missing their cat.'

The girl sniffed wetly, then ran the back of her sleeve across her nose. 'Yeah, s'right. All the cats have buggered off.'

'All?'

She nodded. 'Nemo was the last one to go. After everyone else's went, I tried to keep him inside and safe, but he ran out when me dad set off for work yesterday and hasn't come back. Nemo never stays out for longer than half an hour.'

'And what do you think's happened to him?'

She shrugged. 'You're the detective, you tell me.'

'Do you feel... strange?'

She looked at me oddly. 'Well, I do need to wee a bit.'

'No, no, I mean, the air around here. Does it make you itchy?'

'I'm going to go now.'

The girl slid a poster under the wiper of the nearest car then headed off.

There was definitely something odd going on around here, and it wasn't just the tall guy in the hat and long coat talking to underage girls. Cats were going missing en masse, and the air was tinged with menace. It was clear there was a mystery at play here worthy of my time. Had someone killed the cats? Someone with a cat grudge? Was that a thing? Or perhaps the odd sensation I felt had caused the cats to go missing. It's said that felines are sensitive to all sorts of different spectrums of reality, to the paranormal, even. To things that us humans have no connection to. Perhaps the cats of Oldstone knew something bad was about to happen and made their escape early, like rats from a sinking ship. For now, all I had were questions, it was my job to try and find an answer or two.

I turned, intending to head back to my car to mull things over, when something small and black caught my eye. It was sat watching me from several metres away, its eyes wide and unblinking.

A cat!

I began to slowly move towards it, one foot gently in front of the other, as though I was on a tightrope between two tall buildings and one false move would send me tumbling to my doom.

'Hey there, puss-puss,' I said, kissing my teeth. 'Where've you been, then, eh? Where've you been, little guy?'

I began to crouch as I approached, ready to grab hold of the thing when it turned and bolted. Coat flapping behind me, I sprinted as best I could after the fleeing cat, my boots slapping noisily against the cobbled road.

'I just want to talk!' I yelled after the fleeing moggy, as though that would convince it to reconsider its escape plan.

The thing about cats is, they're fast. The thing about me is, I'm not. Soon enough I found myself stood on a small road on the village outskirts, hand against a wall, panting for breath. The cat had given me the slip, but it let me know one thing: the cats, or at least some of them, were still around here somewhere. Maybe they'd run from home, but they had yet, perhaps, to abandon the village completely.

It was just then that I saw the fox stood upon a dry stone wall on its hind legs, a small, almost Roman-looking helmet upon its head, and an axe in its paw.

Yes, this came as quite a surprise to me, too.

It was a toy of some sort, it must be. A model left on the wall by some child who forgot to take it home.

The fox thrust its axe into the air. 'All hail the Magic Eater! All hail the saviour!'

The fox hopped off the wall and into the field beyond as I approached, a mixture of confusion and fear dampening my brow. When I reached the wall and looked over, the creature was gone.

I yelped and jumped to one side as something brushed against me, only to find the young girl placing yet another poster under someone's windscreen wiper.

'Did you see it?' I asked.

'See what?'

'The fox. The talking fox!'

'You're a bloody weirdo, you are.'

Given the circumstances, I found that difficult to deny.

9

The sky was just starting to bruise as Chloe opened her front door with a grin.

'Hey!'

'I brought wine,' I said as I thrust out the bottle my sweaty hand was gripping tight enough to almost break.

'Come in then,' she said, and with a quick, calming breath, I followed her inside.

We ate bowls of chilli slumped on her couch, the TV playing some old Cary Grant movie. Is it a date if you sit on a couch with a bowl of leftover chilli on your lap? Difficult to say, but whatever it was, I'd take it.

'Are you okay?' she asked.

'Hm? Yes. Yep! Tip-top and ready to rock.'

Christ...

'Cool. You just seem a little off tonight.'

Well, Chloe, I was chasing a cat earlier when an axe-wielding fox spoke to me.

'I am? Sorry, probably just all the, you know, bad stuff lately. The murders. Poor Mary Taylor. Lot of stuff on my mind and not much room up there to hold it.'

She laughed and my stomach released a box full of butterflies that it had been saving for just such an occasion.

'You always make me laugh, Joe.'

It took all my willpower not to fall to my knees and declare my undying love for her. Or, at the very least, my undying I-really-want-to-kiss-your-lovely-mouth.

'So,' I said, clearing my throat, 'I take it no further attempts were made on Mary's life by… the person. The murderer.'

Chloe dabbed up the remaining chilli with a slice of bread and shook her head. 'Nope. And there won't be, as long as the police do the right thing and leave those officers at her door. If you ask me, they should have been there from the start.'

To be fair to the police, they had no idea some sort of hellish octopus person was looking to tie up loose ends.

Chloe curled her legs up on the couch, the ends of her toes touching my outer thigh. I gripped the arm of the couch and did my best not to let loose a plaintive whimper.

She placed her now-empty bowl on the floor and began toying with her hair. 'So, what d'you want to do now?'

A jumble of indecent answers arrived fully formed in my mind, barging their way to the front and causing my mouth to flap silently for a few seconds.

'Are you okay? You've gone all red.'

'Yep, just… toilet. Need a wee.'

'Right. No need to ask, you know where it is.'

I lurched up from the couch, feeling a fool, and headed towards the bathroom. Had that been flirting? What Chloe had been doing, did that constitute a flirt? The hair teasing between her fingers, the bare feet touching my leg, the invitation to take control of what happened next? It definitely seemed like flirting. Then again, it could also have been a tired person passing the time innocently with someone she looked to as a friend.

I locked the bathroom door and sat on the toilet, the seat still down and my trousers still up. I didn't actually need the loo, but this gave me at least a moment or two's respite from the idiot I was making of myself. A few deep breaths, that's all I needed.

If anything's going to happen, just let it happen, and if it doesn't happen, don't sulk about it.

It was then that I felt a prickle dance across my scalp. I was suddenly very sure that I was not alone in the bathroom. I looked to my right, to the bath, with its shower curtain pulled across. My head told me to get out of that small room sharply. My body, ever the traitor, reached out a hand and pulled back the shower curtain.

The axe-wielding fox, Roman helmet still upon its head, was stood on its hind legs in the bathtub.

'All hail the saviour of the Dark Lakes!' it said in its small, Cumbrian voice, waving its axe aloft.

I replied by yelling, 'Argh! Oh, Christ, argh!' in a strangulated voice and falling off the toilet, landing on the tiles with a thump, my left elbow jarring painfully.

'She waits for you upon her throne of skulls, saviour!' cheered the fox.

I was closer than last time, and I could see the fox's fur was thick and messy, and its large, bushy tail cut short, the end missing. It was proportioned like a regular fox that had somehow learned to walk on its hind legs and stood upright with confidence and poise.

A knock at the door. 'Are you okay in there?' asked Chloe. 'I heard noises.'

'Yes! Yep. I'm…' I looked back to the bath to find the fox had disappeared again.

'Are you sure? It sounded like you yelled, *"Oh, Christ!"* in a high-pitched voice.'

I crawled over to the bath and looked for any sign of the bizarre fox, but didn't find so much a muddy footprint staining the white porcelain.

'Should I be worried?' asked Chloe.

I pulled myself up and opened the door, legs a little

unsteady, 'Nope. No worry, just, thought I saw a... spider.'

'Okay.'

'A big spider.'

'Oh.'

'And then I fell off the toilet.'

'Right. You're acting a little oddly, even for you, Joe.'

I stepped out of the bathroom and headed back through to the front room. 'Yeah, sorry, just, blah, head all over the place.'

'Don't worry, me too.'

'Oh?'

'Today's the anniversary of my mum's death.'

I was very much not expecting that.

'What? Really?'

Chloe nodded.

'Right. Shit. Jesus. I'm sorry, I didn't realise.'

Chloe had mentioned her mum a few times, usually after a few too many glasses of wine. Mentioned how she'd died when Chloe was only very young. How it was the entire reason behind her becoming a doctor. Every time she worked on someone, she was trying to save her mum.

'Joe?'

'Yes?'

'Do you want to do a bit of kissing?'

At least three silent seconds passed.

'I'm sorry? Come again?'

'Kissing. I'm sad, and I like you, and I thought I'd invite you over so we could try out a kiss or two to cheer me up.'

'Oh.'

'If that's okay with you.'

'That's okay with me.'

She looked at me oddly, and I suddenly realised I was doing a little jig.

'You're so weird,' she said, laughing.

'Afraid so.'

And then she reached up, pulled my head down, and pressed her lips against mine.

And we did some of the thing you Earth people call "kissing".

Oh, yes.

s the Uncanny Wagon left Carlisle and Chloe behind, and I headed back home, back to Keswick, I felt like a leaf on the breeze.

In other words, I was a bit happy.

The kissing had gone on for some time, enough time for a grope or two to occur before, grinning, she told me that was enough for now. We had plenty of time. No need to rush.

'Are you my girlfriend?' I'd asked, like a ten-year-old boy who'd just given the best girl in the school playground the last of his penny sweets in hope of some affection.

'Maybe. Let's see how it goes, shall we? Thanks for making me feel better, Joe.'

I was so happy and distracted that the fact a talking fox with an axe had greeted me on two occasions had, for a while, slipped my mind. A talking fox that could, apparently, appear and disappear at will. Perhaps the thing was connected to all the cats of Oldstone doing a runner? I supposed that, if I were a cat, I would run from a fox waving an axe at me.

There was also the fact that foxes can't talk, nor wield man-made weaponry, and that I might very well be losing my tiny mind. Then again, octopus men weren't real, either, and I'd met that sucker (no pun intended) twice. Though come to think of it, I was the only one who'd seen the assailant in that way. Mary Taylor had yet to give a statement to the same effect. Perhaps it was all in my head after all. I was a crazy, paranoid man in a fabulous long coat, who thought tramps were stalking him, that foxes could talk, and that there was a killer man-octopus stalking the streets of fair Cumbria.

That felt like it made a lot more sense than the alternative.

It was then that a thick, fetid octopus limb reached out from the back seat of my car, wrapped itself around my head, and caused me to swerve off the road and crash head-on into a tree.

10

The world swayed drunkenly before my eyes as I pressed my weight against the car door. It swung open and I fell onto the grass outside before throwing up my guts. I'd blacked out for a moment or two, and had barely clawed my way back to consciousness. My head felt as though a knife had embedded itself in my right temple.

I couldn't pass out again. I had to stay awake. If I blacked out and that thing was still close, I was dead. Which would ruin an otherwise lovely evening.

I looked up to see the windscreen was entirely gone, my seatbelt having saved me from launching through the hole as the tree brought the car to an abrupt stop. No such luck for the creature that had lunged at me from behind; it had been propelled through the glass and was somewhere ahead of me, hidden in the gloom.

It was almost pitch black out there on the small country road, and the thing could easily be close at hand. I used the car door to pull myself up to my feet, my wobbly legs threatening to send me crashing back to the dirt. I could feel something wet dripping down my forehead and decided to pretend it wasn't blood gushing from an open wound.

I caught a movement in the shadows several metres away, a grunt and a groan.

'I have a gun,' I yelled, holding up my hand with two fingers extended.

Yes, Joseph, that'll fool them...

It seemed like I had two options: leg it, or clamber back into my poor car and see if I could bring the thing back to life. Well, actually, there was a third choice: try to tackle Mr Octopus and find out what it felt like to be horribly murdered.

As I slipped back into the driver's seat, I saw a smear of red on the steering wheel where my head had connected with it. The airbag had clearly failed to deploy, if the thing was even fitted with one.

I peered through the windscreen, or at least the expanse of air where it used to go. The creature was up on its feet and facing me. Its dark body had an indistinct shape, but its giant yellow eyes cut through the gloom like twin suns. I turned the ignition over and the Uncanny Wagon coughed, whirred, wheezed, then cut out.

'Come on, come on,' I muttered, trying again, but each twist of the key only achieved the same result. The car was dead, or at the very least, severely poorly.

I slapped my palms against the dashboard in frustration, then stumbled back out into the night and tried to run. The sudden movement quickly informed me that I was far from over my forty-mile-an-hour steering wheel head-butt. The world weaved before me, my knees turning to jelly, my vision snapping in and out of focus. The world was grey and fuzzy around the edges, and static edged further and further over my eyesight with each desperate step.

The thing was after me, I could hear it. I could hear the sound its beak made, the screeching fury. I could hear its heavy feet mashing the ground. I risked a look over my shoulder. Bad move. Moving forward and looking back was too much for my steering-wheel-bashed brain to deal with, and I tumbled hard to the ground.

'Shitting shit!' I cried as I tried to right myself, tried to stop myself from giving in to my mind's insistence that we just slip into unconsciousness for a quick time-out.

I was up on my feet, almost bent double, trying to move forwards but mostly going sideways. A suckered limb caught my wrist.

'No! Get off.'

I whirled around, swinging a fist in the creature's direction, connecting more by luck than judgment. My knuckles met the side of the creature's head with a squelch, and it stepped back, beak crying with anger.

I did my best to run some more but it was no good. I was exhausted, I was broken, I was moments from passing out. I leaned back against a tree, the only thing keeping me upright, and watched with bleary resignation as the black, multi-limbed creature twitched towards me, convinced it had its quarry beat.

'Fuck... fuck you...' was about as much as I could manage. 'Right in the rear end.'

Its octopus limbs began to dance as though taunting me. I could see my face reflected in the large yellow pools of its eyes, and it wasn't a pretty picture. My features drooped, my face splattered in blood, a large gash streaked across my forehead. Was this how I would die? At the hands—or limbs at least—of some nightmare beast that shouldn't even exist?

It all seemed a tad unfair. I still didn't know who I was. Didn't know what was going on. Just a fool with great hair being buffeted from pillar to post, begging for a straight answer or two. And Chloe had just started kissing me. I'd hoped for a bit more of that. Oh, well.

'Get on with it then,' I demanded.

The octopus man crowed, shrill and piercing in triumph as it prepared to do its worst—

And that's when the front of its head exploded in every direction, dousing me in gore.

I'm not at all embarrassed to say that I screamed a scream only dogs could have heard. I swiped a handful of brains from my eyes to find the creature still standing, held up by the fist that was jutting from where its face had been. Oh, and the fist was also glowing with what looked like fire.

The flaming fist then gave me the finger.

The creature twitched once, then the hand pulled free and it crumpled, wetly, to the ground, quite dead.

The homeless woman flicked chunks of matter from her now not-on-fire hand, then began wiping at it with her coat.

'Nasty bloody bastards, those things,' she noted.

'You... it's you...' I said pointing at her in case she was confused.

'I know.'

'And you just... just...' I pointed at the very dead Mr Octopus.

'You're welcome,' replied the woman, in what seemed to me to be a rather sarcastic tone of voice. She pulled at a cigarette, lit the thing, and inhaled on it deeply.

It was at this point that my body got its way and consciousness finally eluded me.

11

I was looking up at the sky, only it wasn't a normal sort of sky. It wasn't the daytime sky, azure blue with patches of white cloud. Nor was it the night-time sky, jet black and pin-pricked by stars. This sky boiled with fire. It roared and it raged and it spat great, flaming arcs down at the earth as though it were trying to sterilise what lay beneath its endless, angry expanse.

I reached up a hand to my temple—to the wound I'd been dealt in the crash—but I couldn't feel any gash, and my head had stopped throbbing. I was laying in a small, wooden rowing boat, rocked gently by the surrounding water.

Gripping the sides of the boat, I sat up. I was adrift in the middle of a large lake. The Lake District has several large lakes, otherwise, it wouldn't be called the Lake District, it would just be called the District. This lake didn't look familiar, though. I peered over the edge of the boat to examine the water, which, like the sky above, was far from normal. It wasn't clear, or blue, but entirely black. Blacker than the blackest black that you could ever imagine. And then a bit blacker.

Was this a dream? The last thing I remembered was the mad homeless woman enjoying a ciggie after she'd punched an octopus monster right through the head. Life really had taken some turns of late.

I lifted the boat's heavy oars and placed them in the stirrups, or whatever the bits that you sit the oars in on a rowboat are called. I dipped the oars in the water and began to propel myself towards the shore.

I felt strange, and not just because of... well, everything. I felt a sense of déjà vu like I knew this place. Like I belonged there somehow. Perhaps I'd had this dream before and just forgotten about it. People forget dreams all the time. They say you only remember a tiny sliver of the strange trips your sleeping mind takes you on as you lay curled up in bed and the night rolls by unseen.

The small boat buffeted against the shore, and I stood unsteady as the thing tipped back and forth, threatening to throw me off balance. Getting my shoes wet, I leapt out and walked up on to the grass. All around me, hills rose into the roiling sky. There were no buildings to be seen. Just hills, mountains, trees, grass. But again, as with the lake water and the sky, the grass was not the sort you would expect to see. This grass was blood-red. Crimson slashes that covered the ground and clung to the hills. I crouched and ran my hand through it and the grass left a sticky, red residue on my skin. This strange place was bleeding on me.

I stood and decided to explore. If this was a dream, a fantasy my consciousness had retreated to after the car crash, then my brain was being very creative. I wondered what else it had in store for me.

It wasn't long before I found the first skeleton.

It lay on the grass before me, not a scrap of flesh or matter left clinging to it. I peered at the strange skull. It was large and held enormous tusk-like teeth in its jaw. As I walked on, finding more and more bones, until it was difficult to find a path through them, and I had to resort to trampling the remains underfoot. Which I felt somewhat guilty for, but something inside of me insisted I push on, like my feet knew the direction I should be heading. And so my boots crunch-crunched their way over a field of bright, white bones that stretched as far as I could see, with eruptions of blood-red grass forcing their way into view here and there.

I stopped to catch my breath and wondered idly if I'd ever actually been out of breath in a dream before. Is that the sort of thing that happens in a dream? I was also sweating, rivulets of salty water irritating my eyes, forcing me to wipe the sleeve of my coat across them to clear my vision.

Can you sweat in dreams? Feel pain?

As I swallowed and realised how dry-mouthed I'd become, I began to wonder if this really was a dream. Perhaps, instead, I was dead. I'd passed out after the crash, after the attack, and who knows what had happened to me after that? Maybe another of the octopus monsters had popped up and finished me off. That or the homeless woman had done the job. She did punch one creature's brains out. Literally. Maybe she decided to finish me off as dessert.

So was this death? The afterlife? Purgatory? The sky was on fire, which had a definite Hell-y vibe to it. I mean, if I was going to design Hell, I'd certainly have plenty of that stuff around. And bones. Fire and bones. Your standard Hell jazz.

I climbed over a fence and walked on, thankful to be leaving the carpet of bones behind. As I continued, I became aware that I was making my way towards a particular hill. A bulbous hump in the distance. I lost sight of it as I entered a forest, but still, my feet seemed to know which direction to tread. I wouldn't get lost.

The trees were decorated with a red vegetation that matched the crimson grass. The leaves formed a canopy overhead, blocking the view of the furious, burning sky. As I walked beneath it, the unbroken red blanket rained lazy, bloody drops on my head. I left the huddle of trees for a moment and emerged into a clearing. In the centre was an old-fashioned wooden gallows, and from its noose hung a dead body. Steps led up to a wooden platform. The body hung above, a stool by its side, the corpse's feet a half-metre from touching down. It was a woman. She wore a black dress and had long blonde hair that hung down to her waist. I ran towards her, bounding up the steps, but as soon as I touched her I could tell that she was dead. Cold and stiff and gone.

It was far from the most pleasant thing I'd stumbled across on a ramble through a wood.

The woman looked to be in her thirties, and fiercely beautiful. I sat on the gallows steps staring up at her, hoping this really was all a dream, and that I'd hurry up and wake already.

'All hail the saviour!'

I turned to see the fox with his axe held aloft, stood at the edge of the forest.

'You again. What do you want?'

'I've been looking for you. Looking for ages and ages.'

'Well, you've found me. Congratulations. I'm talking to a fox. I'm talking to a fox and there's a dead woman hanging behind me and the sky is made of fire.'

The fox shuffled from foot to foot, then scratched at his chin with his axe. 'You what?'

'Ignore me, I'm just going insane. Who's the woman?' I asked, pointing to the swinging corpse.

'Huh? Y'know who that is. It were your idea, after all. Good idea it was, too.'

'I think you've mistaken me for someone else.'

The fox took a step forward and peered into my eyes. 'No, don't think so. Then again, you all look the same to me. Sorry if that sounds racist.'

'Again, the dead person?'

'That's the Red Woman's sister, ain't it? Blonde Cathy. Was you that told Red to get rid of her. That she should rule alone. "*Family stabs family in the back, so be sure to be the one holding the knife*". Your words, not mine.'

'That does not at all sound like something I would say.'

'Come on, then,' said the fox, gesturing at me with his axe as he turned and walked towards the treeline.

Not knowing what else to do, I stood and made my way down the gallows steps. 'Where are we going?'

'To the hill. She asked me t'come get you, so here I am, and there we'll go.'

I glanced back at the woman, twisting in the light breeze, then turned back and followed the fox into the forest.

'Is it much further?' I asked. The fox licked its paw and held it up above his head.

'Naw, seems like it's pretty close. Always is this time of day, so it's lucky you dropped in now.'

'And where exactly is it I've dropped into?'

'Well, here. This place.'

'A less vague answer would be nice.'

'The Dark Lakes. The land of dread. The veil of anguish. Prison of the restless army of the dead.'

I nodded slowly. 'Right. That place. Got you.'

After what seemed like hours, we finally broke from the forest, and there it was, rising steeply before us: the hill.

'Come on, then,' said the fox, 'top's where you're supposed t'be.'

The hill was so steep I had to bend right over and crawl up the thing, its long, wild, red grasses leaving fresh ruby smears on my coattails and trouser legs.

'Who do I send my dry cleaning bill to?' I asked the fox.

Finally, the hill levelled out as we reached the summit. On top of it was a chair. Well, more of a throne to be honest. A gleaming, white, very uncomfortable-looking throne made entirely of human skulls. Which was creepy.

'Well?' I said, 'what now?'

'Now you take your throne,' came a new voice. She stepped out from behind the chair; a tall, lithe woman, with alabaster skin and the reddest of red hair. Her eyes were piercing green, the smile on her face vicious in its beauty.

Something told me I should be very, very scared.

'I have brought him to you at last, Red Woman,' said the fox, falling to his knees. 'As I were asked to, as I said I would. Now, shall I get my reward?'

The Red Woman approached the fox and removed his helmet.

'You have done well,' she said, stroking the fur on top of his head.

'Thank you.'

And then she tore his head from his neck and the body toppled aside.

'Jesus!' I cried. 'Why? Why did you do that?'

She tipped her head back, mouth wide, as she raised the fox's head high, and allowed the blood to pour into her mouth, over her face, and splash down the dark green leather she wore from shoulder to toe.

She tossed the head aside, smiling at me, her perfect, white teeth stained blood-red.

'I'd very much like to wake up now,' I said.

'Wake up?'

I began to back away. 'This has to be a dream, and I just want to wake up.'

'Oh, but you are waking up, don't you see? You are here again, before the throne, Magic Eater.'

The words gave me pause. That name. That title. It meant something.

Magic Eater.

I looked down at my hands and bright red fire burst from them as the Red Woman laughed and the sky roared in anger.

'No.'

I took a step back and the ground beneath my feet dipped suddenly as the world twisted away.

12

Sometimes, when you're dreaming, you feel like you're falling.

You can't remember how or why, but down, down, down you go, your stomach taking up residence in your mouth as you plummet to your doom. You don't know how this came to be, this endless fall, but you do know one thing with a crystal certainty: if the fall isn't endless, if there is a bottom for you to hit, then you will never wake up. You'll strike down and your bones will shatter, your organs pop, your meat splat. And that's when your eyes spring open and your whole body jerks, a sudden spasm, as though the mattress has broken your fall and saved you from a fate worse than death.

This was one of those times.

I looked around to see the familiar sight of a hospital room. No chairs made of bones or any of that malarkey, just four magnolia walls, a weathered bedside cabinet topped with an empty vase, and an old TV set perched on a swing bracket. I took a wary peek at my hands to find that fire no longer seemed to be erupting from them.

Of course, there wasn't.

I slumped back, my head now resuming its dull throb from the accident, and let out a sigh of relief as the door squeaked open and Doctor Neil, the epic wanker, stepped inside.

Never had I been more delighted to see the sod.

'Doctor Neil!'

'Doctor Smith, you prick,' he spat back.

I almost got up and hugged the man.

'Seems like someone gave you a right going over,' he said, grinning.

'Well, I'm glad my misfortune brings a little light to your horrific, empty life, Doctor Neil.'

'I'll tell you one last time, it's Doctor Smith, you piece of shit.'

'Don't think much of your bedside manner there, Doctor Neil. Real four out of ten stuff, that.'

The door swung open again and Chloe stepped in. 'You two boys aren't fighting again, are you?' she asked with a smile that dulled the throb in my head.

'Doctor Neil here was just telling me how relieved he was that I am fine and dandy and what a testament it is to my remarkable powers of recuperation.'

'Yup, that sounds like something he'd say.'

Doctor Neil looked at us in turn, malice in his eyes, then turned on his heel and stomped out.

'You know,' said Chloe, 'one of these days he's going to twat you one.'

'Oh, he loves me really.'

Chloe pulled up a chair and took my hand. A little shiver ran through me as flesh met flesh.

'What happened?'

A monster with octopus limbs attacked me, then a homeless woman punched its brains out, I took a detour through a hellscape accompanied by a talking fox, and then I went a bit on fire.

'Um. Accident. How did I get here, by the way?'

'Big Marge came back from the toilet to find you slumped across three chairs, unconscious and pissing blood out of your head. What sort of accident?'

I was found in reception? Huh. Well, there is no way I made my own way there. My car was wrecked, and my head almost caved in. Could the homeless woman have brought me here somehow? Carried me here then done a runner? There seemed to be no other explanation, which meant I owed her twice now.

But why on earth was she looking out for me? What did I mean to her? Perhaps she did know me after all, from before I awoke next to Derwentwater ten years ago. I felt my heart flutter a little and sat up straight.

'A woman... did anyone see a woman drop me off?'

'No one saw anything; just there you were. Joe, what happened? Tell me.'

'Just, you know, I was driving back from your place, and... a cat. A cat ran out, and you know me, animal lover, so I swerved, had a bit of a crash, and bopped my head. Stupid, really.'

She looked at me, brow knitted, obviously not buying what I was selling.

'Is that the truth?'

'Of course.'

I hated lying to her, especially post-kiss, but what other option did I have? The truth made me sound like a lunatic, and very few smart, funny, successful, beautiful women are up for kissing lunatics.

She softened. 'Please be more careful next time,' she said, then leaned forward and planted a gentle kiss on my lips. 'You twat.'

I grinned like a fool, cheeks flushing. 'You know, I could get very used to you kissing me.'

'Me too.'

Too agitated, too wired, too just plain ol' freaked out to sit still in a hospital bed when I felt fine enough, I dressed and, against Chloe's orders, checked myself out. Now, true, I'd had a fierce bang on the noggin, so should stay in for observation—plus I'd been informed that the police would be coming by to ask me some questions—but off I went anyway. Telling the boys and girls in blue the truth about what had happened to me wasn't an option, so I'd only be wasting their time.

Plus, I felt fine. Energised, even. I was in the middle of a bunch of clashing, bizarre mysteries and I didn't want to lose time lying on my back eating hospital food and watching daytime TV. Even if there was an episode of *Quincy* on that I'd somehow never seen before.

I felt sure that my past was involved in this somehow. Or at the very least the homeless woman knew who I was. I left the hospital assuming I was due a rest from any shocks, at least for a few hours, but found that not to be the case as soon as I stepped outside to find the Uncanny Wagon in the car park with no visible evidence of ever having been in a crash. The front end wasn't crumpled, and the windscreen was perfectly intact.

'What in the crap of all craps...?'

It was impossible. The crash happened. It actually, actually happened. My car had been wrecked.

I climbed behind the wheel, confused. The pain in my head where it had connected with the steering wheel was evidence enough that the crash really had happened. Not to mention the dried smear of blood from my head that was still on the steering wheel itself. So, well, what the hell had happened? And why was my car not a squashed mess? I turned the key, which sat waiting for me in the ignition. The engine turned over and caught first time.

She's alive!

As I placed my hands on the wheel, I saw a flash of them engulfed in red fire, like they had been in... what had that poor fox called the place? The Dark Lakes? But that was a delusion, surely? My unconscious mind having a merry old time. Then why had it seemed so real? So familiar, even? And why had the fox, who I'd encountered twice in the real world, also been there?

I pulled out of the car park and headed home, to Keswick, making very sure that there was no beast with suckered arms lurking low in the back seat.

After a hot shower and a change of clothes, I grabbed my laptop to check my who-the-heck-am-I? website, more out of habit than expectation, only to find I'd been left a message. I sat up sharply and clicked:

Next time I might not be around to pull your arse out of the fire, you wanker.

The user name was just a string of random numbers and letters, but I knew who it was. The homeless woman. My fire-fisted saviour.

Who are you? I typed, hitting send, then stared at the screen for almost half an hour, hoping for a reply.

Yeah, no reply.

The woman's hand had been on fire, as had mine in my, well, vision, or delusion, or whatever you want to call it. Was that because I'd seen her hand on fire, or because we were connected in our… hot-hand abilities?

I closed my laptop and set it aside to focus on my hands.

'Um… flame on?'

Nothing.

I tried concentrating on them and thinking hot thoughts. After that, I hopped around the room, throwing dramatic shapes as though I were under attack and needed to unleash a fireball from the palm of my hand.

Nothing, obviously.

I sat back down feeling like a bit of a tit.

A lot of very strange stuff was going on, but I did not have superhero powers, and neither did the homeless woman, beyond one hell of a right hook. I'd barely been clinging to consciousness, my mind playing tricks, surely?

I mean, no one can really conjure flames from their fists, right?

13

It was just creeping into the late afternoon as I stepped out of my car and cast my eyes around Oldstone once more.

There it was; that strange, uncomfortable sensation I'd felt on my last visit to the village. It was worse this time if anything. It crawled and itched, a persistent static that prickled my skin. That wasn't the only thing there was more of, either, every available surface was plastered with missing cat posters now.

Missing: Old Tom, ginger tabby, last seen on Friday.

Missing: Blackie, last seen Tuesday morning.

On and on they went. Oldstone had been quite the cat haven before they'd all upped sticks and buggered off.

Actually, that might not be strictly true. I had, after all, spotted one of the elusive buggers on my last visit. Maybe they were all hunkered down someplace safe, put off by the strange atmosphere of the place. But how do you find a cat that doesn't want to be found?

I opened the back of the Uncanny Wagon and pulled out one of those boxes with a little cage door on the front that you force an unhappy mog into when it's time to go to the vets, plus some other bits and pieces. It was time to lay a trap and see what came a-sniffing.

Twenty minutes later, I was sat on a park bench, the cat box resting on the ground several metres away, with a trail of kitty biscuits leading inside. No, it wasn't much of a plan, but at least I was working for Mrs Coates' money.

I retrieved my buzzing mobile from my pocket and saw a message from Chloe: *Are you okay?*

I smiled, the little butterflies in my stomach swirling anew, and set my thumbs to work: *I'm fine.* Send.

Perfect. Enigmatic. Too enigmatic?

Another buzz:

C: *I was thinking... (emoji of a light bulb)*

J: *Ooh, dangerous, never leads anywhere good, thinking.*

C: *Shut up. We should have a date.*

A bit of a pause in replying there as I jerked forward, throwing my phone to the ground. I fell to my knees and scooped the thing up.

J: *Oh?*

C: *A meal. A meal out. (emoji of a chilli)*

J: *Yes. Me and you. Out. Eating. Sounds good.*

C: *Maybe try some more of that kissing. (lips emoji)*

It was very difficult not to just type back a pathetic *Thank you, thank you, thank you.*

J: *It's a date.*

C: xxx *(heart emoji)*

Man alive, that girl is partial to an emoji.

And that was that. A date. An honest to goodness date. We definitely weren't just friends now. I mean, the whole kissing bit was one thing, but a date? A date was girlfriend territory. A date was the sort of thing an honest to goodness *couple* did. Now, it was true that we hadn't nailed down specifics. Time, day, place. Still, no point rocking the boat at this stage. Get out while the going's good. The fact was, Chloe was into me, and I had the emojis to prove it. She was digging me. Digging the vibe that I was... secreting? That doesn't sound right. Well, whatever it was, she had the hots for me. The kissing and eating food in a restaurant kinda hots.

The look on my face at that moment was insufferable, I can tell you. It was just as well there was no foot traffic passing by as they'd have been compelled to slap me silly.

So caught up was I in my new bubble of warm-heart-swelling-loveliness, that I almost failed to see the cat that was creeping towards my trap, munching up one carefully placed kitty biscuit at a time.

I stood, nonchalantly pretending that I had no interest in what the cat was doing as it edged ever closer to the cat box. 'Go on, there's a good kitty,' I muttered under my breath.

The cat poked its head into the box and took a step back. I'd filled that box with enough food to test any cat's willpower. The cat glanced back once, then finally stepped into the trap.

Victory!

I darted forward while the cat chowed down and fell to my knees, throwing the cage door shut and securing it. The poor thing twisted, startled, and began to claw against the secured door of the cat box, against the sides, against the roof. Eventually, it stopped fighting as it resigned itself to its situation. I peered in at the thing, making friendly noises, willing the poor sod to calm down.

'Hey there, little guy, don't worry, I'm nice, me,' I said, then squinted at the thing I'd caught. 'Wait a sec...' I reached into my coat and pulled out the missing cat posters Mrs Coates had given me. Sure enough, one black ear, the other white.

'Well, if it isn't Boris the cat,' I said. 'I know your owner. Small world, eh?'

A few minutes later I was rat-a-tat-tatting at her front door, feeling rather pleased with myself. When Mrs Coates opened up and saw me holding Boris aloft in my cat box, she was so overcome with joy I thought she might faint.

'Boris! Boris, my Boris!'

'As promised,' I said, proudly.

I stepped into her home and placed the cat box down on a sideboard in the entrance hall.

'How did you find him?'

'We detective sorts have our ways, Mrs Coates, but what it truly comes down to is dedication. Dedication and a supreme attention to detail. Nothing gets past these eyes, Mrs Coates. Nothing.'

I opened the cat box to allow Boris the cat to emerge and hop over to his owner. It was then that Boris saw his chance and bolted from the box, out of the house, and off into the distance.

'Ah,' I said. 'Probably should have closed the front door before I did that.'

The look Mrs Coates gave me almost broke the skin.

14

I tried the same cat-catching trick at various locations around Oldstone before finally admitting defeat.

I was annoyed, but as I made my way back to Keswick and home, I at least knew that the one cat I'd seen previously was no fluke. No random stray left behind as the rats fled the ship. The cats were somewhere, either in or close to the town. It was just a case of locating their hideaway now. And, perhaps more to the point, understanding just *why* it was that they all felt the need to make themselves scarce, and whether it was connected to the sense of prickling dread the place gave me.

I'd attempted to raise the matter with Mrs Coates, but she wasn't too keen on chatting after I allowed Boris to leg it again.

Back home, I made myself a strong cup of tea, grabbed a packet of Rich Tea biscuits that I was delighted to find behind a rapidly decaying loaf of bread, and flopped wearily on the couch.

Biscuit in one hand and another in my mouth, I reached for my laptop to see if any further messages had been left for me. There was nothing new. I polished off my tea and headed to the bathroom, parking myself on the toilet for a sit-down wee and a good old ponder.

A village fizzing with a bizarre atmosphere that seemed to be driving out its cat population. Creatures with octopus limbs, murdering people and surrounding their corpses with occult looking symbols, daubed in blood. A talking fox. Let's not forget the talking fox.

Had I gone mad, or had I always been this way? It was the first time I'd explored that option since I came to on the shores of Derwentwater, nudged awake and mind empty. Maybe I was just crackers. Maybe that's why I was suffering from amnesia in the first place. Perhaps my mind had decided it couldn't take anymore and wiped the hard drive clean. Factory settings reset.

That sounded like something that could be true. Maybe. I mean, I'm a believer in the weird side of things, of the paranormal, of there being more to this world than the everyday person generally experiences, but all of *this*? I thought there was something in hauntings, in undiscovered creatures, and yet octopus men and talking foxes? That was a little out there even for me to accept.

So maybe that was it. Maybe I was as mad as a box of tits and I was seeing more and more of this oddness as I barrelled towards another hard reset.

It was only as I finally stood up from the toilet, flushed, and washed my hands, that I became quite sure that I wasn't alone. The bathroom was small, just large enough to squash a toilet, sink, and a small corner bath into. The shower curtain was currently pulled across, hiding the small bath from view, but something was in there. Some dark shape, a black hump that was now dimly visible through the curtain.

This again?

'Hello? What sort of talking animal is waiting for me this time?'

My heart was beating loudly in my chest, banging a coward's tattoo against my ribcage, and yet there went my hand, reaching towards the shower curtain. Being generally afraid but also incurably curious was a damned curse.

'Just so you know, whoever you are, I have a gun. A big gun. Just brim-full of shooty bullets that will turn you into... a dead person. So no funny business.'

One breath. Two breaths. Three breaths.

I yanked back the shower curtain with a little cry of aggression, to find a dead body squashed into the small corner bath. A body with a large hole in its head. A body with numerous octopus arms that had left smears of dark blood all over the white plastic.

Mr Octopus. The creature that had attacked Mary Taylor. The creature that had tried to kill me.

I stumbled backwards out of my bathroom with a pinched cry of surprise and staggered into my living area.

'Finally,' came a voice from behind me. I whirled around, almost falling to the ground, to find the mad homeless woman sat on my sofa. 'Where the fuck have you been? I've been waiting hours.'

I stared at the woman in silent astonishment.

'Very rude way to treat a guest, and I should know, I always treat guests terribly.'

'You!'

She lifted a plastic bag and gave it a shake. 'I just went on a beer run, d'you want one?' She placed the bag next to her on the couch, pulled out a can, cracked it open, and downed it in one.

'You!' I cried. 'Here! In my home!'

She reached into the bag again and retrieved a fresh can of very cheap-looking lager.

A thought struck: 'My car. Did you fix my car after the crash?'

The woman shrugged. 'Maybe. Needed to get your heavy arse to the hospital and I wasn't going to carry you the whole bloody way. I'm not as young as I was, you know?'

'How? How did you do that? Because the Uncanny Wagon was wrecked. And now, it's, well, not.'

'You know,' she said, before burping and carrying on, 'I think there's something I'm forgetting.'

'What?'

'Oh, yep, got it.'

That's when I felt the mad woman's knuckles connect with my left cheek, followed by the floor connecting with my right cheek.

'Ow.'

'Too fucking right,' she replied.

I sat up, clutching my face. 'I think that's a first. I don't think anyone's ever hit me before.'

'Not true,' replied the woman, opening her second drink. 'I've hit you before, you piece of shit. Here,' she tossed a cold can my way. 'Press it against your cheek. Or drink it. Or both.' She cast a look about the room. 'You know, this is a very small flat. You must be doing terribly. I can't say how much that pleases me. Did I call you a piece of shit already?'

I nodded. 'You also punched me.'

'Oh yeah. Ha, good times, you piece of shit.'

I stood, keeping my distance as I opened the can and took a sip. 'You save me, you attack me, you fix my car. You're a very confusing person.'

The woman flopped on the couch then grabbed the remote and turned on the TV.

'So…?' I said.

'D'you get the wrestling? I like the wrestling. D'you remember Big Daddy? Now there was a fighter. And Giant Haystacks. Of course, these days it's all about the American wrestling. Sure, they bring a little extra razz-a-ma-tazz to the thing, but for my money, you can't beat those classic, Seventies and Eighties British wrestlers. Kendo Nagasaki! I met him once. Odd feller. Had me ejected from his home on account of the fact I'd broken in and shouldn't have been there.'

'I can empathise with that,' I replied. 'Can we please get back on topic, though?'

'Ha, that's me, wandering all over the shop. I've yet to meet a tangent I didn't love, you know. Now Rowdy Roddy Piper—if we're talking the American wrestling world—there was a man I *did* have time for...'

It was more than a little exasperating. I tried my best to bring the conversation back on track. 'Me, Joseph, you...?'

'...A woman fighting an overwhelming urge to squeeze your neck until that head of yours pops like a water balloon.'

A mad homeless woman in my front room and an octopus-person corpse in my bathroom. That mental reboot was looking to be right around the corner.

'Listen,' I said, 'I don't mean to be rude, but there's a dead monster in my bath – a dead monster that you killed with your fist.'

She raised her right hand, which was now engulfed in blue flame. 'Right hand of doom.'

'How... how are you doing that?'

'With ease,' she said, and winked at me.

'Yup, I've gone mad. That's all there is to it.'

'No. Not this time. Not yet, at least. And if you do, I'll twat you one.'

'What do you mean, "not this time"?' The woman fell silent. 'Look, you break into my home, dump a body in my bath, drop all sorts of hints about who I am... I think I'm owed an explanation.'

The woman gently placed down her can of beer, then stood, fixing me with darkening eyes. 'Owed? There's only one thing you're *owed*,' she replied, her left fist igniting with blue flames too now.

I backed up until the front door pressed against my rear end, 'Now, come on, let's not get out of hand here. Hulk Hogan! He's a wrestler.'

I yelled in surprise as a sudden, hard knock landed on the front door.

The woman shook her hands and the fire sputtered out. 'See who it is.'

I peeped through the door's spy hole. It was detectives Maya Myers and Sam Samm.

'Well, of course, it is,' I said, then added a 'shit shitting shit,' for good measure.

15

As the door was knocked again I did the dithering from one foot to the other, dancing on the spot thing you only ever see in old, farcical sitcoms.

'Mr Lake?' came Detective Myers' voice.

'Maybe if I stay quiet they'll go away?' I hissed at the homeless woman.

'I can hear you,' replied Myers.

'No, you can't,' I said. It was worth a shot.

'Yes, I can.'

Damn.

This was bad. I had two detectives behind one door, and a weird corpse behind another. It might have been the corpse of a monster, but a corpse nonetheless.

'Yes, sorry, just a... joke?'

I heard Detective Samm with two 'm's' laugh, then stop. 'I don't get it.'

'One moment. Just need to make myself decent,' I said.

'What?'

'Decent. I'm completely naked. Stuff flapping all over the place.'

I turned to the homeless woman and gestured wildly, unable to find the words to accompany the hands.

'Just don't let them in the bathroom,' she said, then shuffled in there, closing the door behind her.

Right, then. Crap.

I smoothed down my clothes, gave my hair a quick ruffle, and opened the door sporting the largest and fakest of fake grins ever committed to a face.

'Detectives! What a pleasure.'

'Hm,' replied Myers, walking in, Detective Samm at her heel.

I closed the door and turned to the two detectives, my eyes involuntarily flicking to the closed bathroom door.

'I like your home,' said Detective Samm. 'Cosy.'

'Yes. Thanks. Thank you.'

'I have a really big, four-bedroom place in Carlisle. Huge.'

'Well, that must be awful.'

Detective Samm nodded, sadly.

Myers was eyeing me. She must have blinked at least once, but it didn't feel like it. Could she sense something was up? Could she smell the corpse on the other side of the bathroom door?

'You seem nervous, Mr Lake,' she noted.

'Me? Nervous? Am I nervous? I don't feel nervous,' I replied nervously.

'Your voice is all high-pitched, you're sweating, and you're breathing heavily.'

'Um… yup. That's because… because of this thing that I am about to say…'

'Go on.'

'Right, well, it's because I was just… jogging? Jogging.'

'Jogging?'

'Jogging.' I performed a little jog on the spot by way of illustration, then stopped as that's obviously an insane thing to do. She knew what jogging was.

'So you've just been jogging, naked, inside your tiny flat?'

'Yep, in here. Forty laps around the front room. I'd jog outside but... all those car fumes and the hard paving stones are murder on my ankles. My body's a temple, Detective.'

Myers narrowed her eyes then turned away. I think I'd gotten away with that. Pretty slick, Joe.

'Bullshit,' barked Myers.

Pretty, pretty slick.

'Is there a reason for this very welcome visit?' I asked.

'Yes,' replied Detective Myers. 'Firstly, you have yet to come to the station to give an official statement about the incidents involving Mary Taylor and Janet Coyle. Any reason for the delay?'

Monsters, cats, talking foxes.

'Just busy. Work and stuff. Slipped my mind. Sorry.'

'And then we were informed that you were involved in an accident.'

'Oh, yes, that was just... a cat. As I told Chloe. Just swerved to avoid a cat. My own fault.'

'Hm. Well, we're going to accompany you to the station and get that statement off you now, Mr Lake.'

Ah, good. Going to the station meant leaving; leaving the madwoman and the monster corpse in my bathtub. This was very, very good.

'Great! Off we go then, can't wait, a trip to a police station, always a pleasure.' I slipped my coat on, ready to skip out of the door.

'Your bathroom.'

And there went my heart, diving into my stomach.

'I'm sorry?' I replied.

'Your bathroom, is it through there?'

'Why? Shall we go?' I said, pointing to the front door.

Myers headed for the closed bathroom door. 'I just need to quickly use your toilet. Too much coffee.'

'No!'

'No?' she replied, turning to me, hand on the door handle.

'It's just, I haven't bleached it in months. I'm... embarrassed to have a lady use it.'

'I'm not a lady, I'm a detective.'

She turned the handle and stepped in. I darted across the room and joined her inside.

'I can usually handle a piss on my own, Mr Lake.'

I looked around, bewildered. There was no sign of the homeless woman and no sign of any monster corpse in the bathtub. There weren't even any bloodstains. I did a little turn, peering around the tiny bathroom in astonishment.

'Mr Lake?'

'Hm?'

'Why are you in here?'

'I just... I thought I'd used up the last of the loo roll, but nope. There it is, hung the right way and everything.'

'I see it, Mr Lake.'

We stood in silence for a few seconds.

'Mr Lake?'

'Yes, Detective Myers?'

'Get out.'

'Yes, Detective Myers.'

With a final, confused look around the bathroom, I stepped out and re-joined Detective Samm.

'She's just peeing,' I said. 'By herself. No one else in there at all. Which is not strange, or scary. It's very, very normal.'

16

I wasn't exactly a stranger to police stations, but I can't say I'd ever exactly felt at ease inside of one.

For a while there, after first waking with a blank history next to Derwentwater, this station had been a regular haunt of mine. Numerous questions on the part of the police, and numerous visits from myself, desperately hoping for an update on my situation. A crumb of hope I could gobble up.

I hadn't visited for several years due to a terminal lack of movement on my case, which I presumed was still, technically, open. The station looked exactly the same. From the looks of things, they weren't planning on renovating the place until it started raining down on their heads.

It was evening now, fast approaching midnight, and I was sat in a small, grim-looking room with Detective Sam Samm sat across a table from me. I feigned looking over my written statement, nodding, and *hmming*, then nodding some more.

'Does that look about right?' asked Detective Samm.

'Yup,' I replied as I grabbed the pen and scribbled my name on the dotted line. 'That sounds about right.' Apart from not mentioning monsters with a beak for a face and giant, haunting, yellow eyes the size of teacup saucers.

'Well, then, that's that,' I said, sliding the signed statement back across the table.

'Great. Very helpful of you.'

'So, any leads yet?' I asked.

'Yes. Well, no, not exactly. Just the strange wiggles painted in blood, but we don't know what those mean. And we've put them through the computer and everything.'

That was a good idea, I should have done that. If the police computer had found nothing, that meant they weren't your everyday occult symbols. These were something else. Or just gibberish.

'I'm sure something will turn up,' I said. 'I have the utmost faith in you, Detective Samm.'

'Thank you very much. I know I'm not the best detective on the force, but I'm learning a lot working with Detective Myers. She really knows her stuff.'

'Yes, she seems very nice for a scary woman.'

Detective Samm laughed. 'Oh, don't mind that. She likes to put on a front, but she doesn't fool me.'

'Hey, why is she working here, anyway? Why would a detective from London relocate to this backwater station?'

'All I know is her last partner was killed on the job and shortly after, here she was.'

Well, that was interesting. And sad, of course. Sounded like she'd left behind a few ghosts.

Detective Samm sat forward suddenly, his brow knitted. 'Wait, I probably shouldn't have told you that. Oh, dear.'

'That's okay, Detective Samm, I won't tell anyone.'

'Phew, thanks,' he replied, relaxing back into his chair. 'She's the best partner I've ever had. The only one who doesn't make fun of me. Doesn't make too much fun, anyway. I think she's making me better.'

The door to the interrogation room opened and Myers stepped in, a styrofoam cup of coffee in hand. 'All done?'

Detective Samm waved the signed statement at her.

'So, am I good to go?' I asked.

'Good to go,' Myers replied. 'Unless there was something else you wanted to let me know.'

'Like...?'

'You tell me. It's obvious you have something on your mind. Something that scares you.'

She was one perceptive woman.

'Nope. Nothing going on up in this noggin.'

She placed the coffee cup down on the table and leaned over until our faces were so close I could feel her breath. 'I don't like it when people lie to my face, Mr Lake, and I don't like it when people keep things from me. You're doing both.'

I went to speak, but she cut me off.

'Don't bother denying it. You have a piece of this thing that you're not ready to hand over for some reason, but hand it over you will. You want to know why?'

I nodded.

'Because people are dying, and it's my job to stop them dying, and that means I will not stop until I have what I need. Do you understand me?'

'Understood.'

She straightened up, lifting her cup to her lips and taking a sip of vending machine coffee. 'Well? Are you going to tell me now or are you going to continue to piss me off?'

I stood and pulled my coat off the back of the chair, sliding it on. 'I'm really a bit bushed. Need to get home, I'm on an early shift at the hospital.'

She grimaced at me. 'Get out of my sight.'

I nodded and headed for the exit.

'Mr Lake?'

I paused.

'You will tell me. Sooner or later, you'll tell me. People are dead, and I have a bad feeling that more deaths are going to follow.'

I pulled my coat closed and strode out the door.

To say I felt like a glob of sputum hawked out of a drunk man's throat was something of an understatement. Myers was right. People had died, maybe more would, and I was keeping my cards under the table. But what else could I do? There was no way she or anyone else in authority was going to believe what I had to say. I wasn't even sure I believed all of it.

The dark outside matched my mood as I steered the Uncanny Wagon home. Maybe it was all over. The murders at least. The thing that had attacked Mary Taylor and me, and that had murdered Janet Coyle, was dead. A crazy woman had punched her fist through the thing's head, and the last time I saw it, its leftovers were curled up in my bathtub. Maybe that would be it. Maybe it was all over.

No, I didn't believe me either, but I was trying to perk up my gloomy spirit, okay?

The first thing I did upon arriving home was dart into the bathroom and check the tub. It was still empty. No monster corpse, no blood, no nothing. I leaned close, even clambered inside the thing, looking for any sign that it had been there. Not a trace. Not a clue.

This was rapidly returning to the, "I'm crazy and about to have a breakdown", idea. Because the only time the body had been there, the only time the homeless woman had been there, was when I was alone. As soon as someone else entered my world, the strange stuff that nobody would believe disappeared.

I saw the plastic bag sat on the couch, three cans from the six-pack still inside.

That didn't prove anything, I told myself. As part of my delusion, maybe I'd gone out and bought the beer and then, you know, forgotten. I sat next to the bag, pulling one out and taking a swig of warm beer before firing up my laptop and heading to my website. The mysterious reply, and my responses, remained unanswered.

Again, what did that prove?

I typed, *Hey, if you're real, you left your beer behind.*

I waited for a few minutes to see if the woman would reply, or suddenly stride back into my flat with a few choice swears to toss in my direction, but I sat alone and silent. I closed my laptop and slumped back, slowly working my way through the rest of my drink. I touched the can to my cheek where the woman's knuckles had connected. There was a bruise there, all right, but still, that wasn't proof of anything. I could have walked into any old door frame.

I needed to talk to Mary Taylor if she was up to it. She was the only one besides me that I knew for a fact was real and had been face-to-face with the killer. Maybe she could settle this, one way or another.

I worked my way through another can then went to bed, where I dreamt about the woman with red hair and her throne of skulls.

17

Far too early the next morning, I marched into the reception of Carlisle Hospital, ready for another shift of poop and puke mopping, bulb-changing, and general dogsbody work.

'Morning, Big Marge,' I said cheerily. Big Marge greeted me with a grunt, not looking up from her magazine.

'Not really a morning person, are you?'

'I'm not really an any-time-of-day person, Joe,' she replied.

'Mary Taylor,' I said, 'is she okay for a visit, d'you think?'

'Let's say she is. Why would she want to see you?'

'I saved her life, remember? I don't like to throw the word "hero" around, but, you know, I have heard others use it. About me.'

'The people you see in the mirror don't count, Joe.'

Early morning banter seen to, I headed up to Mary Taylor's new room. After the aborted attack and the broken window, she'd been relocated to a new private room at the other end of the hospital, with two uniformed officers sat outside, bored out of their minds. I thought I might need to talk my way past them, but it turned out they knew who I was. Most officers around here knew about me. The mystery man. The bloke in the clapped-out car with all the questions. They waved me through.

As the door swung closed, Mary sat up, startled.

'Who are you?'

'It's okay, I work here. I'm sort of a caretaker.'

'Oh. Okay, sorry.'

'Not to worry, I'd be a little jumpy if I was in your shoes. What happened to you was…'

'Not good.'

'Very not good.' I grabbed a chair and sat beside her.

'What is it you want?' she asked, still a little unsure of me.

'My name's Joseph Lake.'

Her eyes widened. 'Oh, it's you. You're the one who found me.'

'Yes. I'm sorry I was too late to do anything about Janet.'

Mary bit her lip and nodded, her eyes turning to shimmering pools. 'Oh, God. I just don't understand it. It's so crazy. So horrible. How can Janet be dead? She's the most alive person I ever met. I know that sounds stupid.'

'No. No, it doesn't.'

A smile twitched at the corners of her mouth for a moment, before the grief pulled them back down again and a tear slipped down her cheek.

'Mary, I'm sorry to ask, but… what do you remember about that night?'

Her hands gripped the covers, knuckle-white. She chewed at her bottom lip.

'Was there anything… anything at all that seemed, off?'

She looked at me again, a realisation dawning. 'You know, don't you?'

'The person who attacked you. Who attacked Janet. It wasn't really what you'd think of as a person at all, was it?'

Rivers ran down each cheek now. She shook her head. 'You saw it?' she whispered, her breath ragged.

'I saw it. More than once.'

'Monsters don't exist, Joseph. Monsters don't exist. I'm not some stupid little girl afraid of things under the bed, but that monster that attacked me, that.... that did that to my friend... that monster exists.'

'What did you tell the police?'

'Something that wouldn't make me sound insane. I just, I'm so sorry, Janet. So sorry. But I couldn't say the truth of it. I thought.... thought maybe it wasn't even true. But you've seen it, too.'

There was no point pretending I was mad anymore. No point in trying to brush this aside, or tell myself I was, I don't know, hallucinating this conversation or something. It was real. It was all real. I only had to look in Mary Taylor's eyes to know that.

Monsters were real.

I placed my hand over hers. 'Don't worry. You're okay now. You're safe.'

We spoke a little more and I tried to distract her from thinking about how scared she was. I think maybe it even worked a little. I left, promising to pay her another visit, loaded with chocolate and a book or two to keep her busy. If almost-deadly encounters with monsters weren't enough to drive her insane, being trapped in a hospital bed and suffering a non-stop diet of daytime TV definitely would.

I'd worked in the hospital long enough to know the computer logins that I shouldn't, and so after leaving Mary Taylor behind, I found the nearest unmanned computer, slipped behind the desk, and gave myself access to the hospital's medical records.

I had a sudden, sure feeling that the attack on Mary and Janet couldn't have been the first of its sort. Searching for anything that looked similar, I found at least two cases in the past couple of months that might fit the bill. A man first, Geoff Smith, forty-two, dead three months ago. And there, Angela Carter, nineteen, died seven weeks back. Both had suffered severe throat lacerations.

I wondered if that would be all, or if there were more. More that hadn't been found. Dead bodies taken someplace else. Some "monster's lair", or even just out of view of any common foot traffic. Dead bodies surrounded by strange, occult symbols, painted in their own blood, waiting to be stumbled upon by a holidaying rambler in the hills. Here to take in the best sights the country had to offer, only to find the worst kind of sight anyone could see.

A hand gripped my shoulder and spun me around.

'What on earth do you think you're up to?'

Doctor Neil, the Lord of Wank-ville, stood there fuming, his usually pallid skin a trembling puce.

'I was only browsing for porn, I swear it, Doctor Neil,' I replied, quickly closing the session so he wasn't able to see what I'd been up to.

'You're not authorised to access these systems, you're only authorised to push a mop across a shit-smeared floor.'

'I'm sorry, I've seen you using the hospital's computers and just assumed that meant any old arsehole could have a go.'

Doctor Neil's face moved rapidly between many different expressions as he took in what I just said. Doctor Neil and I had always had this sort of antagonistic relationship, though I couldn't say for sure why. Sometimes another person just rubs you up the wrong way. At times I did think it might have something to do with the closeness of mine and Chloe's relationship. Perhaps he was jealous. That would make sense. I'd seen the way he looked at her.

A flurry of noisy activity caught our attention as a trolley holding a body burst through the double doors at the far end of the corridor. Doctor Neil switched instantly into work mode and left me behind.

Chloe and Jim, one of the nurses, were working frantically on a body as they moved. Blood poured from a wound on the patient's neck. As they passed me by. I got a closer look at the person on the trolley and recognised him at once.

It was Detective Sam Samm.

18

I found Chloe in the car park half an hour later.

I sidled up and leant against the wall next to her, and she passed me the half-done cigarette she'd been smoking. I took it, inhaled, and handed it back.

'You did everything you could,' I offered quietly.

Chloe rested her head against my shoulder and continued to smoke in silence. The number of times I'd comforted her when she'd failed to hold back death numbered in the hundreds at this point, but it never seemed to get any easier for her. I'd heard that most doctors managed to somehow step away from it, from the crushing reality of all that death, for the sake of their own well-being. Chloe had never learned that trick.

Detective Sam Samm was dead. That nice, odd man had been murdered and every part of me was screaming that it was connected to what had happened to Mary and Janet. What had happened to me. The octopus creature. It had gotten to Detective Samm somehow. Either the creature had managed to renew itself, or there were more of the things out there. Neither option was particularly appealing.

'You know,' said Chloe softly, breaking my chain of thought,

'I don't remember everyone who I've failed to save. It happens, you know? That's part of the job, death. Happens all the time. All the time. Sometimes more than once a day. One goes after the next and you're just there, trying to hold on to their hand as they slip under the water. There goes another one. And another. And another. And I'm just desperately trying to keep hold of them as they're dragged away. There have been so, so many. But I still remember the first person I lost on the job.'

She paused, stomping out the butt of her smoke before pulling a fresh one out of the packet, lighting it, and carrying on, her eyes focused on something I couldn't see.

'It was my second day at work. I'd been allowed one death-free day, then a few hours into day two, in she came. Seven years old. Alice Madders. She'd hit her head playing at the park and her parents had brought her in. Over-cautious is what I thought. She seemed fine. Kids fall, they hit their heads, they shake it off. I did an examination, gave Alice some sweets from the vending machine, assured the parents that everything was going to be all right. Their daughter was just going to have a little bruise on her temple. I even felt vaguely annoyed. Annoyed that they were wasting resources and time that could be better used elsewhere, all because they were nervous parents, wrapping their child in cotton wool. Five minutes after telling the parents everything was fine, Alice Madders began fitting. Her body bent back like she was trying to snap her own spine. Her eyes rolled into her head, her mouth started foaming. I didn't know what to do. The whole world slowed to a crawl. Just a blur. I found out later that the knock on the head had caused a bleed on the brain. There was nothing I could have done about it. The moment she'd hit her head, she was dead. Alice Madders. Red hair in ponytails and her front two teeth missing, a gap for adult teeth that never got to grow.'

We sat and smoked in silence after that, her head on my shoulder, our hands clasped together.

I had no intention of visiting the morgue, but my feet took me there, anyway.

I pushed quietly through the double doors and the lights flickered on, triggered by my presence. The room was empty and the chill of the place prickled my skin. Against one wall were twelve metal doors, hiding gaps long enough to slide a body in. Detective Samm hadn't been placed in one of the drawers yet, his body lay on the mortuary slab in the middle of the room. I approached slowly, placing each foot gently in front of the other. A childish fear bubbled up that if I were to make too much noise I'd disturb the corpse. It would sit up sharply, its eyes black, dead hands reaching for me, clawing at my throat.

I looked down at the poor man. Like Janet Coyle, his neck had been severely injured. Having seen the creature up close, I had to assume it was the large beak that had done the damage. But why? Why were they murdering people? They didn't seem to be eating them. They weren't draining them of blood like a vampire. They were just killing them and leaving their bodies surrounded by strange, cultish symbols. For what purpose? What was the point in it all? Just for the thrill of killing? Some gut instinct told me it had to be more than that. There had to be some reason behind it all.

At first, I didn't even realise that my hands were moving to touch the deceased Detective Samm. It wasn't until the tips of my fingers connected with the chill skin of his temples that what I was doing became clear.

I wanted to *see*.

It was like a locked door in my mind had opened a crack and muscle memory was taking over. I didn't quite understand what was happening, but my body did, as sure as I could tie my shoelaces without thinking about it (most of the time).

I held my breath, and—

I feel fear.

Fear so strong I can taste it. Smell it. Hear it, beating in my ears. A tribal drum beat telling me death is near, death is near, death is near.

I am Detective Sam Samm, and I am afraid. I am Detective Sam Samm, and I am Joseph Lake. I am both. I can't hear Detective Samm's thoughts, but I feel what he feels, the emotions at war within him. I see what he sees.

I am in a house. This is my house. Detective Samm's house. It judders past like a film with frames removed. I can hear my breath, the air sucked rapidly into my lungs and expelled.

I am scared.

Terrified.

I am prey and I am being hunted.

I know this without seeing who's doing the hunting, without hearing Detective Samm's thoughts. The way my heart is beating, my eyes pinned, unblinking, the pure fear powering my limbs; these things tell me everything.

I am prey.

I am being hunted.

They will catch me and I will die.

I'm upstairs, in a bedroom, looking desperately to escape. The way downstairs is cut off. Only one option: the window. As it stutters towards me, my fingers reach for the handle, but then, as though the window had suddenly, impossibly, been pulled away from me, it retreats. I realise then that I am the one who has been pulled away. Something cold and strong is wrapped around my ankle and is pulling me towards it.

I twist, a scream on my tongue, to see the black shape of a monster, its beak clicking and screeching, its octopus limbs twitching, ready, eager, desperate. I'm going to die, I'm going to die, I'm going to—

I staggered back, pulling my hands away from Detective Samm's forehead, gasping for air. Falling to my knees, I clutched at my heart, convinced it was about to give out. Which was not the most pleasant of feelings.

'Hail, Magic Eater!'

I fell back with a yelp at the sudden intrusion. I looked up to see the fox, its axe held high and proud, stood upon Detective Samm's chest.

'Saviour of the Dark Lakes! Eater of worlds!'

'Shut up,' I replied.

The fox blinked twice then lowered its axe. 'Bit rude.'

'How are you back? I thought that woman with the red hair tore your head off.'

'Well, aye, she did.'

'Then...?' I gestured at his head, which was very much attached to his body.

'She'll let my death stick at some point, so she will. It's just I have yet to fully make amends for my past errors, that's all.'

I stood, shaking from what I'd just experienced. From what Detective Samm had experienced.

'What's happening to me?'

'How d'you mean?'

'When I touched that dead body—Detective Samm, the man you are standing on—I felt things. Saw things.'

'Course you did. The doors are starting to open, y'see? Open they go and the real you's peering out.'

I was past the point of questioning this creature's existence by now. What had happened just then, that was no delusion. I'd touched Detective Samm's corpse and been given a glimpse of his final moments. That was *real.* I knew it was. I remembered the flash in the alley before I stumbled across Janet Coyle's dead body. The moment of insight as the creature had brushed past me, our bodies briefly touching, before I discovered Mary Taylor.

Wait a gosh-darned moment—

The fox waved, I could see his face smiling back.

'I saw you,' I cried. 'When this all started, just before I

found Mary Taylor. I had a... feeling. An episode. Like I could sense what the monster was feeling, and then I saw you. Just for a moment. I saw your face.'

'Finally, a flare shot into the dark,' replied the fox. 'I've been trying to find my way to you for so very long. I was starting to think I never would. But I'm patient, me. I wait. And I wait. And I keep these eyes peeled and my axe sharp, so when the moment comes, I can use it to chop my way through to you. Ten years, it took. Ten years before you finally used your powers again. And there I was, eyes as sharp as knives, waiting on behalf of the Red Woman. And now here I am again.'

Ten years? Ten years since I woke next to Derwentwater with no memory.

'You know who I am.'

'Of course, I do. All of the Dark Lakes knows you. All hail our saviour! All hail the Magic Eater!'

I lunged at the fox, grabbing him by the scruff of his neck and shaking him. 'Tell me who I am.'

'What are you doing in here?' asked a voice.

I turned in surprise to find Detective Myers. I turned back, but the fox was gone. Only Detective Samm's corpse remained.

'I said, what are you doing in here?' Myers demanded.

'Nothing. I'm just, working. Cleaning.'

She grimaced and walked towards me. For a moment I thought she might be the second woman in as many days to punch me in the face, but at the last moment, she stepped past me to look down at her dead partner.

'I'm sorry,' I said. 'For your loss.'

She snorted once. We stood in silence for several heavy seconds.

'Do you think...' Detective Myers started, then hesitated, then carried on, 'do you think death can follow you?'

I went to answer, then found myself unable to think of anything.

'Doesn't matter,' she said. 'Now get the hell out of here.'

Perhaps I should have told her. Told her about what it was that had killed her partner. But what would be the point? Why would she believe me? She just lost her second partner in the force – for me to suggest the culprit of poor Detective Samm's demise was a creature with octopus arms would be insensitive at best.

'Really. He was a good one.'

I wanted to say more, to console her in some way, but I felt there was only one thing she wanted from me at that moment.

I walked to the exit and left her alone with her dead partner.

19

I had planned to find Chloe, to suggest we go out and eat something fatty and drink liquids designed to render your brain a train-wreck the next morning, but before I could find her, my phone rang.

'Where's my Boris?' screamed Mrs Coates.

'Ah, yes, fear not, I am on the case. Boris is my number one priority.'

'You found him once, find him again. Today! Or you're off the case. I want my puss puss back.'

I opened my mouth to reply, but she'd already hung up.

I carried on looking for Chloe, but Big Marge informed me that she was in one of the nurse's rooms having a nap, so I decided to leave her to it and find Mrs Coates' damned cat once and for all. Yes, the world was tilting on its axis, but I am a man of my word. I'd been hired to do a job, and I couldn't afford another bad review. My service was already down to two stars on Yelp.

I slipped into the Uncanny Wagon and sped along the empty roads, pulling to a stop in Oldstone some thirty minutes later. Missing cat posters blew past me across the tarmac, a paper tumbleweed.

Unfortunately, my plan for finding Boris—or any of the cats for that matter—had not progressed any from last time. I mean, how exactly do you find a cat that doesn't want to be found? I retrieved the cat box and cat food from the back seat and readied myself for a long, dull wait while I watched my cunning trap.

The fox knew who I was. That was the thought at the front of my mind. As I looked for Chloe, as I drove to Oldstone, as I placed a small pile of cat treats inside the cat box. The fox knew who I was and he'd been looking for me.

I'd often fantasised about someone from my past turning up to say they knew who I was, but not once had that person been an axe-wielding fox. Was he telling the truth? It was hard to say, as I hadn't had much experience telling whether a talking animal was lying to me or not.

Then there was the homeless woman. She, too, seemed to know more about me than I did. The old me, at least. A talking fox and a fighty mad woman were, maybe, at last, the keys to unlocking my past. Now, if only they wouldn't keep disappearing, maybe I could get a straight answer out of them.

I felt my phone vibrating in my pocket and pulled it out to see Chloe's name.

'Hello! Hello, there. You. Hello you. It is me,' I said. Smooth as a mother-fornicator.

'Hey, where are you?' she asked.

'On a cat hunt in Oldstone.'

'Are you getting a pet?'

'No, just helping out an old woman. How are you? I came to find you before heading off, but Big Marge said you were having forty winks.'

'Yeah, I just needed to crash for a bit.'

'Are you okay?'

'Of course. Will you come over later?'

Hello...

'Yeah, I can come over. There. To yours. Where you live.'

'You don't mind?'

I will literally crawl on my belly across poop-smeared shards of broken glass for this.

'Of course not. I had a thing, but I can probably move it.'

'You can?'

'I can move it. Consider it moved. It was here, now it's over there. Moved.'

'Thanks. Thank you. I'll be back a little after seven. Be there waiting for me?'

'Absolutely.'

'Cool. Oh, and Joe?'

'Yep?'

'Bring a toothbrush.'

And then she hung up.

I stood statue-still for several minutes, the phone still glued to my ear. Perhaps her own toothbrush was broken and Chloe was asking for a replacement? A friendly favour?

'Will do,' I replied in a tiny voice, several minutes after she'd hung up.

Well, then. Well, well, wellity, well.

My cheeks ached from over-grinning. I had a few hours before I was due to loiter hormonally outside of Chloe's front door, so I began to set my cat-nabbing trap at different places around Oldstone. I'd put the food-laden cat box down, watch from a discreet distance for half an hour or so, then move on to somewhere else. My mind should really have still been focusing on the talking fox and the fighty mad woman, but instead, my head was full of Chloe and my eyes full of hearts. So much so that, at the final place I rested the cat box, it took me almost twenty minutes to notice that I was sat cross-legged on the grass, in front of a dead cat. I might not have noticed at all if I hadn't decided to stretch back and found myself resting my head on a tiny, furry corpse.

After a suitable amount of yelping and shuddering, I got down on my knees and gave the deceased moggy a closer look.

I wondered how many of the hundreds of missing cat posters pasted all around Oldstone featured this poor cat's mugshot.

'Bad luck, fella,' I said.

It was sad, but a dead cat was not what I'd been looking for. I was looking for, well, alive cats. Boris specifically, but really any live cat would have done. I felt for sure that if the cats had all disappeared over the space of a few days, then it seemed likely all or most had ended up in the same place. For whatever reason.

It was then that a thought struck.

'Oh...'

The strange feelings during the aftermath of the attack on Janet and Mary.

The things I saw when I touched Detective Samm's corpse.

Maybe a dead cat wouldn't be so useless after all. Maybe it could tell me exactly what I needed to know. The fox had said the real me was peeking out. *You finally used your powers again*. I didn't feel powerful, and I'd no idea how I'd managed to make what had happened happen. Worth a shot, though.

I looked down at the dead cat and let out a hard breath, preparing myself.

'Okay, magic brain, I am your master, please do your insight thing.' I punctuated my command with a little hand flourish that felt suitably mystical, then placed my palms on the dead cat. Which was gross.

Of course, a little earlier I'd been touching a dead man, but that had been an almost unconscious decision. This time it was all me. Really there. Choosing to put my hands on a dead thing.

Nothing happened.

I raised my hands to the sky. 'Show me your death,' I commanded, then grabbed the cat again.

Zilch.

Not a thing.

I didn't have powers, that was absurd. There had to have been some other explanation for my earlier "insights". The fox, perhaps. A talking fox is a pretty magical thing, maybe he had the powers and that's what affected me.

But then why would he say that I was using my powers at last?

I grunted in frustrated confusion—not an unfamiliar emotion for me—and placed my hands on the deceased family pet without thinking. No daft commands, no great thought behind it or hand gestures, I just touched the thing with no expectations.

And that's when it happened.

Scents, sounds, everywhere. A new world of information, so vivid, a feeling of poise, of strength, of hunger of...

Show me where, show me where...

I am low to the ground, moving at speed, need to hide, need to go back, fear. I feel fear. My heart is beating so fast. It's not safe, not safe. I see the streets rush by. People, sounds, smells, the giant world around me, and something else, something else. I don't like it. I don't like it. Run, run, run. Back to the safe place. This is not safe. Back to the safe place—

I gasped as the connection was broken, my eyes blinking rapidly as I found myself in a different place to where I'd started. I was out of breath. I think I'd been running. I could see Oldstone a good half-mile away, and in front of me a large barn.

For a moment or two, I let the fact that I'd just experienced the emotions, sights and smells of a cat wash over me. Because that's weird. That's very, very weird. And no fox around, so... it was me. I'd done that. I'd touched the dead body of a cat and been given a glimpse into its life. That was exciting. Or terrifying. One of the two.

I wondered what else I might be capable of.

The barn in front of me didn't look like it was in use anymore, in fact, it looked as though a strong gust of wind might reduce it to kindling. The door screeched a rusty-hinged complaint as I opened it and stepped inside to be greeted by a hundred glowing pricks of light. It was like I was looking into the night sky and stars were twinkling back at me.

I blinked, and as I became more accustomed to the gloom, I saw that these weren't impossible stars, they were eyes. The barn was absolutely packed to the rafters with Oldstone's missing cats.

'I don't suppose any of you are talking cats and can tell me just why it is you're all hiding out in this stinky barn? Daft question I know, but I have recently made the acquaintance of a very talkative fox.'

None of them answered.

Maybe they didn't feel like a chat.

Cats.

20

I was able to spot Boris amongst the crush, but having failed to bring my cat box with me, I settled for taking a picture or two as evidence. Of Boris, and of the rest of the cat-filled barn.

I still didn't know for sure why the moggies had run away from their homes, or why they felt the need to huddle together for safety, but at least I knew where they were.

I told the cats to stay put and headed off towards Mrs Coates' home to bring her the good news.

I'd been an investigator of the peculiar for years now, but my ratio of solved to unsolved was pretty poor. By which I mean I rarely ever came out on top. That's the thing with the bizarre and inexplicable, it rather likes to stay that way. So here I was with a genuine "solved" under my belt, and I'd done it all by myself. Just me and my brand new superpowers.

I walked towards Mrs Coates' home with a spring in my step. Cats located, things of an adult nature waiting for me at Chloe's later, the gratitude of a village of cat lovers incoming. This was turning into quite the day.

So, of course, something had to come along and turn it all to dung.

It was Mrs Coates' front door that did it.

As I pushed open the gate to her well-tended garden, bursting full of brightly coloured flowers and expertly manicured bushes, I saw that the door was slightly ajar. Now, this in itself shouldn't be a cause for concern. Perhaps she'd been doing something in the garden and had stepped back inside for a moment. That's a normal enough thing to have done.

So why was my heart starting to increase its rhythm? Why was a knot forming in my stomach? My body knew something was wrong, even if I had no real evidence for it.

'Mrs Coates?' I said as I reached the door. 'Hello, Mrs Coates? It's Joseph Lake, here about your cat. Well, all the cats.'

A cold, empty silence. I pushed the door open and stepped warily into her home.

'Hello, Mrs Coates? I'm just coming inside now. Is there any reason why my brain is telling me to turn tail and run for the hills?'

Staircase to my right, two doors on the left, a third at the far end. Which way to go? Dealer's choice.

I made my way towards the nearest door and stepped inside.

The front room was neat, but a riot of clashing floral patterns. The carpet, the wallpaper, the furniture. This woman liked her flowers. And a headache, if the way it was affecting me had anything to do with it. Perched on the fireplace was a picture of a much younger Mrs Coates and a beaming man. Ex-husband? I hadn't noticed a wedding ring.

I left and made my way to the second room. This back-room was more subdued than the first and contained a couch, plus a desk with an old foot-pedal powered sewing machine on top.

Kitchen next.

'Mrs Coates?'

There was a cup of tea on the kitchen table. I placed my hand against it. The porcelain was still warm.

I turned back and made my way to the staircase, peering up into the dark second floor.

'Hello? Please say something reassuring so my stomach will stop doing somersaults, Mrs Coates.'

I began to make my way up the stairs, each one creaking under my weight. This was an old house. Well, all the buildings in Oldstone were old. Old Oldstone.

It was halfway up the stairs that I noticed the smudges of dark red on the steps. Splatters against the pristine white of the staircase runner.

Blood. Grisly crumbs leading me up and up.

I stepped on to the landing and saw the door to one of the bedrooms was open. A foot poked out into the corridor, its sole facing me.

'Mrs Coates?'

I ran to her, pushing the door open, and found her stretched out on the carpet, her throat torn out, strange occult-looking symbols daubed on the carpet around her.

'Oh, Christ...'

I crouched, feeling for a pulse as if the truth of the matter wasn't self-evident. Mrs Coates was very, very dead.

I stood, reaching into my pocket to retrieve my phone and call the police, then froze as a dark shape twitched in my periphery. The thick, lined curtains were drawn, lights off, and much of the room was robed in shadow. A perfect place for a monster to lurk.

I backed away as an octopus limb curled out of the shadows.

'Bastard. You bastard,' I said, my anger at Mrs Coates' death trumping my legs' demands to turn and run. Instead, I stepped further into the room as though I'd meant to fight the creature that had killed this poor woman.

The monster screamed and lunged out of the black at me. I stepped back, my heel catching something, and realised with horror that I'd been tripped by Mrs Coates' prone body.

I landed hard, bones jarring, wind jerked out of me, but there was no time to count my bruises. I scrambled backwards on my hands and feet as the creature bent to grab at me, my boot kicking out and catching the thing in the head.

It reeled back, limbs thrashing in fury. Meanwhile, I turned, stood, and ran. The door at the other end of the landing erupted in a blizzard of wooden needles as a second octopus man burst from inside.

'Shit—'

I bolted for the staircase. I was closer, I could make it, I could escape, I could run from the house and not stop running until I was back in the Uncanny Wagon, stomping on the accelerator and powering out of town.

The stairway greeted me. I placed one foot down, then a fleshy limb struck my back foot and the world turned over and over, hard edges assaulting me until my painful whirl of a journey was brought to a sudden stop. My vision blurred and spat stars.

'Up, get up, move,' I said, my voice a slur.

I looked up, time now moving at a crawl, to see the two octopus creatures descending towards me, beaks snapping hungrily. One walked down the stairs, the other scuttled down the wall with its suckered limbs.

'Get up.'

Body aching, knees treacherous, I pushed myself to my feet and opened the front door to find a third monster stood in its frame.

I rocked back on my heels, one octopus man before me, another behind, the third now slithering obscenely across the ceiling above. I was a fly, caught in a web, as three spiders raced to claim me for their dinner.

'Get back,' I yelled, a pointless cry of defiance, as I knew full well I was dead. I was dead, and that was that. There was no way out. This was it: three live monsters and one soon-to-be-dead me.

The creatures were in no rush. Beaks wide, throats clicking, they moved incrementally towards me. Towards my death.

This wasn't fair. Wasn't right. None of it was. Who were these things to take my life from me?

'I said, get back!'

The creatures jerked back as though I'd pulled a weapon. At first, I was confused. What did they have to worry about? Here I was, a nice, fleshy, easy kill, just waiting to have my throat torn open. It was then that I realised my hands were engulfed in bright, blue flames.

Flames meant fire.

Oh shit, I was on fire!

I stepped back, waving my arms around, trying to extinguish the flames and wondering why I didn't feel any pain.

Suddenly over their uncertainty, the creatures rushed me. My world became blue flames and writhing, suckered limbs as death's guillotine came crashing down on me.

21

I assumed I was dead.

Well, you would, wouldn't you?

I was on fire and about half a second away from having three bloodthirsty creatures tear me to pieces.

I was dead. I was an ex-Joseph Lake. Which meant that I wouldn't be going around Chloe's later with a fresh toothbrush tucked into my coat pocket.

Damn.

In that moment, that was the thing that stung the most. Not my death, not my murder at the tentacles of three complete bastards, but the idea that something just beginning, something potentially wonderful, was about to be cut off at the knees.

I'd been infatuated, or in love, or in lust, or all three, with Chloe Palmer ever since I first laid eyes on her. It was a Tuesday. Just a normal, boring, run-of-the-mill Tuesday, and Doctor Alex Kurd was showing a couple of the new recruits around the hospital. I was up a ladder prodding at a light fitting as they passed by.

As *she* passed by.

We met properly the next morning when I drove my car

directly into the back of hers. She was stationary in the car park at the time. She could have been furious. Should have been. But as I waved my arms around, trying to desperately inform her of the bee that had distracted me and caused the accident, she did the strangest thing. She began to laugh. She didn't shout at me. Didn't swear at me. Didn't report me. She just laughed, and I found myself laughing with her.

I was too much of an awkward fool to ever do anything about it, of course, so the years rolled on and I set up shop in the Friend Zone. Which was not at all pleasant at times, particularly when she'd choose to confide in me about her latest man. Her current bedfellow. Those times really slid a shard of ice in the old heart, but then I'd feel guilty for how happy I was each time those short relationships spluttered, coughed, and died. She'd be on the couch, red-eyed, stuffing ice cream into her face hole, and I'd be nodding sympathetically while my insides did a vigorous interpretation of *Riverdance*.

From time to time, I got the feeling she was waiting for me to ask her out. To finally make my feelings known. But the longer time went on, the harder it became. And then at last. At last, at last, we'd gotten past all that. She liked me. She *actually* liked me, and knew for sure that I liked her. We'd done the kissing. And now here I was, dead and massively annoyed that the great romance of my daft life was over before it could begin.

What rotten, shitty luck.

It was all coming together nicely, and now I was just another dead person.

Damn, damn, and double-damn with a cherry on top.

I only realised I wasn't technically dead when something prodded my side and I opened my eyes to find the fox looking up at me, axe in hand.

'All hail, the saviour!'

'Oh, not you again.'

I tried to move but realised that I was affixed to a giant tree by thick chains.

'Wait, I'm alive. I'm alive, aren't I?'

'All hail, the Magic Eater!'

'I'm alive! Chloe Alison Palmer, I am alive.'

This was possibly the happiest anyone who had just awoken to find themselves chained to a tree had ever been.

'I have him chained to the Tree of Anguish. Do you see him, Red Woman?' asked the fox, projecting his words at the rolling red fire of the sky.

I was back in the strange place. What had he called it, the fox? The Dark Lakes? With its fields of bones, fire for sky, and bloody grasses.

'Is this my time? Shall death be my friend at last?' the fox asked in a small voice.

'Why am I here again?' I asked.

'Twas your choice, not mine,' he replied. 'I did not bring you here, you brought yourself as doom descended.'

I wriggled beneath the chains, but they only seemed to tighten as I fought them, as though they were alive and resisting my struggle.

'That's because they are,' said a voice I recognised. I twisted my head as far as I could, to see the woman approaching with her bright, red hair.

'Living chains? Right. Do they have a name? It's rude not to introduce yourself to someone.'

The chains gave me an extra squeeze that momentarily prevented me from breathing.

'Point taken,' I wheezed. 'No more shit-talking the magical chains.'

'Look, here he is again,' said the fox, pointing at me with his axe. 'Surely, now? I have done my duty, yes? Done and done and done, and my weary body craves its prize.'

The Red Woman crouched before the fox and extended a pale hand, scratching at him under the chin affectionately. 'Your time will come. Your time will end. But not yet.'

The fox was close to tears.

The Red Woman stood and turned to me, walking slowly forward. 'Do you know what you are yet?'

'In a lot of trouble?'

A small smile. She was truly stunning, but something about her made my stomach squirm.

'It is starting to become clear though, yes?' She reached out, her long, elegant fingers like feathers of ice across my cheek.

'Am I... magic?'

Her thumb stroked my lower lip. 'You're so much more than that. Shall I show you your future?'

'Depends. Is it a nice future?'

She smiled again. 'Oh, yes. It's... delicious.'

She placed her right hand against my forehead and—

I stride across the face of the earth, a giant, a beast. My skin ripples with flames, my eyes black holes that see and judge and own all.

Screams caress my ears. This is my music. The music of fear. Of pain. Of the world bending to my will. This is my food. I swallow it down but my stomach is never full. Never satiated. Never satisfied.

The Uncanny rise to block my path, and I eat them. I tear them in two and drink their power. I feel their bones crunch between my teeth and I think that this is good.

The end, the end, I am the end. And I am the beginning, too. A new, dark beginning. From the ashes I sow shall rise a new world. My world.

At my side is the army of the dead. My army. We step from the Dark Lakes and shake off the water, and all the world burns and fear and fear and fear and—

'Stop!' My head hung loose and I gasped for air.

'Was it not beautiful?' asked the Red Woman.

'What was that? What was that... thing?'

'It was your choice. You will remember that. You wanted it. You want it. Become the Magic Eater.'

What was this? Besides terrifying and perplexing, obviously. A trick? What was it the Red Woman was trying to get me to do? I wished someone would just give me a straight answer.

'I don't know what you're talking about. Also, these chains really chafe. Could you just let me down? And your hands are freezing. A sign of poor circulation; I'd see a doctor if I were you."

'Look at what you have become. A chattering fool, blind to your true purpose. Your true destiny.'

'All hail the saviour,' cried the fox, and the sky of fire roared its approval.

22

The buzz of a strip light.

I sniffed and caught a smell I knew all too well. I was laid up in a hospital bed again. My eyes creaked open. Someone was sat on a chair at my bedside.

'Chloe?' I said, my dry throat cracking.

'Afraid not,' replied Detective Maya Myers.

I sat up in surprise. Myers handed me a plastic cup of water, which I took after a moment's hesitation and downed in one.

'Thanks. Thank you.'

Myers remained leaning towards me, her eyes narrowed. 'How about now, Mr Lake?'

'How about now, what?'

'Don't you dare give me that bullshit,' she replied with venom. 'People are dying. My partner, Detective Samm, has been murdered. And now you're discovered, unconscious in an old woman's house, and the old woman it belongs to is dead upstairs. Same MO as the others. So why don't you start giving me some answers before I start knocking teeth down your throat.'

Well, that was certainly to the point.

'I didn't do it. I didn't kill any of them,' I replied.

She snorted, kicking back her chair as she stood. 'I know that. You might be many things, but a killer you are not.'

'Well, thanks. Thank you. Just as long as that's clear.'

Myers lunged forward, grabbing me by the collar of my hospital gown, and pulling me forward. 'Tell me what you know.'

'I can't.'

'Tell me!' She shoved me back and turned away in disgust.

'I don't know what I can say.'

'Why? Who's got something on you? We can protect you.'

'No one has anything on me. It's just that you won't believe me. Even if I tell you everything I've seen, or think I've seen, you won't believe a word of it.'

Myers sagged and slumped back on her chair. 'Just tell me. I lost my partner. Lost another partner. Just tell me something. Anything.'

For the first time since I'd met her, Detective Maya Myers looked small. Uncertain. Defeated, even. It didn't look right. This wasn't her. She was strong. I found myself telling some of the truth without even making the decision to do so.

'Do you believe in monsters, Detective?'

She looked up at me, eyes wide. 'Monsters?'

What was that I saw in those eyes? Was that... recognition?

'You *do* know, don't you?'

'Joseph, tell me about the monsters.'

It was at that moment that the door to my private room burst open and a woman I'd never met before stormed in. Her hair was pulled back, the smart suit she wore, fierce, and the briefcase she clutched, shiny.

'Stop talking,' she said. Well, ordered. Every sentence she spoke was a blunt instrument.

'Who are you?' asked Myers, and the woman handed her a card.

'Belinda Washington. I am Mr Lake's lawyer.'

'You are?' I asked, quite flummoxed.

'I am. Detective Myers, have you been questioning my client without proper legal representation present?'

'I just—'

'I'll take that as a yes. Do you intend to charge my client with anything?'

Myers looked at me. I shrugged.

'No, I do not,' she replied.

'In that case, Mr Lake, I suggest you get up out of bed, collect your belongings, and follow me out of this building.'

Myers looked at me again, clearly not done with her questioning. In all honesty, I wasn't done with her either. When I mentioned monsters I'd seen a look of recognition, not a look of confusion, or anger. What did Maya know about monsters? I really wanted to find out more, but Belinda Washington hustled Maya from the room as I dressed. When I stepped into the corridor, only my mysterious lawyer was waiting for me.

'Let's go,' she said.

'Yeah, I don't know who you are, so forgive me for not just following blindly on. It's been a strange few days.'

'Come along,' she said. 'I'll fill you in on the drive. Your car is outside, you can drop me off.'

'My car? How did my car get here...?'

I watched, bewildered, as she turned sharply on her black heels and strode away.

Now, a smart person, after all he'd experienced, would not have followed her quite so willingly, fearing some sort of trap might be looming on the horizon. So what did I do?

'Hey, wait for me.'

I threw on my coat and chased after her.

s we pulled away from the hospital, Belinda Washington sat silently, staring out of the windscreen.'

'Sorry, but when did you take me on as a client? Did Chloe hire you, or...?'

'No one hired me, you tool.'

I turned to her in surprise, only to find that smartly-dressed Belinda Washington was no longer sat next to me. Instead, it was the mad homeless woman, a can of strong lager balanced on her lap where her shiny briefcase had once been.

I did a little scream and jerked the steering wheel. The Uncanny Wagon swerved this way and that, almost hitting a tree, and then I parked up and turned to the woman, my back pressed against the driver's door.

'It's you!'

'You're welcome. I just saved your miserable hide from a prison cell.'

'No. No, you didn't. Myers wasn't going to arrest me, we were just talking.'

'Oh.' The woman opened her can, took a sip, and shrugged. 'We all make mistakes.'

I looked at her warily, trying to find any hint of the person she'd been moments before.

'How did you...?' I waved my hand in front of my face.

'With difficulty. A little illusion magic, a little confusion magic. It stings like a fucker to keep it up for that long. I'll be pissing blood tonight.'

'Magic? That was magic? *Magic*-magic?'

The woman sighed. 'Well, duh.'

'Okay, I'm just not overly accustomed to really-real magic, is all.'

'Well, what d'you think you did to those three soul vampires earlier? Tickle them to death? Idiot.'

'"Idiot" seems a bit uncalled for.'

'How about I punch you in the face again?'

'No, that's okay, I'm fine with being called an idiot.'

'Too fucking right you are,' she replied in a low grumble, turning her attention back to her cheap can of lager.'

Wait a minute.

'I'm sorry, "soul" what now? Did you say "soul vampires"? Was that the thing that you said that I'm just now fully registering? Soul vampires?'

She nodded.

'You don't remember me yet, do you?'

'Yes. I do. I've been seeing you all over the place for weeks.'

'No, you don't remember *me*. My name's Eva Familiar, and it's really very, very shitty to make your reacquaintance.'

'Right. Okay. I sense a lot of hostility in you, Eva. I'm Joseph.'

'No, you're,' she paused to burp, 'not. But idiot will do just fine for now, idiot. Now, shut up and drive me home.'

'You know, you're a very mean lady.'

'Thanks, I do try.'

She collapsed her empty can on her forehead and threw it out of the window. Only the window was closed, so the can bounced off and fell in my lap, leaking its remaining contents on my crotch.

'Right then,' I said, and started up the car.

23

Shortly after setting off again, the woman, Eva, fell asleep.

When she announced her intention to take a nap, I'd pointed out that I was supposed to be driving her home, and as I had no idea where that home was, a few directions might be in order. She assured me that I'd find the way if I just drove, and then promptly fell into a deep snooze that no amount of shaking, shoving, or shouting could rouse her from.

And so I drove.

At first, I felt a fool. I just drove blindly out of Carlisle and into the belly of the Lake District, taking turn after turn at whim. And then a strange sensation began to creep over me. I felt like I wasn't taking random turns at all, but that my hands and feet knew exactly where we were going. As though they were making my decisions for me, and that I just had to leave them to it and we'd get where we were supposed to be going, no problem.

I felt like if I thought too much about it, I'd throw off the trick and drive us into one of the region's great lakes, so I tried to distract myself. It wasn't difficult, considering all of the recent calamities I'd suffered. I thought about the Red Woman.

The thing she had shown me. The thing that had felt like me, but couldn't be. The monstrous beast with skin of fire and dead eyes that sought to lay waste to everything it saw and replace it with something terrible.

The Magic Eater. That's what she called it. That was what the fox had said, too.

Magic Eater.

'Stop!'

Eva's voice snapped me out of my musings, and I stomped my foot on the brake, bringing the Uncanny Wagon to a screeching halt.

'Jesus Christ, don't do that! This poor car has been through enough.'

I stroked the Wagon's steering wheel gently, as though soothing a frightened cat.

'This is it, we're here,' said Eva, pushing the door open and shambling out.

I peered through the windscreen to see nothing. Well, not nothing, there were hills and trees, and all the rest, but nothing that looked like a dwelling.

I got out of the car and looked around for something I might be missing.

'Exactly where is this home of yours, Eva? Is it a home or more of a bivouac sort of situation?'

Eva turned to look at me strangely. 'Christ, don't tell me even your eyes are fucked.'

'My eyes are just fine, thank you. AI vision, sharp as sharp can be.'

'Nope, you can't see shit, idiot.'

'Tell me, then. What exactly am I missing?'

'The blind alley right in front of you.'

Oh, God. Not only was she magic, she was insane.

'We're in the middle of nowhere. There are no alleys. You need buildings for alleys. Streets. All there is around here are hills, fields, rocks, trees, and lakes.'

'Is that so?'

'That is absolutely so.'

'Look again,' said Eva, and then she touched my arm, causing me to yelp as a static shock pricked my flesh.

'What d'you call that then, idiot?' she asked, pointing in front of us.

The entrance to an alleyway had opened up in front of me. A gap between two other things that you could walk down. Only, the two things weren't other buildings, this alley was like a gap in, well, reality. It's sort of hard to explain as it was impossible. But there it was, and it was only visible if I looked directly at it. If I twisted slightly there was nothing, twist back, and oops, a wrinkle in reality. A crack in nothing.

'If you've finished gawping and rubbing your eyes like a cartoon mouse,' said Eva, 'follow me.'

She stepped into the fault in reality and walked down the impossible, insane alleyway. I suspect most people would have fallen to their knees at that point. Collapsed like an overdone flan as their brains objected to this obvious glitch in the matrix, but I'd been attacked by octopus men, and had held conversations with talking foxes, so weird really was my wheelhouse now.

'Okay, then. Impossible alleys nestled between nothing. Of course.'

I walked in after Eva. Inside the impossible alley, the "walls" to either side of me were just the surrounding countryside but warped. Twisted. Stretched. Ahead of us lay a two-storey building made of large blocks of stone. Eva paused at a green metal door.

'Here it is. Home sweet home.'

I felt odd looking at the place. Like it was trying to whisper things to me that I once would have been able to hear. Which I know makes little to no sense, but then most of the last few days had been a confusing whirl of nonsense.

'I'll be honest,' I said, 'I kind of assumed you didn't have a home.'

'Why's that?'

'Well...' I tried to find a tactful way to say, "You look like a tramp", then gave up and gestured at her general mad homeless person appearance.

'It's really very hard not to keep punching you,' she said, unlocking the door and stepping inside.

'And what is it with all that?' I asked. 'The punching and the name-calling? Eva?' I made my way in after her, wary that a fist might erupt from the gloom and break my nose.

It was warm inside. Warmer than I'd expected. I'd prepared myself for a tomb-like chill, but it seemed the ancient place had pretty decent heating.

The floor was bare, dark wood, and a staircase to my left stretched up to the next floor, its steps nude but for a half-inch of dust. It seemed that Eva didn't venture from the ground floor very often.

At first, I thought someone had thrown pots of dark paint randomly against the walls of the corridor, then, upon closer inspection, realised that the large blotches more resembled scorch marks. Fire damage?

The atmosphere within the building was... well, I'm not really sure what it was. But it was something. Not unpleasant, but almost as though the air inside was thicker than outside. I felt as though I'd stepped into an invisible river, and that I could feel the currents rushing past me. I also felt something else.

I felt like I'd been there before.

'Come through to the main room,' said Eva from further inside the house. 'And close the fucking door. Were you born in a barn? Wait, scratch that, I think you actually were. Near some pigs, wasn't it?'

I closed the door as requested, then moved down the corridor and into what she called the "main room". It was large, with an open fireplace dominating one wall. An old metal cauldron hung there, and a large square piece of slate was fixed to the floor before it. Eva stumbled through from another door that looked like it led off to a very rudimentary kitchen.

'Here,' she said, tossing a can of lager my way, then she flopped on one of the tattiest, rankest smelling couches I'd ever laid eyes upon.

'Thank you,' I replied, opening the can and taking a sip.

Eva retrieved a remote control from between the sofa cushions and pointed it at the far wall. A click, and a screen parted to reveal a truly ginormous TV screen. A *Fawlty Towers* repeat came on. This place was literally a burnt-out hovel, but the TV was worth more than my car.

'So,' I said, breaking the heavy, heavy silence, 'I like what you mostly haven't done with the place.'

Eva snorted.

I perched on the end of the couch and we both watched as Basil crouched, holding his head and hopping around in anguish.

'I've been here before, haven't I?'

Eva nodded. 'Say hello to the Cumbrian Coven. Used to look a bit grander in the old days, but it's still standing.'

'Coven?'

'Coven.'

'That's a witch thing, isn't it?' I asked.

'Yup.'

'Are you a witch?'

'Nope.'

'Oh.'

'You're a witch,' she said.

There was quite a bit of silence then as my face did some rather spectacular expression gymnastics.

'Or warlock, if you like. Some of you male witches prefer that. All the same thing, though. Except for the tits.'

A witch. Or warlock. Okay. Well. Hm.

'So I'm a warlock witch thing?'

'That's right, idiot.'

'Okay, I see, and tell me why I should believe a word you say? Who even *are* you? You're just an admittedly quite magic-savvy mad woman. How do I know you're not feeding me a load of old crap, like that fox?'

Eva turned to me, her eyes wide. 'Fox?'

'There has been a talking fox, yes.'

'And a woman? Have you seen a woman with red hair?'

'Yes. Why are you looking at me like that?'

She moved fast, did Eva. Before I had chance to blink, I was on my back on the floor, looking up into her furious eyes, a hand around my throat.

'What did she offer you?'

I choked and burbled a bit until she loosened her grip so that I could actually breathe. 'Rubbish,' I squeaked. 'She just talked rubbish, and I'm pretty sure it was just some sort of weird dream, anyway.'

Eva bared her teeth. 'If you ever see her again, you tell me. You tell me everything. And if I find out you haven't told me everything, I'll fucking kill you. You understand me, idiot?'

I shrank back, which was difficult to do as the floor prevented me from going backwards even an inch. 'Got you,' I said.

Eva grunted in anger, stood, then flopped back on the couch. I sat up, rubbing at my neck.

'That's one punch and a partial strangulation now,' I said. 'Just keeping a tally of abuse, there.'

'Get out,' said Eva.

'But if you are telling the truth, then tell me more. What's my real name? What happened to me? Why can't I remember my life?'

'I'm going to sleep now,' she replied, and lay back. Within seconds, she was snoring like an overweight truck driver after a three-day haul.

'Eva? Eva!'

But it was no good, she was dead to the world.

It was at this point that I remembered an earlier invitation.

'Oh, shit.' I looked at my watch. It was almost ten. 'Oh, shit with some extra shit on top.'

I looked back at Eva, wondered if I should continue to try to wake her up and attempt to get some clear answers to my questions, then thought about how many times she might punch my face if I disturbed her. I had a feeling there'd be plenty of time for more of that.

I ran from the house. From the Cumbrian Coven as Eva had called it. I sprinted down the crazy wrinkle in reality and back into the solid everyday, the Uncanny Wagon there to greet me. I was supposed to be at Chloe's place by seven. Eva had the right name for me.

I was an idiot.

24

Having left the coven behind, my phone sprang to life and vomited up a tide of messages and missed phone calls it had been hiding from me.

Chloe was more than a little confused as to why I seemed to be avoiding her.

'Hey, Chloe, it's me, Joseph. An idiot, I've been reliably informed.'

'Where have you been? I thought we had a date, Joseph. And what's this Big Marge said about you having another stay in a hospital bed?'

'It's nothing. I just found another dead body and, I suppose, passed out. Manly.'

'Jesus, are you okay?'

I nodded furiously, then realised that this was a phone call and head movements in the affirmative were not going to move this conversation along.

'Yep. Yes. I'm oh so good.' Which was a clear lie, but I think I sold it well enough.

'You don't sound good, you sound weird.'

Damn.

'Just, you know, finding another dead person. It's sort of, weirded me out a little, that's all.'

'Are you coming over?'

'Yes, I'm on my way.'

'Good.'

And through the country roads towards Carlisle and Chloe's home I sped.

Okay, so it seems my tardiness had not put the mockers on things. I was still allowed to darken Chloe's door. This should have made me happy, but I was currently full to the trembling brim with all the new information I'd been given, jostling with all the other weird-to-the-point-of-insane sights and sounds I'd collected over the last few days.

Monsters.

Witches.

Magic.

My past life.

Alternate worlds.

Talking animals with a fondness for battle axes.

Any one of those would have been enough to make a man question his sanity; question how real this so-called reality really was. And here I was trying to cope with all of them at the same time. It's a wonder I wasn't curled up in a ball on the ground, babbling like a newborn.

It was like life as I had known it, as I had accepted it, had revealed itself to be only one part of the story. *Look here, under this sheet, see all of this other secret stuff, some of which is going to try and chew your face off with a large fucking beak?*

I was sweating, my heart was beating too fast, my hands white-knuckling the steering wheel.

I needed to calm down.

Everything was fine.

Well, everything wasn't fine, everything was on the terrifying side, but I was going somewhere normal. Somewhere that magic didn't exist and I was plain old Joseph Lake: a gangly, well-meaning doofus with terrific hair and the hots for a very nice woman.

Thirty minutes later, as Chloe opened her front door, I could see in her eyes that I must have looked insane.

'Joe, what's wrong?'

'Nothing. Nothing's wrong. Do you have water? Ha! Of course, you have water; who doesn't have water? Actually, that's insensitive of me, there are many countries in this world where on-hand, potable water is a problem. Thoughtless of me, I apologise.'

Chloe ushered me inside and I tried my best to get my shit together.

'Get your shit together,' I actually said.

'What was that?' asked Chloe, who was stood right next to me.

'Just a normal thing. Normal words.'

She handed me a glass of water, which I gratefully accepted, then downed in three large gulps.

'Ah! Okay, that's better. Now I am calm. And relaxed.'

Chloe looked down at my right leg, which looked as though it was trying to beat out a machine gun rhythm on a bass drum. I gave it a little slap.

'Joe, where have you been since you checked yourself out of the hospital?'

'Just around. Driving. Trying to clear my head after all the unpleasantness. Did Big Marge mention the latest victim was the woman who hired me to find her missing cat? Because she was. That was the woman who died.'

'Shit. No, she didn't say that.'

'Well, it was. So that's shit. Well, even if it hadn't been her it would've been shit. Because dead person. Murdered person.'

I felt Chloe's hand slip into mine.

'Joe, calm down, you're okay.'

'Not really, for many reasons that I can't really divulge at this moment.'

Jesus, I was screwing this up. The past few days had been building an unsteady pile of bricks on top of me, and I thought I'd been handling things reasonably well, but nope, down fell the bricks, and there I was, sweating and trembling in the front room of the woman I was hopelessly in love with.

'Joe, I'm here. I'm your friend. You can tell me anything.'

She looked up at me with those big eyes. Eyes full of empathy and understanding. Eyes that made me feel weak at the knees.

It was at this point I did a very stupid thing. I began to tell the truth. Well, not *tell* as much as *purge* the truth in one volcanic eruption.

'Okay, okay, well, it's just been.... you know, these last few days, with the murders, and my being attacked—'

'You were attacked?'

'Yep, attacked, lied about that, said I just crashed the Uncanny Wagon, but no, attacked, and then there were the monsters with big floppy octopus arms that I haven't told anyone about, and a talking fox with an axe.'

Chloe pulled back, alarm on her face at my crazy unloading.

'Talking fox? Did you say a talking fox?'

'With an axe. And that homeless woman isn't actually homeless, but she is magic, and she lives in a big old house hidden in a wrinkle in reality and she tells me that I am, apparently, a witch.'

'A witch?'

'Or warlock. Witch warlock, that's me, that's apparently what I was before Joseph Lake. I was a witch or a warlock, or whatever, and life is very strange and very frightening, and... oh, dear, you're making a very not good face at me. Shit.'

Chloe let go of my hand and walked slowly over to the couch, then sat down.

'Chloe?'

She didn't answer, didn't look at me.

'I didn't mean any of that. That was all a joke. Ha! Fooled you, you big idiot.'

I squirmed on the spot, my heartbeat loud in my ears.

Moron, moron, moron.

'Look, I'm sorry. I'm just a little... overwhelmed by recent events. Been hit on the head one too many times and I'm talking rubbish. I'm sorry. End of rubbish. I'm not a witch, and foxes obviously can't talk and they certainly don't wear helmets. Can we start again?'

Chloe looked up at me, then at her feet, then back up. 'I'm actually feeling pretty tired.'

'Oh. Yes, of course. Me too.'

'I'll see you tomorrow.'

'Tomorrow it is. Not tonight, tomorrow.'

'Tomorrow.'

'Beautiful.'

Beautiful? Christ, I am an idiot.

'I'll just be off then. Here I go. Off.'

I turned and headed for the door.

'Get some rest, Joe,' said Chloe.

I turned, saluted by way of an answer, and wondered why I'd just done that. Who salutes? A tool. A tool salutes.

I left Chloe's home, got into my car, and drove home, loudly calling myself some very impolite names.

25

I woke the next morning with a groan.

It's not often I wake feeling quite so thoroughly depressed, but then it's not every day I wake from having made myself look and sound like a basket case in front of the woman I want to like me in a sex way.

I reached for my phone and checked to see if she'd sent me any messages.

No messages.

I checked three times just to make sure I hadn't gone message-blind, which I decided to pretend might be a thing in order to make myself feel better.

I stared at my message stream with Chloe for several minutes, debating what to send. And if I should send anything at all. After typing out numerous different possibilities and then deleting each before I had the chance to hit send, I finally went with "Hey".

I waited for a reply.

Twenty minutes.

No reply.

Damn and also bugger with a side dish of balls.

I dragged myself out of bed and shambled miserably into a hot shower, hoping to blast the worst of my mood away. You always feel better after a shower.

So. The big question that I still needed an answer for: did I believe what Eva had told me? Did I believe that I was some sort of a witch? A man-witch. A warlock. Eva certainly had abilities that were out of the ordinary. She also lived in a house hidden in a wrinkle in the fabric of reality. Or something. So, either she was messing with me, or she was telling the truth and I was a magic man. Or, third option, she *thought* she was telling the truth but was in fact wrong about me, because although she herself *was* magic, she was also completely bonkers.

Three options.

I've always hated options. Too much choice turns me into a ditherer. But the fact was, I did feel something at her home. At the coven. Like I'd been there before. Like I belonged there. Like the very air inside the place knew me. And then there was the fire. Not the sort I'd seen in the Dark Lakes, in what may have been a delusion, but the fire that erupted from my hands as the three octopus men readied themselves to pounce and sucker me to death. Or beak me to death. Or a combination of the two. I'd seen Eva do that sort of a thing when she punched her fist through one of the creatures' skulls. She did it, she was magic. I did it, somehow, so maybe I was magic, too. Maybe Eva was telling the truth. Maybe I really was a warlock.

And then there were the strange visions and feelings after touching Detective Samm. After touching the dead cat. More evidence for the prosecution.

One thing was for sure, I needed to find Eva again and wrestle some answers out of her.

I turned off the shower and pulled back the curtain to reveal Eva, stood looking at me.

'Morning, idiot.'

I screamed, jumped back, slipped, and crashed down into the bathtub, jarring my bum-bone something rotten.

'Ha! I like that, because you fell and hurt yourself. That's just good stuff, love,' said Eva.

'Why?' I asked, then added a few more for good measure. 'Why, why, why?'

'To make you scream like a girl and fall over. Mission a-fucking-ccomplished.' Eva high-fived herself, then left me, still curled, nude in the small corner tub, covering my genitals with a flannel.

'Too late, I saw everything,' said Eva from the next room.

I towelled off and dressed before joining Eva, who I found stretched across my couch watching an infomercial about a new set of exercise DVDs that combined tap dance with the power of pole dancing for an easy twenty-minute routine you could do daily in your own home. If your home happened to be equipped with a handy stripper's pole.

'Have you heard of knocking? Ringing a doorbell? Not breaking into people's homes while they're wet and naked?'

'You're out of cereal, love.'

'No, I'm not, I have a box of Bran Flakes in the cupboard.'

'*Had*. Now have not.'

'Why are you here? Do you plan on attacking me again?'

'I never plan that, it just sort of happens. When the muse takes me, know what I mean?'

I poured myself a glass of orange juice. 'Want any?'

'Do you have any vodka or tequila to make it tankable?'

'Afraid not.'

'Then don't waste my time.'

'You're welcome. Is there a reason you're here, Eva?'

'Just curious to know how you're taking the news.'

'That I'm a warlock?'

'Ah. Decided on warlock over witch, have you? Why doesn't that surprise me? Yes, you're a warlock.'

'Then how come I don't know how to do magic?'

'Because you don't really remember being a warlock. Your brain's a blank, which, believe you me, is a good thing.'

'How is not knowing anything about my past life a good thing?'

There was a heavy silence as Eva's eyes seemed to lose focus, like she was seeing something that I couldn't.

'Trust me, love. It's a good thing.'

'How did I get here, Eva? Why can't I remember who I am?'

'Why are you in such a rush for bad news? First things first: soul vampires.' Eva hopped up to her feet, went drunkenly sideways, and almost crashed into my TV set.

'That's the octopus men thingies, right?'

'Those ugly fuckers, yep. They're doing all sorts of nasty shit that they shouldn't. Thought we'd dealt with them, but here they are. Need to find where they're holed up so we can take them out. That's why I brought that body here, so you could feel it up and see if it sparked anything in that noggin of yours.'

'Oh. I can do that. *Maybe* I can do that.'

'No, been dead too long now.'

'It worked with the dead cat.'

Eva blinked at me silently for a moment. 'I beg your pardon?'

'I've been on this case. A village of cats went missing and I was hired to find out where they were.'

Eva slapped her forehead with the heel of her hand and staggered back, which I'd never seen anyone in real life actually do before.

'Of course! Don't you see?'

'I see a lot these days but understand very little.'

'The cats, you wretched, foul, puke. The cats!'

'The cats?'

Eva stepped forward, grabbing me by the collar and pulling me toward her wildly-smiling face. 'The cats know, idiot. The cats always know.' She shoved me aside and bolted for the door.

'The cats always know what? Eva?'

Apparently, this day wasn't going to be any less insane than the one that had gone before it, so I grabbed my coat and ran off in pursuit.

26

As we sped towards Oldstone in the Uncanny Wagon, I peered at Eva in the rearview mirror, stretched out across the back seats, eyes closed.

'You know, you could sit up front like a normal person.'

Eva gave me the finger.

I gave my phone a quick glance; no reply to my *Hey* from Chloe. Damn. I was really in the poop there. Made a real fool of myself. Well, a fool and a loon of myself.

Shit.

'Okay, let's say I'm a witch.'

'I thought you went with warlock, Mr *Look-at-me-I-have-a-penis*.'

'For the record, I have never referred to myself that way.'

Eva snorted. Then burped. Delightful.

'You're magic,' I said. 'You're very magic. But you said you're not a witch, so what are you? Besides violent, terrifying, and gaseous?'

'I already told you. I'm Eva Familiar.'

'That doesn't... oh...'

Familiar. A witch's familiar.

'Are you my familiar?'

Eva opened one eye and glared at me with it. 'Un-fucking-fortunately, yes.'

'Oh. Well, right then. Righty-right.'

'Give me strength...'

'Okay, well, where have you been for the last ten years?'

'Around.'

'Where? Doing what?'

'I forget. Though I know I spent a really cracking fortnight as a French Bulldog in Devon.'

'A dog? Really?'

'Sure. Probably. Why not?'

One thing was very certain, Eva was not a fan of straight answers, nor filling in the whole picture. I wondered what it was she was holding back, and why she was so keen on my not mixing with the Red Woman.

'What does that actually mean, by the way? That you're my "familiar"? Are you sort of, my magical servant, or...?'

'Oi! I'm nobody's lackey, got that, love? I am my own person and I'm the one in charge here, and if you forget that, I'll deck you, got it?'

Sounded like a sore point best left alone.

'Wake me when we get to the cat place.' And with that, her head nodded down and she was sound asleep (the "sound" being a collection of snores, sleep-talking, and violent gassy eruptions).

I'm a warlock. A witch. And I have a coven and a familiar and I am a magic person. Who doesn't know how to do magic. Okay. Well. Big few days. On we go. Despite the fact that the answer seemed to be, "Something that only exists in fiction", it felt rather wonderful to be filling in a blank or two on the real me.

A warlock. That's one avenue I definitely hadn't considered. Because that would have been nuts.

I drove on, glancing down at my phone every few minutes, trying to will the thing to drag a reply out of Chloe. I pulled into Oldstone and parked up without receiving said longed-for reply, so I cracked again and decided to send another message. This time I upped the ante: I sent a smiley face emoji.

As soon as it said "delivered", my insides clenched in horror. I was a moron. No, no, no, I was King Moron. An Emoji? Yes, she obviously loved the things, but I'd just unloaded a whole pile of crazy-bananas on her. A "hey" and a smiley face were hardly going to erase that.

I was done. It was all over. Wave the white flag and embrace a life of quiet contemplation, celibacy, and—

My phone vibrated and I snatched the thing up quicker than The Flash. A reply from Chloe. She'd replied with a smiley face of her own. A yellow circle with a big, toothy, mother-flippin' grin. I hopped out of the Uncanny Wagon and punched the air, followed by a tight, circular strut, chest puffed out like a champ.

'Tosspot,' came Eva's voice as she rolled out of the back seat, shielding her eyes from the morning sunshine.

I pocketed my phone, relieved at Chloe's response. Okay, I could work this. I'd just tell her, I don't know, after the incident with Mrs Coates, that I ended up in a pub and I think someone spiked my drink. She'd believe that. That's the sort of thing that happens. I'd certainly acted like someone who was completely off their tits. Okay. Cool. All was well.

I turned to find Eva down on her hands and knees, sniffing and licking at the ground.

'That is disgusting.'

'I've sniffed worse. This is the place,' she said, pushing herself back to her feet.

'You still haven't actually told me why we're here.'

'Yes, I have, you just don't listen.'

'No. Okay, true. Often true, but not in this particular case. You just had a snooze for most of the journey.'

'Are you sure?'

'Very.'

'Huh. Well isn't it obvious? Can't you feel it?'

I knew what she was talking about. It was the same sensation I'd felt each time I'd visited Oldstone. That creeping prickle across my skin. The sense that something wasn't right with the place.

'I feel it. But what is it?'

'Bad news, that's what it is.'

'I hypothesised that it's why the cats made themselves scarce. The cats could feel the oddness of Oldstone.'

'Cats and soul vampires. They don't get on. It's the magic the soul vampires secrete into the world around them. Messes the cats up, so they move away from it. And that's why we need to catch one of the little buggers.'

'And how are we supposed to do that?'

Eva smiled. 'We need a canary.'

I led us to the barn I found the cats huddled inside of, expecting them to have flown the coop by now. But there they were.

With very little help from Eva (by which I mean no help at all), I managed, at length, to herd one of the unwilling mogs into my cat box. We then spent the next hour strolling around Oldstone, holding the furious cat-in-a-box in front of us, Eva using each twitch, hiss, and flick of the cat's tail to decide which way we should go next.

The theory was that as we approached the point where these soul vampire thingies were holed up, the cat would become increasingly agitated. The theory was successful in practice, and was also successful in encouraging many a passerby give us a wide berth as we speed-walked randomly up and down streets with a cat that was doing its damnedest to pull off a jailbreak.

'This feels a bit predictable,' said Eva as we found a narrow opening in the small hill lurking behind Oldstone's Church, hidden by decades of overgrown foliage.

'I thought vampires hated churches, and crosses, and things of that holy, blessed nature,' I said, as I placed the cat box down and opened the door.

The cat erupted from within and out into the world at such speed that it resembled little more that a furry blur.

'You're thinking of ordinary vampires,' she replied, and kicked aside the scraggle of bushes hiding the thin entrance. 'Those are bloodsuckers, these are a completely different kettle of twats.'

'I take it they don't drink blood, judging by their name?'

'Nope. They eat your essence. Paint an incantation around you in your own blood to trap your soul so they can catch and eat the thing.'

'Oh,' I pulled out my phone and showed her the picture I'd taken of the symbols around Mary Taylor's bed.

'That's them. I'm surprised that didn't clue you in. They literally say, "*Soul, you are mine to feast upon*".'

I squinted at the picture. 'They do?'

'Jesus Christ, you don't even have the basics in there anymore, do you?'

'Well, no, I thought that was pretty obvious. Why is that? If I'm a warlock, why can't I remember any of it? What happened to me?'

'Come on,' said Eva, and began to squeeze into the narrow opening.

'Fine, but you're going to have to tell me at some point,' I said as I followed after. Something told me that if she was so eager to keep the answer to herself, it wasn't going to be anything good.

I'm not generally the claustrophobic type, but I admit to sighing in relief that after a few metres the tight entrance opened up considerably and I could walk head-on as we moved further into the gloom.

'Hey, it's getting a bit dark,' I said, 'I'll use the light on my phone.'

'No need.'

A click of her fingers and Eva's right arm was a torch, her fist wreathed in rippling orange flames.

'Neat,' I said. 'I actually did something a bit like that earlier. Somehow.'

'It's not a competition, love. Come on, and be prepared to run, because these things will happily tear you into a hundred wet pieces.'

'Fear not, running away is something of a specialty of mine.'

Eva grunted and pushed on, her heavy footsteps echoing off the wet rock around us. After a few minutes, we found ourselves in a large cave, the walls dotted with hundreds of holes. It reminded me a little of the mortuary back at the hospital. The openings were of roughly the same size, but there were no shiny metal doors hiding the bodies within. No bodies, either.

'Well,' said Eva, poking her glowing hand into hole after hole and leaning in to take a look, 'this was the place all right.' She ran a finger around the interior of one of the spaces and licked it. 'They were here up until a day or so ago. Still reeks of them.'

It did. A smell like the sea mixed with blood and rot. I can't say I was super upset to find the place empty. One of those things was bad enough. Who knew how many had been stuffed down here? Looking at the number of empty spaces across the cave walls, the answer was: a lot.

As Eva moved the light from her hand around the cave, it revealed symbols painted all across the walls. More of the occult shapes.

'That is not good,' said Eva.

'What? What do they say?'

'Just stuff about being ready to rise up and feast on the souls of all of Great Britain.'

'Yeah, that is definitely not good.'

'Not good, and weird. They're usually the sort that likes to stick to random snacks, but this sounds like something bigger. Something more ambitious.'

A pack of ambitious, soul-eating vampires? That didn't sound pretty.

'Maybe it's time to tell the police?'

'This has nothing to do with the police. This is our job. The Cumbrian Coven's domain. Fuck up monsters and protect people from the Uncanny turds that want to chew on their insides.'

'Oh, so we're, sort of, magic police? I like that. Magic Police! You have the right to remain unmagical; all spells cast can be held against you in a court of law.'

Eva sagged and groaned. 'Don't say that again. It sounds oh so very shit.'

27

I pulled out of Oldstone in the Uncanny Wagon and headed for Carlisle Hospital, leaving Eva behind. She hadn't been too impressed with the fact that I needed to show up to my job to earn money and function in normal society, and called me a number of colourful names, complete with accompanying hand gestures.

I'll be honest, I wasn't really taking to Eva. She claimed to be my familiar, my partner, but seemed like an obnoxious, gassy mess. Not to mention the fact that she'd recently punched me in the face for reasons she'd yet to divulge. What could the old me have done to be worthy of that kind of treatment? Seemed like if anyone should know it was me, and I was increasingly peeved off that she was keeping so many of the puzzle pieces to herself.

Still, for the last ten years, my history had been a complete blank. Now, at least, I saw a sliver or two of the truth. Even if the truth seemed a mite tricky to fully buy into.

I was going a little too fast down an empty country lane when it happened.

I turned a blind corner, only to find a person stood blocking my path. It was a woman with pale skin and long red hair. I yelped, twisted the wheel, and hit the brakes, the world spinning as my poor car screeched and spun before coming to a halt with its rear end in a hedge. Not so much as a near-miss in the last ten years of driving, and now two accidents on the trot.

'I'm okay. Not hurt. Okay.'

I stepped out of the car and looked for the Red Woman, but she was nowhere to be seen.

'That's not funny, or clever, right? You could've bloody killed me.'

'All hail the saviour!'

My shoulders sagged at the voice, and I turned to find the fox stood on the roof of my car, little Roman helmet on his head, axe held aloft.

'You know, a text message would be fine if either of you ever want to get in touch again.'

The fox slid down the windscreen, shuffled along the bonnet, and landed on the road. 'So now you know,' it said.

'Know what?'

'Who you really, truly are.'

'Some of it. Hey, have you got me bugged?' I ran my hands over the fabric of my coat in search of a listening device.

'Ah, but she did not tell you all, that tricksy familiar.'

'Maybe she did, maybe she didn't.'

I felt a cold arm around my waist, then a pair of lips at my ear: 'She didn't tell you about the others, did she?'

I turned to see the Red Woman. 'You know... that was shocking road-sense. I could've hit you. You could have ended up a flesh bag full of bone shards. With red hair on top.'

Her smile could have curdled milk.

'She wouldn't like you talking to me, your familiar, because she knows I tell the truth.'

'Oh? What sort of truth?'

I felt a tug at my coat tails and looked down to see the fox. 'The truth about the other witches of the Cumbrian Coven. Didn't think it was just you and her, did you?'

'Other witches?'

The Red Woman shook her head sadly. 'It pains me that Eva feels the need to keep you so in the dark. You are one of three witches that looked over this county. Now, why would she keep that information from you, Magic Eater?'

It was a fair question.

'Maybe she has good reason not to tell me.'

'What sort of a reason?' asked the Red Woman, her hand trailing lightly across my chest.

'You know, a... good one. Sort of thing.'

The Red Woman pulled me close and planted a kiss on my lips. 'I will never lie to you.'

'Okay,' I squeaked.

'I only want the best for you. Only want you to reach your full, glorious potential. Destiny is waiting for you, Magic Eater. *I* am waiting for you.'

I blinked, and I was alone.

The rest of the journey to work found me deep in troubled thought.

Three witches.

Was that true? And if so, why wouldn't Eva have told me? Perhaps the other witches were like family. I deserved to know about family. I'd often wondered about siblings, about who my parents really were. Perhaps this was it. I was a warlock, and these other two mystery coven members were what passed for my family.

I'll confess to feeling a little burble of excitement in my stomach. Warlock told me what I did, but other people, family, that would tell me who I *was*.

'You're ten minutes late,' said Big Marge as the automatic doors hissed closed behind me and I arrived at her reception area, brow creased, hands plunged deep into the pockets of my long coat. 'It looks like you've got a load on your mind, Joe.'

'A thing or two rattling around upstairs, yeah.'

'You're not built for deep thought, you're built for cleaning up shit. And lucky you, there's a fresh batch of it waiting in the third-floor Ladies.'

With a heavy sigh, I headed for my locker to change into my work things, only to have Chloe open the reception area's double doors as I was about to push my way out.

'Oh,' she said.

'Yes. Sorry, did I hit you with the door?'

'A bit, but that's okay.'

'Good.'

'Yep. Good.'

It felt like awkward had given birth to twins.

'About last night...' I started.

'That's okay, Joe.'

'No, it's not, I was just, all messed up, you know? From the murder. And I was in a pub, and I think my drink was spiked. Someone definitely spiked my drink. I think.'

'Okay. So that's why all the...'

'Crazy faces and witch talk.'

'And the talking fox. It was a talking fox, yes?'

'Mentioned that, did I?'

'Yes, you did.'

'Right. Bloody... spiked drink.'

I could practically see the tension escaping from Chloe's body. I hated lying to her, but the truth would scare her silly, so a lie would have to do for the time being.

'I should have known,' she replied. 'I am a doctor, I should have rationalised how weird you were acting.'

'It's not your fault.'

'Yeah, you always act a bit weird.'

'Ouch, but valid.'

'But not like that. You really had things turned up to eleven.'

She laughed and touched my arm, and suddenly any guilt at having lied to her skipped out of my brain to be replaced by a cloud of chirping love birds. So it was a pity that the moment had to be broken by a terrified Doctor Neil half-running, half-falling towards us down the corridor, his face even paler than usual. And his usual face was almost Casper-the-Friendly-Ghost white.

'Neil, what is it?' asked Chloe.

'They're dead. They're all dead!'

Like I say, moment broken.

28

There's nothing unusual about death in a hospital. People pop their clogs almost every day around these places, and it's always sad. But it's not every day someone is *murdered* in a hospital.

And murdered by people with octopus arms? I'd say the odds on that would be so long you'd end up taking home the GDP of the entire northern hemisphere.

I'm not trying to encourage anyone to gamble here, FYI. Unless you're on to a sure thing, of course.

We took the stairs two at a time, Chloe ahead, me behind. She was nippy, that's for sure. We heard the grim discovery Doctor Neil made before we actually reached it. A high-pitched, electronic whine sliced down the corridor towards us. We both knew what that sound was. Multiple heart monitors flat-lining.

We burst into the small ward that housed six people, now six corpses. Nurses milled round, some trying to help, others just looking on in blank shock.

'Oh my God,' said Chloe, stopping so sharply that I almost ran into the back of her. Instead, I swerved at the last moment and stepped on something damp that caused my foot to slip and sent me crashing to the floor.

Blood.

Around each of the deceased patients, beds were those same occult symbols, painted in their own vital fluids. The soul vampires had paid the hospital another visit.

Chloe ran between the beds, obviously overwhelmed at what she was seeing, frantically looking for any signs of life, trying to help the nurses in attendance.

It was no use, the patients were all dead.

I could sense the creatures in the room. They'd gone, but that magic scent that had infected Oldstone was present. It itched at my skin and made me want to blow my nose.

Eva had been right. These things were stepping up their game. Six people in one go? And inside a room that was so public? They were getting bold. They no longer felt the need to stalk vulnerable people through empty streets in the dead of night or hide in the back seats of cars to lurch out and surprise. Anyone, anywhere, was in danger.

My heart bounced angrily against my rib cage as a thought landed.

'Mary...'

I ran from the room, desperate to be wrong, praying that the protection Detective Myers put on Mary's door had made the things think twice. Or maybe they'd just forgotten about her. Surely one victim was as good as another?

I received my grim answer as I turned the corner to find both of the officers who had been left to protect Mary Taylor slumped on the floor, their windpipes torn out.

'Mary!'

No thought for my own safety, no time to allow fear to infect me, I leapt over the deceased officers and shoulder-barged the door to Mary Taylor's room.

The sight waiting for me was something I'll never forget. Blood was daubed in thick strokes around the bed, but there was something different about the symbols, something unlike the others I'd seen. The word that sprang to mind when I saw them was *active*. An impossible black light was leaking from the occult symbols like smoke, accompanied by a low, gut-shaking hum.

Stood around the bed were three of the octopus-limbed creatures. Soul vampires. And for the first time, I was getting to see what that really meant.

On the bed were two Marys. One was physical: a body, eyes open and rolled back so that only the whites were on show. Her windpipe hung from the tear in her throat, glistening, wet and fresh.

The second Mary was floating just above her corpse. An apparition. Mary Taylor's soul. She thrashed, her semi-transparent form twisting and spasming in horrific torment as the three creatures feasted upon her soul.

It was too late for me to do anything, though what I would have done if it hadn't been, I still don't know. In her final moments, Mary Taylor opened her eyes and saw me. My mouth flapped dumbly, words failing to appear as she reached towards me, imploring me to do something, to do anything.

I did nothing.

And then, with a sudden, piercing scream that put my heart in my windpipe, multiple octopus limbs wrapped around her, pulling pieces of her spirit free to gorge upon.

Mary Taylor was gone.

Her soul devoured.

'Bastards!' I yelled, my fury overriding any sense of personal danger. I'd saved Mary from these wankers twice, and it still hadn't been enough. Police protection hadn't been enough. They'd marked her and they'd taken her. I hadn't saved her, I'd just delayed the inevitable. Made them work a little harder for their supper.

They turned to me, their huge unblinking yellow eyes

bulging from their sockets as though on some sort of high from swallowing Mary Taylor's essence.

'You stupid, ugly, fucking bastards.'

They opened their beaks and screeched at me, each taking a step forward. It was at this point a little clarity worked its way through the haze of anger, and I realised I was in huge and immediate danger.

I wanted to attack them, to wreak terrible revenge for what they had done to Mary. To the other six dead bodies down the corridor. To Detective Sam Samm. To Mrs Coates. To all of them.

Eva claimed that I was a warlock, and considering all that I'd experienced recently, I thought she was very likely telling the truth. She said we were the people who stood against things like this: the monsters. The mythical, the unbelievable, the things that melt away as light filters through your curtains, content in the knowledge that such awful creatures could only exist in nightmares.

I was the thing that protected mankind from the horrible truth that monsters were real, and I had no idea how to do it. No idea how to do magic, how to utilise whatever powers I had. Oh, I'd seen flashes of my potential, in Mrs Coates' house for example, but I had no clue how to manifest such powers when I actually needed them.

As the creatures stalked towards me, I was hopeful of something just... happening. Something that scorched them from the face of the Earth. And quickly.

'Jesus Christ...'

I turned to find Chloe stumbling into the room behind me, staring at the monstrous creatures, their limbs weaving, beaks chittering. I saw her eyes, so disbelieving, so huge that they almost put the octopus men's dilated peepers to shame.

'Chloe, no, get out—'

'Oh,' said Doctor Neil, stood between the two bodies of the police officers, looking past me at the monsters. 'Oh, God.'

I grabbed Chloe and tried to bundle the both of us out of the room, but the door slammed shut. Some invisible hand had thrown it closed to prevent our escape. I turned the handle, shook it, pulled desperately, but the door refused to budge. The creatures had somehow locked the thing and cut off our escape.

'Neil? Neil! Help me with the door.'

'This can't be happening, can't be, this isn't real,' stammered Chloe. I could see her retreating into herself, not able to cope with this sudden upset of how the world should be.

'Chloe, stay with me, I need you to be able to—'

A limb wrapped around my waist and the room streaked and twirled as I spun through the air, crashing against the far wall, the floor catching me and knocking the wind from my lungs. I reached out, tried to call Chloe's name, but only a dry rasp escaped my throat.

'Joe!'

The creatures loomed over Chloe as she slid down the wall, hands up protectively, uselessly.

Gulping down air, I pushed myself to my feet unsteadily. 'Get your filthy octopus limbs away from her!'

I felt a crackle in the air, as though something in the room was flowing towards me. Filling me. It felt like I was some sort of computer game character who had just levelled up. I felt sharper. Stronger. Focused. I had no idea what I was doing, not really, but some instinctive part of my brain did. It had done this a thousand times before. It didn't need me to know, because my inner self knew. The part of me that had lain dormant for ten long years.

'Leave her alone!'

I clapped my hands together and the room shook. One of the creatures broke from the pack and ran towards me. I punched out a fist and flames exploded from my knuckles, catching the creature in the side and sending it smashing straight through the window and landing with a painful crash in the car park outside.

I did that.

Me.

Joseph Lake.

Toilet cleaner and cat-catcher extraordinaire.

I made fire surge from my fists and knock a monster clean through a window. And because I was suddenly so aware of that fact, it was as though I lost a grip on whatever it was I was doing, and the fire I was emanating sputtered and died.

'Come on.' I shook my hands, clapped them together, willed flames to appear, but it was no use. Lucky for me, it seemed my demonstration had convinced the remaining creatures that it was time to make themselves scarce. Unlucky for me, they decided to take Chloe with them.

Before I could attempt to do anything, one of the creatures wrapped a limb around the bed and tossed it in my direction. The other grabbed the screaming Chloe, then all three disappeared through the broken window and after their fallen comrade.

29

Ordinarily speaking, I'm not the sort of person who drops out of a second-storey window. I respect stairs. That's the way to get from one level to another as far as I'm concerned. On this occasion, though, three octopus monsters had abducted Chloe, and I was fairly certain that taking the conventional route would result in my friend ending up dead as a dead thing.

So there I was, casting a fearful eye at the distance I was about to drop, my hands starting to ache.

'Joe! Please.'

And with those two words, any uncertainty evaporated. I let go, the hospital's outer wall streaking past me before the ground met the soles of my feet and my ankles made their complaints loud and clear. This was no time for pain, though. For hobbling around, or curling up in a foetal position and tenderly patting down any sore area to see if bones were jutting through the flesh, white and angry.

No time for that.

No time for me.

The creatures had Chloe. Her eyes were still on me, hands reaching out imploringly.

'Chloe! I'm coming.'

I ran-hobbled after the three creatures, who were rapidly making their escape through the almost-empty car park spaces at the back of the hospital. If I lost sight of them, that was that. I knew it. What reason would they have to keep Chloe alive? Either I somehow rescued her, right here, right now, or Chloe was good as done for; her throat ripped out, her soul shredded and feasted upon by these beaky fucks.

But what could I do? I wished Eva was with me. She knew how to wield her magic with purpose, it wasn't an unconscious bubbling up that she couldn't control. I remembered her fist bursting through the skull of one of the soul vampires, and sorely wished I'd asked her just how the hell she managed to do it.

'Hey, where are you going?' I yelled as I ran after them. 'There's three of you and one of me. Don't you want a snack for the road?'

The creatures paused and turned to look at me, a sharp hissing sound escaping their beaks. Maybe I'd given them an idea.

'Come on flamey hands,' I said, shaking my fists, willing them to hurry up and get magical already, but they stubbornly refused to unleash even a faint spark. 'Oh shit,' seemed a reasonable response as one of the three octopus-limbed creatures broke from the pack and charged towards me, using its extra arms to give it added propulsion, its beak wide and screeching.

I had no clue what to do, so, screaming like a loon, I put my head down and ran right at the thing. A second or two later, I stopped tumbling painfully across the car park surface and lay blinking up at the sky in a daze. Despite my state of about-to-be-killed-ness, I found time to notice that one of the clouds above me was shaped a bit like a horse. Strange, the things you pay attention to when death is knocking on your door.

I pushed myself up, ready to dodge out of the way, only for the creature to descend on me, its limbs like the bars of a cage, slamming down all around to block my escape.

'You probably don't want to taste my soul,' I stammered, 'I think it's gone off.'

The beast threw back its head, beak stretched wide, and let loose a bowel-loosening scream as it prepared to tear out my windpipe.

My life did not flash before my eyes. Instead, I thought about Chloe, and how I'd failed her. I was going to die, which meant she was, too. I hoped they wouldn't hurt her too much.

The creature's noise ceased, and I prepared for the strike, eyes tightly shut, body a hard nugget... only the expected deadly attack didn't come. I opened an eye. The creature was no longer looking at me, it was looking over its shoulder.

It was at this point that a car engine registered.

I peered past the bulk of the creature to see a vehicle hurtling at speed towards us. One way or another, it seemed the world was determined to put an end to me today.

As the soul vampire lifted some of its limbs, I seized the moment, kicking out with a scream and a swear before rolling over and over until a parked car brought my journey to a stop. I looked up just in time to see the speeding car strike the soul vampire square, and carry the thing—its limbs thrashing furiously at the vehicle's bonnet—straight into a wall.

Wham.

The car reversed, and the creature flopped forward, its torso partially crushed, the yellow shine in its eyes weakening. The car idled as if to savour the moment, savour the knowledge that the creature knew what was about to happen, and there was nothing it could do about it. The back wheels spun, the creature screamed, the car lurched forward again. The soul vampire reached out defensively with its many limbs, then the car struck, metal crushed, and the beast screamed its last.

I climbed to my feet, searching for the remaining creatures, for Chloe, but neither were anywhere to be seen. I ran in the direction they'd been heading, but there was no sign of them. They couldn't have escaped in such a short space of time. They should still be in sight.

'Chloe! Chloe, where are you?'

Silence.

She was gone.

Whatever trick the creatures had pulled to hide from view, I was too late. They may have lost one of their number, but they had their prey. They had Chloe, which meant she was dead. Which meant her soul would soon be eaten and there would be nothing left of her but a rotting carcass.

Then a thought struck.

Stupid warlock. Stupid, stupid warlock!

I'd already done this a few times, maybe I could do it again.

I turned and ran towards the dead soul vampire to find the driver stood looking down at its squished corpse. It was Detective Myers, no doubt answering the call Big Marge would have put through when Doctor Neil stumbled, ashen, into reception.

'One of the things I never anticipated when I took this job,' she said, 'was all the fucking monsters.'

I fell to my knees and laid my hands on the dead creature, its blood soaking through my trousers, which was disgusting, obviously.

'I'm pretty sure it's dead,' said Myers.

'Yes, I know, but that's okay, I did this with a dead cat already.'

'You what?'

I closed my eyes, thought about Chloe, about where she could be, and grabbed hold of the dead creature.

'Please,' I said. 'Please show me. Show me something.'

I pushed, I grabbed, I hugged, I even clenched at the pile of spilt intestines, grunting in frustration as I tried to will the darkened corners of my mind to shine a little light. But it was no good, I wasn't getting a thing.

'Mr Lake, what the hell are you doing?'

Distracted, angry, I looked up at Myers' confused face. 'I want to make the dead thing show me its home—'

The world was whipped away and—

A road. There is a road. Hills. Grass. Walls. Home is close. New home. New home that we have moved to. Bring her back here. Bring her back here. Bring her back here—

I gasped and fell backwards, the connection broken.

Myers looked down at me. 'Are you okay?'

I laughed and leapt to my feet, cradling her face in my hands. 'You distracted me. Thank you!'

'You're welcome. Now, get those gore-soaked hands off my face before I knee you in the crotch.'

'Yes, right, sorry.'

I wiped my bloody hands on my coat, then immediately regretted doing so. Hopefully, monster goo came out in the wash.

'You were driving the car,' I said.

'Yes.'

'You could have hit me.'

'That was a risk I was willing to take.'

'Good to know.'

I had a place. An image of an area. It might just have been a road, some scenery, but it was something. It was hope. And right then, that was all I needed to convince myself that I might be able to find Chloe before the creatures murdered her. It was something to hang on to.

I turned to run for the Uncanny Wagon, only for Myers to grab me by the arm and throw me back against her totalled car. She was, it came as no surprise to find out, really quite strong.

'I have questions,' she said.

'There's no time. They have Chloe, and if we don't find her

very, very, very fast, they will kill her. So either help me or get out of my way.'

I half expected her to stop me. Instead, she looked at the dead soul vampire, looked at her smashed car, then looked back to me and nodded.

'What are we waiting for? Let's go monster hunting.'

30

It was only once we were in the car and speeding south of Carlisle and towards the Lake District that what Myers had said actually filtered through.

'Wait, monsters. You know about monsters?'

'I would think that was obvious. The question is, how do *you* know about monsters?'

I ignored the question. 'You first.'

'I'd like to remind you that I'm the police.'

'So what?'

'So answer my question.'

'Okay. Well, it turns out that secret past of mine involved being a warlock. A male witch who fights weird stuff and protects the public from freaky supernatural turds.'

Myers nodded slowly. 'You're a witch?'

'I know, I can't say the knowledge sits too comfortably with me, either. Now go on, your turn.'

Myers bowed her head and began to toy at the hem of her leather jacket.

'What is it?'

'My partner.'

'Detective Samm?'

'No. My partner before that, in London. Her name was Allie Sanders. We were investigating a drug ring operating out of Hammersmith. We thought we'd tracked down the head of the operation, went to investigate, got split up. I heard her screaming and when I found her, she'd been torn apart by... by something I can't even describe. Something that couldn't be real. And... I ran.'

Myers' voice was cracking, it was the first time I'd ever seen her being vulnerable, her armour slipping.

'Go on,' I urged.

'I filed a report. They thought I was crazy, of course. Monsters don't exist. I went to find proof, bumped into a lot of scary shit. Once I'd seen one, it was like the truth was everywhere. Monsters live among us. But I couldn't make my superiors hear me. They made me go to a psychiatrist. Eventually, I pretended it had all been a breakdown caused by Allie's death, and they transferred me up here. Out of the way. Out of their hair.'

I wasn't sure what to say, so I patted her leg.

'Do I look like the family dog?'

'Um, no.'

'Then don't pet me again or I'll break that hand off and beat you unconscious with it.'

'Righto. Sorry about your partner. Both partners.'

'Two dead partners, both murdered by things that can't exist. Maybe death is stalking me.'

'It's possible,' came a voice from behind us. 'Death is a well-known stalker.'

I yelled, twisted the wheel, and yelled again as a truck thundered past, swerving just in time so as not to turn us into a leaky, crushed can. I glared at Eva in the rearview mirror. 'Where did you come from?'

'Ah, well, geographically, organically, or metaphorically?'

'My car! Why are you in my car?'

'Oh. I came to find you, couldn't find you, so broke in here and took a kip on the back seat.'

That was it, after the octopus monster and now this, I was going to make a habit of giving my back seat a thorough once-over before setting off for a drive again.

'You were not in the back seat. No one was in the back seat.'

'You're not too bright these days, are you?' She waved her hands around. 'I'm magic, love.'

'Who is this?' Myers asked, finally.

'Difficult question,' I replied.

'I'll take a simple answer.'

'Who am I?' said Eva. 'Is that what the bird in blue just said?'

'Yes, who are you?'

Eva snorted. 'We met the other day. Bit of a short memory there, love. A bit of a worry that Cumbria's finest have memories like goldfish.''

'I can assure you, I have never met you before in my life.'

Eva looked at Myers like she was insane, then a realisation dawned. 'Oh. Oh! Sorry, that's right, my mistake. We did meet, but I had a different face on. Not your fault, love, my hands are up on that one.'

'*Different face*? Did she just say she had a different face on?'

'It's... tricky to explain.'

'Try me.'

'What are you talking about?' said Eva. 'Piece of piss to explain. I'm magic. He's magic. You're not magic, though somehow you're really pulling off those trousers. Where did you get those anyway? And where are we going? I'm up for pizza.'

'They took Chloe,' I said. 'Those soul vampire things, they killed a bunch of people at the hospital, and then they took a friend of mine and I need to find her before they... well, do things I don't want to think about.'

'Right,' said Eva. 'She's probably already dead.'

'Not helping,' I said, turning almost fully around before Myers shoved my back.

'Hey, driving, remember?'

'Right. Yes. Sorry, Detective.'

'So what happened?' asked Eva.

'Does it matter?' I replied. 'Those things killed people and kidnapped Chloe, and Detective Myers appeared and squashed one dead with her car, and now I'm trying to find out where they've disappeared to, which is really very difficult with you two nattering on.'

There was a brief, strained silence.

'You squashed one with your car?' said Eva.

Myers nodded. 'Rammed into the thing twice. It died screaming.'

'Christ. That is cold-blooded. I like you. You're now my favourite person. Wait, no, second favourite, I'm still number one in my eyes. Drink?'

Eva pulled a can of cheap lager from her coat pocket and offered it over. Myers stared at it for a few seconds, then shrugged and took it, settling back to drain the can dry. 'I know I'm on duty, but monsters.'

'I'm not judging,' I replied.

'So what's the plan?' asked Eva. 'Just drive aimlessly? We still don't know where these arm-heavy bastards have moved on to. I traipsed all over the place, even got a replacement canary-cat, couldn't find a sniff for buggery.'

'I know where they are,' I said.

'Well, then why don't you lead with that?'

'I mean, I sort of know. I don't know where it is exactly, but I know where they are.'

'Does he always talk in riddles?' asked Myers, wiping her mouth with the back of her sleeve.

'He's an idiot, you'll soon come to realise that.'

'Ladies, you're going to make me get a big head here.'

'Just get on with it, idiot.'

'I touched one of them. The dead one. The squished-horribly one. And used my, you know, magic warlock man-witch powers. Not entirely sure how, but it showed me a few images, a few thoughts. It showed me where they are, it's just, I'm not entirely sure where that was as it just looked like, you know—' I gestured at the countryside spread out around us. 'It all looks kind of the same.'

'Oi, racist,' replied Eva.

'What? How? I... what?'

'Do you have another drink?' asked Myers. 'This one was only about ten-percent full.'

Eva produced a full can from somewhere and handed it over. 'So, you have the image. You have the place. Now, use your powers to home in on it.'

'How exactly?'

'How did you see the images in the first place?'

'I don't know how, it's just whenever I'm distracted, whenever I'm not really purposefully trying, it happens. If I come at the thing head-on, I get nothing. If I don't think about it, if I keep it sort of just to the side of my conscious mind, the muscle memory takes over and gets on with it.'

I slammed my foot on the brakes and the car screeched to a halt. Eva tumbled into the footwell, and Myers spilt her can down herself.

'What's with the emergency stop?' she asked, pissed off.

'I don't know, it's like my foot took over.'

'I know,' said Eva as she scrambled back up into a sitting position. 'We distracted you.'

'What do... oh...' I looked out to where we'd ended up. I recognised it. 'Oh!'

'Yeah,' said Eva. 'This ain't my first rodeo, love.'

We were there. We were at the soul vampires' lair.

31

I stepped out of the Uncanny Wagon and turned in a circle, taking in my surroundings in wide-eyed surprise.

'This is it! This is what I saw, this place. I did it!'

'All right,' said Eva, shambling out of the back of the car, 'I was the one that did most of the distracting, and on purpose, I might add. I'm due the credit. Also, have yourself one of these...' She waved a middle finger at me.

'Can we please get past the strange, abusive aggression, Eva? We're meant to be comrades, right?'

Eva snorted, then as Myers joined us, snatched the can of lager back from her, downed it, belched, and tossed the empty receptacle into a bush.

'That's public littering,' said Myers, 'I could have you for that.'

'Just try,' replied Eva, 'I fancy a bit of girl-on-girl.'

There it was again... that tingling sensation itching its way across my skin. The same feeling I'd noticed in Oldstone, but, if anything, even stronger.

'This is it. This is definitely the place.'

Chloe was somewhere near. I'd gotten there as fast as I could, my only hope was that they were still full up from all the food back at the hospital and maybe, just maybe, they'd shoved Chloe into the soul vampire pantry to snack on later. I thought that extraordinarily unlikely, but I had to hold on to something.

'Okay,' said Myers, 'forgive me being non-magic and everything, but it looks to me like we're just stood in the middle of nowhere. All I see is a dirt road, fields, and some hills. There's nothing here. No house, no building, no secret monster hide-out. Where exactly are we supposed to be?'

Before anyone could reply, the ground shook, a giant octopus tentacle burst from under the road, wrapped itself around a still pretty nonchalant-looking Eva, and dragged her beneath the ground.

'Shit!' I cried.

'I hear that,' replied Detective Myers. 'That was... a big monster.'

'Very big monster.'

Detective Myers nodded.

I edged tentatively towards the fissure that had been created in the dirt road. 'Eva?'

A fresh opening led down at an angle into the dark.

'That seems unlikely,' said Myers.

'How d'you mean?'

'Why hasn't that collapsed in on itself? The giant octopus arm has left behind a perfect tunnel for anyone stupid enough to want to explore.'

'Yes. Ah, a trap, perhaps?'

'Seems likely.'

'Still, that's where they must be. Where Eva is. Where, presumably, Chloe is.' A hopefully not-dead Chloe. 'They're in some sort of cavern, or cave system, underneath our feet. So...'

'You're not serious.'

'I really, really wish I wasn't,' I replied.

'If you go down there, you're dead. Did you see the size of that limb? That thing must be ten times as big as the one that lost a fight with my car. Twenty times the size, even. And you're going to crawl down into its conveniently-created tunnel, right onto its home turf?'

'Believe me, I know how stupid this is. I have, for much of the last ten years, been very comfortable in my cowardice, but I belong to the Cumbrian Coven, and I think I'm starting to understand what that means.'

'That doesn't mean anything,' cried Myers. 'I'm an officer of the law. We should get back-up.'

'You do that, see if they believe you. Meanwhile, Chloe is down there, so I'm going to walk—well, crawl—right into their trap and see what sort of trouble I can get into.'

Myers threw her hands up, then walked away. Then back. Then away again.

'Stay and call for backup,' I said. 'You don't need to risk yourself, too. Those are my friends down there, not yours.'

Myers sighed, her head hanging limp for a moment. 'Fine, but if I die down there, I am going to kick your arse.'

'Fair enough. Shall we, then?'

I peered into the tunnel, down into the fathomless black, then had a quick think back to the happy days of a week ago when I had no clue who I was, and that monsters were actually real. You don't know how good you've got it until you're crawling into the underground lair of an octopus-limbed nightmare that wants to eat your soul.

And down we went.

With the way forward partially illuminated by the light from Myers' phone, we crawled for what seemed like hours but was actually closer to three or four minutes.

The experience was—without tarnishing my image of staunch macho-ness—really poop-your-pants terrifying. The only thing that pushed me on was the knowledge that Chloe was down there somewhere, and if she was still alive, she'd more than likely have given up. There was no way she would expect help to appear. She was underground, hidden away in a monster's lair, waiting for the end. There was certainly no way she'd expect someone as daft as me to show up, guns blazing, but I was coming, and I was prepared to suffer whatever consequences came my way so long as I went down doing everything I could to help her.

'I take it you really like this Chloe then?' asked Myers, shuffling down behind me.

I shrugged. 'She's okay,' I said, cool as a cucumber. A cucumber with really nice hair. Which would be disgusting. Scratch that, I'm not eating a hairy cucumber. Also, scratch *that*, as it's just put another image in my mind.

Then all thoughts of salad—hairy or not—slipped from my mind as my hand met nothing and I tumbled out of the end of the tunnel and hit the dirt several feet below.

'Ow.'

Myers stepped on me as she climbed down.

'That's another ow.'

I stood, brushing the worst of the loose muck from my clothes.

'Shouldn't it be a lot darker down here?' asked Myers, turning off the light from her phone and pocketing it. 'Shouldn't it be, like, pitch black?'

'That'll be my doing,' said Eva.

'You're okay,' I cried.

'Always am, love. After getting dragged down here, I bit the fucker and it let go. No one likes getting bit, you know? Not even tentacle monsters.'

'So you're doing the illuminating?' asked Myers.

'You'd better believe it, sugar tits.'

'Do not call me that.'

Eva gave a little salute. 'Understood, twinkle tush.'

Detective Myers sighed and rubbed at her eyes. 'So, this is magic; us being able to see down here... it's down to magic.'

'You're catching on,' replied Eva. 'Shall we head down here then, see if we can pay a home visit?' She lit a cigarette and made off.

'I don't suppose I could bum a smoke, could I?' I asked.

'I'm all out.'

'That tin was full.'

'You are mistaken.'

I was not.

Me and Myers followed on.

'So, that was a big one,' I said. 'Bigger than the others.'

'Probably the queen. Big bitches, the queens. The rest just work for her. Go out, chomp down a few souls, then bring the nourishment back to ol' fatty to help propagate the species.'

'Do we have a plan at all?' asked Myers, 'besides sticking our heads in the lion's mouth?'

'I've got a plan, don't worry,' replied Eva. 'Well, a bit of a plan. Well, no exact plan, technically. We'll improvise.'

Myself and Detective Myers shared a look that was not at all confident.

As we moved forward, a noise started. A sort of droning hum. It was more than a little unnerving.

'What is that?' I asked.

'Hm? Oh, that's probably just a whole bunch of soul vampires harmonising,' replied Eva.

'It's times like this I wish I was a gun-toting, U.S. copper,' said Myers.

'I've got a gun,' said Eva, pulling one from her pocket.

'That's a plastic water pistol,' said Myers.

'Holy water?' I chanced. 'Is it full of holy water? Does that kill those things, like it does normal vampires?'

'No. This is my vodka gun. It's full of vodka.' She fired three shots into her mouth, then pocketed it.

'That's going to be really useful, I'm sure,' said Myers.

'Depends,' replied Eva. 'Maybe they like to party.'

The sound was huge now, echoing around and around, bouncing off the stone walls. There was an opening ahead. This was it. Time for the big, final showdown.

We stepped warily through the opening and into a space the size of a cathedral, packed full of the octopus creatures. There were maybe a hundred of them, all on their knees, arms aloft, worshipping their queen. The queen was, indeed, a big bastard. She looked like Jabba the Hutt's larger, uglier sister, with huge, thick limbs twitching and weaving out of the trembling, oozing flab.

'You see that?' asked Eva.

'Yes?'

'That's your mum, that is.'

For now, all of the creatures' attention was away from us. None of them seemed to have noticed our arrival. I craned my neck, attempting to catch sight of Chloe, but all I could make out were the dark, twitching shapes of the soul vampires.

'Okay,' said Myers, as quietly as she could while still being audible. 'Nobody make a sound. Let's just scope the place out and come up with a plan of action.'

'Agreed,' I whispered back.

Eva stepped forward. 'Oi, wankers, over here!'

Around a hundred pairs of giant, saucer-sized eyes turned our way.

Bollocks.

'My name's Eva Familiar. I bit your Queen earlier. Hello again to you, Tubbs.'

Myself and Myers shuffled in behind Eva. I was desperately looking for a way that this might turn into a win for team Not Octopus Monster, but I was coming up blank.

'Right then,' said Eva. 'We're here to kick seven shades of shit out of you. Who's first?'

A hundred beaks opened wide and screamed in fury, the sound amplified by the vaulted ceiling of the cave, deafeningly loud. Any second now they were going to charge us and kill us and eat our souls.

'Hold on.' A voice.

A voice I recognised.

'Chloe?'

And there she was, stepping out from the shadows. Chloe Palmer.

'Hey, Joe.'

'You're alive!'

She was definitely alive. I felt my grin grow so huge it was almost of cartoon-like proportions.

'Quick, run,' I yelled.

Chloe didn't move towards us. Not even a little bit.

'Chloe? What's wrong?'

'Yeah,' she replied, 'this might break your heart a little. Sorry.'

'What are you talking about? Let's go.'

'Joseph,' said Myers, 'I think your girlfriend is a bad guy.'

I laughed, then turned back to Chloe and saw the look on her face. 'No.'

Chloe shrugged, then nodded.

Shit.

And big hairy man-balls.

32

'No, no, no. No. No, no, no,' I said. Which didn't seem unreasonable, given the circumstances.

All sense of danger had evaporated as I stood rooted to the spot, my limbs useless, my face slack.

'What is it then, love?' asked Eva. 'What're you getting out of this exactly?'

'What am I getting?' replied Chloe. 'I'm getting what should rightfully be mine, and I'm going to do something wonderful with it. Something important.'

Myers stepped forward and flashed her badge. 'Chloe Palmer, you're under arrest, I'm going to have to ask you to accompany me to the station.'

'Really?' replied Chloe, disbelievingly.

'Yeah, I had a feeling that wasn't going to fly,' said Myers, stepping back and putting her badge away.

'Chloe,' I said, 'I don't understand. How can you be the bad guy?'

'I'm not the bad guy, Joe. What I'm doing is for the good of everyone.'

I shifted, trying to ignore my body's desire to crumple pathetically into a melodramatic heap of boo-hoo.

'Look at them all,' said Chloe, turning and waving at the surrounding soul vampires. 'Aren't they beautiful?'

'Not really my type,' replied Myers.

'Boring!' said Eva. 'Come on, love, cut to the chase already, I'm zoning out here.'

Chloe turned to me. 'When I was seven, I had to watch as cancer ate away at my mum... as death took her, piece by painful piece, and there was nothing I, or any doctor, could do about it. I can still hear her screams, Joe. Still see the agony etched into her face. And then I was alone. I never knew much about my dad. I was told he died when I was a baby, but that was about it. Then I got a job at Carlisle Hospital and I started to learn the truth.'

'What truth?' I asked.

'That I'm special. That I'm meant for something more.'

'And who told you that?' asked Myers.

'A fox,' she replied.

Oh...

'That little bastard,' said Eva.

A fox. A talking fox.

'He said things to me, too,' I explained. 'It's just bullshit, Chloe, that's all. Come on, you can still walk back from this. Please.'

She smiled, almost sadly, and shook her head. 'It's not bullshit. As soon as the fox told me, as soon as the Red Woman showed me, I knew it was true. I felt it. My father was from the Dark Lakes. He came here and he fell in love with a mortal woman, and I was what came from that love. My father, with me and my mother by his side, was going to lead an army to conquer Great Britain. This,' she said, arms wide, gesturing to the creatures surrounding her, 'was his army.'

'Shit army,' said Eva. 'Fuckers don't even have swords.'

'Being told the truth opened something up in me,' said Chloe. 'I found them. I found the army that my father was meant to lead. They were asleep, waiting for orders. I woke them up. I was terrified, I wanted to run away, but I couldn't. It was as though I was *meant* to be there. I thought they might attack, but they didn't hurt me. They saw who I was. Who my father was. And they've been growing stronger ever since. Getting ready to emerge from the shadows, with me at their head.'

'Bad luck, love,' replied Eva, 'cos you've got three problems there.'

'Oh?'

'Me, him, and her. I know it doesn't sound like much, but I am fucking scrappy.'

This was too much. It couldn't be real. Couldn't be true. I'd come here to rescue Chloe, to rescue the woman I'd been not-so-secretly in love with for the last several years, and now... what? She was part-evil on her dad's side?

'Chloe, you're a doctor,' I said, 'this goes against everything you've ever worked for.'

'No. Because I haven't told you the best bit yet. We're going to save this country.'

'From what?' I asked.

'From death.'

'Yep,' said Eva, 'she's gone full-blown loon.'

'My dad wasn't altogether nice. He was going to use this army to lay waste to this country. But I've found a different, better use for it.'

I stepped forward, desperate to hear something good from Chloe. Something that would make me understand. 'What do you mean?' I asked.

'These beautiful creatures, they don't have to just eat the souls. Imagine a person, close to death, beyond the help of any doctor. Just not enough time. Not enough tools, or the right medication, or the right knowledge. One of these creatures can remove and hold the sick person's soul. Cleanse it, with my help; with the magic I have inside of me. Infuse the soul with elements of the Uncanny so that when they deliver it back to the body, the patient will live. Will fight against what's killing them and win. Don't you see? They'll cheat death! Isn't that good, Joe? Isn't that a thing worth doing?'

I had to admit, that did seem, well, sort of noble, maybe? Good, sort of?

'One teensy problem: these things need to kill people and eat their souls to survive,' said Eva. 'They're not just going to chew on them and spit them back into their bodies. How are you going to get around that?'

'Oh, they'll still feed, only they'll save their feasting for people who deserve death.'

And there it was.

'And who decides who deserves to die?' asked Myers.

'Me of course,' replied Chloe. 'It's my birthright.'

'What about the people your pets have killed so far?' asked Myers, teeth clenched. 'Were they all deserving? Was my partner?'

Chloe shuffled, looking unsure for the first time since she stepped out of the dark. 'They need to eat to grow strong enough for what's ahead. They've been sleeping for years. They were starving. There wasn't time to—'

'Save it,' replied Myers, almost growling with contempt.

'I remember their names,' said Chloe. 'I'll never forget them. I'll never forget a single one of them. They died so a better world could rise, and they will be worshipped for their sacrifice. Millions will live because of them. *Millions.*'

'I'll be honest, Chloe,' I said, 'this is giving me real second thoughts about kissing you again.'

'Chloe Palmer,' said Myers, 'if you think everyone out there will just fall in front of you, follow you, allow you to decide who lives and who dies, then you don't know shit all about people.'

'They'll accept whatever I say because I'll give them the gift of life. Don't you see? Don't you understand the wonderful thing I'm offering? I'm going to change Britain for the better.

No more mothers crying over their sick, dying children. No more children left without parents, all because of some mutated, evil cells. No more. Not ever again.'

'And those that deserve to die get fed to Mr Octopus?' I said, quietly.

'Yes. Isn't that right? Isn't that a small price to pay for all the good I'll do?'

'Listen,' said Eva, 'all you are is a half-Uncanny and a pile of soul vampires. That's not nearly enough magic. Not nearly enough *power*, to do the sort of thing you're... oh...'

'Oh?' I said.

'Oh,' repeated Eva.

'Oh, what?' said Myers.

'Oh *you*, Joe,' said Chloe.

'Me? What about me?' I asked.

'Besides being the biggest knob-head this side of Manchester,' said Eva, 'you're also a source of crap-loads of Uncanny power. I mean, you're just a potential volcano ready to fire that shit out in every direction.'

'Well, it's not as though I know how to access any of that, and even if I could, I'm not going to help her.'

'Yeah, not really a consent issue,' Eva replied.

'Joe,' said Chloe. 'I'm sorry, you don't know how sorry, but we're going to kill you and feast on your soul. Your special, special soul.'

'See,' said Eva, 'told you.'

'Right. Oh. Great.'

'And then,' said Chloe, 'we'll have more than enough power to change things for the better.'

'For your version of better,' I corrected.

I looked to Chloe, who had an almost sheepish expression on her face. She shrugged. 'Sorry, Joe. Sorry it has to be you.'

'You were using me.'

'No. Not at first. I've always liked you, Joe, you know that. But then I started to realise what you *actually* were.'

'It was the fox, wasn't it? When I mentioned seeing a talking fox.'

She nodded. 'That was the first clue, yeah. I'd been looking for something like you, something so incredibly powerful, that we could all eat and use. That could finally give us the power to take our place up above and *save* people. And there you were. There you'd always been, and I had no idea. Strange thing, life, isn't it?'

'Getting stranger,' said Myers.

'I wish there was another way,' said Chloe. 'I'd hoped you'd be at my side when the moment came. That we could stand together as I beat death at last. I really did like kissing you.'

'Oh,' I replied, 'I've had better.'

'No, you haven't.'

I slumped my shoulders. 'I really liked you, Chloe Palmer.'

'And I really liked you. But I can't wait any longer. People are dying up there. People we can save. People who need me. So now it's time to kill you.'

'Shit. Heads up,' said Myers.

I turned to see the stone burrow that we'd come through was now packed with soul vampires blocking our way. We were trapped. Myers pulled out an extendable baton, ready to smack anything that came too close.

The creatures began to edge towards us.

'One step closer,' said Eva as she pulled her water pistol, 'and you fuckers are going to have a hell of a hangover tomorrow.'

Myers yelled and swung her baton, backing the things up.

'Bring him to me,' ordered Chloe.

The bravest of the creatures descended on us, wrapping its limbs around Eva and Myers and holding them back as I was shoved towards Chloe, towards the huge blob of meat that was the soul vampire queen.

'Chloe Palmer,' said Myers, struggling to free herself from her assailant's grip, 'I am an officer of the law. If you harm a hair on Joseph Lake's head you will have the entire force of the Cumbrian Constabulary to answer to.'

It was a nice try, but it wasn't much of a deterrent at this point. Chloe was now only a few metres in front of me. I felt like grabbing her by the hand and trying to pull her towards the exit. Maybe if I could just get her away from here, away from these creatures, I could talk some sense into her. She was still the Chloe I knew. That part of her must still be in there. And if that was true—and I really, really hoped it was—then maybe there was a chance yet.

That hope was quickly squashed by what happened next.

'It's time for me to become more,' she said.

'More what?'

'Just... more.' She smiled and gave me what you could almost class as a cute, goodbye wave.

'Bye, Joe. Thanks for being a friend. Sorry you won't be able to see the world I'm going to build.'

Then the giant soul vampire queen split open and Chloe stepped inside.

33

'Chloe!'

The wound she'd stepped through healed and the queen began to tremble, twitch, scream, her subjects crying out in reply.

She was changing.

She began to sprout up and up, fresh limbs erupting from her damp, meaty torso. When she stopped growing, she resembled a giant, thick tree of twisted, dark green meat with twitching octopus limbs for branches. A pure, Lovecraftian nightmare made sloppy flesh that screamed from its huge beak, loud enough to make the ground quake.

I staggered backwards, looking up at the terrifying beast before me. Chloe had somehow merged with the queen. There was no talking to her now. No convincing. Chloe was gone.

It was over.

'Hey, idiot,' said Eva. 'You kissed her. Ha!'

And now she was going to kill me and eat my soul. My fists clenched as I willed something to happen. Anything. I was magic. A warlock. If what they were saying was true, I had enough power in me to stop this. To put an end to this abominable army before it emerged above ground. I lifted my hands, screaming, willing the impossible to happen. For fire to burst from me and turn these creatures to ash.

Nothing happened.

Instead, the Chloe Queen reached out with one of its limbs and plucked me from the ground, carrying me towards its giant beak.

This was it then.

Really, really it.

I can't say it was how I'd expected to go.

'Nope,' said Eva. 'He might be a dickhead, but he's my dickhead.'

I craned my head round to see her twist and head-butt the creature holding her, breaking free. She dashed forward, octopus limbs grasping at her, hands burning with livid, orange flames.

'Get your tentacle off my witch, fucker!'

She punched out a fist and a ball of fire shot from her hand and severed the limb holding me. I fell to the ground at her feet as the Chloe Queen screamed in fury.

'Thanks,' I gasped, kicking the dead limb off of me.

'Don't thank me yet, you might still be horribly dead in a minute.'

Eva pulled a piece of chalk from her pocket and drew a quick circle on the rock at her feet.

'Inside, now.'

I didn't ask why, I just hopped in.

'You, too, Detective.' Eva reached out a hand and gripped Myers with some unseen force, pulling her towards us and into the confines of the chalk circle.

'What use is a chalk circle going to be?' Maya asked.

'What she said,' I added.

I soon got my answer. The soul vampires swarmed, desperate to grab us, to pull us apart, to feast on our souls. But some unseen barrier prevented them from getting within the circle Eva had created.

'Magic force field?' I asked.

'Technically, it's a ward of protection,' replied Eva, 'but yeah, "Magic force field" will do.'

'Are we safe?' asked Myers.

'Yep. Well, no. Well, yes. For a bit. I'm not very good at these protection circle jobbies, so sooner or later—and I'm guessing sooner—the spell's gonna break and they're gonna get in. And there's only so many of them I can deal with before they swamp us.'

The Chloe Queen raged at us, her giant limbs as thick as tree trunks, beating against the magical shell Eva had constructed with her chalk circle.

'So what now?' I asked. 'Can we move the circle? Just shuffle out of here before it breaks.'

'Nope.'

'Ah.'

'Then we're still going to be dead, just in a minute or two, rather than immediately?' asked Myers.

'Pretty much,' replied Eva.

'Well, shit,' said Myers.

'Exactly. That is of course unless Magic Joe here pulls his finger out.'

'Me? What the hell can I do?'

'I need you to fuck these twats up.'

Delicately put.

'How?' I cried. 'I don't know how to access the power I have. It's still all locked up and hidden away and I can't get at it. Not when I actually want it, anyway. It plays very hard to get.'

We ducked instinctively as a fresh barrage of limbs assaulted us, the sharp sound of whatever magic shell it was that was protecting us straining and complaining, stabbing at our ears. It didn't sound like it could take much more punishment.

'Wait,' said Eva.

'Wait?' I cried, 'I think we're all out of waiting time.'

'I... no... yes! I've got an idea. Bound to happen, that. Never doubted me for a second.'

'What idea?' I asked.

Eva grinned and waggled her eyebrows. 'Amplifier.'

'Amplifier?' replied Myers, stumbling back against me as the ground began to shake from the relentless onslaught.

'Ampli-shitting-fier! He might not be able to use his magic himself properly, but I can try and force my magic through Mr Idiot here, and he'll act as a booster, whacking up the volume to burn these fuckers to a crisp, and leaving us all nice and safe and alive and ready to party. Sound good?'

'Sounds good to me,' said Myers.

'Will that work?'

'Yep. Definitely work. Well, maybe. Possibly. It'll either work or it'll make your brain go off in your skull like an egg in a microwave.'

'What?'

'Don't worry, you won't feel it if it goes wrong. Okay, you will, it'll hurt like an absolute bastard, but then you'll be dead and you won't feel anything at all.'

'How likely is the egg scenario?'

'Don't worry, there's only an 80/20 chance of that happening.'

'80/20? Is the exploding egg the 80 or the 20?'

'Absolutely,' said Eva, noncommittally. 'Now brace yourself.'

'Is it the 80 or the 20? Eva? Wait—'

Her hands gripped my skull, and suddenly I felt like I'd been dropped from a height into a freezing pool of water. I could still see everything around me. Still see Eva, still see Myers. Could still see the monsters, and the Chloe Queen monstrosity. But it was all in slow motion. Distant. A dot on the horizon.

There were threads of fire in my mind. Burning tendrils, flaming worms. They wriggled their way through my consciousness, forcing connections that no longer existed.

Images flashed before my eyes. Terrible things. Confusing things. Faces and monsters and places and sounds that I knew must be things I'd experienced. Things the old me, the forgotten me, had lived through. Whatever Eva was doing was giving me access to my past. Would it last? Was it just a temporary glimpse that would be locked away again?

I was a witch.

A warlock.

But who was I?

Those things weren't the answer. Not really. It didn't tell me who I really was. What I was like. It didn't give me my memories, my fears, my loves, my hates. Then... two faces, two women, women who I knew, loved, belonged with. Me and them and Eva and we had purpose. Strength.

And then all clear thoughts were lost as it felt like my whole body was being pulled apart. Fingernails dragged down every raw nerve ending, and I heard a horrible sound that I think was me screaming in agony.

I was found. I was lost. My heart was broken, betrayed, scattered to the winds.

Chloe Palmer.

I had loved her as much as I could remember loving anyone, and it didn't matter. It was nothing. I was nothing. I was all just a means to an end. A tool to be used and cast aside.

Anger.

It swamped me. It fed me.

What had the fox said?

The Red Woman?

Become the Magic Eater.

I'd wanted that, hadn't I? I suddenly felt like I had once wanted that very much. Desired it. Coveted it. Obsessed over it. Was willing to burn everyone to the ground to get it.

A beast. I was a beast.

I could see the Red Woman looking at me, only it wasn't me, it was the other me, the forgotten me, and I was holding her hand and smiling. She was smiling back and the sky was on fire and a million-strong army of the dead raised their weapons to the heavens and screamed and hooted and cheered. And they were all mine.

We will do such things together.

The Red Woman was right. I wanted it. The power, the power, the power, and I think I'm falling apart. I think I'm dying. It's not working. It's too much. I don't know how to handle it, and any second now it's egg in a microwave time and that's all she wrote. I needed to control this. Needed to use it. Needed to unleash it. Come on, please, just do it!

'Hey, idiot.'

A voice. Not out loud, in my head. Eva was in my head.

'I can't do it.'

'Yeah, I know, you're useless.'

'Shut up.'

'I never should have come back to the lakes for you. I was having a good time, but here I am, and look what I find. You're pathetic, love.'

'I am not! I am... I am the Cumbrian Coven. I am Joseph Lake.'

I am the Magic Eater.

'You're a twat, is what you are.'

Why was she doing this? Why now, when we were moments from death and... oh....

'Yeah. Distraction. You're welcome.'

And then the cave exploded.

34

I was lying back on something that felt familiar.

'Finally,' said Detective Maya Myers.

I opened my eyes. I was in the back of the Uncanny Wagon, and it was on the move. I sat up to see Myers driving, Eva beside her. 'I'm alive.' I gave myself a quick pat down to make sure. 'I'm alive. How am I alive? How are both of you alive?'

'We won, that's how,' replied Eva, lighting a cigarette and handing it to me.

I took it with a trembling hand and inhaled. 'It worked?'

'Yup. You shat out enough magic to turn every single one of the fuckers to dust. Almost killed us, too. The whole place started coming down while you were sleeping it off. Me and sensible trousers here had to lug your dead weight out of there, sharpish.'

'We did it. We did it!' I laughed, exhilarated. We'd put an end to it. Avenged the murders of Mrs Coates, of Mary Taylor, of Detective Sam Samm, and all the rest.

It didn't take long for the bucket of cold water to be thrown on my high as Chloe's face swam into my mind's eye.

My best friend for years. The person I'd been head over

heels for. Who I thought I might have an actual future with. Dead by my hands. Okay, it turned out she was a half-monster, that she had allowed the deaths of numerous innocent people, but still. She hadn't been all bad. I didn't think I'd be able to just wipe away all the good memories. I didn't want to. They were real. She'd lied to me about a lot of things, but I don't think she had about that.

And now this was real. All of it. Monsters. Magic. What I was, and what I could be. I may not have had most of the pieces, or any of my memories, but I knew more than I had done for the last ten years, even if the things I knew were a mix of crazy and wet-your-pants terrifying.

I wasn't just a half-forgotten local mystery. The man who woke up, naked, without a past, beside Derwentwater. I was *more*. And I was pretty sure this was only the tip of the iceberg.

'Listen, I'm part of this from now on, right?' said Myers.

'You?' replied Eva. 'You were about as useful as a chocolate teapot down there.'

'I'm a detective. I can be useful. Resources, information, access. Also, this isn't a request, it's a done deal. From now on, I'm part of this. I'm the police here, and that means I am involved in protecting people from whatever they need protecting from. Understood?'

'Yes, ma'am,' replied Eva. 'Besides, if it was just me and ol' dickless over there, I'd probably end up killing the fucker.'

'Hey, I have a penis. And balls. Two of them.'

'Seen 'em. Not impressed.'

'Eva, why do you hate me so much? I mean, sometimes you seem okay with me, others you'd be happy feeding my tender, baby-making parts to a wolf. It's very disorientating.'

Eva snorted but didn't reply.

We left Detective Maya Myers at the police station, then I drove Eva back to the coven.

I'd seen the place during Eva's invasion of my mind. Seen memories of my life there, I know I had. Just flashes, but real things from my past. Now they were like fragments on the edge of my vision, just frustratingly out of reach, out of focus. But for a few brief moments, I knew something of my life here. Not just my life. I'd seen other people who belonged here, too.

Other witches.

I thought back to what the Red Woman and the fox had told me last time I saw them. What they had said Eva was keeping from me. I looked at her, slumped on the tatty couch, drinking from her vodka pistol, watching a woman try to convince a couple to spend £300,000 on a large, detached house by the sea.

'There were other members of this coven, weren't there? Others besides me and you.'

'That house is completely overpriced,' said Eva, before shooting vodka into her open mouth.

'Eva.'

She watched the TV in silence.

'Eva, tell me!'

'There were others, yeah. Two of them.'

'So it wasn't just me. What happened to them?'

Eva sat up and rubbed her eyes with the heels of her hands, then looked at me and sighed.

'Eva, tell me, what happened to the other witches?'

'Well, to put it bluntly, you murdered them, love. Shall we go hit the pub, then? You're buying.'

BLOOD STONES

1

Okay, here's the thing, and as far as things go, it is really, really, quite *the* thing.

It turns out that I, Joseph Lake, am a murderer. A killer. A man with blood on his cotton-soft hands.

Yes, the revelation came as something of a surprise to me, too. Particularly as—and you'd agree with this if you knew me—I'm probably the least murdery person you could ever meet.

A well-meaning doofus? It has been said on more than one occasion. A man gifted follically by the gods? Certainly (that's not a brag, it's a stone-cold fact). Someone who knows the lyrics to every song on Fleetwood Mac's seminal soft rock masterpiece, *Rumours*? Guilty as charged, Your Honour.

But a *murderer*?

It's weird how a revelation like that makes you look at yourself differently. There it is in the mirror; that same daft face, that familiar, slightly crooked smile, but there's something new in those eyes. Something grim that you hadn't noticed before.

It wasn't so long ago that I had no idea about my past. Any of it. I mean, *especially* not the murder bit.

Then I found out that I was a warlock.

A male witch.

Which, no, was not something that I'd ever considered a possibility, strangely enough.

Furthermore, I had been just one of three witches, tasked with protecting the local area from mean vampires, naughty wizards, and other assorted magical bastards. A trio of witches that had lived in a coven, with a familiar as our helper. Now it was just me and that familiar left; a rather fighty, drinky, scary woman by the name of Eva. It was she who had, just a couple of days earlier, informed me that I was a murderer. That the reason there were no longer three witches looking after the Lake District, was because I—a man who once danced in the aisles with a sixty-seven-year-old Post Office mistress during a Barry Manilow concert—had killed two of them.

Two dead witches.

Thanks to me.

Oh, but my tally doesn't stop there. No, no, no. Three days ago, I was responsible for the death of Chloe Palmer, a nurse at Carlisle Hospital, where I was employed as a dogsbody-cum-cleaner (and I use that phrase in the Latin sense, not the... you know). Chloe was a woman I had been madly in love with for several years, and who, I had started to believe, felt the same way about me.

Until it turned out that she was, you know, a bit mad.

And in league with some tentacle-limbed, soul-sucking vampire thingies.

And intent on being in control of who got to live and die on planet Earth.

That was a real red flag for me. A definite roadblock to us moving forward together romantically.

Plus there was the fact she was going to eat my soul, which I selfishly like to keep un-chewed.

Long story short, Chloe's dead now, and I felt like a turd wrapped in a different turd. It didn't matter that I'd done the right thing by stopping Chloe, she was still the woman I'd been friends with for years, and in love with since the first moment we spoke.

The whole thing was really tarnishing the rush I should have been feeling since I discovered my real self. And so there I was, sat on my couch, wrapped in a duvet watching my *Seinfeld* DVDs on repeat, and hoping that a little Jerry, George, Elaine and Kramer might prod me out of my blues. The fact that I could be found quietly snivelling as I watched, eyes red, nostrils damp, was perhaps a sign that this gambit was failing somewhat.

'What happened to the pub?' asked Eva, slouched beside me on the couch, ciggie in her mouth, can of beer in her hand, dressed in her usual assortment of black rags.

'What?' I mumbled.

She jabbed a finger at the TV. 'The pub. You know, the pub. The pub they work in. Pub.'

'There is no pub.'

'The pub with the fat drinky man and the man with the brain of a child.'

'*Cheers*.'

'Cheers,' replied Eva, raising her beer can and taking a gulp.

'No, you're thinking of a different... never mind.'

I would love to have been left alone to grieve for Chloe, but Eva had decided that what I wanted didn't matter. She was sensitive like that. So she'd been letting herself into my small, poorly-insulated ground floor flat to slump next to me on the couch for upwards of eleven hours a day.

Perhaps, in some small way, forcing her company upon me was her way of helping me through the grieving process. It was as that thought passed through my mind that an empty beer can bounced off my temple.

'Get me a cold one from the fridge, idiot.'

I already knew better than to argue with her, so up I got and over I went, duvet dragging behind like a stain-riddled cloak.

'You know, this whole feeling-sorry-for-yourself-pity-party is really starting to get on my tits,' said Eva as I passed her a fresh can of lager. 'That woman is dead. It was bloody weeks ago. Move on.'

'It's been three days.'

Eva looked at her watch, then, after a few seconds, realised she wasn't wearing one.

'Are you sure? You've lied to me before, you know.'

'Yes, I am very sure. What's more, this is at least the fifth time I've had to bring that up.'

'The fifth?'

I nodded.

'You sure, love?'

I nodded again.

'In my defence,' she replied, 'I have a massive alcohol dependency issue that is eating away at my brain cells.'

She cracked open her new drink and slurped up a fresh eruption of foam.

'You drink?' I asked. 'Can't say that I've noticed.'

'It's true! I don't think I've been fully sober in ten years. But boy, what a decade it's been.'

'Why, what happened ten years ago?'

I already knew the answer, but since Eva told me about my having murdered my fellow witches, she'd clammed up on the matter. It was as though she couldn't bear to reveal the whole story at once.

'Eva, I couldn't feel any worse, so maybe now's a good time to spill the beans.'

She nodded, downed her empty can, burped with such ferocity that a picture fell off the wall, and stood up with purpose.

'Okay, enough of all this blubbery, it's time to get you in fighting shape.'

I pulled my duvet tighter around my shoulders. 'Maybe tomorrow.'

'No, now,' she insisted, and clapped her hands together, which somehow tore the duvet from me, ignited it mid-air, and turned it to ash before it hit the carpet.

'How did you...? I mean, magic, I get that. Stupid question.'

'That was nothing,' replied Eva, lighting up a fresh ciggie, 'but it's still more than your sorry, good-for-nothing arse is capable of right now.'

'Well, excuse me, but my mind is still pretty much a blank when it comes to all this magicky, warlocky stuff.'

'Exactly, and there are people out there who are going to need our help. It's the whole reason I came back here. We've been out of business for too long, and this whole area has gone to ruin. It's time you learned a few basics.'

'Tomorrow,' I said, curling up on the couch, hugging my knees to my chest.

Another beer can, this time not quite so empty, bounced off my head.

'Fine!' I cried.

I stood, turned off the TV, and followed Eva to the door.

'You know that was my only duvet. I'm going to be freezing tonight.'

2

Eva stretched out across the back seat of my battered little car, the Uncanny Wagon, as we left Keswick behind and the scenic Lake District opened up around us.

'Wake me when we get there,' said Eva, then instantly fell into a deep sleep; a rather enviable skill that I hoped she would teach me one day. I'd always had a bit of trouble with insomnia. Well, "always" meaning the last ten years, since I woke up without a memory, naked, and lying next to Lake Derwentwater.

Recent events and revelations hadn't made it any easier to drift off to sleep either. When I close my eyes now, my mind plays tricks on me. Projects phantom voices into the black. Screams. Monster sounds. Chloe calling my name. Oh, there's a lot of Chloe rattling around in there.

Stupid bloody subconscious.

I was so lost in my thoughts as I steered toward the Cumbrian Coven that it took me a while to register that I now had two passengers in my car.

'All hail the saviour!' said the fox, standing on the front

passenger seat, Roman helmet on his head, battle-axe gripped tightly in its front paws.

The car swerved back and forth two or three times as surprise momentarily overtook me.

'What are you doing here?' I asked in a low hiss, looking back over my shoulder to find Eva somehow still sound asleep. I really, really needed to know her secret.

'You haven't yet returned,' replied the fox. 'To the Dark Lakes, I mean. Been days, it has.'

Ah, the Dark Lakes: the strange, blood-soaked counterpart to the land I was currently driving through. A place inhabited by a woman with the fiercest of red hair. A woman who claimed that I had a throne to accept, an army to lead, a title to take up.

Magic Eater.

I was pretty sure that whole business had something to do with why the other witches were dead, and why I couldn't remember a bloody thing.

'What if she wakes up and sees you?' I asked, gesturing for the fox to sit down, to hide, to not be there at all.

'Makes no difference. Awake. Asleep. Eyes open. Eyes closed. She won't see ears nor tail of me. Not me.'

'How do you know that?'

'Because I don't wants her to, now do I? No one sees me but who I wants. It's only manners.'

Eva had made it clear in no uncertain (and violent) terms that if I saw this strange walking, talking fox again, that I was to let her know. But then… Eva seemed perfectly comfortable keeping secrets from me, so what harm could it do? Until they both told me all the things I needed to know, anyway.

'What do you want?' I asked the fox.

'Just a quick hello,' he replied, waving his axe.

'Yes. Hello. Now if you wouldn't mind sodding off, I'm not in the mood for you or your red-haired master's crap right now, okay?'

'I lost my better half, too, you know?'

I blinked, then looked to the fox, confused.

'Oh yes. You lost you a lady, I lost mine. Two of us were the fiercest team you ever did set eyes upon. She must've slain a thousand with her axe, an' me at her side, doing likewise.'

'What happened?'

The fox shrugged. 'Death has everyone's number. Hers was called, and now here I am, alone and ready to go meet her.'

'The Red Woman, she won't let you die.'

'As is her right. Can't complain. Mustn't grumble. I serve my time, and then my time comes, sure enough.'

'What did you do, fox?' I asked.

'What's that?' came Eva's sleep-bleary voice from behind, causing me to once again take the car on a sudden s-shaped path. 'Who you jabbering at?'

I looked back to the passenger seat, but the fox was gone.

'No one. Nope. Just me having a one-sided chat. Keeping myself company, ha!'

'Idiot,' she said, before settling back down to sleep.

'Right. Yes. Sorry.'

I drove on to the coven.

The Cumbrian Coven—the place I'm told I used to call home—is an old, stone building situated down something called a blind alley. Blind alleys are secret streets, hidden from the sight of most people. The coven basically sits in the middle of nowhere, so there are no buildings either side of this "alley". Instead, it's secreted at the end of a sort of wrinkle in reality. An impossible fissure down which the building lurks like a bug behind a skirting board.

Which is a bit weird, yes.

But then almost everything about my life is weird now. I refer you to my recent conversation with a chatty fox.

I parked up, shook Eva for close to ten minutes until she woke up and almost throttled me to death, then followed her as she weaved her way drowsily into the coven.

'Okay, right, now the lessons can begin,' said Eva, as we stood in the coven's shambolic library, sat just off the main room. There were large, wooden bookcases and giant grimoires scattered all over. It looked as though someone had thrown a fit and trashed the place, but then it had always looked like that.

'One question,' I said.

'What?'

'Why are you holding that large stick?'

To answer my question, Eva struck me across the shins with it. I screamed high and sharp as I hopped around the room.

'Any more questions?' she asked.

'No, no, I'm good.'

'Then let's get started.'

During the past week, I'd proved myself able to perform some aspects of magic, though always by chance. Which is to say, I had no idea how I accessed that part of me, and no clue as to how I might recreate the effect once I had done it.

'We'll start with something so simple a brain-dead sloth could do it,' said Eva. 'So, just do your best, love.'

'Great pep talk.'

I yelped as the stick connected with my legs again. 'Ever hear the phrase, "You catch more flies with honey"?'

'Ever hear the phrase, "I'm going to twat you with this stick if you don't shut your gob"?'

I shut my gob.

'Right,' continued Eva. 'Hold out your hand, palm up.'

I did so with some trepidation, expecting the sting of stick across my mitt at any moment.

'We're going to try fire first. Piece of piss, fire; look...'

Eva held out her hand and a flame blazed into life, hovering in a perfect sphere about an inch above her palm.

'Okay, how do I do that then?' I asked. 'I mean, I've sort of done it before, but I've no idea how, and when I try to think "hot thoughts", nothing happens.'

'*Hot thoughts*,' Eva repeated.

I nodded.

'Jesus Christ...'

I thought it best to move on for fear of another stick incident. 'So, are there magic words, like in *Harry Potter*? Perhaps in Latin, or ancient Greek, or ancient... I don't know, Welsh?'

The ball of fire flew past my head, singeing the left side of my hair. My perfect hair.

'I think I'd just prefer the stick from now on,' I said.

Eva obliged.

3

I arrived at Carlisle Hospital some hours later, legs throbbing from multiple blunt force traumas, and still no closer to becoming a magic whizz.

I strained and strained until it felt as though I was going to pop a blood vessel, but try as I might, fire refused to appear from my hand. I tried to be cheery about the whole affair. It was only my first lesson, after all. Things were bound to improve, I said. Practice would make perfect. Eva had been less sanguine about it, grunting as she walked out, and launching her stick in my direction as she did so.

So I was a witch without magic.

Or at least, without magic that I could properly access.

It was as though whatever happened ten years ago—whatever it was that wiped my memory—had shoved all of my special talents into a room in my mind and locked the door. There was just no getting to it, at least until I found the key.

As the doors to the hospital's reception area slid closed behind me, Big Marge— manning the front desk as usual—looked up from her magazine and waved me over.

'Hi, Big Marge. Have you done something different with your hair, because you are looking particularly striking today.'

'Washed it,' she replied. 'Police are here again.'

Ah, yes. It turns out that when someone vanishes into thin air, as Chloe Palmer had, the police are obliged to take a bit of an interest.

'Oh? Have they, um... heard from her?' I asked.

'No,' replied Big Marge. 'Word on the ward is, she's been kidnapped. Or moved to Birmingham.'

'I don't know which is worse,' I joshed.

Marge grunted. 'Hasn't been in contact with you, has she?'

'Nope.'

But part of me wished that she had. That somehow it was possible for her not to be dead. Just for me. Just for a little while. There was magic in this world, I knew that for a fact. Was it too much to ask that Chloe come back to life? Okay, sure, she'd gone a bit loopy at the end there, but we all have our off days, don't we?

'Have the police said anything?' I asked.

'Say they have a number of leads they're looking into, all the usual crap. Say they're sure they'll find her.'

They're never going to find her, I thought. *There's nothing to find.*

Big Marge crossed herself, then slapped her meaty hands together in prayer.

'I hope they find something. Chloe used to bring me a doughnut every Tuesday. I liked her.'

I didn't feel much like continuing the small talk, so I sloped off to my locker and slipped into my overalls, hoping that a few hours of manual toil would distract me from my woes.

'Joseph Lake.'

Detective Maya Myers stood behind me. Myers not only knew who I really was, but she knew the truth about what had happened to Chloe. She'd been there when it happened. She was still a detective, though, which meant having to go through the motions of an investigation into Chloe's disappearance.

'Hello, Detective. *Detectives.*'

Myers' new partner stood next to her; a tall, broad man with a head like a tombstone. His haircut was severe, his pleasantries absent. Detective Martins. Myers had been teamed with him since the sad death of Detective Sam Samm, her previous partner, who'd been murdered by soul vampires. Soul vampires led by the woman I was still pining after.

Seeing Myers and the lack of Detective Samm—nice, not especially smart, Detective Sam Samm—reminded me that Chloe no longer being around was, on the whole, probably not such a bad thing. No matter how much it knotted my stomach, people had died. Good people. Because of her.

'Has Dr Chloe Palmer been in contact with you?' asked Detective Martins, or rather, *grunted* Detective Martins. Unlike the lovely Sam Samm, Detective Martins was—and I'm thinking of the best way to put this—a complete and utter bastard.

'No. Nope. At least not since yesterday.'

Detective Martins stepped forward. 'What do you mean? Did she contact you yesterday?'

I backed up until my shoulders bashed against the metal of my locker, Detective Martins' sour breath savaging my nostrils.

'No! No, no. Just, since you asked me yesterday. You asked me the same thing then, and she still hasn't been in contact. Believe me, detectives, the moment Chloe Palmer is in touch, you two will be the first to know. Oh yes.'

I looked to Myers, who widened her eyes at me in a, *Get your shit together,* sort of way.

'Make sure you do, Mr Lake,' said Myers.

'And you're sure she *will* contact you?' asked Martins.

'Well, no.'

'Oh, so you think she's dead?'

I knew what he was doing. He was trying to bombard me with questions, to throw me off centre, make me inadvertently say something I might be hiding.

Luckily, Myers also knew what he was up to.

'Just be sure we're the first people you tell if you hear anything,' she said. 'Do we understand each other, Mr Lake?'

I nodded vigorously in the affirmative.

'You better,' said Detective Martins, 'because if I find out that you're keeping anything from me, I'll make balloon animals out of your intestines.' He prodded me hard enough in the gut to leave a bruise by way of punctuation.

'Consider it fully got.'

He sniffed dismissively, then turned and walked away. Myers gave me a quick smile before she made her exit.

At times like this, it's good to know I had an inside woman on the case. And someone, like Detective Maya Myers, who had first-hand experience of the Uncanny.

I grabbed my mop and set off for the first job of my shift, cleaning up some vomit from the second-floor bathroom. It was a job I looked forward to more than my next encounter with Detective Martins.

I suppose you could say that the three of us were something of a team now; that is, me, Eva Familiar, and Detective Myers.

Myers was a London detective, transferred up to the sticks of Cumbria after seeing another partner of hers murdered horribly by... well, *something*. Something not normal and altogether monstrous. Now, since stumbling into the strange case of Chloe Palmer and her army of soul vampires, she'd made it clear that she expected to be part of any future paranormal investigations. Which was fine by me. I liked her and hoped she might act as something of a buffer between me and my violently-inclined familiar.

Plus, like me, she was new to all of this Uncanny stuff. Okay, I wasn't exactly "new", but I may as well have been, thanks to my secretive swine of a brain.

'I know, you know,' came a voice, plucking me from my musing.

A thin, grating voice. The voice of one Dr Neil.

'Good to see you as always, Dr Neil.'

Dr Neil didn't like me. There didn't seem to be any one incident behind the dislike; I think it was just my personality, which I have on good authority can be quite annoying.

'It's Dr Smith! Call me Dr Smith, you lowbrow shit-mopper!'

'You know, name-calling isn't very nice, Dr Neil.'

He glared at me, pacing back and forth across the bathroom like a pasty tiger, wondering whether or not to pounce on the majestic antelope stood proudly before him.

'Where is she? Where's Chloe?'

'As I've already said, I don't know. I wish I did.'

I felt guilty lying about that to most people, but with this particular specimen, oh, it felt good.

'Everyone knows you mooned after her,' said Dr Neil. 'Following her around like a little puppy. She was a doctor, she was one of us, the last thing she would have done was touch a little scrote like you.'

Every part of me wanted to say, *"Hey, I'll have you know that she and I mushed our chew-holes together just a few days ago, before I discovered the whole murder thing, but still! Mouth mushing!"*

I did not say that.

Admitting to Dr Neil, or any police other than Detective Myers, that me and Chloe had recently become more than just friends, would have put me under a very sharp microscope. Woman goes missing? Keep an eye on the boyfriend and see how he reacts.

Well, almost-boyfriend.

More-or-less-boyfriend.

I already mentioned the mouth-mushing, yes?

'Listen, Dr Neil, I've no idea where Chloe is, or what

happened to her. If I did, I would tell you. We were friends. Good friends.'

'I'll never know what she saw in you.'

Dr Neil seemed genuinely upset. Angry, even. I always wondered if he'd been nurturing a little unrequited love for Chloe at the same time I had. That would explain the obvious animosity.

'I'm sure the police will find her,' I told him. 'Safe and sound, you'll see.'

Doctor Neil grunted, then turned on his heel and stormed out of the bathroom. That must be it. A secret love that had festered inside of him for years.

Now, a more unpleasant person than I might have used this revelation to shift attention away from himself and onto that second party. To drop an anonymous tip to the authorities that years of jealousy had become too much for frustrated old Dr Neil until finally he snapped and did something rash.

Tempting.

But no.

No matter the pressure I was under, that wasn't me. Even if Dr Neil was an epic wanker.

It was about three seconds after this thought that I looked up at the bathroom mirror to see Chloe looking back at me.

Yes, the same Chloe who I'd killed just a few days previous.

Which, all things considered, was a bit of a bloody shock.

4

Of course, there's no way that had *actually* been Chloe in the bathroom mirror.

No way.

The explanation was simple: I hadn't been sleeping, I felt a huge amount of guilt over Chloe's death, and, well, I just plain missed the girl I'd known. Loved, even. And so *hello momentary delusion.*

When I blinked, Chloe disappeared. The only thing I saw now was my own slack-jawed reflection, staring bug-eyed at something that was no longer there.

Couldn't have been there.

I decided to cut short my shift. I told Marge I was sick, shoved my overalls in my locker, and hurried out to the Uncanny Wagon. It definitely hadn't been her. I just needed to sleep and to get away from the place we'd spent so much time together. That was all. Hopefully.

Then again...

Were ghosts a thing in this new world of monsters and magic that I'd stumbled into? If there were souls that could be eaten, then that suggested ghosts were a thing. Maybe there was a book on that back at the coven. I made a mental note to ask Eva about it.

I was halfway back to my flat in Keswick when some familiar words rang out for the second time that day.

'All hail the saviour!'

'Getting a mite tired of that,' I told the fox standing on the passenger seat. 'Don't you have any fresh material?'

The fox lowered his axe and slumped his shoulders. 'What?'

'Never mind,' I said. 'What d'you want now? I was hoping to go home and have a bit of a nap.'

'I wish for nothing but my own death.'

'Right. Cheery.'

'She, however, wants much more.'

I wasn't sure exactly when or how it happened, but I suddenly became aware that I was no longer driving down a familiar road. The Uncanny Wagon screeched to a halt as my foot stomped on the brake pedal. I pulled up with such force that the fox tumbled from the passenger seat and into the footwell with a startled cry.

'Sorry,' I said.

The fox grumbled as it clambered back up and twisted its helmet into the correct position.

'Come on,' he said. 'The Red Woman wants to see you.'

I stepped out of the car and looked up at the fire that raged across the sky. No blue, no clouds, just an endless expanse of flames.

I was in the Dark Lakes. The bizarre, bone and blood-smeared counterpart to the Lake District. A place that—so I'd been told—was home to an army of the dead that awaited my orders. Well, they could just keep on waiting. The fact they were dead and most likely evil aside, I didn't feel at all comfortable in a managerial position.

'She has nothing I want to hear,' I told the fox, who was trying to encourage me to follow him.

'How d'you know? Maybe she does.'

'I'm not interested in whatever's going on here. Not interested in any army, especially not a dead one. Not interested in any of your Magic Eater nonsense. Can't you just tell her to find some other poor sap to bother? I'm sure there are any number of power-hungry maniacs out there who'd welcome a zombie army with open arms.'

'Not my job. Not my instructions. Not my duty. I am here in service of the Red Woman, and she commands that I watch you, look after you, and bring you to her when she so desires. Best not keep her waiting.'

The fox turned and strode forward. Well, strode as best as its little legs would allow.

I sighed and followed on. What else could I do? I had no idea how to hop back into my own version of the lakes, so the best I could manage was to do as the fox asked and get this over with as quickly as possible.

The Dark Lakes was an empty, quiet sort of a place. Actually, quiet is probably not the right word. It was more like you sensed an absence. An abject loneliness. A raw longing.

My feet crunched over shards of broken bone as we trudged across a field and headed towards a crop of dilapidated stone buildings. They jutted out at odd angles, squashed together like teeth in need of some serious dentistry. The rot had set in long ago. No window remained unbroken, no rooftop whole. This was the first evidence of civilisation that I had seen in this desolate place.

'Who lives in this town?' I asked.

'Hm? Oh. A few skeletons. A few ghosts.'

Ghosts.

'So ghosts are real?'

'Course,' said the fox. 'You saw them vampires. What are they eating if not ghosts? Ghosts, souls, all the same thing.'

Chloe appeared in my mind's eye for a heartbeat, her hand

reaching out from the bathroom mirror like a woman drowning.

Distracted, I walked into the back of the fox, who had come to an abrupt stop.

'Shit. Sorry, I'm sorry,' I said, as I booted him in the rear end.

The fox stood and righted its helmet again. 'No need for sorries with me, saviour. All hail the Magic Eater.'

'Carry on with that and I'll kick you again.'

The fox shut up.

'So why have we stopped?' I asked.

'Red Woman. She's in there,' replied the fox, using his axe to point at the building we were stood before. It was an old pub. A wooden sign hung from a jib, squeaking back and forth, blown by a wind that wasn't—as far as I could tell—actually blowing.

'The Old Hen,' I said, standing on my tippy-toes and squinting at the faded sign.

'In you go. Doesn't like to be kept waiting, you know? And you've kept her waiting for the longest of long times.'

'Right. Right then.' I yanked at the breast of my coat as I mentally prepared myself, then pushed open the creaking door of The Old Hen and stepped inside.

Music.

It hadn't been at all audible from the other side of the broken door, but as I placed a foot within the pub, there it was. A jaunty piano was being played with gusto as someone sang:

"That's the way to the zoo, that's the way to the zoo; the monkey house is nearly full, but there's room enough for you!"

The music stopped as the skeleton sat behind the keys noticed me, its empty eye sockets turning my way.

'So. You're a skeleton.'

'Who isn't?' he replied.

I peered closer at the thing and noticed scraps of flesh still clinging to its bones, wisps of hair to its skull.

'Personal question, but how long have you been dead?' I asked.

'A long time,' the skeleton replied. 'I was murdered in the summer of 1873 by a man jealous of my skills on the piano. He beat me with an iron rod then strangled me to death.'

'Seems like a thin reason for murder.'

'I was also having frequent intercourse with his wife and oldest daughter. Both fell pregnant with my offspring.'

'That makes more sense. Probably should have led with that.'

'Agreed.'

I glanced around the rest of the pub. A heavy blanket of dust sat over most of it. The bottles behind the bar had clearly not been touched in years.

'I was told a woman would be waiting for me in here. Tall, pale woman. Lots of very red hair.'

'She's waiting on the Hill for you.'

'Right, so why am I here?'

'You're not,' replied the Red Woman.

I spun around in surprise. I was standing somewhere else now, on top of a hill covered in blood-red grass.

'Well, hello,' I said.

'Hello, Magic Eater,' she purred.

'So... how have you been?'

The Red Woman smiled as she stood up from her macabre throne. A throne made of skulls. A throne that was, apparently, mine to take. It didn't look in the least bit comfortable. If I ever did take it, I'd be investing in a nice, plump cushion.

'You know some of yourself now,' she said, 'isn't that right?'

'I know a little. Warlock, coven, familiar, two dead witches.'

The Red Woman stopped before me and traced a single cold finger across my cheek. 'There is so much more. Your familiar told you of the other witches, but not before I did. I wonder why that is?'

'What's the pub all about? If I was coming here, why not just bring me here?'

'The Hill doesn't just stay where you want it. Sometimes it is here. Sometimes it is there. Sometimes it is somewhere else altogether.'

'Right. Not at all enigmatic, that.'

'She refuses to tell you all of the truth, your familiar; isn't that right?'

I shifted uncomfortably under her green-eyed gaze. 'She's not exactly overflowing with a desire to tell me the whole story, no.'

'Whereas I tell you things. I told you about your fallen witches. I told you about your destiny. You can ask me anything, and I will tell you the truth.'

'Tell me why I murdered the two witches,' I said.

'Take your throne,' she said, gesturing to the uncomfortable skull chair, 'and I will tell you the whole story. I promise.'

The way she smiled as she gestured at the skull chair made me very sure that taking up its seat would be a not very nice thing.

'No, thanks. Need to stretch my legs.'

'Such little trust.'

'To be fair, you are keen on me becoming some sort of fifteen-foot-tall, fire-coated monster.'

The Red Woman sat on the throne and slowly crossed her leather-clad legs. 'Here is a little truth. The other witches, do you know their names?'

'No. Eva clams up when I ask about them.'

'Lyna and Melodia. Their names were Lyna and Melodia.'

Was that the truth? It felt like it was. Like, as soon as I heard them, I knew. I knew that those were their names. Of course, those were their names. Lyna and Melodia. My fellow witches. My equals.

And I'd murdered them.

I staggered back as a picture exploded in my mind's eye. Two women, both looking to be in their thirties, but I knew they were much older. And they were laughing. And I was laughing, too.

'What's this?' asked Eva, holding a glass and grimacing from whatever she'd just tasted.

'That's beer,' said one of the witches, the one with blonde corkscrew hair.

'Beer? Well, I don't think I'll be drinking that again.'

And then it was gone. A fragment of ice, bobbing up above the ocean surface for a brief moment before its weight carried it under again.

'I remembered them! Just for a second, I remembered them. And, wow, Eva has *really* changed.'

'I can tell you more,' said the Red Woman. 'I can show you so much more. Just take your throne.'

She stood and stepped aside, and the throne called to me. Not audibly, but I felt its pull, like it was a big magnet made of gross skulls. I wanted to know more. I'd had a taste and now my stomach grumbled for the rest.

'No, I don't think so.'

'Look at what you have become, Magic Eater. Look how your own mind deceives you; keeps the real you under lock and key.'

'Maybe that's the best place for the old me.'

'If you could only remember your true self. Your wants. Your desires. The things you and I did together...'

And then her ice-cold hand was on my temple and—

I am a giant.

Flames burn fiercely across my skin.

All around me I see the magic of this world. Of every world.

I am striding through an ocean of power, waves of every colour wash around me, and I open myself up to it, swallow it, absorb it through every pore, more and more and more and nothing can stop me.

The Uncanny rage against me, but they are like flies raging at a mountain.

My army of the dead awaits me. Awaits my command.

And she waits, too.

The Red Woman.

We are as one.

Together.

Beast and master.

Lovers, two.

And the world shall fall and scream before us, and we shall show it no pity.

No pity.

None.

—just as soon as it started, it was over. I found myself gasping for air, curled in a foetal position on the blood-red grass.

'It is what you want,' said the Red Woman, standing by the throne, 'what you must become. You have no choice. Not in the end. You'll see.'

I pushed myself groggily to my feet.

'I don't care what the old me was up to. If that's the sort of thing that tickles his fancy, he sounds like a right bastard. I've got no interest in all that, thank you very much. No offence, scary woman, but I'm not the murdering kind.'

'What about poor Chloe Palmer?'

That stung.

'That was... different.'

'If you think fulfilling your destiny just means murder, you couldn't be more wrong.'

'Yeah, but not too far wrong, I'm guessing. Just one house over, yeah?'

The Red Woman chuckled.

'If you don't mind, I'd quite like to go home. Where the sky isn't on fire and I'm not wading through bloodied grass.'

She approached. 'Then go.'

'Good. Thank you. You have very nice hair.'

'But know this: you will become the Magic Eater. It is your destiny. You can no more run from it than you can crush a diamond in your fist. You seek only to delay the inevitable.'

I went to answer, but a black wave folded over me, taking me away and away.

5

It was past midnight by the time I finally got home and flopped, exhausted, on my couch.

As usual, I had no idea how I'd returned from the Dark Lakes; everything had gone black, and then I was in my car, a mile from home. Going to that place was never a picnic, but each time I went there, I felt like I was getting more of the puzzle pieces. Each time I spoke with the Red Woman, she gave me more of me than I had. More of me than Eva wanted to share, anyway.

Lyna and Melodia.

I knew their names now. I even knew what they looked like. Well, to a degree. My mind had already scrubbed out most of the memory, but I'd held on to some of it. One of them had a mass of blonde curly hair, wide blue eyes, and a huge smile. The other had straight black hair, brown eyes, and dimples in her cheeks.

Lyna and Melodia. We'd made a trio. Three witches to look after this area of Cumbria. Magic police.

And I killed them.

I didn't know what had happened there, not exactly, but I wasn't stupid. Okay, that might be a stretch, but I'm not *completely* stupid. It had to have something to do with my so-called "destiny"; the Magic Eater stuff the Red Woman kept trying to shove my way. It was more than a teensy bit frustrating to only have these scraps and not know, for sure, the whole picture. But compared to what I knew a week ago, I'd made a giant leap forward.

My phone buzzed in my pocket and I fished it out with a grunt of weary effort. Detective Myers' name flashed across the screen. I hit answer.

'Detective, if this is one of those booty calls I hear about in movies, just know that I am far too tired.'

'Hilarious,' replied Myers. 'A family's just been murdered.'

Which rather took the fun out of things.

It was almost 1 a.m. by the time I reached the scene of the crime. I pulled up to a small cottage in Applethwaite: a tiny village about a mile from my front door. Myers was waiting for me outside and failed to return my rather-too-jaunty wave.

'Sorry, probably not appropriate for a murder scene,' I said.

'Definitely not.'

An ambulance was parked outside with a couple of bored-looking medics sat in the back drinking tea. Scene of crime officers in white boiler suits exited the cottage, and when I say "cottage", I want you to picture a real chocolate box of a thing. You've got it; cob walls, thatched roof, crooked windows, the whole shebang.

'Done?' Myers asked the departing forensics team.

'Yeah,' replied one of the boilersuit peeps, 'got a lovely bunch of pics, all thanks to this fab new lens. Fancy a look?'

'Not interested,' replied Myers.

The man nodded disappointedly and trudged away.

'You really have a lovely way with people, Myers,' I said.

'This is my crime scene. That means I'm in charge here. Do we understand one another?'

'Understood,' I replied.

'People have died within those walls, and it's my job to find whoever did it and make them pay.'

I threw her a little salute. 'Ja vol, mein capitan.'

If it appears that I'm being flippant here, know two things: one, I can't help it, I'm an idiot. And two, I was more than a little uncomfortable. I was being asked to take a tour of a crime scene. A place where people had recently been murdered and where, in fact, their corpses still remained. This was not my natural habitat. True, I had stumbled through a few murders recently, but this was different. This was being asked to help out on a professional basis.

I was, to put it mildly, pooping my pants, both at the idea of seeing more dead people and at the idea that I was then expected to assist in some way. To make sure that whoever—or *whatever*—was behind those deaths was brought to justice. It seemed like a tall order. I clean toilets for a living. This was a lot of pressure for my slender shoulders.

So, jokes, daftness, and distractions.

'I'm guessing there's something a little off about this murder if you're dragging my arse over here,' I said.

Myers nodded. 'This is one for us, all right. Come on.'

I shivered as I stepped over the threshold. 'Brr, what is that?'

'What is what?' asked Myers.

'You don't feel it?'

'The fact that I'm asking would suggest I don't.'

'You make a good point.'

Myers gestured in a *get-the-fuck-on-with-it* sort of way.

'I don't know... it's just sort of... weird.'

'Well, that's really helpful. I'm so glad I called you.'

She carried on through the cottage and I followed. I'd like to have put what I was experiencing more eloquently, but "weird" was the best I could do. As soon as I stepped into the cottage, I could tell something not exactly normal had happened there. Like whatever had intruded and committed the murders left something of its weirdness behind. An imprint in the air around us.

Or something.

I don't know, I hadn't slept properly in a long time.

'He's right, definitely a weird feeling up in this place,' came a voice from behind me. I turned to find Eva laid out on the floor, cigarette in her mouth, eyes closed.

'How did you get here?'

'I called her like I called you,' replied Myers. 'Using a phone. Mystery solved. Wow, I am a good detective.'

'She has your phone number?' I asked Eva, incredulously. 'I didn't even know you had a phone.'

'Of course, I have a phone. I'm not Captain fucking Caveman.'

Eva opened her eyes and pushed herself vertical, briefly staggering to one side before getting to grips with the idea of walking again.

'Why don't I have your number?' I asked.

'I only give my number to friends, you don't want just anyone bothering me, know what I mean?'

'Well, that has to sting,' said Myers.

'What? Nope. Completely unstung.'

It definitely stung a teensy bit.

'Is this crime scene catered?' asked Eva. 'Only I could murder a bacon buttie. Haven't had anything solid pass my lips in hours.'

'No. Because it's a crime scene,' Myers replied, 'not a children's party.'

'Ah, so no pass the parcel, either?'

'No.'

'I see. Makes sense. Make a note of that for the future, though.'

'I will not.'

'Okay,' said Eva, rubbing her hands together and striding forward, 'let's see some bodies.'

'And you think I'm annoying,' I told Myers with a grin.

'Yes. I do.'

'Right.'

Myers walked to the next room after Eva, with me at her heels. The room had patio doors that led to the back garden. The doors looked as if a wrecking ball had smashed into them from outside, smothering the room in shards of wood and glass. Eva crouched down by something that used to be alive. Used to be a person. Now it resembled a large chunk of cured meat.

'Well, isn't this something?' asked Eva.

The body was completely mummified; lips pulled back in a final grimace, cheeks hollow.

'How long since they were killed?' I asked.

'A few hours at best,' replied Myers.

'A few hours? But... well, look at them.'

She nodded. 'Exactly. That is one Mr Mark Watterson. He was forty-two years of age, married, and a father. The wife and child are upstairs.'

'Is the mummy a mummy, too?' asked Eva.

'Yes,' replied Myers, 'and the kid. Dead and dried out, like they've been left out in the desert for months.'

Eva ran a finger across the desiccated corpse, then stuck it in her mouth.

'That seems inappropriate,' said Myers.

'Yeah,' replied Eva, 'tastes like shit, too.'

'How do you know they haven't been dead for ages?' I asked.

'Because they were at their neighbours only a few hours ago, and they were very much alive at the time.'

'So, some sort of vampire again?' I asked.

'No,' replied Eva, 'this was something else. Show me the others.'

Upstairs, huddled together in what must have been the parents' bedroom, were what remained of the wife and daughter; two strips of people jerky, clinging to each other in one corner of the room. I won't deny that I felt my stomach churn as I looked at them. Especially at the smaller of the two withered bodies.

The mother had died trying to shield her child, but it hadn't worked. What sort of a monster would kill a child?

'Something's wrong,' said Eva, pacing the room and waving her hands around like she was conducting an invisible orchestra.

'Three people are dead,' I replied, 'so I'd say there's quite a lot wrong, yeah.'

'Hm? What? Not the dead people. The dead people are obvious, they're dead, you can see them. No, something else... aha!'

'What is it?' asked Myers.

Eva grinned, then clapped her hands together. The far wall seemed to ripple, then it whipped away like a tablecloth to reveal a hidden room. Inside of the room was a cauldron, magical texts, robes, and pentagrams chalked on a square of slate. Basically a full-on, secret magic room.

Someone had murdered a family of magicians.

6

I stepped into the secret room, happy to leave behind the dead mother and child.

'Were they witches then?' I asked. 'Like me?'

'Nah,' replied Eva. 'Things like you aren't just spread around willy-nilly. Plus, I'd know if there were any in my own backyard. These are just low-level magicians. By the look of this set-up, they've been trying to fly under the radar.'

'Well, it looks as though they didn't fly low enough,' said Myers.

'So you're saying they were murdered because they were magical?' I asked Eva.

She sighed. 'Not the sharpest, are you, idiot?'

'Wait a minute, how did you not realise they were magic right away? I thought you were able to sense that kind of thing.'

'I didn't clock that they had anything about them that was magical straight away 'cos that Uncanny spark has been drained almost entirely out of them. They're practically normals now.' Eva shuddered and made a "yuck" face.

'No offence taken,' replied Myers.

'Oh! I think I've got it,' I replied.

'Go on,' said Eva.

'Someone or something is feasting on magic? On magical people for… reasons to be determined.'

'Obviously. I basically just said that.'

'No, you didn't.'

'Oh. Well, I said it in my head. Same thing.'

'It's really not.'

Eva changed the subject. 'Something is feeding on the Uncanny. I wonder what. And also why. And also what.'

Myers pulled out her notepad. 'These aren't the first bodies to fit this MO. In the months before I met you two, there were six other cases across the county. Forced entry—really forced entry—and dried out bodies. We've been keeping the weirder details out of circulation because, well, they're weird.'

She handed the pad to Eva, who scanned the details.

'Okay, at least two of these are Uncanny types of one kind or another. Melinda Smith was a gnome.'

'That explains why she was so small,' said Myers. 'And was found clutching a fishing rod.'

I laughed, then felt bad. Because of the murdered thing.

'Another one here: Bob. Big Bob. Troll. Hard bastards to kill, trolls, but some bugger's managed it.'

'What about the other four?' I asked.

'Don't know 'em, but it's safe to assume they were some flavour of Uncanny.'

Myers took back her pad and pocketed it. 'The pattern's clear enough, and the attacks seem to be increasing in frequency. The first few were months apart, the last three have happened in the last week alone.'

'Someone's either getting bolder or stronger,' said Eva.

'And they're targeting weird-arse things like you two.'

'Right,' I said, 'which means we're probably in, sort of, danger.'

'Yeah,' replied Eva, 'gives life an extra spice when you feel the shadow of the noose, don't you think?'

'I prefer not living in constant fear, but different folks and all that,' I replied.

I noticed that Myers seemed to be looking at me expectantly.

'What?' I asked.

'Well, go on then. Do the thing.'

'What thing?'

'Like you did with the soul vampire. You were able to touch the body and get a picture from it. Do that again and tell me what we're looking at here.'

Ah, right, that. One of the magical power thingies that I'd managed to tune into recently was gaining insight into a recently deceased person—or monster's—life. Or, to put it more specifically, their life very close to the point of their death. Problem was, it did mean touching dead things.

'Who's it gonna be then?' asked Eva. 'Little or large?'

I wasn't too keen on touching a dead child, so mother it would be.

Trying not to look too closely at the corpse, I knelt down beside it.

'What's it like?' asked Myers. 'When you see the things you see?'

'It's... odd. It's like watching something underwater, but their emotions, I get those *sharp*.'

'Get on with it then, idiot,' said Eva.

'Don't rush me. I'm just preparing my... whatever it is that needs preparing.'

The truth was that this had never worked when I really wanted it to. Not directly, at least. Something had always needed to distract me from focusing too closely on what it was I wanted to do. To force whatever it was inside of me to click into place and allow the magic to happen.

But not this time.

As soon as I laid my hands on the waxy skin of the dead woman, it was like I'd been dropped into a freezing lake. The "real" world was yanked away as a new one rushed headlong towards me. My body trembled. I could hear a child chattering somewhere behind me. I knew I was seeing the woman's memories, but part of me was scared that if I turned around I'd see the tiny, withered corpse of the child creak into life, its locked jaw cracking as rough, garbled words forced their way out.

It was night. There was no colour in the memory; everything was shades of black and grey, but I *felt* the night. I could feel the woman's contentment. She had a husband she loved, and a child she would die for. A child that she struggled for years to conceive before it finally happened. And now her life was complete and she was looking forward to the future. I felt the powerful love of a mother for her child coursing through me, and it was intoxicating, frightening. The strength of it. The sure and happy knowledge that there was nothing she wouldn't do. That her own life would be a small price to pay in return for her child's safety.

On that night, giving up her own life wasn't going to be enough, though, because something was hungry for more than just *her* existence.

A voice from the next room. Her husband.

'What did you say, love?' she asks.

'There's something in the back garden.'

'What? What is it?'

'Mummy, look at this picture of a cow I drew.'

The small, smiling girl holds up the wonky, crayon drawing of a cow that looks nothing like a cow, scrawled in purple and red.

'Oh, that's wonderful! What an artist.'

'I know!'

'Do you think you'll be able to sleep now?'

The child frowns, her forehead wrinkling, obviously pondering the question deeply. Finally, she nods.

'Good girl.'

'After one more bedtime story, Mummy.'

'There's definitely something in the garden.'

I try to stop the woman from moving towards the back room, from walking through to see what her husband is talking about, but it's useless. I have no power over her actions. This has already happened, I'm just along for the ride.

'Is it a fox? I saw a big one back there the other week.'

No, it isn't a fox. Not this time.

Things move fast then.

A large, wide shape, taller than a person, hurtles through the patio doors, sending shards firing out, cutting into her flesh. Her husband yells and falls to the floor. What has come through the glass doors isn't a person or even an animal. It isn't a living thing at all.

It's a stone.

A large standing stone, the kind you see in ancient stone circles, with strange pictures and symbols chiselled across its surface. Clear but weathered with age.

'Mummy, what is that?'

Panic, terror. The woman rushes towards her daughter, picking her up and running for the front door.

'Daddy! What's the stone doing to Daddy?'

I can hear his screams, but she doesn't look back. All that matters is getting her daughter to safety. To the front door. To the car. To anywhere but here.

But the front door opens and there stands a second stone. Giant. Filling the door frame. Purple sparks ripple up and down its surface.

No way forward, no way back, only up.

I know where this is going.

The woman screams, I scream, my throat raw and—

'What the fuck is this?'

I felt like I'd been rear-ended in my car. I jolted forward, falling on top of the woman's dried-out corpse, then yelped in disgust and hopped backwards.

'I said, what the fuck is this?'

Detective Martins, Myers' new partner, stood in the doorway.

'I brought in a couple of independent experts to give the crime scene a look over,' replied Myers, 'that's all.'

'Who's the prick?' asked Eva, gesturing towards Martins with her cigarette.

'What did you say?' replied Martins, taking a threatening step towards Eva.

Eva didn't even blink.

'This is my partner,' said Myers.

'Tough break.'

'And this is the guy who's neck-deep in the missing nurse case,' said Martins, jabbing a finger in my direction.

There was a lot of finger-pointing going on suddenly. Far too much for my liking.

'Neck deep?' I replied. 'I'm not neck-deep. I'm not even ankle-deep, am I?'

Myers arched an eyebrow. 'You're a person of interest.'

That did not sound good. Not at all.

'You never told me you knew him,' said Martins.

'It wasn't relevant. And I don't know him. I just know that Mr Lake and Miss Familiar here have a deep knowledge of local lore and strange events.'

'And action films of the 1980s,' added Eva. 'I'm a bloody Mastermind on that shit.'

Martins approached Myers, a scowl creasing his face. 'Because of what happened to Detective Samm, I've been giving you a pass, but this here is bullshit. This is official police business, we don't need a cut-price Mulder and Scully to help us out. Am I understood?'

Myers looked coolly at her partner. 'I wouldn't push any further at that, Detective.'

'You know, I really don't mind just... leaving,' I said, the tension in the room so thick it could crush a bear.

A really big bear.

'Stay where you are,' said Myers, not taking her eyes off Martins. 'This is the seventh case of its kind, and an outside perspective is appreciated. All that matters is stopping any more deaths. Not ego. Not pride. Understood?'

Martins glared at her.

'Okay, now kiss,' said Eva.

Martins snorted and turned to me, fists clenched. For a horrible moment, I thought he might be about to propel his large knuckles into my face.

'I don't trust you, Lake.'

'Understood.'

'A man with no past who likes weird stuff, and a friend who's dropped off the face of the Earth. I don't care what Myers here thinks of you, I think you stink, and I am watching you.'

'Thank you?'

Martins cast a cold look back to his partner then stomped out.

'Well, that was all very arousing,' said Eva, taking a drag of her cigarette.

'Don't worry about him,' said Myers, 'his bark's worse than his bite.'

'Really?'

'Yes. Well, no. His bite is really, really bad. What happened to the secret room?'

'Oh,' said Eva, shambling over to where the room had been and now wasn't. 'Soon as I heard that big lump of rage and repressed sexuality lumbering in, I snapped the spell that was hiding it back in place. Best not to involve him in certain aspects of this case, right love?'

'Right,' agreed Myers.

'So?' Eva waved her cigarette towards me, spilling ash like confetti, 'what did you see when you touched up that dead woman?'

'Did you see the killer?' asked Myers.

'Yeah, I saw them.'

'So who is it then?' asked Eva. 'What did the shit-head look like?'

And so I told them about the sentient killer rocks.

Myers might, *might* have been a little sceptical.

'Bullshit.'

Just a little.

7

I was woken the next morning by the insistent electronic beeping of my utter swine of an alarm clock, which needled me from my too-short slumber. It was seven in the morning and I was due for my shift at the hospital in less than an hour. I slapped the alarm quiet and zombie-walked my way to a hot shower.

As the water battered my face, I replayed the previous night's events. Something was murdering people with a connection to magic. "The Uncanny", as Eva would say. People like me. And the something doing the killing—or *pair of somethings*, going by what I'd seen through the eyes of the dead mother—were giant rocks. Monoliths; the kind you see parked in circles in countryside fields. Ancient rings of standing stones where sprites and fairies frolic when the moon is full. Or naked, thrashing ladies, like in *The Wicker Man*.

Clean, dry, and dressed, I slumped on the couch with a cup of tea and a slice of toast. I checked my phone to see Eva had sent me a text.

Me. You. Stone hunting.

Apparently, I'd earned the privilege of having her phone number.

I messaged back that I'd catch up with her after my shift, then scrolled through my emails. There was one there from someone I didn't know, with the intriguing title, 'Please Help Me'. It had come from someone called Annie Royal. The message was sent to my "professional" weird investigations site (emphasis on the speech marks). Before I started to find out who I was, I ran a not-at-all-successful sideline job, investigating strange goings-on in the local area. In doing so, I'd hoped I might stumble across something that shone some light on my past. Having learned what I know now, I sometimes wonder if I should have just stayed quiet and kept the blinkers on.

The email was sparse. It simply read, *Mr Lake, I'd like to hire you. Annie.*

A week ago, I'd have replied right away, but on this day, after everything I'd been through, I found my thumb swiping and deleting the message. No time for anything else right now. I was already up to my nose in weird.

The message did remind me of something I'd been meaning to do, though: namely shutting down my other website. That one was really just a cry for help into the digital wilderness. My face, the point of my discovery ten years previous, and a question: 'Who am I?' There was a space to leave messages – not that anything ever got left there these days. I used to check it more out of habit than hope, refreshing the page on a thirty-second basis on my worst days, but now I didn't need it at all. Time to shut that puppy down. But as I fired up my laptop and accessed the site, something gave me pause.

A new message.

Joe, help me. I don't know where I am.

The name next to the message read "Chloe".

Well, that was some low-down, mean-spirited, nasty, trolling right there. What kind of person pretends to be a missing woman? A missing woman who was actually dead.

An image of Chloe reaching for me from the hospital's bathroom mirror flashed through my head.

It was a nasty trick, that's all. Some local kid with the emotional depth of a cockroach or Piers Morgan, hoping to get a rise out of me. But a little part of me wondered. Maybe even hoped. Either way, the laptop closed without the website being decommissioned. Because maybe. Just maybe.

Hey, it wouldn't be the strangest thing to have happened recently.

'You look worse than usual, and you usually look like shite,' noted Big Marge as I stumbled through the automatic doors to the reception desk, trying not to trip over my own feet.

'Thanks for sugarcoating that, Biggie.'

'You still not sleeping?'

'Oh, I slept. Unfortunately, for a rather stunted length of time. I was out painting the town red. Wine, women, and song; you know how it is.'

'I do. I get the distinct feeling you don't, though.'

After the usual stimulating rounds of floor mopping, toilet tissue replenishment, and lightbulb replacement, I found myself back in the bathroom where I recently had my Chloe vision. I approached the mirror, nervously scanning for any sign of her. It was a trick of the mind, that's all. Had to have been. But that didn't stop the hairs on the nape of my neck from standing up and doing a little boogie. Hope is a bastard.

'Hello? Are you there?' I asked.

Silence.

No sign of her.

I reached a hand towards the mirror, part of me wondering if it would go right through the glass, *Alice in Wonderland* style. What if there was a hidden world beyond it, where Chloe, now magically alive and not evil, was waiting for me with a smile and a hug, and much mouth mushing?

My fingertips met the cold, very solid surface of the mirror. Of course.

'Chloe, are you there? Did you leave me a message?'

'I knew it, you're mental.'

I turned with a yelp of surprise to find Dr Neil standing in the doorway, arms folded.

'You know, we really must stop meeting like this,' I said, 'people will talk.'

I headed towards the exit, but Dr Neil stood his ground.

I squared up to him. 'I'm not possessed with the power to walk through people, so if you could shift your pasty body to the left, I'll be on my way.'

'Still no sign of Chloe,' he growled. 'Where is she, Lake?'

I sighed. 'How many times? I don't know. I really wish I did.'

'The police have got your number. That detective was very interested in what I had to say about you.'

'You rotten bastard,' I shot back. 'This isn't a game. Someone's missing.'

'Right. And yet for someone who claimed to be oh so close to Chloe, you don't seem all that upset. Word on reception is that you were out living it up last night, having a rare old time.'

'What?'

'Charlotte from the canteen overheard you and Big Marge talking. Bragging about the women you were cavorting with. Isn't that right?'

'You're wasting your time with me, Dr Neil. I appreciate that you want Chloe back—I do, too—but I'm not your man.'

'I'll catch you out, Lake. Or the police will. Don't think we won't.'

Great. Not only had Dr Neil taken his crazy up a notch, now he was involving a detective in a case that—unbeknownst to him—I was already up to my neck in.

Hang on. A sudden thought struck. 'Did you leave a message on my site?'

It wasn't Chloe, obviously, or even some kid with too much time on their hands and a sociopathic streak. It was this piece of work trying to get me to confess, or let something slip.

'What?' he said. 'I haven't left you any messages. What are you talking about?'

'*Exactly* what the message-leaver would say!' I cried. 'Checkmate.'

But Dr Neil's expression of bewilderment told me I was barking up the wrong tree. I can read him like a book, and this book was titled, *What the Flying Fuck are You on About*?

'Nothing,' I said. 'Forget about it.'

'What message?'

'Sorry, I'd love to stay and chat, but I dislike you immensely. Bye-bye.'

I levered Dr Neil aside and made my exit.

8

Two hours later, I was standing with Eva in a stone circle, peering at a crude pencil drawing that I'd scrawled of the rocks I saw in the dead woman's memories.

'Well?' asked Eva.

We were high up, and the afternoon wind toyed with my magnificent hair.

'No, I don't think it's any of these. Plus the tallest stone here comes up to my waist. The ones I saw were at least as tall as me.'

'Lanky stones. Got it.'

This was the third local stone circle we'd paid a visit to that afternoon, and we had, so far, struck out at all three. All of the circle stones I saw were much too small. Too narrow. Too weathered. And none of them featured the engravings I'd witnessed on the murder stones.

We made our way back down the hill and clambered inside the Uncanny Wagon, setting off for circle number four. You'll find these sort of things dotted all over Cumbria, the county of England I live in. Evidence of a lively past, they say. Pagans dancing to the setting sun of the Summer Solstice, druids with sickles, blood sacrifices, fun for all the family.

'Is there any truth to the story of, uh, naked women dancing around stone circles?' I asked as nonchalantly as I could.

Eva was settled in her usual position, stretched out across the back seat of my car. 'Wicker Man?'

'Yep.'

'Oh, yes. Tons of that stuff.'

'Blimey.'

'And not just women. I remember you on at least six separate occasions skipping around the circle we were just at, moonlight bouncing off your man-bits.'

'You're kidding me.'

'Nope. Or maybe. One of the two. Reality and fiction don't really get on in my head.'

The next circle we arrived at was another bust. The stones were the size of children, barely poking their heads above the grass.

'This one feels a bit... familiar,' I said. 'Did I...?'

'Yup. In fact, I think you grazed your penis here,' she said with a cackle, slapping a particularly pointy-looking rock.

We piled back into the car and on to stone circle numero cinq.

The whole time we'd been driving around and completely failing to find either of the standing stones I'd witnessed, I had one thing rolling over and over in my mind.

'So, uh, about Chloe...'

'Hm?' replied Eva, eyes closed and arms across her chest on the back seat like the scruffiest vampire you ever did see.

'I said, I've been thinking about Chloe. There's been some... *stuff* in the last day or two.'

'Who's this bint, Chloe?'

'Are you...? Are you being entirely serious right now?'

Eva opened her eyes. 'That's a very deep question, love, but I like to think the answer is "never".'

'Chloe! Chloe Palmer! My sort-of-girlfriend who was about to unleash a load of those octopus-limbed soul suckers!'

'Oh, I got you. I like to file that shit away once we're done with it. Don't need a lot of clutter in my conscious mind, know what I mean?'

I gripped the wheel and drove on, sulking.

'Well?' said Eva. 'Is there a reason for bringing up that very dead, very crazy tit?'

'Just an annoyance, that's all. Someone left me a message on one of my websites claiming to be her.'

'Oh. Yeah?'

'Yeah.'

'Well, guess what?'

'What?'

'This is gonna blow your mind.'

'Tell me!'

'It wasn't her.'

'I see.'

'She's dead,' said Eva. 'You made her go splat-bye-bye.'

'I know.'

Well, I sort of knew. I knew that's what Eva and Myers *said* I did, but I had no actual memory of Chloe's final moments, or of any of the monsters' for that matter. All I recalled was a giant build-up of power being unleashed, and then I woke up in my car.

Maybe they were hiding something from me. It was possible. I mean, it's not as though Eva had been overly forthcoming with information. She had still yet to tell me everything about myself, for example. Instead, I had to rely on a talking fox and a scary redhead who wanted me to become some sort of almighty doomsday monster.

Almighty Doomsday Monster is also the name of the heavy metal band I plan to form one day.

'It's not just the message,' I said, 'I know that's nothing.

Probably. I also, sort of, maybe, possibly not, but perhaps… saw her.'

Eva sat up. 'Come again?'

'I saw her. Just for a second—less than a second, probably—in a bathroom mirror at work.'

'Were you on any sort of hallucinogenic drugs at the time?'

'What? No!'

'Okay. Do you have any hallucinogenic drugs on you right now? A nice baggie of 'shrooms, perhaps?'

'No.'

'Pity. They would really liven up this tragic afternoon.'

Yes, Eva was a very frustrating sort of person.

'I know it's probably just kids messing around on my site, and my mind playing tricks on me. I mean, I killed her,' and boy, oh, boy, did I not I enjoy saying that out loud, 'but there's a lot of strange stuff that seems to happen these days. What if some part of her, you know, clung on? Somehow. In some fashion yet to be determined.'

'It hasn't. You burnt that bitch to ash.'

'But what if…?'

Eva sighed and leaned forward. 'Listen, idiot, she's dead. She's gone. I know that stings, but you killed her. She isn't coming back, and that's a good thing, because she was off her rocker.'

'I remember.'

'I mean, just a complete fruit loop.'

'Right.'

'But—and this "but" is larger than the one the receptionist at your hospital sits on all day—if her soul has managed to avoid judgment and hang around, that would be a very bad thing. So if you see or hear from this person who definitely doesn't exist anymore, you tell me.'

'And then we help in some way?'

'Yes.'

'Okay.'

'We help by shredding that fucker's soul to make sure she never comes back. Not ever. You don't give people like that a second chance. Well, not usually.' Eva's eyes darkened before she shook free whatever bleak thought had gripped her and got back to the ritual of rolling up a cigarette with her carrot-coloured fingers.

And that was that.

And it was all daft, anyway. Chloe was gone. She was gone, and I was seeing things that weren't there. Guilt, sleep deprivation, the product of a creative mind, that's all. But still, as I drove and stole glances at Eva in the rearview mirror, I realised two things. One, I hoped that I wasn't seeing things. I hoped Chloe was still alive, even if she was a ghost and so, I suppose, not technically "alive". And two, if that was true and she came to see me again, there was no way in hell that I was going to tell Eva about it.

I killed Chloe once; I really didn't want to be responsible for it happening a second time. Everyone is redeemable in the end, right?

'How much further to the next circle?' I asked.

'Couple of miles.'

It was at this point that a strange feeling washed over me, as though someone had thrown a bucket of ice water over my head. Which, no, wasn't at all pleasant.

I let out a little cry of pained surprise and stomped on the brake pedal. Eva threw out her own cry at the force of the sudden stop, and her refusal to wear a seatbelt sent her flying off the seat and onto the floor.

'Oi!' she yelled amongst several swear words. 'You just destroyed my ciggie!'

'Sorry, sorry, it's just... I had a feeling.'

'Tingle in your pants? You dirty bastard.'

'Not that sort of feeling.'

'Can't get it up, eh? It happens,' said Eva, before letting

loose a filthy cackle and beginning the process of rolling a fresh smoke.

'My penis is fine thank you very... this isn't about my penis!'

'Well, thank the Lord for small mercies. *Very* small.'

I ignored her. 'I think I just had a magic thing happen.'

'What sort of magic thing?' she asked, popping her cigarette between her lips and lighting it with a flame that appeared from the tip of her finger.

Bloody show-off.

'I don't know. I was just driving along and a sudden, overwhelming urge to stop gripped me. Like something inside me was saying, "*We're here, this is the place, you found it!*"'

'What place?'

'I think this is where the stone circle is.'

Eva looked out of the window to her left. Then to her right. Then turned around to look out of the rear window before flopping back down. 'There are no stones out here, idiot.'

Which was, unfortunately, true. All I saw were fields and hills and a distinct lack of large standing stones, in a circle or otherwise.

'Drive on,' said Eva, 'we've got another six circles to check out yet.'

I turned the engine over but my foot stubbornly refused to press down on the accelerator. No matter how hard I tried to ignore it, the weird feeling continued to insist that we were already where we were supposed to be. I killed the engine.

'We're here. This is the place.'

Eva half-grumbled, half-growled, then shoved open the door. 'Okay, we'll look, but unless these are invisible stones, you're just wasting our time.'

'I'm supposed to be a warlock, right? This is my hidden magic self telling me something, I'm sure of it.'

And I was. Every nerve ending tingled; telling me that the things I'd seen, the killer stones, were close at hand.

We walked an ever-widening circle around the car, but

soon realised that there was nothing to be seen; barely a rock, never mind a person-sized standing stone or ten. Eva called me a variety of colourful names before making her way back to the Uncanny Wagon. I gave the area one last curious glance, then got back behind the wheel and drove us to the next stop.

9

I dropped a decidedly grumpy Eva back at the coven, then headed to my flat as the sun dropped and a chill began to nip at the air.

The circle hunt had been a waste of time. Circle after circle, and not one had a single stone that looked anything like the rocks I'd seen, the rocks I had done my best to render in pencil. Which meant we were in the delightful position of having an extraordinarily bizarre set of killers on the loose, and no leads to go on.

The stones belonged to a circle, Eva was sure of it, but this was a world where creatures with octopus limbs ate souls for supper, so who's to say these mobile stones stayed in one place when they weren't busy killing? Or whether the circle they belonged to wasn't somewhere out of sight and inaccessible, like the middle of a mountain, or the bottom of one of Cumbria's great lakes.

Ooh!

That made sense. Maybe. Perhaps the death stones skulked at the bottom of a lake, out of sight, hidden from view.

As I parked outside my flat, I was so deep in my musings

that I didn't notice the woman sat on my doorstep until I was two feet from my door and preparing to slot my key home.

'Mr Lake?' asked the woman, rising to her feet.

No, I did not yell out in surprise and do three bunny hops backwards, hands to my aghast face like an over-emoting actor in a silent film.

'Sorry, did I startle you?' asked the woman.

'Not at all.'

The woman looked to be around thirty or so, and wore her hair in a blonde bob.

'Sorry.'

I straightened out the lines of my long coat as I gathered myself. 'Don't worry. It takes more than an unexpected guest to scare me.'

'Oh. What was the screaming and jumping about then?'

I made to speak, paused, then brushed it aside. 'Can I help you?'

'I hope so. My name is Annie. Are you Mr Lake? Mr Joseph Lake?'

'Yeah, for the last few years. It's a long story. Well, not that long a story. I woke up next to a lake with no memory and decided to use "Joseph Lake" as my name.'

'I see.'

'You're probably not here for that, though.'

'No.'

'Right.'

'Mr Lake, I emailed you about a job, but you didn't reply.'

'You what now?' I remembered the email I recently deleted. 'Sorry, I don't recall any email. At all. I definitely didn't delete it.'

Smooth.

'No worries. I didn't get a response, and I'm in a bit of a rush, so here I am! Initiative, you see?'

'Yes. Well done. Look, I don't mean to be rude, but I'm not really looking for work right now.'

'Oh.'

'There's a very large, big case that I'm on at the moment.'

'Oh?'

'Yep, several murders. I'm assisting the police, all very hush-hush. And then there are the hospital toilets on the third floor that need a good seeing to tomorrow, so as you can no doubt appreciate, my hands are pretty full. Sorry.'

I slid my key into the door and pushed it open as I gave Annie an apologetic shrug/sorry face combo and placed one foot inside the flat.

'Please, Mr Lake. I don't know who else to turn to.'

I stopped and turned back to her. It figured that a woman who took it upon herself to track me down at my door after one unanswered email wasn't going to be brushed off so easily.

'Okay, what about if you send your information to me in another email, and this time I won't delete it.'

'I thought you said you didn't delete the first one?'

'Yes. Good. And I also won't delete this next one. Put all the stuff into it, and if I get a moment, I'll give it a look. Deal?'

Annie bit her lip and shook her head.

'Really, Annie, I don't want to sound rude, but I am rather tired and would like to go inside. Alone.'

'I'm in danger, Mr Lake.'

Damn.

'Have you gone to the police?'

'No.'

'Then maybe go to the police? They should really be your first port of call, not a man who mops floors six hours a day.'

'I can't! I can't go to the police!'

She was starting to become emotional. She'd been calm and collected up to this point, now the strain of whatever was bothering her was starting to crack her perfect surface.

'Why can't you go to the police?' I asked.

'Because they won't believe me, just like you don't!' she bawled. 'Coming to you was a mistake. You're just some crank cheating people out of their money by pretending to investigate ghosts and what have you.'

'Whoa there, take it easy.'

Something was definitely eating at her. I won't deny feeling a little bit guilty about brushing her aside. And the whole email deletion thing.

'Why won't they believe you, Annie? Tell me what's wrong.'

Annie's eyes filled with tears. Her shoulders trembled as she tried to hold back sobs.

'Annie, you can tell me. Why do you need my help?'

'I need your help, Mr Lake,' she replied, 'because I sold my soul to the Devil.'

Now, that was quite the revelation. Unfortunately, I didn't have much time to sit with it, as it was only three or so seconds later that a large, vicious eagle swooped out of the sky and attacked her.

10

Annie's cries of pain were masked by the Uncanny Wagon's screeching tyres—not to mention the tribal anxiety drums beating out a frantic rhythm in my head—as we hurtled at unsafe speeds toward Carlisle.

'Annie, are you okay?' I asked, like everyone's favourite dead celebrity paedophile.

I glanced at her in the rearview. She was sprawled across the back seat, leaking blood from the wounds she received at the claws of the eagle.

Right. The eagle.

Now, eagle attacks are not exactly a common event around these parts. Or, to be honest, any parts. Maybe if you're a vole, but not a fully-grown human lady.

'Annie?'

'I'm okay. My head hurts.'

She'd cracked her skull pretty viciously having taken a fall during the eagle's second dive-bomb. I'd tried to shoo the thing away, but it turned out that a man timidly saying, "Go away! Shoo! Go away, please!" wasn't all that off-putting to a huge bird of prey with dinner on the brain.

The eagle got four good shots in at Annie, leaving behind

deep lacerations and torn clothing before I managed to bundle her into the back of my car. I had the choice to duck into the house or the car, and in the moment, I chose the motor. Which, in retrospect, had definitely been the wrong choice. Annie was losing blood, so I decided the best thing I could do was get her away and to help, which is why we were currently breaking the speed limit on our way to the hospital.

'Told you,' said Annie, her voice groggy, 'I told you. Wants to… I'm gonna die.'

'No negative nellies in here, Annie. Come on! It's just a few gashes and a bash on the bonce. You'll be right as rain in no time.'

'Kill me. They want me dead. All of them, they want me dead.'

'Who wants you dead? Annie?'

I twisted in my seat and looked back to see that she'd passed out, blood pooling under her head.

'Shit. Balls. Annie? Annie!'

I gave her a shove to try and rouse her. She managed to bat my hand away but didn't come round. I stomped on the accelerator and my poor little car lurched forward, the engine sounding not in the least bit happy about the thrashing I was giving it.

'Sorry old thing, but this is an emergency. Woman in peril.'

As if responding to my plea, the car sped up, the needle passing the hundred-mile-an-hour mark. I must confess to feeling quite proud of the battered thing; I had no idea it could go at such speeds. My admiration was cut short, however, as a shadow fell over me and I looked up to see the eagle—beak wide, giant wings spread—swooping directly at the windscreen.

'Shitting shit!'

I yanked the wheel to the left and the car went into a screaming spin, the eagle's wing brushing the side as it rushed past, letting out a squawk of frustration.

'You crazy, kamikaze death bird!' I yelled. Which is not something you say every day.

I twisted the wheel and reversed back into the road from the grass verge where our spin had deposited us. Annie was on the floor now, still unconscious.

'Don't worry, we're not far from… oh fuckity fuck-fuck!'

The eagle's head crashed through the rear window, screeching and snapping at Annie. If she hadn't tumbled from the seat as we spun, the thing would be up to its eyeballs in her already.

I grabbed the metal steering wheel lock and leaned back, striking the crazed bird's head as it struggled and thrashed, trying to force its way through the window.

'Get out, you rotten, feathery bastard!'

But each hit I landed only seemed to make the thing madder, more determined to get inside. Now, I'm no expert on birds, but I'm pretty sure if one rushed head-first at a car window, its skull would come off second best. Despite that, this thing showed no sign of injury, just a devilish determination to get at its quarry.

The steering wheel lock proving to be less than useful, I tossed it aside, shifted position, and began to strike out at the thing with the sole of my boot.

'Go away! Please! Thank you!'

My boot mashed against the eagle's skull six or seven times before I got a lucky hit in and dislodged the thing. The bird fell from the back of the car, wings going like the clappers.

'Don't worry, Annie,' I told the unconscious woman lying prone on the floor of my car. 'I sorted the bastard out. Everything's going to be okay.'

That is, of course, exactly the sort of thing a stupid person would say right before things got many times worse.

I contorted my body until I flopped back the right way in the driver's seat, but as I reached for the key, it turned suddenly dark outside.

'That can't be good,' I said, leaning to look out of the window and seeing what had cast its huge shadow over us.

The sight that greeted me elicited a slight squeak of terror. Okay, a big one.

'Hold on, Annie!'

I turned the key and stamped on the accelerator. The Uncanny Wagon lurched forward, its tyres not the only thing screaming as they struggled for traction.

There were more eagles after us.

Not one, not two, a *lot* more.

Blackening the sky.

I'm talking Hitchcock turned up to eleven. I didn't have time to make an exact count of the birds as I was in a state of blind terror, but let's say it looked like about a hundred of the bastards. It's possible I'm rounding up.

'Everything's going to be okay, Annie, just a few ticked off birdies, that's all.'

A dent appeared in the panel of the driver's door as the first of the feral beasts dive-bombed us.

'Leave my car alone! It's an antique!'

The eagles, strangely, paid no heed to my demand. Rude.

I gripped the wheel so tightly that my fingers ached as I tried to keep control of the thing; tried to will it forward as the birds attacked again and again, buffeting the outside of the Uncanny Wagon like one of those plagues from the bible, only worse. I don't know about you, but I'd take a swarm of locusts over a swarm of razor-beaked, knife-taloned birds any day.

A crash, and a bird's beak was through the driver's side window and in biting distance of my face. I grabbed the steering wheel lock again and swatted at the animal as I tried to keep the car moving. There was no time to stop to try and dislodge the maniac, we'd have been swamped by the rest in seconds.

'Ours, ours, ours!' said the eagle.

That's right, *said* the eagle.

Despite everything happening in that moment, it still came as something of a shock to hear the animal talk.

'What did you say?'

'Ours!'

Not quite the extended vocabulary of my fox friend, but it was getting its point across clearly enough.

'You can't claim ownership of a lady these days,' I told it. 'This isn't the Fifties.'

I struck out again; the talkative eagle doing its best to dodge my blows and wriggle its way further into the car.

Another crash, an eagle head screeching, this time from the left passenger window.

'Ours! Ours! Ours!' it yelled in a sharp, grating rasp.

Things were not going well, and we were still several miles from Carlisle, let alone the hospital.

A thud from behind. One of the eagles had found the hole made by the first attacker and was attempting to widen the gap. It's times like these that knowing how to access a little bit of magic would have really come in handy. I grabbed my phone and called Eva, trying to ignore the eagle's beak to my right, which was inching ever closer to my eyeball.

'I'm not here,' came Eva's sleepy voice.

'Eva!'

The call ended.

Even dockers don't swear the way I did then.

'Ours! Ours!'

'Invest in a thesaurus!' I cried.

I hit Eva's number again and she picked up on the fifth ring.

'I told you, I'm not here, idiot.'

'Birds! Eagles! Lots of birds eagles beaks claws very very danger and scared and need help and magic!'

There was a pause.

'Who is this?'

'Eva!'

'Rubbish, you sound nothing like me.'

I screamed some more anguished gibberish at her.

'You finished?' she asked.

A beak scratched my cheek, drawing blood. Further obscenities followed.

'Ours! Ours!'

'Oi, is that a talking eagle?' asked Eva.

'Yes!'

'Thought so. Horrible voices, that lot. Like nails on a blackboard.'

I was driving at quite an obtuse angle now, one hand on the wheel, the other holding my phone to my ear as I leaned as far from the snapping beak of the eagle as possible, whilst still being able to see out of the windscreen. How I was still managing to keep us on the road and more or less in the right lane was a mystery.

'Eva, loads and loads of eagles from I don't know where are attacking me. Help me!'

'How? I'm here on my couch, enjoying a rather cheap lager, and you're there, trying not to get pecked to buggery.'

'Tell me how to do some magic to stop them! I know I've done it before, so tell me how!'

Another kamikaze eagle bombed into the side of the car. The tyres met the grass verge before I yanked the wheel to the right and the Uncanny Wagon swerved back into the road, a large lorry honking its horn as I just about avoided ploughing into its front end.

'Eva!'

'Okay, well, the thing is, magic is all around you, see? It's just a case of being able to will it into your horrible, skinny, good-for-nothing body.'

'Okay, okay, it's all around me.'

'Ooh!'

'What? What is it?'

'I don't think I've seen this episode of Columbo before. That's sort of magic in itself, isn't it, love?'

'Eva!'

The eagle stuck in the drivers-side window had now wiggled close enough for its beak to nip at the sleeve of my beautiful long coat. Now it was just pissing me off.

'Nope. False alarm. Seen it.'

'Magic! Magic!'

'Hm? Oh, right, well, it's all around you, all the time. Everything emits a natural background trace of it, you've just gotta allow yourself to see it.'

'Right, what does it look like?'

'Sort of, colourful waves, washing around the place.'

'Okay, okay...'

I had a look around. 'No waves.'

'Look harder.'

'That's your advice? "Look harder"? I can't see any colourful magical wave thingies!'

'Listen to me. You can. You can see them better than almost anybody.'

Something about Eva's voice had changed. It was almost... soothing.

'The magic is yours, warlock,' she said. 'You are born of it. It is part of you.'

I felt calm. Well, as calm as a man barely in control of a speeding vehicle that's under attack from a swarm of murderous, talking eagles can feel.

'It wants you to see it. It wants to make itself part of you. For you to soak it in and use it. To realise its potential. Can you see it now?'

And then a strange thing happened.

I *could* see it.

It's like someone flicked a switch, or placed those magic shades from *They Live* in front of my eyes, and now a world that had been hiding from me was revealed.

Magic was everywhere.

Great, multi-coloured stripes of noisy, beautiful energy

swishing this way and that, sparkling with possibility. And it called to me. Almost sang.

'I… I see it.'

'Just let it in.'

'Hello, lovely magic,' I said, and the waves responded, changing course, flowing toward me. I felt it enter the fabric of me, bathing me in a warming static shower.

'Make demands of it,' said Eva. 'It's your tool. Make it your weapon.'

The eagle's beak tore through the material of my coat and scraped my skin. But that was okay, because it was about to be very, very dead.

'The magic is mine,' I said. 'I control it. It is my instrument to play.'

It felt right. Natural. For a moment I wasn't Joseph Lake anymore. I was a warlock. A witch. And I was about done with all these bloody eagles.

'Do it,' whispered Eva. 'Tell the magic what you want of it.'

I sat up and grabbed the eagle by the neck, my hand glowing with white-hot fire. It struggled and screamed in my grip.

'Ours! Ours!'

'No,' I replied. 'Mine.'

And with that, the fire in my hand consumed the bird, turning it to ash. Which, yeah, was pretty cool.

'All of you,' I said, my whole body glowing now, tendrils of pure white energy weaving out of me like flames from the sun, 'you can piss right off.'

And piss off they did.

11

The ancient coffee machine in the corner of the hospital reception rattled as it spat black tar into my Styrofoam cup.

The eagles were dead, burnt to a crisp by my own hands. How I pulled that little trick off, I had no idea. I'd seen magic everywhere in that moment, washing around me in colourful, evanescent waves, but peering around the room now, I saw nothing. Nothing of the magic that I'd used. That I'd willed into myself and turned into white-hot fire.

As terrifying as the whole eagle episode had been, I'd be lying if I said I didn't feel a touch thrilled at the way the situation had resolved itself. At the momentary access I'd been given to the world the old me had lived in. The world that I'd used as a weapon.

For a few minutes there, I'd been an honest-to-goodness warlock. A witch. A powerful bastard capable of unleashing fire from my—

'Shit!' I swore and blew on my fingers as the spilt coffee scorched my skin.

'A bird?' said Big Marge from behind her desk, eyebrow cocked.

'Yup. A big one. Insane. Just dive-bombed down at poor Annie.'

'You're telling me an eagle did that to her?'

'That is true, yes.'

'Don't see a whole lot of eagle action around here.'

'Yeah. Weird, eh?'

'Mm-hm. You know, this is not the first lady in distress you've brought into this hospital in the last few weeks. Add that to the disappearance of poor Chloe, and people are going to talk.'

'If you mean Doctor Neil there, then I think you are unfairly stretching the definition of "people".'

'Funny.'

'Most people laugh when they find something funny.'

'I will when it happens,' said Marge.

A fresh burn to join my recent coffee mishap.

'All I'm saying, Joe, is watch yourself. You know those police have your number. Don't give them any more reason to be suspicious of you.'

'Aw, I'm touched. Touched that you care about me, Big Marge.'

'Well, I'd hate to have to go to the effort of finding a new mop boy. Not easy to find someone willing to clean up piss, shit, and vomit on the money this place pays.'

With that delightful conversation at an end, I went to find Annie, who was laying in a ward now with around ten other people. I approached her bed, pulled the curtain closed around us, and sat beside her.

'Sure you don't want me to get you a coffee? Tea?'

'I'm okay, they gave me water,' she replied, nodding toward the plastic jug perched on the bedside table.

'So, what's the verdict?' I asked.

'Just a few cuts and bruises mostly; nothing serious. Gave me a few stitches.'

'Oh good. Great.'

'They're making me stay in overnight, though, for observation. They said I must have bashed my head pretty hard, so they don't want me going home yet.'

'Better safe than sorry.'

Annie nodded, then winced and put a hand to the bandage taped around her head.

'So, assault by a cloud of angry talking eagles,' I said. 'That's a bit... weird.'

'Just a bit. How did you get rid of them in the end?'

'My car's pretty nippy. I know it's not much to look at, but that baby can move.'

Annie's face scrunched up for a moment before she shrugged and said, 'Okay. Lucky you were there, really, otherwise I'd be dead and they'd have me.'

Ah, right, the whole selling her soul thing.

'So you're saying that those eagles were, what... the Devil?'

'Yes. Well, maybe not the Devil exactly. Demons. I've spoken to a lot of different things over the years.'

'Right. Let's say I believe all of this "selling your soul" stuff...'

'You should, it's true.'

'Eagle attack aside, I've seen a lot of strange things recently, so I'm going to take you at your word until I have a good reason not to. Now, why don't you fill me in on the details.'

Annie frowned and nodded, reaching over to the jug, pouring herself a cupful, and taking a sip.

'It all started a few days after my seventh birthday. We lived in a little farmhouse, no neighbours house in sight. I liked that. Liked to run wild. Out the back of the house was an old stone well. It didn't have a bucket or anything, and the opening was covered by wooden boards. My dad was always telling me to stay away from the thing, that it wasn't safe, but I was seven. So I would try to lift up the boards to see down into the well, and sometimes I'd haul myself up on them and stomp my feet like I was tap dancing. One day, they were both out, and I climbed up on the boards and I stamped and stomped and made a real racket. You can guess how that went. The wood gave way and down I went, into the bottom of the well.'

'Christ,' I said, on the edge of my seat, coffee forgotten, imagining Annie being swallowed by that black mouth. This girl knew how to tell a story. 'What happened then?' I asked.

'I landed. It hurt like nothing else. I got the wind knocked out of me so bad, I thought I'd never be able to breathe again. But it passed. I got control of my lungs, got my breath back, and up I stood. Lucky for me, the bottom of the well was pretty soggy, otherwise I'd have been dead for sure.'

'What happened next?' I asked, riveted.

'What do you think? I yelled and screamed, and screamed some more. No one came, though. My parents weren't going to be back for hours, so I had a go at climbing up. I never got more than a few feet before slipping back down again. I was stuck. Stuck down a dark, stinking well, with no way to get out, scared out of my mind. I bawled my eyes out; great, heaving sobs as I sat there hugging my knees. That's when I made a mistake. A mistake much worse than tap dancing on those rotten boards.'

'What? What did you do?'

'I asked for help. Again and again. I said I'd give anything if I could just get out of there without my parents finding out what I'd done. I suppose I was trying to bargain with God, like you do when you're in a bad spot—whether you believe in a god or not—but it wasn't God who answered.'

'You got the Devil on the line.'

Annie nodded.

'Or something close to it. I didn't hear it at first, I was so taken up with my crying and begging, but then I caught it. A whisper. It was coming from a crack in the wall of the well. I put my ear to it, and as I did, the voice became clearer.'

'What did it say?'

Annie took another sip of her water, then looked me dead in the eyes for the first time since she started her story.

'It said, "What wouldst thou like?" Just that. Just those words, over and over.'

'Well, that sounds pretty wet-your-knickers terrifying.'

'It was. Although I didn't piss myself.'

'You go, girl.'

'I thought it must be an angel, so I answered. I said more than anything I wanted out of the well and for my mum and dad never to find out. The voice said it could help me, but it would need something in return. I said I'd give it anything I had: my best dolly, all my music tapes, even my piggy bank, which was almost full. The voice said it wanted my soul. I said, fine.'

'Just like that?'

'I was a scared seven-year-old, I wasn't thinking it through.'

'Right, yes. Sorry.'

'The voice asked me to repeat my consent, so I did. Then I blinked and I wasn't in the well anymore. I was standing beside it, and the boards across the opening were intact like nothing had ever happened.'

I sat back and sipped at my coffee. 'Well, blimey. That's quite a story.'

'I haven't finished yet.'

'What more is there? I get it, you were stuck and you sold your soul.'

Annie shifted uncomfortably in her bed, her face flushing.

'What?' I asked. 'What is it?'

'It might not have been the only time I... sold my soul.'

'Pardon me now?'

'In my defence, I was seven and thought I'd discovered a wish-granting angel or a genie or something. What would you have done?'

'You went back down the well, didn't you?'

'I did, yes. More than once.'

'How many times more than once?'

'I lost count. Any time there was something I needed—

money, an answer to a question, some bitch at school who was giving me a hard time and needed dealing with—I would go to the well, push the board aside, and talk to my wish-giver.'

I could understand that. If all you had to do to get what you wanted in life was sign over a soul you'd already given away, why not?

'One thing I don't get,' I said, 'why did this thing keep granting you wishes? I mean, it already had what it wanted...'

'Yeah. It turns out I sold my soul to a lot of demons. I mean, *a lot*. At first, I didn't really notice, but I began to realise that each time I spoke to my wish-giver, I was hearing a slightly different whisper. Whatever connection that well was giving me to these things, it wasn't directed at just one demon. Every time I connected, it was as though I dialled a different number out of the book at random.'

'So you promised your soul to a different demon over and over again.'

Annie nodded.

'That's a good way to piss off a whole bunch of monsters. I mean, they can't all have your one little-bitty soul.'

'Yep. Hence the eagle attack and my seeking out your help. I stopped going down into that well years ago once I realised what I'd done, what I was talking to down there.'

'I don't get it. Why are they only coming after you now?'

'I think it's because I almost died eight months ago. That's my only guess. I was in a crash and bashed my head. The doctors said I was technically dead for a few minutes.'

I figured out the rest. 'A bunch of demons you promised your soul to were lining up to claim what you promised them, only to find the waiting room a touch on the crowded side.'

Annie nodded. 'That's what I'm assuming.'

'They're not waiting for you to die to claim your soul. They're rushing to be the one who kills you so they can have you for themselves.'

'Yep.'

'Wow. They're going about it in a very odd way. Why not just, I don't know, wait until you're asleep and draw a big demon claw across your throat?'

'I think, technically, I'm supposed to die normally before they can claim what they're owed. But because so many are owed it, and they don't want a big fight when I finally do die, they're each trying to off me in a subtle way. A not-obviously-by-their-hand way. They're cheating, basically.'

'Yes, well, a vast army of talking eagles attacking a moving vehicle in the north of England. What could be more subtle? If this is really all true, and you're not just some loony who pissed off a bunch of eagles, then you are in one ginormous amount of trouble.'

'Thanks, I know,' replied Annie, indicating her current circumstances. 'So, will you help me or not?'

I finished the last of my terrible vending machine coffee.

'I'll help,' I replied.

Of course, I did. Shame I had absolutely no idea how.

12

The Uncanny Wagon wasn't looking its best.

To be fair, even on a good day it looked like I'd stolen the thing from a scrap yard, but tonight, under the glow of the moon in the hospital car park, it looked an absolute state. Three of its windows had holes in them, feathers were plastered to the bonnet with eagle blood, and the bodywork was peppered with dents from all of the kamikaze impacts.

'My poor baby,' I said, gently patting the roof. 'You'll be okay, don't worry. I'll nurse you back to health.'

The thing rattled and complained the whole drive home. As I pulled up outside my flat, I thanked the Lord that I hadn't passed any police cars along the way. I'm sure they'd have had a thing or two to say about the roadworthiness of my vehicle.

At this point, I really should have collapsed into bed. I was exhausted, my body heavy, brain frazzled. But instead of grabbing some shut-eye, I flipped open my laptop. There was a new message waiting for me on my 'Who Am I?' website.

A new message from Chloe.

'Help me, Joe. Help me.'

I sat up, suddenly very awake.

'Where are you?' I typed, and hit reply.

She wouldn't answer, I knew that. She wasn't there, waiting with bated breath for my response. She wasn't anywhere. This was just some idiot kid mucking me about. Had to be.

My heart thumped as my laptop pinged and a reply landed.

'I think I'm where you left me. I'm scared. I'm waiting for you. Please help.'

I put the laptop down and paced the room for a few minutes. This was absurd. It couldn't really be her, could it? Eva said as much. Chloe was dead.

But what if it was her? Somehow. People were selling their souls, and foxes could talk, so why couldn't Chloe have survived?

'I'm on my way.'

I hit send, grabbed my coat, and headed out the door.

I *think I'm where you left me.*

That's what Chloe had said. So there I was. The road where a giant octopus arm had erupted, grabbed Eva, and dragged her down to where the soul vampires and Chloe had made their home.

There was no evidence of that now. No hole to prove that what had happened had actually happened. Eva said she'd cleaned things up afterwards. The last thing you want in this line of work, she said, was for some "normal" to stumble across a loose end that led them into a heap of trouble. Only, Eva had said "fuck-load of trouble", not "heap".

The battered driver-side door of my car closed on the third attempt. I looked around nervously and pulled my coat closed for comfort. This was probably a very daft idea. How did I know that I wasn't walking into a trap? I had no idea who'd want to spring a trap on me, or why, but that didn't mean the possibility wasn't there.

I should have brought Eva with me.

Then again, if I had, and it turned out that Chloe really was waiting for me, I had the distinct impression that Eva would have applied a *throw fireballs first, ask questions later* policy to the situation.

Plus, Chloe wasn't going to be there, so Eva would only have gotten pissed off and hit me with a stick again. And I am no fan of being hit with sticks.

'Chloe? Chloe, it's me. It's Joe, I'm here.' I felt silly even saying the words, but sometimes hope makes us do silly things.

The moon was high and the stars were out. That's something I love about living up here, away from the cities, in the far north of England. The Lake District is free of the blight of light pollution that smothers the majesty of the night sky. Out here, the stars come out in force every night.

'Chloe? Where are you?'

I reached the spot where—more or less—the octopus arm had appeared from. I crouched and ran my fingers across the dirt.

'Chloe?'

The only response I got was the hoot of a distant owl. No one spoke, no one replied, and no one appeared. Like an idiot, I waited for another half an hour, then got back in the Uncanny Wagon and drove home, trying to decide if I was heartbroken or furious.

By the time I got back, I'd settled on furious.

Some bastard was playing a malicious trick on me, that's all there was to it. Had to be. That, coupled with sleep deprivation, was giving me hope where there was none.

I grabbed my laptop and fired it up, ready to reply—none too pleasantly— to the little shit leaving messages on my site. It was just then that a heavy *thud-thud* landed on my front door.

I closed the laptop and put it aside, looking to the door in confusion. I checked my phone; it was almost three in the morning. Who could possibly be making a house-call at this ungodly hour?

Thud-Thud-Thud.

Whoever they were, they were heavy-handed.

'Who is it? It's late, you know!'

Thud-Thud-Thud.

Eva, perhaps? That must be it. Probably drunk out of her mind and this was the closest place to crash.

'Eva? Is that you out there?'

Thud-Thud-Thud.

'Eva, if that is you, then please call me an idiot and I'll let you in.'

Thud-Thud-Thud.

I'd never known her fail to call me an idiot before. Or, for that matter, to wait for me to let her in. My home, my car; Eva seemed to have a poor grasp of ownership laws or personal space.

Thud-Thud-Thud.

At that point, I wasn't sure if it was the door or my own heart beating in my ears.

I moved quietly over to the door and placed my eye against the peephole.

'Oh,' I said when I saw what it was that had dropped around for a visit. 'Oh shit.'

This was somewhat of an understatement.

Stood at my door was a stone. A stone taller than me with ancient words and pictures etched into its surface.

And then it moved.

I staggered back with a startled yelp as I saw it—quite impossibly—glide back a few feet and then hurtle forward. Apparently, the stone was done knocking politely and was now employing a more forthright approach.

Crash.

The door flew open as the lock shattered.

'I'm... not in...?' I said.

The fact that I was both standing before the stone and talking to it, may have clued it into the notion that I wasn't being entirely honest.

Turning slightly to gain access to my home, the stone bolted forward, its top scraping the uppermost part of the door frame and sending splinters flying. I half-walked, half-fell backwards until my spine was up against the wall.

'Stop! Stop right there or...' I rather feebly raised both fists and shook them.

The stone was terrified by my fearsome display.

Probably.

Shut up.

Now, the way I saw it, there were two paths out of this situation. The window to my right—which I would need to hop over the couch to get to—or the front door, currently behind the giant moving stone. There was a door leading to a bathroom, but the bathroom had no window, and the flat lacked a back door. It was basically two small rooms with one entry and exit point.

Oh, I suppose there was a third option, but that one was death. I thought I'd leave that option till last.

The stone edged forward.

'Wait! Wait a second, please. You've got the wrong person! You like magic people, but that's not me. My name is... Jimmy. Jimmy Jimson? Jimmy Jimson.'

Hey, I never claimed to work well under pressure.

'I'm just staying here for a bit. Joseph is out doing stuff. Drinking. Or dancing. Something. And I'm here, being non-magical and very ordinary and my name is Jimmy Jimson.'

Purple energy rippled across the surface of the stone and arced out towards me. I leapt to the side, the energy just missing me as it struck the wall and left a giant scorch mark. I landed heavily, scrambling to right myself again. I turned, ready to make a run for the window, only for the stone to lunge forward.

'No!'

I raised my hands defensively and they pressed against the killer stone as it came to a halt before me. And then a strange thing happened. I felt as though I heard a voice. The voice of the stone. And it said one thing:

Elga and her Kin.

The energy the stone was emitting coiled around me, grasping me tight. My mouth opened wide in a soundless scream as I felt myself being drained. Fed on. It was killing me. Taking my magic and anything else I had. I was going to die. Death by hungry stone.

It's not exactly how I pictured ending my days, but it would make for a hell of an obit.

I tried to picture the world as Eva had revealed it to me. Tried to see the magic that was all around me. If I could see it, maybe I could access it again. Maybe I could use it to free myself and escape. But I couldn't see anything, and the room was turning to static.

Actually, that's not quite true. I did see one thing, or thought I did: a small furry shape in the corner of the room, an axe gripped in its paws. Its mouth moved and it said things, but I couldn't hear the words. Didn't need to. I already knew what they were.

'All hail the saviour!'

I am a colossus. I am draped in fire and hundreds die beneath my feet.

I am no warlock. Nothing so small. So weak. So wretched that I can be killed by an enchanted standing stone.

I am the killer. I am who others shrink from. Die for.

Magic Eater.

Magic Eater.

Magic Eater.

I could feel the Red Woman's ice-cold touch upon my face.

Before I even realised I was doing so, I was standing up. The stone tried to fight back, I could feel it. Feel it intensifying its attack, trying to drain me of my strength. My magic.

'You cannot hurt me.'

'Magic Eater,' said the fox, bowing down on one knee as he faded from view.

I saw the world as it was once again. Saw the magic that we swam in every day. I fed upon it and felt myself grow. Felt the flames lick across my skin.

'No! No!' I cried.

I pushed out and the stone flew away from me, its grip broken.

'Stop this!'

The flames on my skin died as I ran for the door, for the car, over the hills and far away.

13

Dawn was breaking by the time I returned to my flat with Eva and Myers in tow.

'Any sign of the stone?' I asked nervously, staying back with Myers as Eva poked her head into my flat, the door of which hung off its hinges.

'Nope. Doesn't look like anyone stole anything, either. People are far too nice around here.'

'Yes,' replied Myers, 'I too wish we lived in a place rife with rampant burglary.'

The Detective delivers sarcasm like a boss.

'Come in then,' Eva shouted from inside.

We found ample evidence of a struggle. Scorch marks on the wall, gouges in the floorboards, plaster cracked from where the front door had burst open and the handle had struck home. Could have been worse, though. I could be a dried-out corpse on the floor.

'So,' said Myers, 'definitely killer standing stones then?'

'Definitely,' I replied.

'Well, great. That's great.'

'At least there won't be any long, boring speeches when we

track the fuckers down,' said Eva, helping herself to a beer from my fridge, 'always hate those things. Give me a mute killer stone any day of the year.' She flicked the top off and took a swig before belching with such ferocity that a piece of broken plaster from above the door dislodged and crashed to the floor.

'So, any clue where the thing is?' asked Myers.

I shrugged. 'Although, it's funny you said that, Eva, about them being mute, because I don't think they are.'

'Aw, and just as I was starting to like them.'

'When I touched it, touched the stone, I heard it say something.'

'What?' asked Myers.

'It said, "Elga and her Kin". Just that.'

'Elga and her Kin?' Myers repeated.

'Yeah. Does that mean anything to you, Eva?'

'Yup. That definitely means something. Good work.'

I looked at her, then to Myers, then back again. 'You don't know what it means, do you?'

'Not exactly. Not entirely. Sounds familiar, though. Familiar to a familiar,' she laughed and took another swig. 'Look, I can't be expected to know every little detail of every little thing. Plus there was the whole, you know, incident that fucked up my head a bit. Just like it did yours.'

'What incident?' asked Myers.

'Oh, forgot you were there,' said Eva. 'Forget I said anything.'

Okay, that was interesting. Apparently, the thing I did didn't just mess me up; Eva had caught some of the flack, too.

'Elga and her Kin, eh?' she said. 'I'll have a look in the library, back at the coven. Probably something in one of those big bastard books. Bound to be. Sounds like just the sort of boring, ancient thing that'd be in one of them.'

Eva grabbed another two bottles of beer, saluted, then headed for the door.

'Wait. Wait a second,' I cried.

'What, love? D'you want a bedtime story, too? Tucking in before I go? Cup of warm cocoa?'

'What if that thing comes back?' I asked. 'Am I safe?'

'No one is ever safe, idiot.'

'Well, that's comforting,' said Myers.

'Don't piss your pants, I wasn't just standing around drinking beer the last few minutes. I also laid down a few protection spells on the place. Multi-tasking like a mother-fucker. Probably should have done it a lot earlier, come to think of it.'

'Oh, you think so?' I said, gesturing to the sorry condition of my flat.

'Nobody's perfect, idiot. You should know that. You did murder the other coven witches.'

And with that, she left.

'What was that about murder?' asked Myers.

'She means, uh, metaphorically speaking.'

There was a rather uncomfortable second or two after that, I can tell you.

I managed to squeeze in almost ninety minutes of solid sleep before my alarm screamed in my ear and I had to drag my body out of bed.

I told Annie I'd pick her up the morning she was discharged. Of course, when I made that promise, I hadn't realised I'd be kept up all night by a home-invading henge.

I drank some disgustingly strong coffee, grabbed a slice of white bread to eat on the way, then left, locking the door Myers had helped me fix. I say "helped", but my role was largely supervisory. By which I mean I had no idea what to do so stood by and watched Myers do everything.

Eighty minutes later, I was helping Annie into the Uncanny Wagon.

'Oh my god, the state of your car,' she said.

'It has seen better days, true.'

'It stinks of bird poo.'

She was not wrong. I got in and we drove out of Carlisle towards her old family home.

'How are you feeling now?' I asked. 'How's the head?'

'Okay. Throbs a bit, but they gave me some killer pain meds.'

I whistled appreciatively. 'Must be nice.'

Annie smiled. It was actually quite a nice smile. If I hadn't been grieving for Chloe, I might even have fallen madly in love with that smile. Or at least, madly in unrequited lust.

'The farmhouse, who lives there now?' I asked.

'Oh, nobody. My parents are dead, so it was left to me.'

'Right. Sorry. Dead parents. Rough.'

'Yeah. Partially my fault. I went down the well and wished they were dead.'

I looked at her at least three or four times in silence before I was able to scramble my thoughts together and form a sentence.

'I'm... what... sorry...?'

Well, roughly a sentence.

'Joke.'

'Oh,' I said. 'Edgy material. I get it.'

'It happened a year ago. Car crash. I actually thought about going down the well to try and bargain for their lives. I hadn't been down to ask for anything in years and years. But I didn't. Was that selfish of me?'

'I wouldn't say selfish. You knew what you were getting into then. That you were playing with fire.'

Annie teased at the hem of her coat. 'Damage was done. I should have gone down anyway. But I was afraid.'

'So the old house is just sitting empty?'

'Yeah, I kept it that way. I mean, what if I were to sell it, have someone else move in, and they discovered the well's secret, too? No. I'll keep it empty.'

Twenty minutes later, the car tyres crunched over gravel as we pulled up in front of a farmhouse. It was perfectly charming, except for the boards nailed over its windows, which gave it a slightly sinister edge.

'Where is it?' I asked.

'It's around back. Come on.'

I followed. I'll admit to feeling a little worried. What if there really were demons at the bottom of that well? I wasn't equipped to deal with demons. But then, I wasn't equipped to deal with killer standing stones, either, and I'd survived those. I thought back to what had happened just a few hours earlier. To what I'd tapped into.

Magic Eater.

For a few seconds, I'd felt a whisper of that power.

I hadn't told Eva the truth about how I escaped. I told her that I got lucky and managed to slip the thing before it did me any serious mischief.

What really happened had been... intoxicating. Being so close to the power the Dark Lakes was offering me. To feel that strength. That invulnerability. That certainty that I could swat aside anything that stood against me. That I didn't have to feel worry or fear ever again. If I had that power—if I could access it whenever I wanted—I'd be capable of anything. A situation like this wouldn't be terrifying, Demons in a well? A walk in the park.

'Here it is,' said Annie, snapping me out of my trance and startling me. My train of thought had pulled me into a new way of thinking. Of *wanting*. I shivered and tried to push the thoughts aside.

'This is the well,' she said.

A circular brick wall stood a little above my waist, fashioned out of large blocks of grey stone. A simple, moss-covered board sat over its opening.

'It looks like something the girl from *The Ring* crawled out of,' I said.

We pushed the board aside and peered down into the darkness.

'Hello,' I said into the void, my voice echoing down. 'Are there any demons down there?'

None answered, surprisingly.

'What do you want to do?' asked Annie.

'I'll be honest, I didn't think this through past, "Say hello to well".'

I took out my phone and turned on its light, leaning over the wall and trying to see if the glow reached to the bottom of the hole. It should go without saying that I, of course, dropped my phone into the well.

'Balls.'

It looked as though I was going down to the bottom no matter what. Annie showed me the ladder she'd taken to using to get in and out of there over the years. I dragged it over, then fed it down into the well until its feet touched the bottom.

'Is there anything I should be, you know, worried about?' I asked.

'I don't think so. They just talk to you.'

'Right. Just demons having a bit of a chin-wag. What could be terrifying about that?'

Feeling like I might throw up at any moment, I clambered onto the stone lip then began my descent down, down, down into the well.

'It's okay, Joe, nothing to worry about,' I told myself, as the temperature dropped with each step.

This was something new at least. Climbing down into an old well to chat to some Hell people. They do say variety is the spice of life.

I stepped off the ladder onto the soft, damp ground and found my phone there waiting for me. I picked it up carefully as though cradling a baby bird, and brushed off the muck. It had survived the fall. I sighed with relief. Over a bloody phone. What have we become, eh?

Using the torch, I studied my surroundings. It was as if I'd arrived on an alien world, colder than the one I knew, and tinged with dread. It set my skin crawling. Something wasn't at all right down there. In fact, something was entirely wrong.

I tried to imagine what it must have been like for seven-year-old Annie to have been in this place; all alone, frightened, no way out. I'd only been in the well for a few moments and could already see myself agreeing to do just about anything to avoid being trapped there.

'Well?' came Annie's voice from way up high. 'Anything?'

'Not yet.'

I traced my hands across the damp brickwork surrounding me. Something was down here. Annie was telling the truth. The knots in my stomach told me so.

'Hello?' I said. 'Are there any demons down here? Sorry for the unannounced drop-in; I hate an unannounced drop-in, myself. If you want to come round, phone first, it's only polite.'

My nose twitched. There was a strange smell, increasing in intensity. A sort of sulphurous odour. I knew what that meant.

'Please,' I said, 'I need help. I'll give anything for help.'

Silence. Maybe for it to work there had to be something you genuinely desired. Something you really wanted. But what did I want? What could I possibly be after that I was willing to go this far for? Oh. Well, of course.

Her.

'My friend is lost,' I said. 'Her name's Chloe. Can you find her?'

I pictured Chloe in my mind; beautiful, funny, turned-out-to-be-a-maniac, Chloe. I thought about the good times. Thought about how it felt when we first kissed. Thought about how much I'd like to kiss her again.

'You miss her.' The voice was an arid whisper.

'Hello? Who is that?'

I turned in circles but couldn't see any sign of where the voice was coming from.

'What dost thou desire, Joseph Lake? What dost thou crave?'

'Forgive me for being a bit, familiar, but who am I speaking with? Feel free to not be scary.'

'You lost someone.'

'Yes.'

'Would thou desire her return?'

'Yes.'

'A small price is all we ask.'

I found myself dithering, tempted. Could I really ask and Chloe would be back? As simple as that?

'Annie. You know her?'

'We know her.'

'I would like to, well, request, or demand—no, demand's a bit strong—let's stick with request... I'd like to *request* that you all stop trying to kill her. Please. Thank you.' I threw in a little bow for good measure.

'Her soul is promised. Promised over and over. She is ours.'

'Well, what if I told you I'm a warlock—a warlock of the Cumbrian Coven—and she's under my protection?'

'We would say she is in even greater danger.' There was a noise then that might have been laughter. I rocked back on my heels in fear.

'We will take what is ours. Take it. Eat it. Make it scream. It shall be delicious, the agonies. The music of our world.'

A sharp cry from above.

'Annie? Annie, what's wrong?'

More screams.

'What are you doing to her?'

'Taking what is owed, Magic Eater.'

I grasped the ladder and left the horrible laughter behind as I did my best to run upwards without slipping.

'Annie!'

I emerged from the mouth of the well, squinting, the world suddenly turned bright and warm. My clothes clung to my skin, either with sweat, or the clamminess of the well, I didn't know.

'Annie!'

I couldn't see her, but a distant scream told me where she was. I hopped off the stone well and ran around the house to where I'd parked up.

Annie was in the car. A large wolf was throwing itself wildly against the door, trying to get at her. Yes, a wolf. Like eagles, you don't exactly see a lot of wolves around here, generally speaking.

'Joe, get back!' yelled Annie, helpfully drawing the wolf's attention to my presence.

It turned, its face a twisted, drool-spitting snarl.

'Now, now,' I said slowly backing away. 'Nice doggy. Nice doggy. No need to get upset or tear my throat out.'

But this doggy wouldn't be placated so easily. It sprinted for me, eyes burning like hot coals. I turned to run and managed to trip over my own clumsy feet, sending myself crashing to the dirt. I rolled onto my back just in time to see the beast flying through the air towards me, mouth wide, fangs flashing white.

'Shit!'

Somehow, I caught the thing by the neck as it landed on me, my arms rigid, trying to keep its snapping teeth from making friends with my face.

'Ours!' it growled. 'Ours! Ours! Ours!'

I screamed and caught the wolf's rancid breath in my throat. My arms were weakening. I couldn't hold on. It was no good; as the wolf's paws scrabbled at the dirt for purchase, I knew my grip was going to give way at any second, and then it would make mincemeat of my jugular.

The wolf made a high-pitched noise, its face switching from

a snarl to surprise, and then it sagged unconscious on top of me.

'Holy. Mother. Of shit.'

I wheezed as I rolled the thing off, and found a wide-eyed Annie staring down at me, the lock to the Uncanny Wagon's steering wheel gripped knuckle-white in her hands.

14

It turned out that Annie had been telling the truth all along. Without a doubt. One-hundred percent. She'd sold her soul, multiple times, and now a bunch of pissed off demons were vying to claim her spirit as their own.

I took her to my flat, which I thought would be a safe place for her to hide out now that Eva had covered it in protection spells. With Annie dropped off, I gave my wolf slobber-coated face a good scrubbing, then headed for the coven. I needed to bring Eva in on this, as I obviously had no idea how I was going to get Annie out of her fatal predicament.

Not that I told her that, of course. I assured her that all would be well. Demons? No big deal. Just another Wednesday in my line of work.

I parked up and made my way down the blind alley that hid the coven from prying eyes.

'What?' barked Eva, refusing to look up from the bong she was huffing god knows what from.

'Why does that thing look like you fashioned it from a human skull?' I asked.

'Because I'm fucking metal, that's why. Now get on with

whatever it was you came here for so I can get back to you not being here.'

'It's about Annie. She came to me for help. She's got a bunch of demons trying to kill her to get at her soul.'

Eva inhaled then offered the bong my way. 'Get in on this, it'll put hair on your frigging eyeballs.'

'As nice as that sounds, I think I'll pass.'

'Pussy.'

'Thank you.'

'Sold her soul, eh?' said Eva. 'What a prick. Complete prick behaviour, that.'

'I don't think she's a prick. She seems nice.'

'Yes, but you're a prick, too, so you would think that.'

'Charming.'

'Has she or has she not sold herself to multiple demons who are now scrambling to off her so they can be the one to claim her everlasting soul?'

'Well, when you put it like that, yes.'

'What a prick.'

'Okay, fine,' I conceded, 'she's a prick and she did something stupid, but we have to help. We can't just let them kill her.'

'Yeah, we can. We can easily do that. Really easily. Look how easily I'm doing exactly that, right now.'

She took another mighty hit on her bong then collapsed back and let the—somehow—purple smoke drift out of her head's exit holes.

'Hey, idiot, we should order takeaway! Pizza! Pizza, pizza, pizza, pizza, pizza. That's a funny word: pizza. Double Z. Not many double Z words.'

She broke out in a full-body laugh that took almost three minutes to end.

'Are you done?' I asked.

Eva nodded. 'Hey, what happened to that pizza you were going on about? I am famished.'

'Eva, focus! There's a woman in danger. Isn't this what we're all about?'

'Normally, yeah, but she sold her soul to a demon. To *lots* of demons. Those contracts are locked up tight. There's no wiggling out of them. You can't take them back. What's theirs is theirs. Whatever we do, whatever magic we try, it'll only—at best—delay things. Sooner or later, your prick of a pal is going to get what's coming to her, and one lucky demon is going to get her rancid soul to use as a punching bag for the rest of eternity.'

'Shit. Shit it.'

'But there is some good news.'

'Good news? Okay, good news is good. Hit me with it.'

'I just remembered I have three slices of leftover pizza in the fridge. Pizza, pizza!'

Eva rolled onto the floor, managed to pull herself up to her feet, and staggered to the kitchen.

'Eva, come on, she's at my flat!' I said, chasing her heels. 'I can't let her die without at least trying. Just give me *something*.'

She retrieved a pizza box from the fridge, opening it up and inhaling its contents with an almost sexual ferocity.

'Want a slice?'

My stomach growled. 'Yeah, thanks.'

'Well, you can't. This is my pizza.'

'Eva, there must be something.'

'Nope. The only way you can get around it is if you can find someone to agree to take on the debt. Then the original person would be free of it, and whoever took it on would find themselves marked. But really, what kind of a brain-dead, moronic dumb-dumb would willingly do that to themselves?'

She grabbed the box and wobbled back through to the main room.

Well, this was less than ideal. I had a woman banking on my help, and yet I had no help to give. Brilliant.

I sighed and slumped onto the couch beside Eva. 'What

about the other thing? The murder stones. Any news on Elga and her Kin?'

'Still looking into it,' Eva replied.

'How much have you looked into it?'

'Loads.'

'How much.'

'I'm about to start at any moment.'

'Eva, people are dying!'

'People are always dying, idiot. Like your friend, Annie. She's dying, any day now by the sounds of it. Shit happens. Death happens. I'll get to it. Now, if you don't mind, me and these three slices of cold pizza are about to become very intimate, and we'd appreciate some privacy.'

I drove away from the coven, away from Eva, a familiar cocktail of annoyance, frustration, and confusion doing somersaults in my belly. Plus hunger. I hadn't realised until now, but in all the hullabaloo, I'd been missing out on food as well as sleep.

So, to sum up: according to Eva, Annie was up to her neck in it and that was that. The deal had been done. If you sold your soul, that was it. There was no breaking a contract. A soul was owed and a soul would be taken. The only loophole: a second party could take on the debt, but doing so would mean sacrificing their own life.

I already didn't like the direction this was heading in.

I swung by a local pizza place on my way back to the flat and grabbed a couple—one for me and one for Annie—then headed home. Unfortunately, those pizzas would find themselves abandoned in my car as I pulled up outside of my flat to find Detective Martins, Myers' new partner, lying in wait.

Life really did seem keen on kicking me square between the legs.

15

There I was again, sat by myself in a police station, miserable and exhausted. It had barely been a week since I last found myself here, held in custody and being subjected to a barrage of questions. Same room, too. Perhaps they'd name it after me one day. The Joseph Lake Memorial Interrogation Room.

'I don't like you, Mr Lake,' said Detective Martins as he entered the room and sat down opposite me.

'Oh?'

'No. And you smell bad.'

'I'll have you know I'm very scrupulous about hygiene.'

'You're also not funny.'

'About the smell thing... I was down a well earlier, and before that, I had a run-in with some large birds, so it is possible I'm hosting some left-over stench.'

Detective Martins leaned over the little table and sniffed me. He took two great lungs full and grimaced. 'I can smell a liar, and that's what you are. You reek of it.'

The questioning did not seem to be going well. I would have asked for a lawyer but thought that might have made me look even more guilty. Plus, I had a friend on the inside.

'You still haven't actually told me why you dragged me here. You realise there are two pizzas in my car, and I didn't even get a chance to crack a window so they can breathe.'

The door opened and Myers entered, taking her place beside Martins.

'The gang's all here, then,' I chirped.

'Mr Lake,' said Myers, 'have you been in contact with Miss Chloe Palmer recently?'

Myers was completely unreadable. Obviously, she knew what had happened and was on my side, but she had a poker face and a half.

'Answer the question,' said Martins, rather aggressively.

'No, I haven't seen or spoken to Miss Chloe Palmer.'

'Really?' said Martins, 'because I happen to think otherwise.'

'Well, that's nice. Believe me, if I'd spoken to her, if I knew where she was, you would be the first to know.'

Martins smiled and took out a sheet of paper, sliding it towards me. 'Do you recognise this?'

I looked to Myers, a little confused then took the paper. It showed the comments section of a website. My website.

'Ah...' I said.

'*Ah*,' repeated Martins. 'I told you, Lake. I can smell a liar.'

'Look, no, this isn't really anything.'

'It's you conversing with Chloe Palmer,' he replied.

'How did you even see this?' I asked.

'An informant,' replied Myers.

'An informant, who would be...?' Doctor Neil of course. Oh, that pasty bastard.

'Where is she, Lake?' asked Martins.

'This is nothing. It's less than nothing. Honest.'

'You have at best a loose association with that word, don't you?' asked Martins.

'No, I'm honest, I'm very honest. You could say honest is my middle name, but I wouldn't because that would be dishonest and I hate dishonest people. Can't stand them. Horrid lot.'

'Mr Lake,' said Myers as I floundered, trying to keep my head above water, 'we're just trying to understand what this is and why you didn't tell us about it.'

'I understand,' said Martins. 'It's because he didn't want us to know. Isn't that right, Lake?'

'Okay. Okay. Yes, I read those messages, but I knew they came from someone playing a sick joke.'

'You *knew*?' said Martins. 'How would you *know*, exactly? Is there any reason it couldn't be her?'

'Yes!'

Myers widened her eyes at me in a *shut-it-you-moron* sort of way. She gets a lot of information across with the slightest facial tick, that one.

'I mean, no. Obviously, it could be her, it's just... that'd be a really weird way to get in contact, wouldn't it? That's not a thing you do, so I assumed it was just kids pissing about.'

'I see. But then it appears you came to believe it was her,' said Myers.

'I hoped. I knew it was dumb, but I hoped anyway because I wanted it to be her. Because I'm worried about her. But it wasn't. It isn't. It's just, like I said, kids or something.'

Martins sat back, arms crossed, eyeing me evilly.

'Even if it actually had been her, I mean, so what? Wouldn't that have been a good thing? It would show she was still okay, right? Also, can I go now, please?'

Martins stood up and kicked his chair back dramatically. 'I know you're up to your neck in this, Lake, and I'm going to be the one to finger you.'

'Please,' I replied, 'I'm not really into that sort of thing. Not that I'm judging.'

Martins lunged forward, fist clenched. Lucky for me, his partner stood and placed a placating arm between us.

'Okay, Martins, that's enough.'

He shot her daggers, then turned and stormed out.

'Well, he is just an aneurysm waiting to happen,' I said.

'Why didn't you tell me about the messages?' asked Myers. 'Or at least delete them?'

'Because they were nothing. Well, probably nothing. You do remember what happened, right?'

'Yes, and I'm the one trying to protect you from the fallout, and this sort of thing does not make it any easier. An officer like Martins gets tunnel vision, and now, thanks to your stupidity, all he sees at the end of that tunnel is you.'

Detective Myers drove me home. I retrieved the pizzas from the Uncanny Wagon before heading inside.

'I was starting to worry about you,' said Annie, as I entered with a cheery hello.

'I come bearing very cold gifts.'

We sat on the couch eating delicious microwaved pizza, drinking beer, and letting some bad sci-fi movie burble along in the background as we talked.

'Anything happen while I was gone?' I asked.

'Nope,' replied Annie, muffled around a mouthful of pizza. 'You said this place had protection on it. What did you mean by that?'

'Magic. It has magic stuff on it to keep me safe from... things.'

'I'm sorry, what? Are you saying you're a magician?'

'No, of course not.'

'Oh.'

'I'm a witch.'

'Oh again.'

'Though, I tend to prefer the term warlock. Is that sexist of me? It feels sexist.'

'A little bit,' she admitted. 'Though warlock does sound more bad-arse. I'd probably use that, too.'

She smiled and I found myself laughing. It might be the first time I'd felt in any way relaxed since Chloe died. It felt.. a bit weird. A bit wrong.

'So you believe me, then?' I asked. 'You're going to take my word for it that I'm a warlock?'

'Joe, I've been climbing into a well to talk to creatures from Hell since I was seven years old. I can cope with the idea that warlocks exist.'

That made sense.

'I'm going to be completely honest here' I said, 'it wasn't until about a week ago that I even knew warlocks existed. My past is a bit, well, completely empty. But then I found out there's magic, and monsters, and talking, axe-wielding foxes, and now, demons. It's been quite the few days, let me tell you.'

'Axe-wielding foxes?'

'Oh, yes.'

Annie smiled. 'That sounds sort of cute. And awesome.'

I went over to the fridge and grabbed a fresh couple of bottles. 'Another beer?'

Annie nodded and made grabby hands. 'You know, I actually feel... relaxed,' she said. 'I've been walking around like I have a target on my back for weeks, because, well, I *do*. It's so good to finally have someone on my side. Someone helping me.'

Ah. Yes. I had yet to actually go into the details of my conversation with Eva. About how, apparently, Annie was pretty much screwed in the bottom.

'It's not just me I'm scared about,' said Annie.

'What is it?'

'I mean, if it was just me, I'd be scared, of course. Terrified. But... I'm a mum.'

Ah. And oh. And shit.

'A little girl. She's three.'

I thought back to the earlier crime scene; to the dead mother's fierce, all-consuming love for her child. It was the most powerful love I'd ever seen. The sort of love I'd likely never know.

'What's her name?' I asked.

'Millie. She's great. Well, I would say that, but it's also true. The best thing that's ever happened to me. The only good thing I ever got out of her dad before he upped sticks. And now...' her voice faltered, a catch in the throat.

'Where is she?'

'She's staying with my best friend. I had to make up some bullshit for why. I just... I couldn't risk her being near me. Getting caught in the crossfire. Joe, I'm going to die and Millie is going to be left without a mum.'

Tears were rolling down her face now, so I said something stupid to cheer her up.

'That's not gonna happen. I'll protect you. I'll get those demons off your back.'

'You promise?'

Don't do it, Joe.

'I promise. Absolutely.'

Well, crap.

Of course, I knew I'd made a promise that I had no idea I could keep. In fact, I was pretty sure I couldn't, but what else was I supposed to say? I thought about her little girl finding out her mum was dead, that she was never going to see her again, and there was nothing I could do but make a dumb promise.

'What's with the face?' asked Annie.

'Hm?'

'You looked sad.'

'Me? No. Always happy, me. Not smart enough to be miserable. You need depth to be sad.' I tipped her a smile and a wink.

'I've seen that look on you a few times, Joe. Tell you what, I've shared my sad story, why don't you tell me what's going on with you?'

'It's nothing.'

'Ah, a woman.'

'Wow. You are very perceptive.'

'I know. That's another one of the things I sold my soul for.'

'Is that true?'

She laughed. 'Maybe. So someone broke your heart? Been there, done that.'

'Probably not like this, you haven't.'

'Try me.'

'Okay,' I said, taking a deep breath. 'Well, it turned out the girl I'd been in love with, who was into me, too, planned to eat my warlock soul so her army of octopus-limbed, soul-sucking vampires could go marching across the country and bring it to its knees.'

Annie nodded thoughtfully as she sipped her beer and took in my story. 'Yep, definitely been there.'

I laughed and leaned back. 'Life is strange, isn't it?'

'Amen to that.'

We tapped our bottles together, drank another three, then fell asleep where we sat.

16

I returned bright and breezy to the hospital the following morning for another shift. I'd be lying if I said switching out dud light bulbs was topmost of my mind that day. No, I had a much more pressing matter to deal with.

'Ah, Doctor Neil, there you are.'

He turned from the sink in the second-floor men's toilets and glared at me as though he were attempting to force lasers from his eyes and burn twin holes through my head. No doubt he would pretend he hadn't dropped me in it with the police, but he knew that I knew that he knew, and it was only a matter of time—of expert linguistic chokeholds—before he admitted to the whole dirty—

'Yes, I told the police and had you dragged down to the station. That was me. All me. And I'll do it again the next chance I get.'

Ha! He stumbled right into my trap.

Shut up.

'Nice try, Doc, but I had nothing to do with Chloe going missing, and those messages came from nasty kids who haven't developed empathy yet. Or maybe it was you all along...'

'Pardon me?'

'Have you been leaving messages on my site?'

'Why would I do that?'

'To keep the police from looking too hard at you. Where were you the day Chloe Palmer went missing, eh? Answer me that.'

Dr Neil stared at me, jaw silently moving up and down. I'd say the blood had drained from his face, but I'm not sure given the nature of his sickly albino skin.

'I had nothing to do with it,' he roared.

'With "it"? What "it", Dr Neil? Is it an "it" we're dealing with now?'

'I, well...'

'Sounds like you know an awful lot if you know we're dealing with an "it". Maybe I should go and have a quiet word with Detectives Myers and Martins; ask if they've given you a proper look yet.'

'You know what happened to Chloe. Sooner or later, the police will find out. I only hope I'm there to see it.'

'Please let this sink in, once and for all: I had nothing to do with Chloe's disappearance, and if you keep trying to make trouble for me... well... that isn't nice. So stop it.'

Dr Neil grimaced and stormed out of the room, leaving me alone but for the company of the piss-scented floor. Christ, he had a bee in his bonnet about this. It was annoying. Especially annoying as he was, basically, correct. Tunnel vision malice on his part rather than any deductive prowess, but correct all the same. I refused to credit him with a high-functioning brain, or even just a brain, really.

I sighed and leaned against the sink, looking up into the mirror and expecting to see my haggard face staring back.

Instead, I saw Chloe.

'Holy buggering mother of poop,' I said as I staggered back from the unexpected appearance.

'Joe, help me. Please.'

'Chloe?'

I took a tentative step forward as she reached out a desperate hand. Any moment she'd disappear again, surely. Just another brain-addled flash. I looked away and shook my head. This wasn't happening. Chloe was dead. But this time she didn't go away.

'Joe, please, I don't know where I am.'

'Chloe? Oh my god, it is you! It's really bloody you, isn't it?'

'Please!'

I almost ran at the mirror but held firm, which was sensible given that I'd have cracked my face on it something fierce.

'Chloe, can you hear me?' I pleaded.

The apparition nodded, a tear rolling down her cheek. 'Joe! Please, I keep trying to reach you, but I'm weak. I think I'm nearly all gone.'

I wanted to help her—of course, I did—but there was the lingering matter of how things had ended between us. What with her squid-man army and that.

'The things you were going to do, the things you'd already done, that's not the person I knew. Thought I knew. Thought I loved.'

'That wasn't me,' she replied. 'It was my dad.'

'What are you saying?'

'My dead dad from the Dark Lakes. Somehow, when I moved back here, some part of him infected me. Possessed me, somehow. I couldn't resist it. I wasn't strong enough.'

'Is that true? Please, I need to know. I'll help, but I need to know.'

'It's true, Joe. You know it is, don't you? Deep down. You know me, Joe. You know me like no one else ever has. Is that really something I would have done? It makes me sick to even think about it.'

I didn't answer.

Yes, deep down, I found it hard to believe that the Chloe Palmer I knew would wind up going down the road she had, but that wasn't to say it didn't happen. Didn't mean it was anyone besides herself calling the shots.

But I wanted to believe it. And if monsters, and demons, and souls were real, who's to say an evil spirit hadn't possessed her?

'Joe!'

Chloe was starting to flicker like one of the dud bulbs I should have been seeing to.

'Tell me where you are, Chloe. I'll find you.'

'I don't know. I think I'm trapped between worlds somehow. And I think something is coming to get me. I can feel it.'

'I'll find you, I promise.'

Chloe reached out one last time, and then the only person I saw in the mirror was me.

As I drove to the coven, I knew I was about to attempt something absurd. I knew I was taking a risk. I knew that just because Chloe said one thing, didn't mean it was true. The strange, magical world I found myself living in could be a duplicitous so-and-so, but I had to try, didn't I? Had to hope.

One way or another, I was going to figure this thing out. My first port of call was the coven, where I expected to find Eva. I knew that talking to her was most likely a waste of time—after all, she'd already made her position on Chloe's apparent resurrection quite clear—but I was prepared to chisel away at her some more. Eva wasn't home, though, which lead me to Plan B.

The library.

Maybe there was something among all of those books that could help me. As I stepped into the room and cast my eyes across the jumble of anonymous, identical-looking tomes, my heart took a cliff dive. This was a fool's errand, in more ways than one. How on earth was I going to find anything useful among all that knowledge when I had no idea where to look or what I was even looking for?

'It's probably in this book here,' came a familiar voice. I turned to see the fox, sporting, as always, its Roman helmet. It pointed its battle-axe at a large tome discarded in a far corner.

'You didn't say your catchphrase,' I said.

'My what?'

'You know,' I shook a fist at the roof, *"All hail the saviour!"* You always say that. It's your thing.'

The fox shuffled from foot to foot and scratched at its head. 'I do?'

'Is there a reason you're here?'

'Yes, help! I help. Helped you with that stone, didn't I?'

'I thought I'd seen you.'

'Gave you a little taste. Made you feel strong, yes?'

I closed my eyes and remembered that feeling. That amazing, terrifying feeling.

'You sleeping?' asked the fox.

'Not enough, no.' I opened my eyes again and strode across the room. I picked up the heavy volume the fox had indicated. 'How do you know this is the book I need?'

The fox shrugged. 'I see things, I know things. That's me.'

I lugged the book over to the library's gnarled desk and dropped it with a thump. A mildewy cloud of odour spewed out as I spread the book open.

'So, what spell will I need?' I mumbled.

The pages of the book whipped past of their own accord before settling on a spell.

'Okay, that was a bit not normal.'

'That's the spell,' said the fox. 'Can save her. Bring her back.'

I looked into the fox's eager eyes.

'Why exactly would you be helping me?'

'I am the fox. From the Dark Lakes. I help you.'

'I'm not going to accept your redheaded mistress' demand

to take up any throne, you know. Especially not a throne made of skulls that will turn me into some sort of super-powered hellion.'

'You say that now. Say something different later, yes.'

'Nope. I'm a good person. In the main.'

The fox tutted and picked at the blade of its axe. 'You have been good for ten years. It's a phase, that is all.'

I ignored the fox and started to look through the spell. I came upon a problem pretty sharpish.

'What language is this exactly?'

'Magic.'

'Magic? The language magic?'

The fox nodded.

'Can you read it?'

'I am just a fox. Foxes cannot read, in my experience.'

'Yes, but then most foxes can't talk, either.'

'We talk plenty,' he sulked.

'Sorry. So, what do I do now?'

'Be magic.'

'Oh, just that?' I replied. 'Just be magic?'

'The Red Woman could help.'

'Yes, I'm sure, with no demands attached. Just doing little old me a no-strings solid.'

The fox looked at me, confused. 'No. She will expect you to become the Magic Eater.'

'You don't really get sarcasm, do you?'

I jumped at the sound of the front door opening. Eva was back.

'Shit it. Shit, shitty, shit it! You've got to hide.'

But, of course, the fox had already done his customary disappearing act. I closed the useless magic book, smoothed down my clothes, put on my best nothing-dodgy-going-on-here smile, and sauntered through into the front room. Whereupon Eva threw a fireball in my direction which narrowly missed my head.

'Christ!' I cried.

'Oh, it's you,' she said.

'You could have killed me!'

'Lots of times. Lots and lots. There you stand by my good graces. What're you doing here?'

'Nothing weird. All above board, I can assure you of that.'

Eva narrowed her eyes and looked past me. 'What were you doing in the library?'

'Just, you know, browsing. I was going to try a bit of magic revision, but it turns out the books are all written in gibberish.'

'You're nervous, idiot. What are you nervous about?'

I dithered this way and that before Eva became distracted by her ringing phone.

'What?' she said, answering the call. 'Right. Give us twenty.' She pocketed the phone and lit a cigarette.

'Good news?'

Eva shrugged. 'Depends on your predilections. We've got another dried-out stiff.'

I can't deny feeling a teensy bit grateful for the timing of this latest horrific murder, which really didn't make me feel too good about myself, I can tell you.

17

The scene of the crime was a little different this time. No house; instead, I found myself parking up near a small humpback bridge.

'Aw no,' said Eva, sitting up from her usual position on the back seat. 'Aw no, no, no.'

'What? What's wrong? I mean, besides the obvious deathy situation?'

'Come on,' she said, and stepped out of the car, heading down the bank towards a small stone bridge surrounded by a huddle of police officers and a forensics team.

'Eva?'

I followed her down the damp incline to the underneath of the bridge, almost slipping as I did so. And then I did slip, landing in a heap at someone's feet. I looked up to see Detective Myers.

'Don't worry,' she said. 'No one saw.'

I looked around to see several officers laughing and nudging each other.

'Apart from everyone over there, I mean.'

'Good. Great.'

I stood and regained my composure as best I could then

followed Myers to the body. Eva was already crouched by its side. As with the others, the corpse was completely shrivelled and dried out.

'Is it another one of you magic people?' asked Myers.

'Yup,' replied Eva. 'He's an Uncanny, all right.'

'We couldn't find any sort of I.D. on him,' said Myers.

'No need. I know this fella. A troll who went by the name Tony. Tony the troll. Me and him used to drink like demons in our younger days. He could really hold his booze. Well, for a troll.'

'A troll,' said Myers, nodding. 'Okay. Dead troll. Of course.'

I patted her on the shoulder. 'It just carries on getting weirder, doesn't it?'

'Do I look like your loyal family pet?'

I stopped the patting.

'You can see drag marks to and from the body here,' said Myers, pointing at the dirt.

'The stones,' I said. 'Elga and her Kin.'

'Are you two any further along with that?' she asked.

'Ah, well, no. Not as such,' I replied.

'I have someone we can talk to about it,' said Eva. 'Local know-it-all.'

Mickey Finn's is a pub on the outskirts of Keswick, the small town I live in. It's a pub that—up until this moment—I had neither seen nor heard of, which, if you knew Keswick, would seem impossible. Live there for even the shortest length of time and you'll have seen and visited every place there is to visit.

But not Mickey Finn's. Mickey Finn's was only meant to be seen by a certain very specific type of clientele: namely, Uncanny people. Like the coven, it sat at the end of a blind alley, and this time it lived up fully to its name.

'What am I supposed to be looking at?' asked Myers, staring at what looked to her like a solid brick wall.

'Mickey Finn's,' replied Eva. 'Not much to look at, but it's got booze, crisps, and a jukebox containing nothing that came out post-1976, so its fucking belter. Come on.'

Eva walked into the alley.

Myers made a small, strangled sound as she stagger-stepped back. 'She disappeared!'

It was a nice feeling, not being the one struggling to keep up for a change. The one floundering, wide-eyed, at the latest impossibility.

'It's called a blind alley,' I explained, swaggering around in a somewhat insufferable manner. 'We magic sorts use them to keep certain places secret from unwanted visitors.'

Eva stepped back out of the alley, causing Myers to let out another cry and bunny hop back.

'You coming or what?'

'Blind alley,' I said.

'Huh? Oh!' Eva placed her hand against Myers' head. 'See.'

The Detective swatted the hand aside, went to give Eva a piece of her mind, then stopped. 'Oh.'

'Yup,' I said. 'Come along, you two.'

I strode into the alley towards the little pub nestled at the far end. Eva and Myers followed on.

'No one likes you when you're smug, idiot,' said Eva. 'Or just in general, actually.'

Mickey Finn's was what you might call an old school pub. By which I mean it looked like something from medieval times. That's apart from the jukebox, which was currently playing *Jolene* by Dolly Parton.

The floor was dirt scattered with hay; the beer decanted from large barrels with simple taps hammered into them. We stepped inside and the drinkers paused their conversations to see who we were. I was very aware of the harsh looks and whispered curses thrown specifically in my direction.

'Stay cool,' Eva told the patrons of Mickey Finn's. 'The idiot's with me. If anyone wants to start something, I have my fighting fists on.'

The drinkers went back to their conversations.

'Not too popular in here, then,' said Myers.

'I've never even been here,' I replied.

'Yeah, you have,' said Eva. 'And everyone here knows what a piece of shit you are. Were. Whatever. Come on.'

Eva wandered over to the bar as I tried to put on a brave, not-at-all-scared face.

'What exactly did you get up to in the past?' asked Myers.

'Oh, you know, we all do stupid things when we're young.' I scampered after Eva, who already had the broken-nosed, shaven-headed barman filling three jugs with beer.

'So, who's your source?' asked Myers.

'Malden,' said Eva, taking her drink from the barman and blowing off the froth. 'Still an expert at giving head I see, Grunt.'

The barman grunted.

'Appropriate name,' I said. Grunt glared at me and shoved my drink over, spilling about half of it in the process. 'Thank you.'

'Come on, he's over there,' said Eva.

We joined a rather ratty-looking man, sat by himself in one corner. And when I say ratty, I mean ratty. His clothes were a tattered jumble, his fingernails filthy, his ears and teeth tapering into points, just like a rodent's.

'Malden,' said Eva, nodding and taking a seat opposite the man.

'Eva, how nice to see you. When was the last time we spoke? Oh, it must have been years and years and years and years ago. How many years is it? Now, it must be more than six. I bet it's more than six, isn't it? Maybe eight.'

'You'll have to forgive Malden,' said Eva, 'he is massively boring.'

'It can't be ten, can it?'

'Yup. Ten years. Only got back to the Lakes recently. Been doing a tour of the country since, well…' she gestured in my direction.

'Janto,' said Malden, raising his glass to me.

I raised mine in return. 'Oh, Janto to you, too.' I leaned over to Eva. '*Janto*; is that magic for hello?'

'No, that's your real name.'

I took a few silent seconds to digest that one. 'Janto is my name? My real name?' It occurred to me then that I'd never thought to ask what my old name—my real name—had been. I'd given myself the name Joseph Lake. Seemed I got the first letter right at least.

'Do I have a second name?' I asked.

'No, just Janto,' said Eva. 'Witches don't need second names. They're like Cher that way.'

'Sorry,' said Myers, 'but, what exactly are you, Malden?'

'I'm an eaves,' he replied.

'An eaves.'

'We like to lurk about. Listen to things. Gather secrets and sell them on. It's a very interesting line of work, actually.'

'No it isn't, Malden,' said Eva. 'Now stop going on about nothing. We need something from you.'

I raised my hand. 'Is it okay if I keep going by Joseph? Joseph feels more me.'

'Fine,' said Eva. 'Janto has a really shitty association for me. What's your price, Malden?'

'The usual.'

'Are we paying for this intel?' asked Myers.

'No,' said Eva. 'Well, yeah, but not in cash, Malden and his kind trade info for magic.'

'So, Eva, Janto, Officer, what is it you would like to know?'

'Malden,' I said, 'there's a stone circle we're looking for.'

'Lot of stone circles around these parts,' he replied. 'I've got a long, winding, fascinating story about stone circles, actually, if you'd like to hear it.'

'No, thanks,' said Eva, 'but I'll keep the offer in mind if I want to be bored to death.'

Malden laughed. 'See, that's what I like about you, Eva. You're so rude. You also have a very nice bottom. For a familiar.'

'He wouldn't say it if it wasn't true,' said Eva, waggling her eyebrows at Myers.

'We want to ask about a specific stone circle,' I said, getting us back on track.

'Shoot.'

'Elga and her Kin.'

Malden nodded and scratched at his scabby chin with his sharp yellow fingernails, skin flaking off and drifting down to his jumper like some sort of really disgusting snowfall.

'Elga and her Kin, eh? Yeah, I know that.'

'Brilliant! Is there a reason we didn't come and ask this question right away?' I said, turning to Eva.

Eva shrugged. 'And go the easy route? Where's your sense of fun?'

'I'm sure Tony the troll would have an answer to that,' I replied. 'Except he wouldn't because he's dead.'

Myers slid a pad and pen across to Malden. 'Could you write down an exact location for us?'

'Be my pleasure.'

He scrawled down the name of a place. There was only one problem....

'Actually, we've already tried there,' I said. 'Remember when I got that weird feeling and stopped? That was the place. There was nothing there.'

'Didn't happen to go during the day, did you?' asked Malden.

'Yeah, why?'

'Of course!' said Eva, slapping a palm against her forehead.

'Of course what?' asked Myers.

'It's a night circle, isn't it?' said Eva.

'Complete night circle, yeah,' said Malden.

'What's a night circle?' I asked.

'Well, for starters, it's only visible at night,' replied Malden. 'You can't see it while the sun's up.'

'The stones only attacked at night,' said Myers. 'So that makes a sort of sense.'

'You know,' said Malden, 'I've got a nice story about that circle, too, if you've got thirty or forty minutes to spare.'

Eva downed her drink, then Myers', then mine before unleashing a burp that could have brought down a passing plane. 'Sorry,' she said, 'looks like we're all done.' She clicked her fingers and the air around her hand began to sparkle and glow. 'Get that down you, love.' She flicked the sparkles and they drifted over to the grasping Malden, who gobbled them up with his dagger-like teeth as if he hadn't eaten in days.

'Now, that's good magic,' he said, licking his lips.

As we headed for the exit, I was feeling sort of good. We had new information: we knew what and where the circle was. The investigation had stepped forward. We were actually getting somewhere. I may even have been smiling. And that's when my phone started to vibrate.

It was the hospital.

'Hello?' I said, answering. 'I'm not late for a shift, am I?'

'Joe,' said Big Marge, 'it's your friend, Annie.'

I felt my body turn cold. 'What about her?'

'You'd better get over here.'

I pocketed my phone and ran from the pub.

18

Annie did not look at all well as I entered her hospital room. Hardly surprising, really. You tend not to look your best after a car has smashed into you, throwing your ragdoll body through the air, and leaving you in a bloody heap on the side of the road.

'Annie?'

I moved to the side of the bed. Her eyes were closed. Unconscious or sleeping, I wasn't sure. Her face was badly bruised, one of her arms in a cast. Had there been another attempt to grab her soul? Or was it just a coincidence? People are hit by cars all the time.

'Jo-Joe...?' Annie's eyes fluttered open, her cracked lips parting to speak again before receding into a pained grimace.

'Hey, it's okay, I'm here.'

I dragged a chair over and sat by her side as she struggled into a semi-seated position and reached for a plastic cup of tepid water on the bedside table.

'What happened?' I asked. 'Why did you leave the flat?'

'I had work. I don't know. I was stupid.' She reached out the hand that wasn't set in plaster and gripped my arm like a woman holding on to a life belt in the middle of a stormy sea.

'It's okay, I'm here, they didn't get you. It was, you know, "them", I take it?'

Annie nodded. 'One of them almost got me. Almost took me out and claimed my soul.'

'But they didn't. You're still here. You're still alive.'

'I'm never going to see my daughter again, am I? I'm never going to hold Millie, never going to hear her laugh, ever again.'

'Don't talk like that. They haven't won yet. You'll see your daughter again; I promised you, didn't I?'

Yeah, I promised all right. I had no right, but I'd gone ahead and done it, anyway. Would I have done that if she hadn't been a mother? If I hadn't experienced the love that dead magician had for her daughter? Maybe, maybe not. But it felt like the sensation of that love had infected me a little. Seeped into my bones. I didn't just want to protect Annie, I felt like I had to protect her daughter, too. I didn't want a child growing up without her mum on my conscience.

'I'm frightened, Joe.'

'I know. Me too.'

I could feel her trembling as she held on to me, and my stomach twisted. All she had was a life of fear ahead of her, and a short one at that the way things were going. And there was nothing I could do about it. Nothing Eva could do, either. The bad guys were going to get her. She was going to die, and Millie, her kid, was going to grow up with barely a memory of her.

That's unless I did something massively stupid and epically dangerous. Something that would save Annie as I promised—would let her go back to her life, her child—but put me in the firing line with no clear exit points marked. I thought about the dead magician one more time. How that love *burned.*

Crap.

'Annie, I think I have a way to get you out of this.'

Crap crap crap.

Annie's eyes widened and she sat forward sharply, wincing

in pain as her body let her know how much of a mistake that sudden movement was.

'Really? You can help, after all?'

'Sure,' I said, as nonchalantly as I could while my knees knocked and my heart raced. 'I said I would help, didn't I, and I'm not one to disappoint a lady. Well, that's not true, but not on this occasion.'

A tear raced down Annie's cheek. She leaned forward as best she could and hugged me.

'Okay, no need for that,' I said, 'just doing my job.'

'What is it? Some sort of magic spell?'

'Yep. Well, sort of. I'm not entirely sure.'

'Oh. Okay.'

'Basically, you can't cancel your contract with the demons, but you can pass the debt on. Pass it on to someone willing to take what you're offering.'

Annie looked confused. 'You're saying you'd take on my debt?'

'Yep,' I said, my voice something of a squeak. I cleared my throat and tried again. 'Yes. Yep. I will take on your debt, and problem solved; no more animal attacks, no more dodgy drivers.'

'But wouldn't that just make them all turn their attention on you?'

Please don't point out the terrifying, stupid flaw in all of this.

'Yes, well, there is that, but don't worry, I'm not like you. I'm a warlock, remember, and I know lots of other magic... stuff. And people. They wouldn't help a non-magic person like you, but they will me. Honest. No worries.'

Annie didn't look like she was buying a word of it, which wasn't surprising as I'm a terrible liar.

'I don't want to be responsible for your death, Joe. This is my fault.'

'Death? Who's dying? Trust me, all will be well. Or are you

happy with the constant stream of close shaves you're currently enjoying? Happy with Millie never seeing you again?'

Annie wrestled for a moment.

'Trust me. I'm a witch. I shit demons for breakfast.'

'That's a strange way to phrase that.'

It was.

'Shall we?' I said, holding out my hands.

'How do we do it?'

'Not sure. I thought we might just hold hands and, I don't know, you could offer me the debt, and I could accept, and we'll see how it goes.'

Annie reached out toward me then pulled away. 'Promise me you can solve this. That you can have the debt cancelled.'

'Cross my heart and hope not to die.'

'I mean it. I don't want to be responsible for anyone's death.'

Me neither, though I have at least three on my record so far.

'Trust me,' I said. 'No one is dying.'

I waggled my open hands and Annie reached out, grasping them. 'So what now?' she asked.

'Offer me the debt,' I said.

'Just that? Just offer?'

'I am playing this part a little by ear, but yeah. Offer.'

'Okay. Okay. Joseph Lake, will you take on my debt?'

The lights in the room dimmed a little and I could have sworn I heard the sound of crackling flames way down in the mix.

'Do you hear that?' asked Annie.

'I hear it. Okay, it's working, I think. Ask me again.'

'Joseph Lake, will you take on my debt?'

'Yes,' I replied. 'Yes, I will. I would really like and want it, please and thank you.'

We each pulled back with a sudden cry as our hands unleashed a painful shock.

'Was that it?' asked Annie, blowing on her fingertips. 'Is it done, did it work?'

I closed my eyes, holding my hands tight to my chest. I could feel something new and uncomfortable inside of me. Something that hadn't been there before.

'Do you feel different?' I asked.

Annie looked confused for a second, then her face brightened. 'Yeah. Yeah, I do. Sort of, lighter. Like I had something inside of me all this time, something uncomfortable, and I didn't even notice, I'd had it there so long.'

'Yup. I have that now. That or I'm about to have a heart attack.'

Annie smiled and, despite the pain, insisted on leaning forward to hug me.

'Thank you, Joe. Thank you for saving my life.'

19

As I left, I wondered how long it would take before a demon made an attempt on my life. Yes, I felt somewhat heroic, somewhat good about myself. What had happened with Chloe had been necessary, or it had seemed so at the time, but it had left me with no satisfaction. All that had given me was a mixture of guilt, sadness, and heartbreak.

But this?

This was a purely good thing. I was a witch of the Cumbrian Coven, tasked with helping the people of the Lakes when they were threatened by the Uncanny, by monsters, and I'd done my job. I made sure that a little girl would get to grow up with her mum by her side. Just me, off my own back.

Unfortunately, even this unselfish act wasn't something I could enjoy, as I was absolutely, completely, and totally crapping my pants over it.

Evening was fast approaching as I drove from the hospital to meet Eva and Myers. I was twitchy, on edge. My head bobbed this way and that, expecting the worst to come my way at any moment. It had worked, the transfer of debt, I just knew it. I felt it, sitting inside of me. I owed my soul to an unknown number of demons now; a rabble of rotten, squabbling monsters fighting over which would be the one to torment my eternal soul. Eva had told me that there was no way out of it. All I could do was pass it on. I wondered if the Red Woman would agree with her.

After perhaps the slowest drive I have ever taken—nervously keeping below the speed limit, waving other annoyed drivers past—I arrived at the stone circle's location to find both Eva and Myers already there.

'You're late, idiot,' noted Eva.

'Sorry.'

'Apology not accepted.'

'Good, because actually, I'm not sorry. I was at the hospital with Annie, who was almost killed earlier.'

'Who?'

'Who? Who!'

'Okay,' said Myers, stepping between me and Eva. 'I don't know what all this is about, but we've got an investigation to get on with, so get your heads out of your arses and let's get on with it.'

It's not often I lose my temper. It didn't suit me. As Myers walked off ahead to the exact location of the apparently invisible stone circle, Eva stepped in line beside me.

'You didn't do anything stupid, did you?' she asked.

'What? No, of course not. Nope.'

'Good.'

'Sorry about the whole...' I mimed my little moment of crossness.

'Oh, was that you being angry? Huh. You know, in the past, decades ago, you *really* used to get pissed off. I mean, your temper was the stuff of legend.'

'Really? That doesn't sound like me.'

'To be fair, you don't sound like you. Not the real you. The other you.'

'What did I get angry about?' I asked.

'Mostly Lyna and Melodia.'

The other witches. The ones I murdered.

'Why, what did they used to do?'

'Oh, you were like family. No, you were family. But you were the oldest by a few hundred years, so they were like your annoying younger sisters. Big brothers always get pissed off with their bratty younger siblings.'

It was strange to hear Eva being so open with me about something from my past. So lucid, too. No divergence, no swearing, no insults. I wondered if this was what she'd been like before... well, before everything.

And then part of what she had said suddenly hit home.

'I was the oldest by a few hundred years? A few hundred!'

'Yeah, about that. Two or three hundred.'

'Wait, so I'm... no... how old am I?'

Eva shrugged, plucked a battered chrome hip flask from her pocket, and unscrewed the lid. 'Fucked if I know. A few thousand years, at least.'

I stopped dead in my tracks. Eva carried on, flask to her mouth, before pausing and looking back at me, confused.

'What's up?' she asked. 'Need a piss?'

'I'm thousands of years old? Me?'

'Yup. You don't look too bad on it, I suppose.'

I couldn't compute that sort of bombshell. It was too big a number, too out there, impossible to grasp.

'Hey,' said Myers, waving us forward, 'this is the spot, right?'

Eva took a swig, slotted her flask away, and carried on.

A few thousand years old. Well, holy crap. They didn't bake a birthday cake big enough to hold that many candles.

'Yeah, this is it,' said Eva, twirling around.

'I can't help but notice a distinct lack of stones,' noted Myers.

'The moon is on the rise,' said Eva, 'any second now, we'll see the fuckers.'

And see them we did. It took another twenty minutes for the light of day to fully fade away and be replaced by a moon, bright and full. At first, it was like a smear on a pair of glasses. Something indistinct, not quite there, that you'd get rid of just by wiping the lenses. And then, as if by magic (actually, entirely by magic), there they were. Elga and her Kin. A stone circle, solid and real, surrounded us.

'Thirty stones,' said Myers, making a note in her pad. 'Do you recognise the one that attacked you?'

I walked around the circle, trying not to get too close to the stones as I passed. I remembered the crackling energy that flew from the one that had invaded my home.

'This is the one,' I said, pointing to one stone in particular. 'And this stone next to it, I think I saw it in the vision I saw when I touched the mother's body back at the magician's house.'

Eva leaned forward, squinting at the stone. 'Yeah, look at those dark splashes.'

'Dried blood,' said Myers.

'Bingo fucking bango,' replied Eva.

It was a strange feeling, being in that circle. No doubt you'd get a bit of a shiver running up your spine, standing in the middle of an ancient stone circle at night, but this one had an extra something-something. I felt like I was being watched.

'If,' said Eva, 'I was the sort of dick who got creeped out, I would be creeped the fuckity-fuck out right about now.'

'Me too,' said Myers, but the way she shifted, the way her eyes darted around a little more sharply than usual, told me that was a front. She was wigging out just as much as I was.

'So what now?' I asked. 'Do we, I don't know, blow them up?'

'Good idea,' said Eva, rubbing her hands together. Energy, thick and brightly-coloured, began to form between her hands. 'Stand back, I'm about to fuck a bitch up.'

With a grunt, she threw her right hand towards one of the stones as though she were pitching a baseball. A sphere of crackling energy exploded from her palm and struck the stone squarely.

And nothing happened.

'Well, that's rude,' said Eva. 'Didn't even leave a mark.'

'We have another problem,' said Myers.

'What is it?' I asked. 'Feel free to say something ordinary, like your phone is almost out of battery, or you think you might have left a window slightly ajar.'

'There were thirty stones,' said Myers.

'Yes, there are thirty stones.'

'I said *were*. Count them.'

I counted. And then counted again. There were now only twenty-nine stones.

Someone, somewhere, was about to get murdered.

20

It only took an hour for Myers' phone to buzz.

A man had been roused by the sound of a ruckus next door: loud thumps, breaking glass, furniture smashing. When he went to take a look, he found his elderly neighbour curled up on her kitchen floor, quite dead. He didn't have to check for a pulse to make sure as she—like the other victims—was a withered, mummified horror. His screams alerted a passer-by, who informed the police, who informed Myers.

There was no need for Eva and me to tag along. We knew what we'd see and we knew what had happened, so we stayed with the stone circle with Elga and her Kin.

The missing stone reappeared shortly after Myers left. There was blood sprayed across its surface, and not dried blood, like the other stone. This blood was very much wet.

'This is crazy,' I said. 'I mean, soul vampires with octopus limbs and demons buying souls at the bottom of a well, those are all crazy, too, but a crazy I can wrap my head around. But these are stones. Stones aren't alive.'

'There's always a first time,' said Eva.

'What's more, stones don't kill unless they're being used as a tool by a living, breathing creature.'

Eva cut short her visual examination of the stone and stood bolt upright, looking at me in surprise.

'What?' I asked. 'What is it? Is there a wasp on me?'

'No wasp.'

'Phew.'

'If there was a wasp,' she said, 'I would give you no indication, and wait for it to hopefully sting the shit out of you.'

'Thanks.'

'But what you said, that flicked a little switch in the old brain meat.'

'What did I say?' I asked.

'The stones. The stones. They're just the tip of the iceberg. I think? Yeah. Or…? Something else. Someone else.' She kneeled down and placed her hand against the ground in front of one of the stones.

'What is it?' I asked.

'Not one hundred percent sure.'

Eva flopped down, placing her ear against the muck.

'Hm.' She waved me over. 'Come and have a listen.'

'Listen? To the soil?'

Eva continued to waggle her hand at me, so I did as she asked, pressing my ear to the grass.

'What am I listening for?' I asked.

'Anything.'

'Right.'

So I listened. Then listened a bit more.

'Not sure I'm getting anything.'

Eva hopped up to her feet and began striding away, lighting a cigarette as she did.

'Oh, are we off?' I asked.

'Yup,' replied Eva, blowing a cloud of smoke into the air.

'But what about the circle. What about Elga and her Kin?'

'I think we need to go and ask Malden the dull as ditchwater eaves a few more questions. I reckon we didn't ask the right ones last time. Come along, idiot.'

I flicked a spider from my ear and hurried after her.

Mickey Finn's, the drinking hole for magical and monstrous types, was still open, despite the fact that it was gone two in the morning.

'This place never closes,' said Eva, as if reading my mind. 'Half the things that drink here only wake up at night, so they keep the place running twenty-four seven.'

Malden was at the same table we met him at the first time. He smiled a ratty, toothy smile and waved us over.

'Greetings and salutations, my coven friends.'

'I'll get the drinks in,' said Eva, leaving me to keep Malden company.

'So,' I started, 'how's your evening been?'

'I've been to the toilet eight times in the last two hours. Eight times.'

'Okay.'

'Four were merely to deposit urine, as you would expect from all of the alcohol imbibing.'

'Goes right through me, too.'

'But, and this is where it gets interesting...'

'I'm all ears.'

'...The other four were a combination of urine and solids.'

'Your use of the word "interesting" may have been a stretch, I think.'

'Four times! In such a short space of time. I don't know what to think. It's a new record. I've made a note of it.'

Eva sat next to me, placing a pint before me while she gulped from her own. Which, I noticed, had a shot glass sat inside of it.

'Thank God you're back,' I hissed from behind my glass before placing it to my lips.

'No need to whisper, idiot,' replied Eva. 'Malden here knows he's as boring as marital sex, don't you, Malders?'

'It has been mentioned over the years. Can't see it myself, mind you. Would you like me to fill you in on my toilet situation?'

'You really don't want to hear it,' I said.

'How many times?'

'Eight within two hours, four for solids.'

Eva whistled. 'A new record.'

'That's what I said,' replied Malden.

'Perhaps we could get to the stones?' I said.

'Elga and her Kin?' asked Malden. 'How'd you go? You find them?'

'Yes, we found them,' I replied.

'Lovely example of a night circle, that.'

'I think you held out on us, Malden,' said Eva.

'Oh?'

'It's not just your ordinary night circle, is it?'

'Depends. Everything is ordinary to someone. Just depends who you are.'

'Those stones are moving,' I said. 'They leave, they kill someone, then they return to their place in the circle.'

'Oh,' said Malden, wiping at his crusty nose with the back of a filthy sleeve. 'Suppose that makes sense.'

'What is the circle, Malden?' asked Eva.

'It's a graveyard, really,' he replied. 'The stones themselves aren't Elga and her Kin, they're just, well, headstones I suppose is the best way to describe them.'

'Headstones?' said Eva. 'Headstones for who?'

'Don't you know, Janto?' asked Malden, using my—apparently—real name. It felt a bit weird to be addressed that way.

'Should I?' I asked.

'Well, it was you and your witches who put them down. Elga and her Kin.'

'We did?'

'I don't know the details, but Elga and her Kin were a powerful cabal of some sort. You sorted them out and that's where their bodies lay: trapped under the circle forevermore, one under each stone marker.'

'Sorry, but why didn't you tell us all this the first time we asked?' I said.

Malden looked at me, utterly confused. 'I recall you asked *where* it was, not *what*. It may sound pedantic, but I answer what I'm asked, you see. It's good to be accurate and not add in extraneous details that the question-asker may find tedious, and in any way not apropos to the answer they actually require.'

'Four poos?' asked Eva.

Malden held up four fingers. 'Four. And each of them quite sizeable.'

21

Eva compensated Malden for the fresh information with some sweet magical succour, then went to the bar to get another round. Meanwhile, I made my way to the Gents. Yes, the scene of Malden's now-infamous four poos.

If Malden was correct—and Eva seemed confident that he was—it seemed that the stones themselves were not the problem. They were merely the blades used for the cutting. It also seemed that I had, in my empty past, dealt with whoever Elga and her Kin were, and that their current situation was all mine and my fellow witches doing.

I asked Eva why she hadn't known about it, but Malden said it was before her time.

As I emptied a pint-full into the urinal (honestly, my bladder is weaker than an Adam Sandler comedy), I thought again about Eva's earlier revelation about my age. About how I was thousands of years old. To have lost so much experience, so many memories... I thought losing twenty or thirty years was horrific, but this took it to a whole new level. If I access to my memories, I'd have known immediately about the stones, about who Elga and her Kin were, what they were capable of, and how to defeat them. I'd done it once; it stood to reason that I'd be able to do it again. If only, if only I knew the what, the how, the everything.

But I didn't.

I didn't know a shitting thing, and being told about it sparked naught. No half-memory, no sense of déjà vu, no prickle of familiarity.

I shook off, zipped up, and went to wash my hands. Chloe was waiting for me in the mirror when I looked up.

'Joe!'

'Jesus, Chloe!'

She looked awful. Okay, she was dead, but the other times I'd seen her, she still looked, well... healthy by comparison. Now she was drawn, grey-skinned, her body trembling.

'Please, Joe. You're the only one that can help me.'

'I don't know how.'

I didn't want to look at her. It gnawed at my insides. Why couldn't she just be dead? And by dead, I mean dead-dead, not whatever this was. And as soon as I thought that, I felt a wave of shame crash over me. How could I even think that way? And how could I let myself become so distracted by everything else that I just put Chloe on the back-burner?

'Chloe, what's happening to you wherever it is you are?'

'They keep coming for me,' she said, her voice a stammering whisper, her head twitching this way and that, terrified that someone was going to creep up on her.

'Who keeps coming for you?' I asked.

'I don't know,' she replied, barely keeping it together enough to speak. 'They want me, Joe. They said... they said they're going to eat what's left of me, and then that'll be that. I won't even have an afterlife. You've got to get me out of here!'

I pressed my hand against the mirror, wishing I could push through and grab hold of her, pull her back into this world, make her safe.

'I'll ask Eva. Make her help.'

'She won't help. You know that. It has to be you, Joe. I know you can help me. You can help me, and then we can finally leave this behind and be together. Properly together, forever.'

I saw a blur of movement to her left and pulled away from the mirror in surprise. 'What is that?'

'They've found me! Please, Joe, please be quick! I know you have the power to help me.'

'Chloe!'

She turned and ran as I slapped the cold surface of the mirror.

'You'll never believe it.'

I jumped at the voice and turned to find Malden standing in the doorway, shaking his head. I looked back to the mirror, but there was no sign of Chloe, of whatever it was that was after her.

'Go on,' said Malden, 'never in a million years will you believe me.'

I turned back to him and sighed. 'What won't I believe?'

'Guess who's about to clock up his fifth solids deposit of the night?' He pointed at himself, then shook his head. 'What a crazy, crazy day.'

He chuckled as he shuffled over to the toilet stall. I gave a last glance into the mirror, my heart beating way too fast, and left in search of a drink.

I joined Eva, downing half of my pint in one.

'Oh, now we're talking,' said Eva, rubbing her hands together. 'Big boy drinking time, is it, love?' She raised her glass high. 'To Malden's fifth shit of the evening,' and then she downed her drink before pulling out her tobacco tin and rolling a fresh smoke.

'Another two over here, Grunt,' said Eva, waving her hand at the barman.

'So, Elga and her Kin... who were they exactly?'

'Beats me. Before my time. We could go back to the coven,

search through all those boring books and see if there's any record of them, or...'

'Or...?'

'Or I could do some more potentially dangerous fucking with your brain.'

'More?'

'Yeah, like with the magic amplification trick I banged together to take care of all those bastard soul vampires the other day. Sorted those fuckers out, but forcing me through you left you with a bit of brain damage. Won't be able to pull that trick again.'

'I'm sorry... brain damage? You gave me brain damage?'

'You probably won't even notice it considering how fucked that lump of shite between your ears is anyway.'

Grunt placed a couple of fresh pints before us.

'Thank you, garçon,' said Eva. 'Grunt, how's the magic-dampening in here?'

'Is good,' grunted Grunt.

'Should be possible to do a little bit of memory work, though, right? Only I can't be fucked to go outside to do it, not with us getting so comfy here.'

'Is possible.'

'Nice one.'

Grunt moved away as Eva somehow inhaled a lungful from her cigarette and took a gulp from her pint at the same time.

'Magic-dampening?'

'Oh yeah. All of these holes employ a bit of the old magic-dampening. Imagine two Uncannies in here, loaded up and pissed off. Not a happy end to that story. So these places sit in a dampening bubble. They don't stop magic entirely, but it stops anything too naughty going down.'

That certainly made sense. Flying fists were one thing, but literal flying while two pissed up blokes lobbed fireballs at each other would definitely constitute an issue.

'Okay, then,' said Eva, 'seeing as—for once—you know

more than me, I'm going to see if I can rattle a memory or two loose.'

'How are you going to do that?' I asked.

'With great fucking difficulty.' She reached out, placed the tips of her thumbs on my temples, and closed her eyes.

'What should I do?'

'Just think about Elga and her Kin. Think about that title, and think about those stones. I'll try and throw a rope in and see if anything climbs up.'

'Right. Okay. Thinking now.'

And so I did. I closed my eyes and thought that name, over and over like a mantra. At first, nothing happened, but then Eva's fingers began to feel hot. The temperature slowly rose until it felt like my skin was burning. My whole face. My whole head, in fact.

'Eva.'

'Shh, I'm getting something.'

The temperature rose higher and I felt myself pulling away.

'Stay still, idiot.'

'I can't.'

'Aha! Got something.'

'Eva, that's starting to hurt.'

'Well, this is gonna hurt a fuck-tonne more.'

'What is?'

I opened my eyes in time to see Eva pull a fist back and throw it at my head.

She was not lying. It hurt like a mother-shitting bastard, though not in the way I was expecting. Rather than her fist connecting with my nose—her knuckles cracking bone and me falling back off the stool and onto the floor—Eva's hand passed through my face and into my head. You could say it was like her hand had become ghost-like, insubstantial, only I felt it. I felt jagged shards of pain shoot through every bit of me. I'm pretty sure I was screaming by that point. I mean, you would, wouldn't you?

Then I saw them.

Elga and her Kin.

It was night and I entered the dark place with Lyna and Melodia either side of me. They were waiting for us, Elga at the front, her head encased in a goat mask, a freshly torn-out heart in her hand, blood dripping through her fingers.

'Elga!' I heard myself say, only it didn't sound quite like me. There was a different flavour to the voice. I looked down and saw my hands throbbing with power, with fire, and—

The picture skipped, on to another memory, another shard. A jumble of shards. Dead bodies strewn across the ground, broken, hundreds of them. No, thousands. Tens of thousands. Generations torn apart by Elga and her Kin; unstoppable. But then there we were again, the three of us, the three that stop the unstoppable.

But only just.

Only just.

I could see Lyna, see Melodia, battered, bodies criss-crossed with wounds, exhaustion ready to take them down.

'Janto,' said Melodia, her voice a weak whisper. 'Stop them. You have to stop them.'

I blinked and the visions, the memories were over. I was still at the table, Eva wiping her hand with a napkin, Malden sat opposite.

'Did... did it work?'

'Sort of. I definitely saw the twats, but nothing exactly useful. Apart from seeing how strong they are. Fuckers nearly wiped you three out. That's some crazy, next-level power, that.'

I reached for my drink, hand trembling, and took a sip, spilling a little down my chin.

'Did you put your hand inside my head?'

'Sort of. Also sort of not. Spells can be complicated, know what I mean?'

'I really don't.'

'Yeah, sorry. Forgot who I was dealing with, love.'

Malden raised his hand, 'If you're interested, that was a mission aborted on my end. From my end. A false alarm.'

'Better luck next time,' said Eva.

'I still have the memories in my head,' I said. 'The memories you shook loose.'

Eva shrugged. 'Yeah, well, you would, wouldn't you?'

'Couldn't you have done that before?'

'Could have, yeah, but it hurts me more than it hurts you, and it hurts you like a motherfucker.'

'But you could help me remember more about my past, about me. Not just me hearing about things, but actually experiencing them, knowing them. You could do that with your ghosty fist trick, there, yes?'

'Yes.'

I laughed and clapped my hands together.

'Not gonna, though.'

'What? Why not?'

'Neither you nor I want you remembering any of that shit. You don't want to remember being Janto.'

'Of course, I do!'

Eva met my gaze. I saw fear in her eyes, saw sadness, just for a moment. She looked away. 'Trust me. You don't.'

There followed a silence so heavy it could crush a diamond.

'Well,' said Malden, breaking the tension, 'unless my arse is playing silly beggars again, it looks like number five is a go after all.'

22

I left Eva and Malden to it shortly after that. It was late—beyond late—and I had a shift the next day. I'd also had a bellyful of being awake.

I left the Uncanny Wagon at the entrance to the blind alley and made my way on foot through the empty, silent streets of Keswick, the night air crisp and soothing against my skin.

For those of you keeping score, I now had three seemingly insurmountable problems pressing against me...

There was Elga and her Kin, who were apparently some sort of deadly, ancient killer cult buried under a bunch of murderous standing stones. From the flashes of memory Eva had teased out, it didn't look like they were going to be as easy to deal with as the soul vampires. Especially as the amplification trick Eva employed that time was now off the table (I tried not to think too much about the brain damage revelation – there's only so much awful a man can deal with at any one time. Ah, self-delusion is a wonderful thing).

Then there was the fact I now owed my eternal soul to a bunch of very competitive demons who were in a hurry to facilitate my untimely demise.

Last but not least? Chloe. I'm a glass-half-full sort of a

person most of the time, and I like to think the best of people, even rotten buggers. I knew Chloe long before her bad side made a show, and she did seem to have an excuse for that. Provided I believed her about the spirit of her dead dad possessing her, anyway. I mean, that sounded plausible, right? We've all seen parents living out their failed ambitions through their offspring. And I knew Chloe. I was sure of it. I'd spent years with her, laughing with her, whiling away the hours, becoming closer. She couldn't have been hiding a dark side like that the whole time, surely? No, I had to believe her, had to give her the benefit of the doubt. I was going to try and save her, and I had an idea how to go about it. I just needed to have a word with a certain talking, axe-wielding fox.

'Hello?' I said as I walked one of Keswick's backstreets. 'Hello, Mr Fox, are you there?'

I wasn't sure how it worked exactly—whether he watched me the whole time—but since the little blighter seemed to be able to pop up at will, I thought maybe if I asked nicely, he'd appear. Not much of a plan, no, but it was all I had. I could hardly ask Eva to put me in touch with the fox, could I? She'd made it quite clear what she'd do if she found me messing around with the Dark Lakes.

'Mr Fox, Mr Fox, this is the Magic Eater, please pick up if you're in.' I snorted, laughing at the ridiculousness of it all.

I cupped my hands around my mouth. 'The Magic Eater will see you now!'

A noise off to my right, something down a creepy, darkened alley.

'Hello? Is that you in there?'

Could it be the fox? He did favour a surprise appearance. Of course, it could also just be some poor, rough sleeper, roused from his slumber by an idiot yelling nonsense in the middle of the night.

Another noise. A shuffling.

'Fox, is that you in there?'

I walked slowly toward the mouth of the alley. This wasn't of the magical, blind variety. This was your common or garden, rubbish-strewn sliver tucked between two buildings. A likely spot for a man caught short, or for someone to do something not exactly above board, out of sight of any passersby.

'Hey, Mr Fox, it's me. You know, the saviour.'

I took a couple of steps into the alley, squinting to adjust to the drop in visibility. A movement, just ahead by the large rusted bins.

'Hello?'

Was that fur? I was sure I could see fur poking up over the lip of the bin.

'It is you! You're not usually so reticent to shoot your mouth off,' I said, relaxing as I walked forward. As it turned out, relaxing was a mistake.

What I saw when I looked behind the bin was not a fox stood on its hind legs, a Roman military helmet perched upon its head. What I saw was a rat.

A big rat.

A rat the size of a large family dog.

Its yellow eyes were fixed to mine. Large, jagged teeth dripping with saliva chattered in my direction. I'm no expert when it comes to rats, but I was fairly certain that what I was seeing was somewhat on the impossibly large side. I began to slowly back away from the thing, my stomach churning.

'There, there,' I said as the rat thrashed its thick tail back and forth. 'No need to, you know, sink those disgusting teeth into my neck or anything.'

'Ours!' hissed the giant rat.

I stopped in surprise. 'I beg your pardon?'

'Ours! Ours! Ours!'

Oh. And ah. And oh shit.

One of the demons was trying to call in the debt. I turned to bolt from the alley and back into the street, only to pull up short, almost falling over my feet as I forced my body to suddenly stop moving forward. The entrance to the alley now had three more oversized rats sat in it, blocking my escape.

'Ours!' they said as one. 'Ours! Ours! Ours!'

Rats to the front of me, a rat to the side, all ready to rip me apart so a demon could reach in and pluck out my soul. Well, balls to that.

I turned and ran to the other end of the alley, the heavy-footed rats thundering across the cobbles after me, screaming their claim on me over and over.

Of course, the alley led only to a dead end. Of course.

'Shit! Shit it!'

I turned, my back pressed against the crumbling brickwork. It wasn't even a wall I could scramble over, it was a three-storey building. No sign of a window to smash my way through. I was trapped, and the rats knew it. All four of them had stopped their hurry and now slowly, oh so slowly, padded toward me, relishing my fear, their long nails scraping the ground like knives.

I held out my hand, palm up, doing my best to ignore how much it was trembling, and tried to think hot thoughts.

'Come on, come on. I'm magic, very magic. It's time to actually do some shitting magic!'

The rats chittered, apparently amused as I tried to wriggle my way out of my untimely end. They were moments away from rushing me, sinking their rotten teeth into my flesh, spilling my blood across the black cobbles.

'Ours! Ours!'

'Come on, hot thoughts. Fire, flames, come on!'

I strained, I gritted my teeth, but nothing was happening. It wasn't going to work.

I heard a low chuckle that made me feel as though the ground was about to disappear and I would fall, fall, fall. It wasn't a natural chuckle.

I could see a shape near the mouth of the alley; an indistinct, grey shape against the black. It moved slowly, step by step, closer and closer. It was the demon: the one responsible for these rats. It must have been. It was here to enjoy its victory. It had won, and my soul would be his. Not any of the other demons who Annie had promised hers to. His.

The magic wasn't happening. This was it. Come in, Joseph Lake, Janto the warlock, Magic Eater, your time is up. Apart from the time I was going to spend being tormented in Hell, anyway.

I shifted and something metal attached to the wall on my right glinted in the moonlight. A metal ladder. A fire escape. A Joseph escape! No time to consider what to do next – I ran and leapt for the bottom rung of the ladder. There was no way the rats would be able to make the leap up to follow. It would have worked, too, if it wasn't for my lousy, some would say non-existent, upper-body strength.

I dangled from the ladder, legs bicycling as I strained to pull myself up. The rats screeched as they pogoed into the air, teeth scraping at my boots. I kicked them away, straining at the ladder, urging myself on. My whole body was shaking, limp as wet lettuce. I wasn't going to make it.

No.

I refused to die in some Keswick back alley. One more push would do it. That's all. I was so close. Just a little higher and I'd be out of there. Come on, Joseph. You can do this!

Except, I really couldn't.

My aching, sweaty fingers lost purchase, and I fell to the ground below, cracking the back of my skull on a cobble. Stars exploded in my head, dancing among the very real ones that shone down from the night sky.

Foiled. Cause of death: massive rats and lack of a gym membership.

I could hear the demon laughing, no longer a chuckle, now an unhinged screech of hysterics. It was a sound that pissed me right off. I sat up, grimacing. I touched the damp area on the back of my head and found my hair slick with blood.

‘Fuck you,’ I said. ‘Fuck you right up the fucker.’

And then, without forcing it, without thinking about what I was doing at all, I reached out both hands and flames burst from them, rolling down the alley, filling it, burning the screaming rats to black ash.

23

I awoke, head throbbing, eyes gummed and bleary, tongue replaced with a sheet of sandpaper.

How I made it home was a mystery. I looked at my phone. It was midday already. I sat up, happy to discover that I'd placed a glass of water next to the bed, and downed the lot. Water had never tasted so good.

I tenderly touched the back of my head. The hair was matted, and there was a gash there, too, but my tender probing suggested it wouldn't need stitches. So that was good.

I stood, a little wobbly, and staggered to the shower, letting the water run colder than usual as it bashed some life into me.

I'd done that.

Magic.

The demon sent a pack of giant rats to take me down, and I messed those suckers up with flames that shot from my hands. I looked down at them. They didn't look any different, but I knew better.

Eva hadn't helped me that time. That had been all me. I created fire from nothing. I couldn't help but feel a little, well, hugely bloody thrilled. That's what I was, what I really was: a witch, a warlock, and I had, off my own back—without help—made magic happen.

Maybe soon, I'd be able to do it whenever I wanted. Whenever I needed.

I dried, dressed, and grabbed a bowl of Rice Krispies. Eva had left a text reminding me that we'd agreed to pay Elga and her Kin another visit that night. Hopefully, she had some kind of a plan as the group I'd seen in the jumble of old memories were absolutely not going to be a pushover, flamey hands or no flamey hands.

The most pressing matter on my mind was not the stone circle, though, or the previous night's magical outburst, nor even the fact that I had several demons after my soul. No, the most important thing on my mind was Chloe. I had to find a way to get back to the Dark Lakes, and sharpish. For all I knew, it was already too late.

With that in mind, one of the first things I did after I arrived at Carlisle Hospital for my shift was make a beeline for the bathroom and look in the mirror. She never appeared when I wanted her to, she'd always surprise me by suddenly just being there, but I had to try and find out how she was doing. The last time, in the bathroom mirror at Mickey Finn's, she hadn't looked good at all.

I checked all of the stalls were empty and went to the mirror. All I saw was me looking back.

'Chloe? Chloe, are you there? Can you hear me?'

I asked for ten full minutes, but there was no sign of her.

As my shift came to an end and the sky was beginning to darken, I made my way to Annie's bedside to pay a visit.

'Well, look who's looking at least eighty percent better,' I said as I pulled a chair over and sat by her bed. It was true. She seemed so much more alive, so much brighter than she had before.

'Joe!' she chirped. 'I was starting to think you'd forgotten about me.'

'What, the woman who I recently—rather heroically, some might say stupidly—took a death sentence from? Fat chance.'

Annie's smile dropped and I realised what a stupid thing that had been to say. In my defence, I make a habit of saying stupid things.

'It's okay,' I said in my best cheery voice, 'you didn't make me do anything I didn't want to.'

Looking at Annie closer now, it really was remarkable how quickly her banged-up body was healing.

'I know what you're thinking,' she said, touching the cheek that was bruised the last time I saw her, 'this was another of the things I sold my soul for. I was eight and fed up that I kept getting sick, so I went down the well and asked that I get better faster. Heal quickly.'

'Why didn't you just ask never to get sick or hurt?'

'That's exactly what a more forward-thinking eight-year-old would have done. But then, a more forward-thinking person wouldn't have sold their soul to a bunch of demons.'

'You make a good point, Annie.'

'How's it been?' she asked, trying to smile even if her eyes looked watery.

'Great. Well, nothing deadly, yet,' I said, choosing not to bring up the previous night's giant rat assault.

'Are you lying to me, Joe?'

'Never.'

She stared at me, willing me to break, but I held firm. 'Any luck getting rid of the debt?'

'I've been busy with some killer stones, but it's next on my list. Well, next to next on my list.'

'What could be more important than making sure a demon doesn't kill you?'

'Normally, I would agree with you, but I'm in the habit of putting myself in the sniper's scope for women in distress, and I've got another one on the docket. The difference this time is that it's my fault, and I need to right that wrong.'

Don't I sound noble as all hell?

'Who are you trying to impress?' asked Annie.

'The girl. Myself. It does mean doing something very, very dumb, though.'

'Dumber than making yourself the target of a demon hunt?'

'Yeah, I think so. No one could ever accuse me of being smart, eh?'

Annie laughed. 'Maybe not. But kind. I think I could accuse you of that, right enough.'

Talking with Annie had cheered me up a little. Seeing the good I'd done distracted me from how stupid it had been, and how I was likely going to do something off-the-scale stupid.

If only I could get a hold of that bloody fox.

Of course, I found him waiting for me in the passenger seat of the Uncanny Wagon.

'All hail the saviour!'

'Where were you last night?' I asked, starting up the engine and pulling out of the hospital car park.

'Last night? Time has no place in the Dark Lakes. Day and night, no such thing.'

'How do you know when you're supposed to sleep?' I asked.

'I dunno. When I'm tired?'

'Makes sense. So why are you here now?'

'You called, I came.'

'I called about sixteen hours ago before a pack of massive mutant rats attacked me!'

'Eh?'

'Never mind,' I sighed. 'Listen, I have a question for you.'

'I may answer, I may not,' replied the fox with a haughty sniff. 'I am not your answer fox.'

'How amenable is the Red Woman when it comes to granting favours?'

The fox looked at me with an extremely confused expression upon its furry face. He then, rather annoyingly, burst into great gales of laughter. The kind of laughter that makes tears run down your cheeks. Or in this case, wet the fur of your cheeks.

'You know that's pretty obnoxious?' I said.

'Favour? Is that what you have asked me?'

'I take it that the answer is, "Not at all", right?'

'What kind of favour would you even ask of her?' he said, the fit of laughter at last breaking.

'I want to bring someone back from the dead,' I replied.

24

I pulled up close to the location of Elga and her Kin and found Eva and Myers waiting by the detective's car. I waved as I approached.

'So what is it we're hoping to do tonight?' I asked.

Eva sipped from a can of cheap lager, and I wondered for a moment where she got the money to pay for her endless supply of booze and tobacco. I also wondered if she was ever sober.

'We continue the investigation that I'm in charge of,' replied Myers. 'Tonight we're going to ask the suspect a few questions.'

'Suspect?' I replied. 'They're a bit more than *suspect*.'

'Procedure,' said Myers. 'We follow this properly and assume nothing until we have the facts.'

I was going to ask a few how's and what's when I was interrupted by Eva, who coughed and fired beer out of her nostrils in a very unladylike manner.

'Whoa there,' said Myers, patting her on the back.

'You,' said Eva, pointing at me.

'Yes, it's me. Hello.'

Eva waggled a pointy finger at me. 'You did magic, didn't you?'

'How do you...?'

'How do I know? I can see it on you. I can smell it!'

'Well, I suppose I might have done a bit of magic.'

'Is that something to celebrate?' asked Myers. 'I feel like it's something we're supposed to be celebrating.'

'Firey hands, wasn't it?' asked Eva. 'A bit of the old *pew-pew.*' She mimed firing twin guns into the air, actual flames exploding like bullets from her fingertips.

This was the first time I'd seen Eva actually being pleased for me. It was almost as disconcerting as talking to a demon at the bottom of a well.

Almost.

'Yup. Still not sure how I did it exactly, but I did.'

Eva's face fell a little. 'Wait, why were you doing firey *pew-pew* hands?'

Because I have a bunch of demons clamouring to claim my soul.

'I was... having a gentleman's wee in an alley. A rat startled me and flames shot out.'

'Flames shot out of your...' Myers nodded to my crotch.

'No! No. Just my hands. Which, thankfully, were not touching my penis at the time.'

Eva narrowed her eyes at me. It seemed she wasn't buying what I was selling, but luckily for me, she's a flighty one, and Myers was there to unwittingly nudge her off course.

'Enough small talk,' she said. 'I'm on duty here, which means the both of you are, too.'

Eva replied with the most sarcastic salute you or anyone else has ever witnessed. It's difficult to describe just how devastatingly sarcastic it was, so just take my word for it.

'I have my regulation extendable baton on me,' said Myers.

'Oh, good. I've gone weeks without a solid spanking. Shall we?' Eva pointed to the location of the still-invisible night circle and wandered ahead as Myers looked to me and sighed.

'I hear you... sister?' I tried.

'Don't do that.'

'Right you are. That didn't feel good.'

Suitably chastised, I stepped in beside the detective and followed Eva.

'So. Magic, huh?' said Myers. 'You really did that? On your own?'

'I really did. It's sort of... exciting, I suppose.'

'You know, the stickler side of me is kind of uneasy about you two.'

'Oh? Is it because we're such bad-arses?'

Myers rolled her eyes. It was well deserved.

'You two are basically unlicensed firearms. Not to mention vigilantes, if I go by the book. And I've always been a big fan of the book.'

'I've got a book for you,' said Eva over her shoulder. 'It's called *Let Eva Do What the Fuck She Wants, But Feel Free to Arrest the Idiot*. It's a page-turner and a half, that one. Rave reviews in all the posh press.'

'What I'm saying is, I'm allowing you both to do what you are doing because it needs to be done, and it's an area the police can't walk into. But I want you to know that I'm allowing it, and I set the boundaries.'

'Right,' I replied. 'Got it. Understood.'

'Good.'

'Is it wrong that I like it when you're stern?'

'I also have a Taser on me.'

'Oi!' said Eva, waving us forward. 'It's starting.'

We caught up and saw the stone circle shimmer into view once again.

'Yep,' said Myers, 'that isn't any less freaky the second time around.'

'So what's the plan, exactly?' I asked, trying not to have any of the stones in my blind spots for longer than a few seconds at a time.

'The plan is to have a chat, and hopefully blow these fuckers up,' said Eva. 'It's a pretty solid plan, yes?'

We stood in silence for almost twenty seconds looking at the stones. Nothing much happened. Or, to put it another way, nothing at all happened. Finally, I heard a soft snoring to my right.

'Did she just fall asleep on us?' asked Myers, not turning to look.

Eva was, indeed, asleep. Stood upright, can of beer still gripped in one hand.

'Eva?' I said tentatively.

Snore.

'Eva!' said Myers, very much not tentatively.

Eva's eyes snapped open. 'What happened? Did we win? Was I very brave and sexy and brave?'

'How exactly are you going to talk to them?' asked Myers, ploughing on through.

'Well, they're under there, somewhere,' said Eva, wandering closer to a stone and patting it like a favoured pet. 'Headstones is what Malden said, so it stands to reason each marks where either Elga or one of her Kin are buried.'

'So they're dead?' I said. 'As in, dead. Not alive.'

'Dead. Undead. Between alive and dead. It's all a spectrum, love. Doesn't mean life stops.'

Eva didn't know how much I hoped that was true.

'Okay, so they're dead or half-dead,' said Myers. 'How are you gonna chat to them?'

'Magic request,' replied Eva, dropping her trousers, squatting down, and taking a thunderous piss on the grass.

It went on for some time and was accompanied by a series of sighs and groans of satisfaction that made me feel more than a little grossed out. Finally, she grabbed a fistful of grass, wiped her... lady bits then stood and pulled her pants up.

'That should do it,' she said.

'Assuming the answer isn't just, "Because you're insane and disgusting", why should that do it?' asked Myers.

Eva looked at her, incredulous, then to me, pulling a, “Do you believe this idiot?” face. ‘Piss magic.’

‘Piss magic?’ I repeated.

‘They’re under the soil, so I put the magical request into my piss, took a slash, and right now it’s soaking its way towards whoever’s down there. They’ll get the message any second now.’

‘You know, it’s at times like these that I’m not sure how much of this I should take seriously,’ said Myers.

Eva pulled out a smoke and lit it. She had her back to the stones, which meant she didn’t see what Myers and I saw next.

A hand.

A hand pushing its way out of the earth.

What was left of a hand, anyway. There was no flesh, just ragged scraps of skin and sinew clinging to weathered bones.

‘Um, Eva…?’ I started.

‘Up already, eh,’ she said. ‘Nice of a host not to keep their guests waiting. Just ‘cos you’re a murdering zombie bastard, doesn’t mean you can’t have decent manners.’ She flicked the remains of her ciggie into the distance and turned on her heel to face the emerging… thing. ‘Hello there, love. I’m Eva, that’s Myers, and that twat over here is Joseph. We’re here to ask what in the name of fuck it is you think you’re doing.’

The corpse wore a dark crimson robe, soil crumbling from it as it stepped fully out of the ground. Its head was covered by a large mask fashioned to look like a goat. Basically, your classic satanic cult look.

‘Oi, wanker, you listening or do I have to make you?’ asked Eva, taking a few steps in its direction.

‘Careful,’ I said, but she waved me back, smiling, not at all concerned.

The corpse raised a hand and pointed to me. ‘Warlock.’

Not sure what to do, and attempting to ignore my body’s treacherous trembling, I smiled and gave a little bow. ‘Hello.

Yes, that's me. I believe we have met before, though my memory recently is a little, well, let's say *hazy*.'

Myers stepped forward, baton in hand. 'How about you fill us in on why you're sending stones out to kill people?'

'Uncanny people at that,' added Eva.

'Because we can,' said the corpse, its voice a dry scrape. 'Because we must. Because life shall return and death shall follow us as we step out into this new world.'

More movement in the ground as, in front of each of the twenty-nine remaining stones, hands began to push out of the earth.

'Looks like the whole family's up,' said Myers.

'I am Elga, and I shall lead my Kin back into life. Back into a life that you,' she stated, punctuating the word with a bony finger jabbed in my direction, 'you and your unworthy witches took from us. The stones bring us power, bring us life, and we shall drink until we break the bonds placed upon us and step back into the world of the living to take our rightful place as gods.'

'You're a real talker for a dead bastard, aren't you?' said Eva.

Elga's masked head twisted sharply. 'We will eat our way through all of you,' she hissed. 'Drink down your power to put flesh on our bones.'

'What if you just, I don't know, didn't do that?' I suggested. 'It sounds like a lot of hard work. What if you just didn't kill anyone and carried on being dead? Or sort of dead. Whatever it is that you and your friends are.'

Each member of the circle raised their hands to point at me and began to speak as one. 'You, the last remaining witch of Cumbria, last remaining member of the three that took our lives, our freedom, our future from us. Could not kill us entirely, instead, reduced us to this. Trapped until ten years ago, when your coven fell and the barriers became weak enough for us to push through.'

I glanced at Eva, but she was too busy yawning to react. Ten years ago, when the coven fell, when I lost my memory.

'Over the last decade, we clawed our way back into being. At first, we were just thoughts. Ideas. An ache of nothingness. We had to be patient, but piece by piece, we forced our way back into reality.'

'Ah, so that's why the attacks are increasing,' said Eva.

'As every night fell, we became more. And then, finally, the stones responded to our demands. Now we cannot be stopped.'

'If you're so powerful, why only send out one stone at a time?' I asked.

'Good point,' added Myers.

'I'll tell you why,' said Eva. 'It's because they're all mouth and no trousers. They're still too weak, which means they can be beaten.'

'Oh, well that's good news,' I said. 'Big fan of good news, me.'

Elga hissed. 'We shall drain you dry and curse your soul forevermore, warlock.'

Little did they know that there was currently a bit of a queue for my soul.

'I've got some bad news,' said Eva, 'for you and the rest of the Addams Family here. Do you wanna know what it is?'

'What?'

'Me, motherfucker.'

Eva's hands burst into flames. She hurled globe after globe of burning power in the direction of the cult until the view was entirely obscured by fire and smoke. Finally, she stopped and blew the tips of her index fingers.

'You can pick your jaws up off the ground now,' she told us smugly.

Unfortunately, Eva had spoken a wee bit too soon. With a yelp of surprise, she was lifted from the ground by an unseen force and tossed in the direction of my car. The smoke cleared to reveal Elga and her Kin, perfectly unharmed. All that magic, all that that power, and it hadn't even touched them.

'I think maybe we should retreat,' suggested Myers, baton twitching in her hand.

'Well, you did say you were in charge, and I always respect authority.'

'Death will come for you,' boomed Elga. 'Death shall come for all.'

'Yup, I think we've more or less got the picture,' I replied, and with that, Myers and I beat a hasty retreat to the road. We found Eva sprawled across the roof of the Uncanny Wagon. I'd say I was upset about the dent she created, but after the beating it had taken recently, I couldn't see the difference.

'Are you okay?' asked Myers, helping Eva to the ground.

'Fit as a fiddle,' she groaned.

'So,' I said, 'they're still pretty strong, eh?'

Eva nodded. 'That, "Me, motherfucker", bit would have gone over way better if they hadn't handed me my arse, right?'

That was definitely true.

25

Myers left to drop Eva off at the coven. Eva was being her usual self, but I'd been around her long enough to see that she wasn't as blasé about the situation as she'd have liked us to believe. She was worried. Very worried.

It wasn't difficult to see why. The sort-of-dead cult, Elga and her Kin, were already too strong for her to just brush off. To barrage with fire and magic. Eva had thrown her best at them and hadn't even scorched their scarlet robes. Which was a bit of a pisser. I mean, that's going to knock anyone's confidence.

They were too strong for her to tackle head-on. If the fragments of memory I'd seen had taught me anything, it was that Elga and her Kin were almost more powerful than the Cumbrian Coven when the three of us were at full strength. Now they were on the rise again, and there was only one witch left. Just me. And I could barely work up a flame when I wanted to.

Yeah. Bit of a shitty wicket.

Eva said she'd search the coven's library, that there were bound to be spells, records that would sort the situation out lickety-split. Can't say I felt too confident about that. But there was more than just worry on my mind as I steered the Uncanny Wagon back to Keswick, back to my flat. There was the message I'd tasked the fox with delivering to the Red Woman.

What exactly did I think she'd want in return for her help? I thought I knew, but I'd deal with that when it came to it. My mind was too clouded by the burning desire to help Chloe—to pull her back from whatever limbo I'd banished her to—to dwell on what the consequences of asking the Dark Lakes for help might be. Just like Annie, I wasn't a very forward-thinking person.

Or even a thinking person.

I looked in the rearview mirror and saw a pair of eyes looking back at me.

'Chloe!'

I instinctively looked over my shoulder expecting her to be sat in the back of the car, but of course, the seat was empty. I returned to the mirror to find Chloe, still there, slowly fading from view.

'Please, Joe. I'm almost all gone... almost all...'

'Chloe, hang on! Just a little longer, please!'

As my heart beat a furious tattoo in my chest, Chloe disappeared from view. I gripped the steering wheel, teeth clamped. I was running out of time. Chloe was running out of time.

'Fox, where are you?' I said, bashing the steering wheel with the heel of my hand.

So preoccupied was I with my thoughts, that I didn't notice the van hurtling towards me. Its front end clipped the back of my car and sent me in a spin. My head bounced off the driver's side window, and bright lights exploded in my vision as the car shuddered to a stop.

'Ouch,' I said.

There was a frantic knocking on the passenger door, then a wide-eyed man bending over to look at me. 'Sorry mate, sorry!'

I smiled weakly and held up a hand, opening the door and stepping out.

'Sorry. Van went fucking mad, I swear. Weren't my fault.'

The skin on the back of my neck began to prickle. The thing I'd taken from Annie, the debt, I could feel it growing heavier inside of me.

'Oh shit,' I said, looking around.

'Honest. Van suddenly lurched forward, like, and the brakes wouldn't work. You all right?'

'Get back in your van.'

'What?'

'I'm fine, I forgive you, it wasn't your fault. I think a demon took control of your vehicle to knock me off the road.'

The man, not unreasonably, looked at me like I was a shitting lunatic. 'I think you might have bashed your head, mate,' he said.

'Probably. Actually, definitely. But don't worry, you can go.'

The man resorted to looking merely confused. 'What about insurance? Don't you wanna swap details?'

I had been trying to get rid of him before whatever was about to happen happened, but he was being rather stubborn about the Get Out of Jail Free card I was waggling fiercely in front of him. And so, of course, a wolf showed up.

'Is that... is that a wolf?' asked the man, looking into the field beyond me.

I turned to see what appeared to be the same animal that had attacked Annie while I was down the well. Only the man was wrong.

'No,' I replied, 'that appears to be six wolves.'

Five more melted out of the gloom to join the first, teeth bared in saliva-dripping snarls.

'I might actually go now if that's okay,' said the man.

'Quite okay.'

He jumped back into his van, the wheels kicking up dirt as he hurriedly reversed away. I would have done the same—clambered back inside the Uncanny Wagon and left this out-of-place wolf pack far behind—but as I pulled the handle, the door refused to open.

The wolves howled as I swore, then one bolted towards me. I scampered to the next door and tried the handle. No dice.

'Shit, shit, shit.'

Round to the other side, both doors, same story. Whichever demon was making a play for my soul this time, he wasn't taking any chances. I considered legging it but quickly realised what a stupid and short-lived gambit that would be. Instead, I ran up the back end of the car and scrambled on to the roof, removing a boot to use as a weapon. Yes, I'm sure I'd have no problem seeing off six hellhounds on a mission to tear me to pieces using a worn-out old boot.

The wolves circled my poor car, growling at me, in no rush. They knew it was all done but for the actual eating me part.

'Piss off, you toothy bastards,' I said, waggling my boot.

I thought back to the alley, the rats, and balled my right hand, trying to find some of the old magic. The car rocked, almost sending me tumbling from the roof and to the ground below, a tasty-treat for the jaws beneath.

One of the wolves leapt up on the car bonnet, its front paws on the windscreen. 'Ours!' it said. 'Ours! Ours! Ours!'

I swung my boot, catching the animal flush on the nose. It fell yelping off the car.

'Who's next?' I yelled, brandishing my footwear at the other wolves. 'Fire hand, fire hand.'

Sparks and sputters of flame danced into life for a half-second at a time above my palm, but nothing held.

'Firey-firey-fire-hand!' I screamed, and laughed in surprise as a globe of magic, of white-hot flame, appeared, spitting with fury.

'I did it! I bloody well did it!'

And then one of the wolves barged forcefully into the side of the Uncanny Wagon. The impact sent me off balance and tumbling to the ground, where I landed heavily on my right shoulder. The magic puttered out, my boot spun away, and my lungs refused to do their job properly.

I rolled onto my back—throat desperately trying to force air in the right direction—and saw three sets of giant, hungry teeth hove into view above me.

I would have said, "Oh shit", or something to that effect, but I was still struggling to take a breath, never mind speak. My number was pretty much up at this point. I'd done a daft, reckless thing taking on Annie's debt—not to mention keeping that information from Eva—and now here I was. The debt was being called in. My throat was about to be made a chew toy for a pack of wolves, and a demon would step in to pluck my soul out of the mess they left behind.

Well, at least I'd die doing something nice. Something kind. Or I would have if a small fox hadn't jumped into the fray, laughing like a loon as he went at the wolves with his two-headed battle-axe.

I sat up sharply, pushing myself back until I rested against the car, finally managing to take in some shallow breaths as the fox deftly defended himself. The wolves attempted to swamp the small, fierce thing but failed miserably. Beast after beast fell, their blood and guts flying across my vision as the fox sunk his axe into stomachs, ribs, and skulls. Finally, the last wolf collapsed, its back legs giving a final spasmodic kick before the fox raised his axe high and swung it into the creature's brain with a mighty battle cry.

The fox wiped dark red gore from his axe using the fur of one of the fallen wolves, then wandered over to me.

'All hail the saviour,' I said. Or rather, wheezed.

26

The blazing sky of the Dark Lakes opened up above me.

'Cheers for the assist,' I said, thanking the fox again for his timely intervention.

'Doing demon work, those wolves,' said the fox. 'Sneaky demons.'

We were stood atop the red hill. The same hill that the throne fashioned from skulls sat upon. The throne made of skulls that I was, apparently, fated to take as my own.

'So... where is she?' I asked.

'Hm?'

'The Red Woman. I take it that's why you came to find me.'

'Oh yes, that's it.'

'Well?'

I felt an ice-cold hand snake around my waist.

'Here I am, dearest,' said the Red Woman, her voice a purr in my ear.

I stepped away from her grasp with a shiver and turned to face her. She smiled, and for once the smile seemed to reach her eyes.

'It seems you cannot stay away from here,' she said,

running a finger across the arm of the throne. 'Perhaps you're ready to take your rightful place after all?'

I dithered, shuffling from foot to foot, uncertain as to what it was I was going to ask.

The Red Women narrowed her eyes at me. 'You have demons on your tail.'

'I'll do anything to impress a woman,' I replied.

She shook her head and tutted. 'So cavalier. That's the Janto I remember. So eager to dive into the new. The unknown. The dangerous.'

'Tell me something...' I said.

'...Anything.'

'Why did I make the choice to join you back then? Back when I was Janto the warlock.'

She took a seat upon the throne and slowly crossed her legs, her fingers gripping the armrests. 'Because you wanted to know what true power felt like. What it meant to be a god.'

Well, didn't Janto the warlock sound like an overachieving prick?

The fox nudged me with his axe. 'I told her your wants,' he said.

'Oh, a warlock who wants. Déjà vu, yes?' said the Red Woman.

'There's a woman. A dead woman. Or a maybe dead woman. I killed her, I think. It's all a bit confusing, but she's talking to me in mirrors.'

'In mirrors?' repeated the Red Woman.

'Yeah. Bit mad, I know, and no one else seems to see her, but I think she's real and I want to help her.'

'I see. You believe her to be trapped between realms? Between life and death? Between this short, ugly existence and the next?'

'Yes. Well, I think so. I'm pretty sure. Seventy percent. Or I'm off my rocker, which is also a distinct possibility.'

The Red Woman smiled, her teeth almost blinding in their whiteness.

'Is it possible?' I asked.

'Is what possible?'

'To save her. To save Chloe. If she's there, between whatever she's between, can she be saved?'

The Red Woman stood. 'She can.'

My heart gave a little leap of joy. If it had heels, it would have clicked them together, but it didn't, because hearts don't have heels. Or feet, generally.

'Please save Chloe,' I said, putting it plainly as I took a beseeching step toward the Red Woman.

'Me?' she replied, placing her hands to her chest. 'Oh no. I don't have that kind of power.'

My heart did the exact opposite of what it had just done.

'Oh. Right.'

Not even the Red Woman could help me. But wait a second... 'You said she could be saved. Why say that if you can't save her?'

'Because she *can* be saved.'

'How?'

'You know how. Whether you're aware or not, there's a reason you came back here to ask, and it wasn't because you thought I would be the one to lend a helping hand.'

'It wasn't?'

The Red Woman rested her arms on my shoulders and laced her fingers behind my head. 'No. It wasn't.'

'Then... why was it?' I asked, trying not to look into those sparkling green eyes of hers, which was difficult to do since we were practically touching noses.

'Because you remember what it was you once wanted. You remember the power that the Dark Lakes has for you. A power that can slay demons, turn all-powerful death cults to ash, and pluck the dead from the veil of shadows and back into the world of the living. *Your* power.

'Magic Eater,' said the fox.

Here I was again with a choice to make. A power to resist or embrace. I suppose I'd hoped the Red Woman could help, but at the back of my mind, hidden there so I wouldn't look too closely, was the only real option. I'd felt that power. Felt it burning inside of me like a supernova. If I wanted to save Chloe, it meant sitting on that throne.

'You see it now, don't you?' asked the Red Woman. 'You see what you could do if you just accepted your destiny. Nothing will ever hurt you. No cult, no demons. You could shrug off their debt as though it were nothing more than a winter scarf, cast aside after coming in from the snow.'

'I could,' I said.

I knew it. I walked over to the throne, a hundred rictus death grins smiling at me. I reached out a hand and touched an armrest. It felt softer than I imagined. Warmer. Inviting.

'Become the Magic Eater, at last,' said the Red Woman, her voice now seeming to be more in my head than my ears. 'Take your throne, accept your power, and save Chloe Palmer.'

I blinked and shook my head upon realising that I'd turned and begun lowering myself into the seat of the throne. 'Wait,' I said, hopping away from it.

'What?' said the Red Woman, her face momentarily twitching with irritation, an expression I'm very much familiar with.

'When the stone attacked me, I felt some of the power of the Magic Eater, which means you must have let me, right?'

The Red Woman didn't answer.

'I felt that power. It helped me escape. I didn't have to sit on a throne or accept some destiny. Can you let me taste it again? Just enough to save her?'

She shook her head.

'Please,' I said, looking to the fox, who glanced at the Red Woman, then turned away.

'Please. I can't become this monster you want me to be.'

'Monster?' she replied. 'So judgmental. You will not be a monster. You will be... magnificent. Glorious. A giant.'

'But I won't be me. I can't.'

The Red Woman shrugged. 'Then she dies.'

'No!'

'You're right. She doesn't die, she's already dead, by your hand. You think yourself so righteous, and yet you killed the woman you loved. Now you will leave her in the grip of the demons, phantoms, and hellish creatures that torture her, all because you're too scared to take up a mantle that you once burned like a star to possess.'

I looked back at the throne, at the skulls that seemed to be imploring me to take my place upon them.

'Sit,' she hissed. 'Become the Magic Eater.'

The Red Woman lunged forward, pushing me back, and as I raised my hands to stop her, we touched. My hand gripped her arm and her eyes widened.

'What are you...?'

Her voice trailed off and I saw the world around me alter. The air was full of colourful waves now, just like it had been when Eva helped me access my magic days earlier. I saw it, I saw the magic that surrounded me, and without thinking, without needing to know how, I pulled it into me. The waves rippled and flowed through my body, through the hand that gripped the Red Woman's arm... and I saw the truth.

I was in my car, in the Uncanny Wagon, looking at Chloe in the rearview mirror, only now I saw it wasn't Chloe at all.

I was at Carlisle Hospital, staring in the mirror of one of the bathrooms, Chloe wide-eyed, terrified, reaching out to me, imploring me to rescue her. And it wasn't Chloe.

Over and over, each time she had come to me, I saw the truth.

I saw the Red Woman reaching out towards me.

I saw the lie.

'No!'

The Red Woman pushed me away from her and the spell broke, the magic waves fading from view.

'It was you,' I cried, my whole body shaking. 'Chloe isn't trapped. She isn't looking for my help. It's just you.' Anger rose within me, knotting my stomach.

The Red Woman grimaced, her hands crackling with black lightning. 'Do not test me, boy,' she snarled.

'You were trying to trick me. Playing on my guilt, on my love for Chloe. All to make me sit on your stupid throne.'

'It is your destiny!'

'Then destiny can go fuck itself right in the arse,' I replied. Which wasn't quite the cool, James Bond retort you'd hope for in this sort of situation.

I turned and ran down the red hill. Again, not exactly 007 behaviour.

'You cannot escape your throne, Magic Eater! Fate will always win!'

I didn't reply, didn't look back, just ran. I lost my footing, took a spill, and the flaming sky above me seemed to flash on and off as though someone was playing with a light switch. I rolled over and over and—

I woke with a start as though from a falling dream and found myself on the couch in my flat. I looked around, befuddled, raising a trembling hand to wipe at my damp forehead.

'Shit,' I said, not liking how spooked I sounded.

My phone was ringing. I pulled it from my pocket. Eva's name lit the screen.

'What is it?' I asked.

I could hear breathing on the other end.

'Eva?'

'Malden's dead,' she replied.

27

As I walked into the dark alley, the moon lighting my way, I felt a combination of anger and sadness, which you'll be surprised to discover was not a pleasing cocktail.

It was a lie.

All of it.

The Red Woman had given me hope. She'd play-acted as Chloe and made me believe I could save her. Could get her back. Reverse what I'd done. Convinced me that Chloe hadn't been a terrible person after all. That she'd been convinced by her dead dad into doing his dirty work. Of course. Of course, she had. The Chloe I knew, loved, would never have turned like that.

But no.

Chloe was the only one to blame for the things she'd done. For the things she'd intended to do until we stopped her. Until I stopped her. Killed her.

'Well, look at the face on this fucker,' said Eva, turning as she heard me approach.

'We're at a crime scene, Eva,' said Myers. 'It's not generally the place for happy grins and a swagger in your step.'

On the ground were the remains of poor, dull Malden. As with the others, his corpse was a shrivelled, dried-out thing. An unwrapped mummy.

People I knew didn't die before I started to find out who I really was. Chloe, Detective Sam Samm, Mrs Coates, and now Malden; it seemed like death followed me everywhere these days.

Perhaps I'd have been better off not knowing. Plain old Joseph Lake, working in a hospital, with no memories of who he really was. That guy was okay. He had a life, a girl he liked, and no one was being murdered by people with octopus limbs, or killer standing stones. At least, not to the best of my knowledge.

'Eva,' said Myers, 'tell me you have a plan. Some way to make this the last person Elga and her Kin do this to.'

'Yup, totally have a plan.'

'Good,' replied Myers.

'Well, not a plan exactly.'

Myers looked to me, her eyes hooded, and sighed. 'What *do* you have then?'

'A bit of a plan.'

'Tell me the bit.'

'A bit may be stretching things a little.'

'What do you have, Eva?'

Eva frowned and crouched to look closer at poor Malden. 'What I have is anger.'

'Anger isn't enough, though, is it?' I replied.

'No, but it's a bloody good start.'

'Eva,' said Myers, 'tomorrow night, someone else is going to die.'

'And the night after that,' I added.

'And the night after that,' said Myers, 'until those bastards have enough strength to crawl out of their graves, leave the circle, and do whatever nasty shit they've got on their half-decayed brains.'

'Don't you think I know that?' said Eva, standing, eyes blazing.

'Then tell me something,' replied Myers, not raising her voice, not blinking.

'I'll find something. I will. There'll be something in the library, or... there'll be something.'

Eva's eyes momentarily flickered to mine and they told me everything I needed to know. She had no idea how we were going to stop this.

Well, shit and damn and bugger on top.

I said my goodbyes, turned, and left them to pick over the crime scene. I just wanted to go home.

I didn't make it into work the next day. I sounded so dreary, so defeated that I didn't even have to fake a sick voice when I called Big Marge.

'Jesus, you sound worse than shit,' she said.

'Thanks,' I replied, and hung up to get back to my busy schedule of curling up on the couch in silence.

Chloe was dead. She wasn't coming back. We had no way of stopping Elga and her Kin, and I'd never seen Eva look so helpless. I also had demons coming after me for my soul. I could feel the debt sitting heavy inside of me like wet concrete. A debt I could only get rid of if someone agreed to take it off me.

I had no interest in interacting with the outside world. At least staying inside, I felt sort of safe from attack, what with the layers of protections that Eva had placed over my flat. I could lie inside feeling sorry for myself, grieving the pretty-evil-after-all Chloe, and not have to worry about any demons getting at me with their eagles, or wolves, or giant frigging rats.

I was safe.

Nothing could get in.

I heard feet shuffling on the wooden floorboards.

'How did you get in?' I asked the fox.

'I get in where I needs to,' he chirped.

So much for protection spells.

'Then you can get right back out again,' I told him.

The fox dithered, teasing nervously at the head of his battle axe.

'What is it?' I said, sighing.

'Feel... bad.'

'Yes, I feel bad. Now piss off.'

'Not you. Me. Feel bad.'

I sat up and looked at the fox, who did indeed seem to be looking a little shameful.

'Bad that you got caught?' I asked.

'Not my idea. I do as the Red Woman asks. That's me. That's my job.'

I narrowed my eyes. Something wasn't right here. What was the game this time? 'What are you trying to do?'

The fox placed a hand to his chest. 'The debt. Your soul. You must get rid of that or you die, yes?'

'Thanks for reminding me. I'd totally forgotten my soul is promised to a bunch of demons. Funny the things that slip your mind, eh?'

'I do what I do for selfish reasons,' said the fox.

'You want to die to join your partner.'

His eyes welled up and tears dampened the fur on his face.

'What are you doing?' I asked. 'Stop that. I can't stand to see a fox crying, it makes me very uncomfortable.'

'I work for the Red Woman because I must,' he said. 'My destiny is to rejoin my partner.'

'And what's my destiny?'

'You know, Magic Eater.'

'Well, good luck persuading me of that one, foxy.'

'She does not know I am here,' he said.

'Why should I believe that? Why should I believe anything that you have to say?'

The fox shrugged. 'Because it's true. I tell the truth. I am here on my own, and I wish to help you, Magic Eater.'

'Fine. Help me how, exactly?'

And so we spoke further, and I decided to do something very, very stupid.

But then when didn't I?

28

The sky was beginning to darken as I pulled the Uncanny Wagon to a stop and looked out over the green hills of the Lake District.

'Right then...'

My phone buzzed again. Eva. It was the fifth time she'd tried calling since I messaged her and Myers to come and meet me at the night circle. At the site where Elga and her Kin lurked, growing stronger with each passing night.

I rejected the call, stepped out of the car, and made my way to the circle. The sun had almost dipped below the horizon, and I could already see a faint smattering of stars above.

I might be about to die.

I was willingly putting my head into the lion's jaws just to see what would happen.

Part of me was terrified, another part—the grieving part, the angry part—wasn't worried at all.

The stones shimmered into view. I rested my hand against one. It was strange to feel something that looked like a flickering image have such solidity beneath my fingers.

I felt my phone buzz again and pulled it out. A message from Eva: *Don't do anything stupid, stupid!*

I smiled and messaged back: *Since when have I done anything else?*

I looked up at the moon, shining down on me like a polished silver coin. The circle was complete. Ready to send one of its number out into the surrounding area to find a new person to murder and drain of power. The stone would return to its place and feed that power, that strength, to the bodies that lay beneath the ground. To revive the cult trapped in an undead state by me, by my coven, hundreds of years ago.

I rapped my knuckles against the standing stone. 'Knock, knock. Janto the warlock will see you now.'

That was me. Janto. Witch of the Cumbrian Coven. And here I was, doing what I was supposed to do. Putting myself in harm's way.

The air was still, not a sound.

'I said, Janto the warlock will see you now!' I screamed, my voice cracking. I could feel my pain in that cry. My grief. My anger.

A hand reached up from the dirt a few stones over; the same stone that Eva had peed in front of the previous night. Elga was answering my unannounced drop-in. I stepped back out of the circle.

'Sorry if you were having a lie-in,' I said, 'but this really can't wait.'

Her head emerged, her shoulders, as she dragged herself fully into view, her scarlet robe fluttering in the breeze. 'Janto,' she hissed, her voice like leaves blowing across a crypt floor.

'Yup, that's me, apparently. The ancient magical bad-arse that sentenced you to live like a worm for centuries. How's tricks?'

I was vamping, trying to hide my fear, as all around the circle, other hands began to break the surface: the rest of this zombie death cult dragging their decaying bodies into the night air.

'Must be good to get up and stretch your bones every now and again, eh?' I said.

Elga snapped her fingers and all thirty stones twisted to face me. Which was scary as hell, make no mistake.

'Why do you come here again?' she asked. 'Do you wish to die?'

'Maybe,' I replied.

'We could... accommodate that.'

I stepped closer, heart beating so hard it felt as though it might crack my ribcage. 'Do you know what I am?'

'You are a witch,' replied Elga.

I smiled and shook my head. 'No, not just a witch. Do you have any idea of the power I have access to now? The magic that I could give to you?'

Elga tilted her head to one side. 'I do not understand.'

I pulled something out of my jacket pocket. It was grass. Blood-red grass.

'Do you know what this is?' I asked, and threw the grass to Elga, who reached out and caught some falling blades.

'Dark Lakes,' she said, and the other cult members whispered the words over and over.

'I'm not just a witch. I'm the Magic Eater.'

The stiffened lips of the half-dead thing before me drew back to reveal crooked yellow-brown teeth.

'Yeah, you know what that is, don't you?'

'Such power,' hissed Elga.

'Such awful, boring power,' I replied.

'You... offer us this power?'

I swallowed. I could feel my pulse beating in my neck. 'I do.'

'Why?'

'Because people keep dying. All I ever wanted was to know who I am. Who I really am. And nothing about what I've found out so far has been good. I'm a murderer. I killed the rest of my coven. And I killed the woman I've loved for almost as long as my memory goes back.'

'So?'

I stepped forward, practically snarling. 'So I want revenge on a world that would let any part of that happen. What good is life if all it is, is shit and pain and loss? If that's life, if that's my truth, then it can go to hell.'

I stepped inside the boundary of the stone circle.

'Idiot, what are you doing?'

I turned to see Eva and Myers racing up from the road toward me.

'I'm getting out,' I replied.

'We... feel your power...' said Elga, her voice taking on an awed quality as all around me the rest of her cult writhed and moaned in pleasure.

'Joe, get out of there,' cried Myers, her baton out, warily eying the groaning corpses.

'What point is there in doing good if everyone dies anyway?' I asked. 'Why not just get the whole thing over with?'

Eva yelled and threw a ball of fire at me, but it bounced off of some unseen barrier that protected the circle.

'No!' she screamed. 'Janto, you fuck!'

Eva threw volley after volley, but it was no good, the barrier held. The cult was too strong for her. Soon, they'd be too strong for anyone.

'I'll see you soon, Chloe,' I said, and smiled.

The stones throbbed with energy; scarlet trails of power strobing up and down the grey of each stone, ready to feast on what I had to offer. Ready to take it all and feed it to Elga and her Kin.

'Joe, please,' said Eva, 'don't do this. Chloe's dead, but she had to die. The bitch was evil.'

I ignored her; didn't turn my head to see her or Myers. I didn't want to see their faces. All I could do was concentrate on me. On Elga. On not falling into a terrified bundle on the ground.

'The power of this witch shall be ours!' cried Elga, hands

aloft, her Kin cheering, swaying back and forth. 'The power of the Magic Eater, all that he has shall be ours and we will at last step out of this prison and tear the world down!'

I thought about Chloe, curled up on the couch beside me, her bare feet touching my leg as we watched television together. That had been real. No matter what else I discovered about her after, that had been real. Those moments. Those feelings. The pain I felt now. The ache that only a lost love could inflict.

I fell to my knees, tears streaking my cheeks. 'Just take it. Take it, please.'

The energy from one of the stones burst forward and wrapped itself around my body, making me gasp as it sank into me. Probed me. Scraped against every nerve ending I had.

'Feed us!' screamed Elga.

The stones shone fiercely in the black of the night, then all thirty of them fired their energy at me, invading my body, making me shake and spasm in pain. I saw bright yellow explosions in the periphery of my vision. Eva not giving up, trying again and again to break in. To save me? No, probably to kill me.

'Do you... want it?' I asked, forcing the words out like kidney stones. 'Do you want... what I have?'

'Yes!'

I could barely speak now, the pain was so intense. It felt as though every atom of me was being torn apart. But I had to carry on. Had to say the words.

'Do you... accept my magic... my power?'

'Yes!'

'Do you accept... everything that I am? Every... part of me?'

They chanted as one. 'Yes! Yes! Yes!'

'Then say it!'

'We accept it! Give it to us! Give us all of it!'

And so I did.

A scream erupted from me, cleaving the air like a blade. I

threw my head back, arms outstretched as the stones siphoned off my power. I felt them leaching my essence, draining me dry, then the energy that gripped me shot back, striking each member of the cult in turn. Their dead forms shook as they screeched in unison, desperate for everything I had to give.

It was too much. The pain, the feeling of being pulled apart, I couldn't take it.

But no—

No—

I had to concentrate—

Ignore the agony, the fear, the instinct to just let it all go. I had to concentrate on one thing and one thing alone. Push that forward. Give it to them. Let them have it.

'Take it!' I yelled.

I felt the weight leave me and I smiled. Somehow, through all the pain, I smiled. I may even have laughed.

'Now!' I said, or thought, I wasn't really sure. 'Take what is yours. Take it all!'

The ground trembled and the energy bursting from the standing stones crackled and died. I fell to one side and felt the cold grass against my face as I twitched at the mercy of my frazzled nerves.

'What is this?' asked Elga.

I pulled air into my lungs as I weakly pushed myself up to my feet.

'Oh,' said Eva, who looked at me dumbfounded. 'Oh, you absolute motherfucker.'

'What? What did I just miss?' asked Myers.

'Oh, you total and utter motherfucker!' said Eva.

'You know it,' I said.

Elga's hands raked at her chest. 'Take it back! I do not accept it! Take it back!'

'No backsies,' I said and staggered out of the circle as the ground within began to crack. I fell to my knees and Eva knelt down to help me.

'You're an idiot,' she said.

'I know.'

It was the fox that gave me the idea. I had a debt. A soul that a group of angry demons would kill to own.

'What's he done?' asked Myers, staring at the circle as grey smudges with burning red eyes began to seep out of the ground.

'He tricked them,' said Eva.

All those demons owed, and only one soul in the pot. So I drove to the well and I climbed down inside, and I offered them an alternative. Thirty souls. Enough for them to all have their fun. And the best part? They could claim what they were owed right away. No need to fight amongst themselves, no need to expedite any deaths using overgrown animals. The things taking on the debt were already, in most ways, dead. Easy pickings.

Myers' eyes widened as Eva filled her in. She looked from me, then to the circle as the demons tore out what was theirs and dragged the screaming souls to Hell. The vessels they'd been occupying crumbled to dust at last, dead, empty, defeated.

It had been a risk. No, a bit more than a risk. I really didn't know how it would go. A big part of me assumed I'd never walk out of that circle. That Elga and her Kin would drain me dry, killing me and giving them all the power that waited for me in the Dark Lakes.

But no.

I'd only gone and bloody well pulled it off.

I smiled at Eva, whose face was flitting somewhere between impressed and really shitting annoyed.

'Go team Coven,' I said.

Then high-fived myself like a really cool idiot.

Then blacked out.

29

I was in no shape to do anything for the next few days, let alone work. Luckily for me, I'd already phoned in sick, so it wasn't a stretch to keep that going for a little while longer.

Eva stayed pissed off at me. On the one hand, I'd just done something legitimately awesome: scrubbed the debt on my soul, and destroyed a super-powerful zombie death cult that was days from breaking free of their prison and bringing about Hell on Earth.

On the other hand, I hadn't told her the truth.

To my mind, the first one massively outweighed the other, but in the days since the circle fell, I hadn't heard diddly squat from her, and every message I sent remained unanswered.

Four days later, I limped into Carlisle Hospital to take my first shift since, you know, saving the world.

'Either you've set yourself up as a pimp or your leg is fucked,' said Big Marge as I approached the reception desk at a slow hobble.

'I'm afraid there aren't many openings for a pimp in Cumbria,' I replied, smiling. 'I just fell down the stairs.'

'You live in a flat. A flat doesn't have any stairs.'

'I know, that's the weird thing.'

Big Marge raised an eyebrow then went back to the magazine she was reading. 'Glad you're better. There's something awful needs mopping in the Ladies on the second floor. Something devastating.'

Ah, it was good to be back. Well, it was until a few hours later, when I walked into a corridor on my way to shove a fistful of coins into the vending machine, only to find Dr Neil and Detective Martins huddled in deep conversation.

'Shit,' I muttered.

Those were the last two people I wanted to see. Apart from the Red Woman. Or some horror movie reappearance of Elga, her bony hand bursting out of the ground in a *surprise, fucker!* jump-scare ending.

I tried to change course, only for the door behind me to bang closed and draw their attention. Apparently, I'd used up all my luck in that stone circle.

'Mr Lake,' said Detective Martins, walking over to me. 'I don't suppose you've anything new to tell me about the disappearance of Chloe Palmer?'

I bowed my head and sighed.

'Just tell us where she is,' demanded Dr Neil. 'I know you've got something you're not telling us.'

'This is your last chance, Lake,' said Martins. 'Your last chance to tell me something useful and make things easier on yourself. Tell me where Chloe Palmer is.'

'Um, I'm sort of, over here.'

To say all three of our faces were slack with amazement as we turned to see Chloe stood before us was something of an understatement.

'Chloe?' said Dr Neil.

'Yeah. Who's that?' she asked, pointing at Martins.

'My...' Martins coughed and straightened his tie, trying to put his gruff, snake-eyed demeanour back in place. 'My name is Detective Martins.'

'Ah, right, I was meaning to come into the station and put your fears to rest.'

'Chloe, where have you been?' asked Dr Neil.

'I know, I know, dick move to just ghost out on you like that, but I was so tired of the pressure of this job. Of my life. And, actually, so sick of you, you boring, dumb piece of shit. Oh, I couldn't wait to get away from you, you Casper-looking motherfucker.'

I tried to swallow back the smirk that was fighting its way out of my mouth. I completely failed.

'Detective Martins, I'm sorry. I took myself away for a few days. I meant to text work to let them know, and just completely forgot. I'm so sorry for the trouble caused, I really had no idea.'

'People have been trying to call you,' he said.

'I'll bet, but I lost my phone. I've been camping. In Scotland.'

'Scotland?'

'Yup.' She smiled and winked at me.

'I've decided to live off the grid from now on. Just sick of all this modern shit, you know?'

'I see,' replied Martins, his voice emerging between gritted teeth. 'Mr Lake, you're off the hook.'

'Thank you. I did tell you,' I said.

Martins grimaced at me, then left.

I found Eva leaning against the side of the Uncanny Wagon, a can in her hand and a smoke between her lips.

'Thanks,' I said.

'Hm? What for?' she replied.

'For doing that. For being Chloe. Now she can disappear again and no one will think anything of it.'

'Yeah. Well, you're not the only one with good ideas.'

I smiled. 'So it was a good idea?'

'I never said that.'

'You totally said that. Just then.'

Eva turned to look at me, scowling. 'I was about to say that was the dumbest move you've ever pulled, but in all honesty, it's not even close.'

'But it worked. I couldn't tell you, you wouldn't have let me do it, and it was the only way.'

I climbed behind the wheel, and Eva slumped across the back seat, her feet sticking out of the open window. As I turned the key and the engine coughed into life, she patted me on the shoulder.

'What is it?' I asked.

'Nothing. Just... Malden would say thanks. And then probably go into some very dull story about his bowel movements. I'm going to miss those.'

I looked in the rearview. Eva smiled back at me. I don't think I'd ever seen her smile at me with anything even close to affection before. The last thing I wanted to do was ruin the moment.

'You know, I think you're starting to like me.'

Well, there we go, I went and ruined it. A stick thwacked the back of my head.

'Oi!'

'What? It's my whacking stick. It's a callback.'

'A what now?' I said, rubbing at my sore head.

'Call Myers.'

'Why? Not more trouble?'

'Nah. We're going to the pub, and I'm not getting wasted with just you, idiot.'

I smiled and steered out of the hospital car park.

PAST SINS

1

I was strolling by a lake with a chill Northern air nipping at my exposed genitalia.

Which is to say, I was very naked.

Completely nude.

Starkers.

And outside.

Now, believe it or not, I'm not normally the type to go for a naked stroll, which told me one of two things: either I'd gone quite mad—a distinct possibility considering my life lately—or I was dreaming.

And dreaming I was. Which was a relief.

Usually, I'd be ashamed to be caught outside in the nude. The naked male body is not something to present to a wide audience, at least not mine. I look my best dressed. Preferably three layers between people's eyes and my skin. But, as I already explained, this was a dream, and I was out and proud.

Quite liberating, really, even if it was all in my head. So much so that I whistled as I moseyed along the beach, bare feet slapping the mud, my undercarriage lolloping from side-to-side. The lake stretched out before me, brilliantly blue, lush green hills squatting just beyond its rim. I was at Lake

Derwentwater; the body of water by which I'd awoken ten years ago with no clue as to who, or what, I was.

This giant hole in my memory had remained with me until quite recently when I found out a number of surprising things. Chief of these was the fact that I was a warlock—a male witch—and several hundred years old. That alone would have been more than enough information for one tiny mind, but the surprises kept on a-coming. I also learned that monsters were real and that other planes of existence... well, existed. Then there was the part about me being destined to sit upon a throne of skulls so I could become a living apocalypse called the Magic Eater who brought about Hell on Earth.

Yup.

A bit much to take in, really, at least all in one go.

Luckily, I did have someone I could talk to about it.

Unluckily, that someone was a foul-mouthed, drunk by the name of Eva, who was as likely to punch me as she was to lend an understanding ear. More likely, if I'm honest.

Anyway, enough backstory, let's return to nudey dream time...

It was always at this point, with my toes wriggling at the water's edge, that I remembered I'd had this dream before. I'd been having the dream several times a week for the last month, in fact, so I knew what was going to happen next.

I was going to get in that lake and have a bit of a swim.

Being aware of this should have allowed me to take control of things and deviate from the script, but for some reason, I never did. The moment I considered taking a left instead of a right, I'd realise I was up to my waist in water and about to kick off swimming. And off I went, slicing through the water with all the grace of an epileptic buffalo. You'd think I'd allow myself to be a better swimmer in my own dream, but apparently not.

When I reached the centre of Derwentwater, I took a big gulp of air and ducked under the surface, kicking hard, driving down, down, down into the belly of the lake.

'Swim down.'

'Swim down, Janto.'

The voices were distant, tickling at the edge of my hearing, my own mysterious cheering squad.

'Swim down.'

The voices were familiar, but I couldn't quite place them. All I knew was that I trusted them, and so down I swam.

'Swim down.'

'Swim down, Janto.'

As my lungs began to burn and my vision blurred, the voices were replaced by a sharp ringing sound and—

I woke, bleary, bolting upright, gasping for air. Clearly, I'd taken my dream a little too literally and had been holding my breath in real life, too. I flopped back on the pillow, wanting nothing more than to drift off back to sleep, but my phone had other ideas, keeping up its annoying, insistent cry.

Being woken from a strange dream by an alarm is a bit of a clichéd way to begin a story, yes, but this was a phone call, so an entirely different, and not at all hack, opening.

Honest.

I struggled out of the corkscrew I'd turned my duvet into during my nocturnal swimming and grabbed my phone.

'Hello?'

'Fuck sake, idiot, can you answer a bit slower next time?'

Ah, the sweary, punchy woman I mentioned earlier. She with the riot of black hair, a favoured ensemble of black ragged clothing, and a coat of many pockets, many stains, and many unpleasant smells that I swear she must have stolen from a slumbering tramp.

'And a good morning to you, Eva. You have heard of the concept of sleep?'

'Yeah, you can waste a lot of your day doing that. Think of all the drinking hours people give up just so they can lie down with their eyes shut for a bit. Waste of time.'

'I've seen you sleep, Eva.'

'Resting my eyes.'

A smile teased at my lips. 'Is there something you wanted?'

'Hm? Oh yeah, right. We've got a job. Missing baby. Monster baby. Thing.'

'A monster baby?'

'Take a piss, put your coat on, and come pick me up, idiot.'

The thin woman who answered the door of the pretty thatch-roofed cottage was grey and wide-eyed, her hands trembling. Clearly she was feeling somewhat emotionally frazzled. I see a lot of this sort of thing at the day job, over at Carlisle Hospital, so I knew tact and a soft touch were required.

'Jesus, love, you look like you fucked a ghost,' said Eva, always one to be counted on for her sensitivity.

The woman burst into tears. Of course. Eva offered her a sip of her can of beer, but for some reason, the woman refused this generous offer.

'Suit yourself,' said Eva, shrugging, and pushed past the woman and into her house. Literally pushed past. A two-handed shove.

'I'm very sorry about...' I said, gesturing in Eva's general direction, then meekly slid past the still bawling woman.

Moments later, we were gathered in the front room of the cottage. Flames roared in the open fireplace. The room was neat and ordered to an insane degree. This pair took being house proud to the next level.

The woman had taken it down a notch or two now, and was merely whimpering on the plump pink couch as her husband—an imposingly-sized man with a beard of such mighty proportions that it looked like a bear cub clinging to his chin—sat beside her staring daggers at Eva. Clearly, he'd had dealings with her before. By this point, I'd grown used to Eva having this effect on people.

'So where—' Eva paused to unleash a burp of such ferocity that it knocked over a family portrait on the mantelpiece, '—where is the fucker? Little baby monster, fuck-face fuck.'

Now, Eva was always inebriated to some degree, but I was getting the distinct impression that she was a little deeper into her cups than usual.

'It's upstairs, in the nursery, sat in his crib,' replied the husband, drawing fresh wailings from the wife.

'There, there,' I said. 'Don't worry, we deal with this sort of thing all the time.'

I was trying to ease their worry but realised they weren't paying me the slightest bit of notice. I turned to what was drawing their attention: Eva, leaning against the mantel, still somehow upright despite being sound asleep.

'Eva,' I said, nudging her and almost getting a right hand to the face as she jolted awake, wide-eyed.

'Baby's room?' said Eva, using her sleeve to wipe drool from the corner of her mouth.

The parents nodded.

'Right. Here we go then. Let's get the fucker.'

Eva headed for the stairs and I followed, offering a quick, sympathetic smile to the parents as I left.

'Eva, do we have a plan?'

She paused halfway up the stairs and swayed at such an alarming angle that I thought she was going to tumble back and crash into me. Somehow, she pivoted forward and carried on up.

'Twat the twat,' she said.

'Right. Good plan. Intricate.'

Eva had more or less filled me in on the latest bit of bother on the drive from the coven to the house. We were dealing with a cuckoo. Not the beaked kind, but the Uncanny variety. A creature that imitated a young child and replaced it in the family home, feasting on the psychic power generated by a loving, devoted set of parents.

Usually, they go unnoticed, but this time the cuckoo had chosen poorly, replacing the child of a couple of magicians, who managed to clock what was going on.

The door in front of us had a small plate screwed into it that read *Jacob's Room*.

'Hey, if they're magicians, why couldn't they deal with this themselves?' I asked.

Eva patted herself down, then pulled out her tobacco tin and began rolling herself a fresh smoke.

'Hm. Bit above their pay grade. Pair of useless fuckers, really, far as magicians go. Bit of telepathy. Make stuff, sort of, hover. They can do that. Not much else. And this thing, this cuckoo twat, has to be handled carefully, otherwise, the real kid'll be buggered. Not literally. I mean, it'll be fucked.'

'Not any better.'

'Dead. Lost. Dead lost.'

'So how do we kick the cuckoo out and get the real child back?'

'Got this shitting, you know, magical thing. Magical totem sort of thing.' Eva began going through pocket after pocket before finally locating the item and pulling it out. A gold coin sat on her palm

'We pay it to leave?'

Eva stared at me with hooded eyes.

'Okay. We don't pay it.'

'Idiot. We make it eat the coin. It eats the coin and the magical magic coin does what it does and hey-de-ho, drinks all round. Come on, let's get in character.'

Eva stood in front of the door to Jacob's room while I tried to calm the two sides waging war in my stomach: reckless excitement and abject fear. This wasn't my first monster. In the months since I'd met Eva—or re-met, as it happens—I'd faced plenty of horrific, powerful, horrible creatures. But

I'd yet to get used to it. Yet to feel confident in the face of danger.

And still...

There was that excitement there, too. More and more, I felt it. This is what I was meant to do. What I had done for hundreds of years before the death of my two fellow witches. Before they died at my own hands, and the Cumbrian Coven fell. And now here I was again, performing my duty; risking my life to keep people safe.

I'd also been able to get to grips with some rudimentary magic. Nothing too flashy, but I could manifest a fireball without too much of a struggle, and I could, on occasion, fling objects through the air without touching them.

I'd yet to impress Eva, who continued to tell me I was a terrible student, but at least I wasn't entirely at the whims of chance now. When I walked into a shoot-out these days, I wasn't doing so empty-handed.

'Okay,' said Eva, dropping her almost-dead cigarette on the carpet and stomping it out with the heel of her boot. 'Let's get this little turd.' She opened the door and we stepped inside.

The boy was sat in his crib, playing with a toy car. He didn't look much like a monster, but then I suppose that was the point.

'Quick question: is there a way of making absolutely sure that we're not about to force a large coin into an actual toddler's stomach?'

'Hm? Oh yeah, good point. Good idea.'

Eva staggered over the crib and glared down at the oblivious toddler.

'Oi. Hey! Hey, you down there, you tiny, dumb, baby thing. Are you a monster in disguise?'

'I think you're being a bit subtle,' I said as the toddler blinked in confusion at the woman glaring down at him with drool forming in the corners of her downturned mouth.

'I'm Jacob,' said the toddler, lifting up the toy car he was playing with. 'I'm three years old and I like trains and... and... cars, too. But not boats.'

'I didn't ask for your life story, idiot,' replied Eva, then held up the magic coin. 'Know what this is?'

Young Jacob looked at the coin, then at Eva, then over at me. 'I like cars,' he said.

'I don't think that's a monster,' I said.

'Well, forgive me, Mr Big Pants, if I don't take your word as gospel,' replied Eva.

Jacob began to cry and call for his mommy.

'Now look what you've done,' I said.

'You really think this little shit-machine isn't a monster?' asked Eva.

'Well, maybe not, I don't know. He seems very toddler-ish. Not that I have an extensive amount of experience with toddlers.'

Eva shook her head, her face twitching between disappointment, anger, and exasperation. It was quite the display of facial gymnastics; a solid nine on the scoreboard.

'Oh, and you're so sure, are you?' I said, pouting.

Eva sighed. She turned, pointed at little Jacob, and yelled some sort of gibberish that may or may not have been close to, 'Ala Mur Kala Phot!'

The result of this string of odd words was that, for a brief flash, Jacob was no longer a pudgy human toddler. Instead, he was a festering, hate-filled blob of horror that sent me rocking back on my heels.

'What in the name of balls was that?' I cried.

'I just made the little arsehole show his true colours,' Eva replied. 'Now, can we all agree that it's a fucking monster?'

I nodded briskly, eyes fixed on Not-Jacob in case the real him decided to make a leap for my sweet neck meat. 'Use the coin,' I said. 'The magic coin. Now. Get it down his neck.'

'All right, I'm getting to it, what's your hurry?'

'I just think, when it comes to monster killing, that sooner is better than later.'

Eva sneered. 'The moment I start taking orders from you again is the day I put a gun in my mouth.'

'He'll die,' said Not-Jacob, which rather pulled us out of our back and forth.

'I'm sorry?' I replied.

'The human child,' said Not-Jacob, toy car set aside now, the pretence over.

'Look, you little cuckoo nutsack, the jig's up,' said Eva, rolling herself a fresh smoke. 'The parents know what you are, and so do we. Time to mosey out of town or prepare to be fucked up in the most fuck-uppest way possible. Understand?'

Not-Jacob laughed. No, laughed makes it sound pleasant, and the noise that came out of the thing pretending to be a toddler was anything but that. It was a sharp snigger that made the hairs on the back of my neck stand up and dance. That made the contents of my stomach curdle.

'Bit of a boo-boo on your part, trying to set up shop in the home of a family of magicians,' said Eva. 'Might wanna do your recon a bit more thoroughly next time.'

'Is that so?' the creature replied.

'Where's the real Jacob?' I asked.

'In a dark, dark place, Janto,' replied the cuckoo, using my old name. My real name from back when I was an all-powerful witch, and not a man employed to mop up puke.

'How does it know my name?'

'Bad news travels fast, idiot,' said Eva. 'Okay, bored now.'

She grabbed Not-Jacob by the nape of his neck and lifted the screeching, wriggling thing aloft, sending his fat legs whirring on invisible bicycle pedals.

'This,' said Eva, 'is a magic coin. I'm gonna shove it down your neck, and then it's bye-bye baby.'

Not-Jacob smiled.

'Why is he doing that?' I asked.

'Why are you smiling?' said Eva.

Then Jacob's face tore open and a flood of blood and gunk poured out over Eva's hand. It looked a little like that scene in *The Shining* with the elevator doors, only, you know, with a toddler's face. So not at all similar, now I think about it. Forget that.

'What's it doing?' I screamed.

'Fucked if I know,' replied Eva.

Suddenly, what it was doing became all too clear as the creature hiding inside its compact disguise burst from within, all giant green limbs and gnashing teeth. It began to expand, rapidly, like one of those inflatable rafts that are the size of a small satchel until you pull a cord and it fills an entire room.

Only this didn't fill the entire room.

Because the entire room was too small.

There followed much swearing and noise, and I'm not ashamed to admit that I ran for the door as the creature pushed against the cracking walls and ceiling as it continued its unexpected growth spurt.

'Did you know it would do that?' I asked as I ran down the shaking stairs, Eva at my heels.

'No, it looked smaller in the drawing.'

'How much smaller?'

'Well, the size of the page.'

I would have tossed back a devastating reply to that, but any further conversation was cut short as the bedroom wall crashed down and one of the beast's limbs burst rolled out and along the staircase, knocking us down the rest of the way. I landed on the floor with a cry, Eva thudding on top of me, expelling the wind from my lungs.

'What's happening?' shouted Jacob's mother. 'Jacob!'

Eva staggered up and grabbed the gawping parents. 'Out! Fucking out!'

She shoved them toward the door and out into the garden

as I regained my footing and followed, gulping down some air as I regained control of my breathing.

The cold night air greeted me as I lurched out of the house and ran past Eva and the parents before tumbling down into the dirt road.

'Well, there it goes,' said Eva.

I turned, breathing heavily, to see the creature—the cuckoo—had now grown larger than the house itself, and was shaking off brick walls and roofing tiles like a chick bursting from its eggshell.

'Our home...' said the wife, her voice a wailing stammer.

The cuckoo opened its giant mouth and roared, its many tree-length limbs thrashing around furiously.

'Now what?' I asked.

'Well,' said Eva, pulling a can of beer from her pocket, opening it up, and putting it to her mouth to catch the escaping froth, 'that's a good fucking question.'

'Jacob,' said the husband. 'Where's Jacob?'

The cuckoo roared again.

'Shall we, I don't know, attack?' I asked. 'Or run. Maybe run?'

'No,' said Eva, 'first one. Attack. We attack.'

'Oh dear,' I replied, not unreasonably.

I raised my fist and felt some of the surrounding magic flow into me. I concentrated, moulding the magic to my will, and a ball of fire ignited around my hand. I looked to Eva and couldn't help but smile.

'All right, no reason to look so smug about a little bit of fi—'

Eva's sentence was cut short as a giant green limb coiled around her waist, yanked her off the ground, and deposited her into the monster's gaping mouth.

I looked up at the cuckoo, dumbfounded, the flame around my fist puttering out as my concentration fell away.

'Eva? Eva!'

She did not answer. What with having been eaten by a huge monster.

'What now?' asked the husband.

I looked at him, at his wife, then back to the house-sized beast that had just swallowed my friend.

It couldn't be. Not Eva. She'd never go out like that. Not without a fight.

'Eva! Get back here right now!'

The cuckoo roared as I strutted towards its flabby, juddering mass, the fire reigniting around my fist. As if that would scare something of that size. I might as well have tried taking on an elephant armed with a single lit match. But forward I strode, disbelief and anger momentarily pushing aside fear and reason.

'Eva Familiar, I am Janto of the Cumbrian Coven. I created you and you will do as I say!'

Nothing.

'Did you hear me, you demented cow? Get out here, right now!'

The cuckoo was still enjoying a good roar when the noise caught in whatever it had that passed for a throat.

And then it exploded.

It was disgusting.

The eruption sent me fifteen feet in the opposite direction before depositing me on my back. I sat up, ears ringing from the blast. I was coated head-to-foot in the creature's blood, as well as great, wet, lumps of its flesh and innards.

Lovely.

Eva looked down at me, equally coated. She brushed the worst off her face, then reached into her coat and retrieved her tobacco tin.

'What...? What happened?'

'Hm?' said Eva, as she rolled herself another cigarette with blood-damp fingers. 'Oh, it did what I was wanting it to. Swallowed the magic coin that'd destroy it.'

'And you, too.'

'Yeah. Third time I've been swallowed now. It's uncomfortable.'

I sat up to see the husband and wife retrieving their child, the real Jacob, from the wreckage of the cuckoo.

'He was inside the monster all along?'

'Yup. Don't ask me how it works, but he's fine. Job done.'

'What about our house?' asked the husband, stood in the gore-splattered ruins of their formerly picture-perfect cottage.

'We saved your kid,' said Eva.

'Yes, but... just look at the place,' said the wife, starting to shudder with tears again.

Eva looked down at me. 'No pleasing some fuckers, is there?'

She headed towards my car, the Uncanny Wagon, and I stood, shrugged apologetically, then hurried after her.

2

We arrived back at the Cumbrian Coven with the cuckoo's innards still coating us, though now it was dried and cracked as we moved.

While Jacob's parents had been house proud, Eva's sense of domestic pride really threw the lever in the opposite direction. So far the other way that the lever snapped. In stark contrast to the picture-perfect cottage (well, previously picture-perfect), the coven was little more than grey stone walls covered in cracks and scorch marks. Most—if not all—of the furniture in the place looked as though it had been liberated from tips and skips. You don't even want me to paint a picture of the kitchen, it would only give you nightmares. But know this: something was growing out of the sink. Something that I swear once opened an eye.

Eva watched TV and drank cradled by a couch so ragged and broken that even a crack den would have turned its nose up at it. She fished around on the floor until her hand found a half-drunk can of beer, and swallowed the lukewarm remains in one. I braved the kitchen and grabbed a cold can from the fridge. As usual, there was little in the way of food inside, unless you consider mould food, which I don't. I took a mouthful or two of cheap, strong beer, then pressed the cool tin to my eye, which throbbed from being struck by a fat ball of exploding cuckoo flesh.

'Have you got anything to eat?' I asked. 'Preferably something out of a tin that's free of contamination.'

'What am I, your mum?'

'Sorry, but fighting monsters gives me a bit of an appetite.'

Eva sighed. 'Brown paper bag. Freezer compartment.'

I opened the fridge again and reached into the freezer drawer, pulling out a large, brown paper bag.

'This?'

'Is it brown?'

'Yes.'

'Is it a paper bag?'

'Yes.'

'Then I'll let you put the rest of the pieces together, idiot.'

I'd gotten quite adept at allowing Eva's many, many insults roll off me. It's not as though I could really complain about them, anyway. I had, after all, been responsible for the death of her other two creators, Lyna and Melodia. The two witches who should be making up the trio of power with me, to look after Cumbria, the county in northern England we reside in. It's a wonder Eva gave me the time of day, really.

The rumble of my stomach shut up any further introspection, and I reached into the bag to pull out something to chew on. The 'something to chew on' that I pulled out came as something of a surprise, as it appeared to be a tiny person. Not a model, not an ornament, but an actual living creature, frozen stiff. I let out a strangled whimper that Eva found quite hilarious.

'What the... what is this...?' I asked, waggling the tiny corpse popsicle (corpsicle?).

'Fairy, that. Very tasty.'

'A fairy?' I peered closer and saw a pair of gossamer-thin

wings flattened fast to the little thing's back. 'Like… a real fairy?'

Eva hauled herself upright and wandered over, plucking a second fairy from the bag. 'Yup, a really real fairy.'

'Whoa.' I looked at the magical little creature in my hand. It was beautiful, perfect; a piece of a fairy tale brought to life.

And then Eva ripped hers in half and began to slurp on its innards.

'Jesus Christ,' I cried.

'I know,' said Eva, her pupils huge, 'they're bloody fresh.'

She grabbed the rest of the bag from me and headed for the couch. I paused, looked at the fairy in my hand—at the two halves that Eva had discarded on the floor—then slowly moved to join her on the couch.

'Sorry, daft question I'm sure, but… why are you tearing fairies in half and slurping out their insides?'

Eva stuck her finger into one half of her second snack and teased out something gross, which she then slurped down. 'Don't feel sad for these bastards. Fairies are rotten, evil little fuckers. Lay eggs in homeless people, and when they hatch they eat their way out of the poor sods.'

'Oh.' It was definitely an 'oh' sort of a realisation. 'Well, that's… disappointing. But, well, why are you eating it?'

'Fairies are good for one thing: they're packed full of concentrated magic. Crack one open, get it down you, and ride the wave. Feel that undiluted power rushing round your body.'

I looked down at the fairy in my hand, then passed it to Eva.

'Wuss,' she replied before feasting on it, then standing up and doing a spot of vigorous shadow boxing. 'This is some really good shit. You sure you don't want some, idiot?'

I took that as my cue to leave.

'No thank you. I've got a shift in a few hours, and it would be nice to get an hour or two of sleep before the drudgery begins.'

'What? It's the weekend! Who works weekends?'

'First of all, I do. I work weekends. Hospitals don't close on the weekend.'

'Pff. Needy lot, the sick.'

'Second of all—and I probably should have led with this—it's not the weekend, it's Tuesday.'

Eva eyed me suspiciously. 'You sure?'

'Very.' I showed her the date on my phone. Her face dropped and drained of colour. She slumped back on the couch and turned on the TV.

'What? What's wrong?' I asked.

'Go if you're going.'

'Okay.' I turned to leave, then paused, dithering. 'It's just, it seems like maybe something's up? Is it the day?'

'We're not pals, Joseph,' she reminded me.

'Oh. Well. Okay.'

'Today is the fifteenth of July. You know what that means?'

'No.'

'It means it would have been Lyna's birthday,' said Eva. 'Still is. The dead can celebrate birthdays, too.'

I worried at the buttons on my coat, not knowing quite what to say. It was obvious that Eva was hurting, and she was only hurting because of me. Because of the old me. The me I couldn't even remember.

'I'm sorry,' was the best I could do as I headed for the exit.

'I'll never forgive you, you know,' said Eva. 'They'd want me to, but tough. I'm not forgiving a fucking thing, got me? Not forgiving, not forgetting, and not trusting.'

I nodded, then left, feeling just about as shitty as it's possible to feel.

Which was very shitty.

And then a little worse than that.

3

It turns out that being reminded of what a worthless, reprehensible human being you are can really interfere with your ability to drift off to sleep. Strange, that. Five hours had passed since I said goodnight to Eva, and I'd slept for literally none of them.

I wearily trotted into Carlisle Hospital for my shift and headed for the reception desk, the cold glow of the strip lighting wrapping its arms around me. As usual, people were dotted around in uncomfortable chairs, waiting. Waiting to be seen. Waiting for people who were being seen. Waiting for news that might ruin their day, or their entire life.

Big Marge, the ever-present receptionist with the barmaid hair, greeted me with her usual judgemental expression. 'You look like crap,' she said. 'As always.'

'You know, you're really not very good at flirting, Marge.'

Big Marge raised an epically scornful eyebrow. If Big Marge were ever to lose the power of speech, her eyebrows would be able to take over the communication role, no problem

'What happened to you this time, then?' she asked, indicating my eye, which had become puffy and bloomed with a rosy red glow.

'Oh, nothing. Nothing weird,' I replied. Which, even as I said it, I realised was in itself a weird thing to say.

'You come in here banged up a lot. Exhausted, covered in bruises, cuts. Smelling like you needed a shower three days ago. What's going on with you?'

A plausible excuse was required.

'Fight club.'

Thanks for nothing, brain.

'Come again?' said Marge.

'Fight club. Like that film.'

'Which film?'

'*Fight Club.*'

'Hm. Yeah. I do like me some Bradley Pitt.'

'It's just a fitness thing,' I explained, caught up in the lie. 'Me and a few, uh, lads, we duke it out in a church basement. It was either that or a book club, and I don't have time for reading.' I grinned, hoping for charming.

'Bollocks.'

'Okay, I do read. Sometimes. But only books with pictures.'

'There's no way your skinny arse is fighting grown men.'

'And why is that?' I asked, bristling slightly.

Big Marge raised a fist and made as though she was about to hit me. I leapt back, squealing, throwing my arms up in front of my face.

Dignity, I know not your presence.

I straightened out my long coat, ignored Big Marge's smug look, and headed for my locker.

As I trundled through the workday in a sleep-deprived fug, I found myself thinking about how utterly bizarre my life had become. I watched the mop in my hands sweeping back and forth across a dirty corridor floor—hands that I could ignite with flames should I wish to—and wondered how long I could keep juggling both sides of my life.

If only this warlock thingy paid a living wage, I could drop the day job and actually get enough sleep to function properly. That'd be nice.

But no, apparently, monetary reward wasn't part of the gig. The best I could expect for rescuing someone from a bloodthirsty werewolf, or saving the entire world from a long-dead cult ready to rise up and enslave humanity, was a glow of satisfaction and a busted nose.

I yawned and leaned on the mop for a quick rest. Sooner or later, the wheels were going to come off, I was sure of it. Brain or body, one had to fall to bits eventually.

'All hail the saviour!'

I turned to see the fox, Roman helmet on his head, axe held aloft, grinning up at me.

'You know, I'm really, really over that greeting. How about a simple *Hi* from now on?'

The fox lowered his axe and frowned.

'Well, suits yourself,' he said. 'You are the mighty one. The eater of magic.'

'No, I'm not. I keep telling you this. Are you hard of thinking or something?'

The fox looked up at me, eyes huge and watery.

'Sorry,' I said. 'Sorry, that was mean, I apologise.'

'It was very mean, yes.'

'Yes.'

'Very, very mean, it was.'

'I said I'm sorry.'

'I forgive you, saviour.'

'Joseph,' I corrected.

'Saviour Joseph.'

'Just Joseph. Or Joe. Just call me Joe.'

The fox considered this, then offered me a big grin. 'Joe. Hi, Joe.'

'Hello, fox. Now, is there something you wanted? A message from the Red Woman? Some dire warning you need to pass on?

Some demand to take my throne that you both already know I have absolutely no intention of taking so I can become an evil monster I have absolutely no intention of becoming?'

The fox considered my questions as he scratched at his chin with a claw, then nodded. 'Yes. Mostly all of that.'

I sighed and went back to mopping.

'She's very upset, the Red Woman. Very much.'

'Is she now.'

'Says you're a disappointment. A big one.'

'What else is new?' I asked. 'I get the feeling I'm a very disappointing sort of a person.'

The fox began to idly swing his axe back and forth, apparently at a bit of a loss.

'Look, you go back and tell that scary, persistent red-head that she can stick her throne where the sun doesn't shine. By which I mean her ice-cold bottom.'

The fox frowned.

'I do not believe it would fit. Very big chair, very small bottom.'

'Is there anything else, only I am at work here.'

The fox went to speak, then stopped and shook his furry little head. He was a bit of an adorable annoyance, I had to admit.

'I don't wants to help her, you know.'

'Is that so?' I replied.

The fox nodded. 'Have to, don't I? Doing what I must, so one day I'll be allowed the sweet relief of death and rejoin my beloved.'

Now he was just making me feel guilty. I found myself turning back to say I understood, but the fox had disappeared, as silently as he had arrived.

After many torturous hours, my shift finally ended, and I shambled toward my beat-up little car, the Uncanny Wagon. How the thing still passed its MOT, I had no idea. I stroked its roof as though it were a beloved family pet, feeling all the dents, many of them caused by a recent attack from a swarm of demonically-possessed eagles. *Swarm* of eagles? Is that right? Probably flock, right?

'Joe!'

I turned to see a woman speed-walking across the hospital car park toward me.

'Annie?'

Annie had sold her soul to a demon. Actually, to lots of demons. Not to toot my own horn, but I'd been very, very brave and saved her neck. I hadn't seen her since, so this was a pleasant surprise.

'Caught you,' she said, a nice smile upon her extremely nice face. Her eyes seemed to sparkle when she smiled like that.

'Caught? I can assure you I wasn't doing anything wrong.'

'I was in the neighbourhood, so thought I'd drop in on the off-chance,' she said, pushing her blonde locks behind her perfectly formed ears. 'The receptionist said you just clocked off.'

'Yup, this is me, clocking off.'

'What happened to your eye?' she asked.

'A fight club, would you believe?'

'Was it a very nasty monster?'

'Oh, an absolute rotter. But never fear, the righteous prevailed.' I posed heroically, chest out, hands on hips.

'Come on, you can take me for a drink and fill me in.'

I'd been day-dreaming about my bed, and having almost sexual fantasies about the plump coolness of my pillow, but only a prize pillock turns down a beautiful woman asking to be accompanied to a bar for refreshments.

4

Twenty minutes later, we were sat in a brightly-lit, soulless pub, and I was setting a glass of white wine in front of Annie as I slurped the froth from a pint of lager.

'I needed that,' I said, feeling refreshed in a way that sometimes only alcohol can provide.

'So, the eye,' said Annie, 'what happened there?'

'Oh, no biggie, just a giant monster that had replaced a toddler.'

'Well, that's something,' said Annie, sipping her wine.

Never been a fan of wine, myself. And the hangovers from that stuff? Good God.

'Long story short, I was a hero, monster exploded, little kid fine and dandy.'

'Congratulations,' she replied, smiling warmly.

Yes, I could have mentioned that I did little more than get hit in the face by a chunk of exploding monster, but that didn't sound half as impressive.

'How's the little one?' I asked. 'Millie, isn't it?'

'She's good. Actually, she's great. I've never known someone so full of beans. She really brightens up a day.'

'Gets it from you, no doubt.'

'Well, aren't you a charmer?'

'I've been called a lot of names in my life, but never that.' I saluted her with my pint glass and took another gulp.

'How goes the magic practice?'

'Pretty good. Eva hardly ever hits me with the stick now. Well, not for my magic, anyway. She did thwack me across the back of the legs the other day because, and I quote, "I just wanted to."'

Annie giggled, and I found my face flush with heat.

'Show me,' she said.

I cast a glance over my shoulder to check the coast was clear. The pub was sparsely populated, and we were tucked away in a quiet snug. 'Okay then, mind your eyebrows.'

I concentrated and the air around me seemed to flicker. As I understood it, the Uncanny was everywhere. Anything and everything emitted a certain amount of magic, and we walked through this invisible wash every day of our lives. Sometimes, when I concentrated hard enough, I could sort of see it. See the multicoloured waves that rolled and weaved all around us, like the vivid swirls in a Van Gogh painting.

I lifted my hand, palm up, and willed some of the magic to flow towards me. To do what I wanted it to do. To perform the impossible.

Annie sat back and gasped as a perfectly spherical ball of orange flame appeared an inch above my palm.

'Doesn't it burn?' she asked.

I waggled my fingers and the ball of fire began to spin around. 'No,' I replied. 'If it were to touch *you* it would burn, but not me.'

I closed my hand and the flame vanished.

'Consider me impressed,' said Annie. 'So I was wondering...'

'No, I can't fly.'

'—I was wondering if you'd like to take me on a date some time.'

I coughed into my pint as the beer slipped down the wrong pipe. 'I'm...' a bit more coughing, then I tried again: 'I'm sorry?'

'A date. We could go on a date. If you like.'

Apparently, saving a soul from eternal damnation could really turn a girl's head. No one ever tells you that.

'Joe?'

'Hm?'

'Are you going to answer, or...?'

'Yep. Yes. I am.'

'Well?'

And then, dear friends, I said something epically stupid and dumbfounding.

'Can I think about it?'

Feel free to pick up whatever's closest to you and hurl it in my direction.

The look on Annie's face was quite something. 'Oh sure,' she muttered. 'Yeah. Of course.'

Shortly after dropping that utterly bone-headed sentence, I'd made my excuses and left through the empty streets towards my parked car.

Can I think about it?

I checked the time on my phone. It was almost eight. All I wanted was to get home and have an early night.

Can I think about it?

What in the name of all that's unholy did I say that for?

Yes! Yes, please, thank you. That's the correct response when a beautiful woman you really, really like asks you out on a date.

So why had I dithered? What was holding me back from grasping this rare romantic opportunity that had landed in my unworthy lap? I was definitely interested, and I'd come to terms with the whole Chloe thing now. Plus, she was dead, so even if I hadn't, the chance of a happy ending there seemed fairly remote.

So why the uncertainty with Annie?

I would have continued to muse on my unlikely reaction if I hadn't been surprised by a cathedral.

There it was, stood on the back street where I parked the Uncanny Wagon. Now, I may have been working on a limited amount of sleep, but I'm pretty sure I'd have noticed pulling up next to something of that magnitude. Especially as it appeared to have been plucked directly from a gothic-themed nightmare.

I leaned back and took in its impressive if crumbling facade, gawping in awe at the giant spire that reached so impossibly high into the early evening sky that its tip was hidden by clouds.

The smart thing to do at this point would have been to leap behind the wheel of the Uncanny Wagon, speed off home, and forget all about the gigantic, shadow-drenched nightmare building that had definitely not been there before. So of course, I made a beeline for the place.

I stopped before the cathedral's massive, imposing entrance. Its twin doors were made of thick mahogany and studded with rusted, metal spikes. Very inviting, yes?

As I stepped closer, I thought I could hear the church organ playing inside. Okay, this was clearly something Uncanny and potentially dangerous, and now was really the time to get in my motor and drive away.

I pressed my hand against the door and, with a little effort, it creaked open. Damn you, curiosity. My footsteps echoed around the huge, vaulted space as I entered, and I found myself shivering as the temperature seemed to drop around ten degrees.

'Hello?' I said, trying to stop my teeth from chattering.

At first, I wasn't sure what the tune being played on the

church organ was, then I became convinced it was *Bohemian Rhapsody*.

I slowly made my way around a fat stone column, and the main space revealed itself. Wooden pews lined the floor, all pushed over, broken and coated with moss. It was clear that no one had sat down to listen to a sermon here in a long, long time.

Dominating the far wall was a ginormous stained glass window depicting what appeared to be residents from a lunatic's worst nightmare. The figures tore the heads from terrified soldiers, holding them above their open mouths and drinking down the blood that poured out. Which seemed a bit much for a house of God.

The cathedral's pipe organ was situated to one side of this gory window, with a strange yet familiar figure tickling the ivories.

A skeleton.

'Hello again,' I said, and threw in a jaunty little wave.

'Here at last, are you?' replied the skeleton.

I'd met this musically-gifted set of bones on a previous visit to the Dark Lakes, which told me that the mysterious cathedral must be connected to that unpleasant place.

'Do you know any other Queen songs?' I asked. 'Maybe a little *Don't Stop Me Now*?'

The skeleton scratched at his skull as he had a think with, well, whatever it is that skeletons think with, then launched into a not bad version with some gusto. I found my foot tapping, and began to hum along. When the song came to an end, I gave the skeleton a round of applause.

'Thank you, I thank you,' he replied, standing and taking a bow.

'As lovely as that was, is there a reason you're here?' I asked. 'Is there a reason this whole creepy, battered cathedral with the heavy metal stained glass window has appeared on the streets of Carlisle?'

'Death, Janto. Death is why we're here.'

I didn't like the sound of that. Not one bit.

'In what way?' I asked. 'A nice way? Like with Tarot cards: you know, "Don't think of it as an end, but the beginning of something new"? That kind of death?'

The skeleton idly teased at the organ's keys as his empty black eye sockets stayed fixed on me. To add to the creep, I noted he was playing the theme tune from *The Exorcist.*

'I see a lot, you know, Janto.'

'Good for you.'

'I see death in your future. Unavoidable.'

'My death?'

'That would be telling. But it's there. Clear as night. Tragedy. A fall is coming. A fall that stings and shocks and changes.'

I'd be lying if I said this conversation was lifting my spirits any.

'Right, well, I'll be off home if that's okay,' I said. 'Oh, and don't feel like you have to transport a whole evil cathedral into the middle of town when you fancy a chat. Just text next time, okay?'

I turned to head off into the night, only to find the Red Woman perched, legs crossed, on one of the overturned pews. Her thick, red hair tumbled down her shoulders, and her skin was as pale as a ghost's. She wore a form-fitting, green dress, the skirt split to an almost obscene level. She looked like Rita Hayworth playing the part of a femme fatale, and here I was, some poor sap in way over his head.

'Magic Eater,' she said, her voice a lusty purr.

'Oh good, you're here, too. I was just off, so I'll leave you and the skeleton to it. Hi and goodbye.'

As I passed, the Red Woman reached out and took my wrist in her icicle fingers.

'What's the hurry, Magic Eater?'

'It's Joseph. Not Janto, not Magic Eater: Joseph.'

She smiled, then bowed her head once. 'As you wish. What's in a name, anyway?'

'What's all this in aid of?' I asked, gesturing to our surroundings.

'I just wanted to see you.'

Apparently, I was in demand with beautiful women today. Twice in one lifetime. Pretty good going.

'This building is not in your world,' said the Red Woman. 'I have extended it from the Dark Lakes so we could have this conversation..'

'Right. Thanks? Is this a "thanks" situation? Thanks.'

'Sit down, Joseph, I don't bite. Well, that's not strictly true.'

The Red Woman smiled and rubbed a hand up her thigh, towards her, well... her you-know-what.

Lady bits.

I did my best to ignore the sexy display and went to sit down on a pew. Unfortunately, I completely failed to ignore the sexy display and missed my perch, landing with a jarring thump on the flagstone.

'Ha!' exclaimed the skeleton. 'What an idiot. And this is your great hope?'

The Red Woman clicked her fingers and the music-playing skeleton disappeared.

Trying to reclaim my dignity, I stood, brushed down my coat, then finally took a seat.

'I apologise for that nattering bag of bones,' she said.

'Look, I know why you're here,' I said. 'I know what you want. You've made your intentions clear over and over, and I'm, well, sort of sick of hearing it. Okay? I'm never, ever, going to fulfil my stupid destiny.'

The Red Woman smiled, her white teeth dazzling. She began to chuckle. It was not in the least bit reassuring.

'What? What's so funny?' I asked. 'Do I have food in my teeth?'

'Can't you feel it? Doesn't it prickle at your skin?'

'I... what?'

'You don't sense the inevitability?'

'All I sense is how cold this place is. Saving money on heating bills, or...?'

'Chatter on, but your throne is waiting,' said the Red Woman, 'and you are heading towards it, whatever you may think.'

'No, I'm not.'

'Something has changed. Something is coming, I can see it. I can see you taking your seat on the throne at last, and I won't have to lift a finger to make it happen.'

I pulled my coat tight, feeling a fist of anger grip my stomach. 'You're wrong.'

'No,' she said, tipping her head back, a look of pleasure washing over her face. 'Something has changed, I know it; every nerve-ending I have aches with the knowledge. You will become the Magic Eater at last, and soon. Oh, so very soon.'

I didn't bother replying. Instead, I walked across the cathedral floor, my boots echoing with each footstep, and did my best to ignore the seed of worry that had taken root in my belly.

5

I blinked in surprise as I stepped out of the cathedral. It was nighttime. It had been early evening when I entered, but now it was pitch black outside. I checked the time on my phone. It was almost three in the morning. I turned back to look at the cathedral, only to find it had vanished, and that I was now standing in front of a plain brick wall. I'd only been inside the cathedral for a few minutes at most, and it had spat me out hours later before disappearing the moment my back was turned.

Rude.

My phone buzzed in my hand. I looked down to see I'd missed multiple calls from both Eva and Detective Maya Myers.

I groaned and wondered what the chances were that I could just slink home and finally get some sleep.

My phone rang. Detective Myers.

I considered ignoring it.

I answered.

Damn it.

'Yeah?'

'Well, don't you sound like you're just full of the joy of existence?' said Myers, her familiar sarcastic lilt making me smile despite myself.

'You know, I think I'm going to start turning my phone off at night,' I replied. 'What's wrong?'

What was wrong, according to Detective Myers, was that something had killed a whole barn full of sheep at Hunter's Farm.

I made peace with the idea of never sleeping again, climbed into the Uncanny Wagon, and steered it towards the scene of the crime.

Myers greeted me when I arrived, her leather jacket done up to keep out the frosty morning air. She held a metal thermos of coffee in a gloved hand.

'Can I have a sip?' I asked.

'Do you have a cup?'

I patted myself down. 'Not on me, no.'

'Sorry, then that's a no. Germs.' She smiled and gestured for me to follow her to the barn.

Inside, it was, well, a bloody mess. And I mean that literally. Shredded sheep littered the place; chunks of flesh, pools of blood, and dangling entrails covered almost every square inch of the building. It was disgusting. I mean, really disgusting. Like a bomb had gone off in a butchers shop.

Eva was on the scene already, crouching down and using a stick to poke at an unidentifiable portion of sheep.

'He's here,' said Myers.

Eva grunted by way of reply.

'Frosty greeting, even for her,' said Myers, quietly, as she sipped at her coffee.

'Yeah, well, we had a bit of an awkward moment.'

'Couldn't most of her moments be considered awkward?'

'Good point,' I said. 'So, what happened here, exactly?' It was all I could do not to end the sentence with the word, *'Aliens?'*

'It's not fucking aliens,' said Eva, lips clamped around a freshly-rolled cigarette.

'I didn't say a thing,' I said, raising my hands. 'But... maybe? I mean, I've read about this sort of thing. Aliens love to pop down and mess around with farm animals. Cutting them open to see how they work, that sort of thing.'

'Okay, demons, ghosts, maybe even vampires,' said Myers, 'but I draw the line at policing little green men.'

'Already told you,' spat Eva, 'it's not fucking aliens.'

She removed a thermos of her own from the inside pocket of her tatty coat.

'Coffee?' I cried, dumbfounded to see her drinking anything beside cans of super-strength lager.

'Whisky,' she replied. 'I'm not an animal.'

I was going to point out that the purpose of a thermos was to store hot drinks, not spirits, but I let it go. Particularly as she still had a stick on her person.

'Well then, a barn full of slaughtered sheep,' I said. 'What do the farmers have to say? Did they see anything? Hear anything?'

Myers nodded. 'Mr Hunter says he did. Got up for a piss in the middle of the night and saw movement outside the barn. Left the house with a cricket bat to investigate. Stepped into the barn to see this horror show.'

'But no sign of who did it?' I asked. 'Maybe a glimpse at a departing flying saucer?'

Myers shook her head. 'This isn't the first local farm to see something like this recently, though it is the first on this level. A few others have seen a cow killed, or a couple of pigs, but nothing on this scale.'

'So whatever's behind the killings has taken a step up,' I said.

'Exactly,' said Myers before putting a hand to her head and scrunching her eyes up. 'Christ, I've got a bastard of a head coming on.'

'Oi, long streak of piss, go on then,' said Eva.

'Go on then what?' I replied.

Eva gesticulated at the nearest lumps of dead sheep. 'Do your thing, get your hands dirty.'

Ah, yes. One of the few abilities I seemed to still have access to was that I could touch the bodies of the recently deceased and see flashes of their experiences close to the point of death.

I looked around at all the disgusting, blood-soaked bits strewn around the barn among the straw and dung.

'But... I don't want to touch them,' I said, my voice a toddler's whine.

'You're good for practically fuck all,' replied Eva. 'Transportation, and this. So go over there and touch some dead things.'

I looked to Myers for support.

'She has a point.'

'Traitor.'

Myers shrugged.

I sighed and picked my way carefully across the gore-coated floor until I found a mostly-intact sheep corpse. This one only had a couple of its legs torn off and its intestines trailing out like a grim bridal train.

I forgot to mention the smell. It really smelled. A lot.

I grimaced and lowered myself into a crouch, not wanting to dip my knees into the crimson pooled at my feet.

'Okay, nothing disgusting about what I'm about to do. All perfectly normal and not at all nightmare-inducing.'

'Get on with it, idiot,' encouraged Eva.

'Okay!'

I breathed in a couple of times, then closed my eyes and tried to connect with the magic around me. I felt it respond. Felt it flow towards me. And then, without thinking too much about the disgusting mess I was reaching for, I placed both hands on the dead sheep and waited for a miracle.

And waited.

And waited a little bit more.

The miracle did not happen. Not at all. I opened my eyes, confused, and looked back to Eva and Myers.

'Well?' said the detective. 'What did you see?'

'I don't think it's working,' I replied.

'Great. So now we're just down to transportation,' said Eva, swigging from her thermos.

'Try again,' suggested Myers

I turned back to the dead animal and tried to concentrate. This always worked. This "sight" power. Even before I knew how to control it, it had worked. I'd touch a thing and all of these images would come rushing in. Dreadful little home movies of a living creature's final moments.

I focused.

I looked around me this time, as the magic in the air flickered into view. Other Uncanny types see these washes of colour all the time. They live in it. But not me. Not anymore. I have to really *want* to see it. Have to force myself to.

I gritted my teeth and the magic soaked into me, more and more, and I made my demands of it. Told it who I was and what I wanted.

I touched the dead sheep again. And saw nothing. Not a bloody thing.

I grunted and pushed harder, my hands starting to tingle as though being swarmed with static. And yet no pictures, no insight, popped into my mind's eye.

I climbed to my feet, confused.

'Well?' said Eva.

'Something's not right,' I replied.

'Well, yeah,' said Myers. 'I mean, we are stood in a barn full of dead bodies.'

'What did you see?' asked Eva, growing irritable. Well, more irritable. She has levels. Grumpy, all the way to absolutely fucking livid.

'I didn't see anything, it felt like I was being blocked. Like there was a wall between me and the sheep's final moments.'

'So try another one,' she shot back.

And so I did. In the end, I must have stuffed my hands into twenty different sheep, but always the same story.

Something had murdered all of these animals in the most brutal of ways, and whatever it was, it knew how to stop me from seeing it.

6

Sleep.

I'm a big fan of sleep.

And yet I was getting so little of it that I'd found myself literally lusting after the stuff.

After my failure at the barn, I excused myself, drove home, and collapsed into bed, still fully dressed. I was asleep in seconds. Sadly, I wasn't able to glean any enjoyment from it, thanks to the troubling dream I'd been having playing on repeat.

There I was again, stark bollock naked and about to step into Derwentwater for a bit of a paddle. It wasn't that the dream was a nightmare exactly. Nothing explicitly scary happened, but each time I experienced it, I felt a strange uneasiness that stuck with me well into my waking hours.

I waded into the chilly water, feeling the stones beneath my feet, slick and hard.

'Swim down.'

'Swim down, Janto.'

Those distant, familiar voices, teasing at me again.

'Swim down.'

I turned and looked back at the beach to see two figures staring across the lake at me. Two women.

'Swim down, Janto,' said one of them.

And now I knew who the voices belonged to.

I knew who the two women were.

Lyna and Melodia. The two dead witches of the Cumbrian Coven. The two dead witches that I murdered after becoming some sort of power-crazed lunatic with murder on his mind.

'Swim down.'

I turned from them quickly and ducked into the water.

I'd like to say that when I eventually woke up I was refreshed and ready to attack the day a new man. I'd like to say that. Instead, I woke to find I'd slept all the way through to late afternoon, and with a head full of cotton wool. Which was no big surprise. Somehow, sleeping for too long always makes me feel worse than not having slept at all.

I cursed my stupid body and dragged myself to the shower, hoping the water might pummel some sense into me. Feeling a little more with it, I made a late-late-late breakfast of eggs and toast, and started to think about Annie. I had no idea why I'd delayed answering her offer of a date. I liked her. She liked me. What was I worried about? My life was full of monsters and fear and the threat of becoming a world-crushing, flame-skinned beast. Wasn't I owed a little romance?

'Hi.'

The unexpected greeting almost caused me to spill my eggs. The fox was stood on my couch, almost sheepishly.

'Getting better,' I said, decanting my freshly-scrambled eggs onto a plate and reaching inside a cupboard to fish out the brown sauce. 'You can still do some work on the surprise element. It would be nice not to jump out of my skin every time you showed up.'

The fox looked at me, confused. 'But you are still within your skin.'

'Right. My mistake.' I dolloped the sauce on, grabbed a fork, and sat on the couch next to the fox.

'If you're hungry, there's crisps in the cupboard,' I said.

'I am not hungry,' he replied.

'Suit yourself.'

The fox paused, then hopped off the couch and grabbed himself a packet of crisps. Salt & Vinegar. A gourmet's choice.

'Thank you, Magic Eater, for sharing your rations.'

'Joseph. It's Joseph.'

'Yes. Joseph.'

He hopped up on the couch again and we watched a *Frasier* re-run in silence for a few minutes as I finished my eggs and he munched on his crisps.

'Your den is not tidy,' said the fox.

I looked around my snug little flat. It was true that it looked more like a student's bedsit than the home of a man in his thirties. Or, in my case, a man in his nineteen-thirties.

'Your Red Woman paid me a visit last night,' I said, placing my plate on the floor.

'Oh?'

'Yeah, and she didn't come alone. Brought a skeleton. And a very run-down cathedral.'

The fox nodded. 'I know of the place. And the skeleton. He will not stop playing no matter how much you threaten.'

'I thought he was pretty good. For a skeleton. So, are you here to convince me to take up the mantle of Magic Eater? To fulfil my shitty destiny?'

'No.'

'Oh. Well. Why are you here, then?'

The fox studied his hind paws. 'I do not like the Dark Lakes anymore. I do not want to stay there.'

I wasn't entirely sure where to go from there. Was the fox looking to have a heart to heart? He seemed so glum, the poor little sod, that before I could stop myself, I reached over and gave his belly fur a little ruffle.

'There, there. Chin up.'

The fox grinned. 'She is very sure that you will soon take the throne.'

'Yeah, she said.'

'Very sure. She does not tell me why. I think perhaps she does not know. But yet she knows.'

'Well, she's out of luck. The only throne this arse sits on is in my bathroom.'

'You have a throne there?'

I looked at the fox for several seconds. 'Yes. I have a throne there.'

'Ah...' said the fox, impressed.

I felt my phone vibrate and plucked it from my pocket, expecting it to be either Eva or Detective Myers with more news on the dead sheep. Instead, I saw that someone had contacted me through my spooky website.

A little background: before I knew who I was, I used to investigate weird stuff. It was more of a hobby than anything. I'd look into all sorts of spooky goings-on; anything from suspected hauntings, to claims of vampirism. None of it ever added up to anything, but it got me out the house and kept me distracted from the gnawing mystery of my own identity.

I'd packed all that in, though. I barely had enough time as it was, what with the day job and my coven duties, without running around the countryside chasing non-existent ghosts. Still, something about this message caught my interest. If I had to put it down to anything, I think I'd say it was the last line, which read: *PLEASE HELP, MONEY NO OBJECT*. I don't know why, but something about that part really snagged my attention.

Two hours later, I was sat in Brewer's Café, just off the main street in the centre of Keswick. Keswick, the small town I lived in, was a market town, huddled within the Lake District, surrounded by mountains. It's close to Derwentwater, which is how I came to set up shop here after waking there without my memory.

I phoned the man who left me the intriguing message and suggested we meet the next day, but he seemed very keen to talk as soon as possible, so here I was, nursing a mug of tea and waiting for him to show up.

I took out my phone and clicked on my contacts. Annie's name was top of the list. I took a breath.

'Okay. Well. Okay.'

I hit 'Call'.

She answered in three rings. Neither keen, nor unkeen. 'I was wondering if I was going to hear from you, Joe.'

'Yes, right, sorry.'

'So?'

'Look, first of all, let me apologise for whatever that was yesterday.'

'It was a bit weird, yeah.'

'A bit weird is a good description of me, so it's very on-brand.'

There was a bit of a pause.

'And?'

'And yes. Sorry. I would very much enjoy being in a romantic date type situation with you, Annie.'

'Would you now?'

'Yes. Please.'

'Well, I'm sorry, the offer's off the table.'

I felt as though I'd shrunk about ten inches. 'Oh. Of course. Of course it is. Sorry to bother you.'

Annie started to laugh.

'You rotten sod,' I said, and couldn't help but laugh, too.

'Enjoy a taste of your own medicine.'

'I really am sorry, you just caught me a bit off guard.'

'You can make up for it by taking me out for a meal on Friday.'

I felt butterflies bashing around in my stomach. 'Absolutely. A meal. This Friday. That I can do.'

'Good. I'll see you then, Joe.'

'Yes you will, Annie.'

I finished the call and pocketed my phone, cheeks aching from the grin I was wearing.

Well, well, Joe. You old womaniser, you.

'Mr Lake?'

I looked up as the voice snapped me out of my warm fuzzy-wuzzies. A jittery-looking man in an ill-fitting suit hovered a few feet away.

'Mr Lake? Are you Mr Lake?'

'That's me, but Joseph will do,' I replied. 'You're Paul Travers, I presume?'

The man looked over his shoulder then quickly plonked himself down on the seat opposite. I took in the strange specimen before me. He didn't look in the best of ways, in fact, he looked bloody petrified. His eyes bulged, his fingers clenched and waggled and interlocked and wouldn't settle. His hair was plastered damp to his forehead, and he had a good four days worth of growth on his face. Something was causing him considerable distress.

'Are you okay?' I asked.

'What?' he replied, looking nervously around the busy café, which was full of rotund old women with hair dyed shades of purple and pink, chomping down on cream buns.

'You seem a little on edge. In fact you seem fully on edge. The whole of you is just one big edge.'

'I need help.'

'Okay, so what is it I can do for you, Mr Travers?'

'We all need help,' he replied. 'Not just me, it's all of them. They think I don't know yet, but I do. I see it. I see them all.'

I was starting to suspect that this man might be a little on the insane side.

'What is it you know, exactly?' I asked.

'They're all in on it!' he cried, his voice a high-pitched shriek that drew disapproving eyes from the rest of the room.

'It's okay, you're safe here, Mr Travers. No need for shouting. Can I get you a cup of tea?'

He stood, kicking his chair back and raking both hands through what was left of his sweat-drenched hair. 'No! No, no, no, no! He's coming! He's coming!'

I stood up slowly, worried that he might be about to hurt himself. Or worse, hurt me. Not a fan of being hurt.

'Calm down, you're okay, there's no need to panic.'

'This was a mistake. That's all. A mistake. Simple mistake. Mistakes happen, happen, happen!'

He turned, and in his haste to leave, stumbled over his fallen chair. Careening to one side, he spilled into a neighbouring table, causing a couple of fellow diners' drinks to tumble and crash to the floor.

'Sorry, sorry, this was a mistake,' he said, answering their noisy complaints.

'Mr Travers—Paul—tell me what's wrong!' I called after him, but he didn't answer.

Mr Travers rushed out of the café and was gone.

7

A couple of days passed uneventfully until Friday arrived, the day of my big date with Annie.

In the meantime, I tried to get in touch with Paul Travers a couple of times, but he didn't respond. I decided it best to assume he was just on something of the illegal variety and put the whole business out of my mind.

'You are dressed finer than usual,' said the fox, who was sat eating crisps on my couch (salt & vinegar, of course).

'I'm going to have to start charging you rent soon,' I replied. 'And for the food.'

The fox grinned back, his spiky teeth full of mashed potato. He'd popped in a lot over the last few days, which should have bothered me, I suppose, considering it had been his job to help coerce me into being, you know, an evil, murdery bastard. Instead, I found myself enjoying the company. It was like having a pet. A talking, crisps-loving pet.

I sat next to the fox as he stared, transfixed by another episode of *Frasier*.

'Can I ask you something?' I said.

'Anything. You are the oncoming darkness, the eater of magic, the—'

'Yeah, about that. You knew me. The real me, from before. Janto the warlock.'

'That is so, yes.'

'So, what was I like exactly?'

The fox scratched at his chin with the edge of his battle-axe as he considered the question. 'You looked the same.'

'Obviously, I looked the same. That's not what I meant. I meant personality-wise.'

'Oh, you were very good.'

'Good?'

'Yes.' The fox frowned. 'Well, not good. Opposite of good. Very bad.'

'Right.'

'Very, very bad.'

'Got it.'

'Horrible.'

'I see.'

'Very nasty.'

'I said, I see!'

We sat in silence for a few seconds as I huffed. What exactly had I expected him to say? From what little scraps I'd been fed—and the knowledge of how things had ended up—I knew I wasn't exactly a saint. I was the exact opposite, in fact.

'Was there anything good about me?'

'Your hair,' said the fox. 'Always had very good hair.'

It's true, I do have very nice hair. And I don't even do anything special to it. That's not a brag, just a stone-cold fact.

'Most people, when they first find themselves at the Dark Lakes, they are afraid,' said the fox. 'I was the first creature there that you met, and I saw no fear in you. None at all. I saw determination. I saw someone who knew that they were where they belonged. I saw a hunger that would chew through worlds.' The fox shivered then turned his attention back to his crisps.

'Do you have any more salt & vinegar?'

I was on my way to Annie in a little Italian place down a back street in Keswick. It was a short distance from my flat, so I left the fox to *Frasier* and headed over on foot. My stomach was in knots at the prospect of meeting Annie, and I hoped the cool, early evening air might help me get a hold of myself.

It may come as some surprise to you, but my romantic history was somewhat patchy. I know, I know, I'm tall, reasonable-looking, and possess at least one good outfit, but when it came to women, my experience was scant.

There were a couple of reasons for this. Number one, I didn't remember the vast majority of my life. Perhaps before waking naked next to a lake, I'd been a legendary lover in the Uncanny world. For all I knew, hundreds of women throughout history had considered me the finest sex person they'd ever lain with.

You don't know, it could be true.

The other reason is that for the chunk of my life I do remember—the last ten years—I'd spent most of it in love with Chloe Palmer, a doctor at the hospital I worked at. This unspoken love had stopped me considering any other options, and when we finally did get together, it turned out that she was secretly an insane person who planned to lead an army of octopus-limbed soul vampires into battle against humanity.

As I say. A patchy romantic history.

I peered through the restaurant's glass door to see Annie already sat at the table I'd booked. I took three deep breaths, straightened out my coat, then entered.

'Hello!'

The greeting came out so loud that it not only startled her but everyone else in the place. Trying to ignore the glares of the rest of the eaters, I hastily made my way over to the table and took a seat.

'Sorry, did I just shout really loudly?' I asked.

'You did a bit. And at quite a shrill pitch, too.'

'Why, thank you,' I said, which made her laugh.

Okay, so I hadn't blown things just yet. Actually, that was a bit of an understatement. Not only had I not blown things, but what followed was one of the nicest hours I remember experiencing in a long time. The nerves melted away within seconds, and we spoke and ate and drank and laughed.

So yes, of course, I ruined everything. Come on, this is me you're dealing with here.

Having paid a visit to the Gents, I exited the cubicle and washed my hands. I'm not an animal.

I gave myself a little wink in the mirror. 'You're doing good, kid,' I told myself. Awful.

'Swim down, Janto.'

I jerked around, looking for the source of the voice, but I was alone.

'Swim down.'

Of course, I knew the voices. They belonged to the two witches I'd murdered.

'Where are you?' I asked.

Previous to this, I'd only heard them in dreams, which made me think this was definitely a bad sign.

'Hello? Can you hear me?'

'Swim down.'

'I don't understand. Why? Why do you keep saying that?'

A movement in the mirror caught my eye. Ripples. The glass was now the surface of the lake from my dream. I found myself moving closer to it, squinting, trying to see what was in the water.

'Swim down.'

It was an army.

It was my army.

An army of the dead, waiting for me at the bottom of the Dark Lakes. Waiting for my command.

'Swim down, Janto.'

A hand shot from the mirror towards me and I stumbled back, yelping with surprise.

'You all right, mate?'

I spun around to find a fellow diner had entered without me noticing. I looked back to the mirror, but that's all it was again. No ripples, no water, no army.

'Seriously, are you all right?' asked the concerned diner.

'No. I mean yes, sorry.' I patted my stomach theatrically. 'Dodgy scampi. Playing havoc with my insides.'

I glanced at the mirror again and headed out of the bathroom, back to my table. Annie beamed up at me, but her expression soon crumpled when she saw the face I was wearing.

'Hey, are you okay? What happened?'

'What? Nothing. Fine, I'm fine.'

Why was I lying to her? She knew weird stuff existed, she'd sold her soul to demons for God's sake.

'Would you like to see the dessert menu?' asked the waiter.

'What?'

'Can you give us a moment?' asked Annie.

The waiter gave me a bit of side-eye, then smiled at Annie and left.

What I saw in the bathroom I'd only ever experienced in my dreams, so why here, why now? Was Annie being present somehow connected to the visions? If she was the kind of person who'd courted demons, how did I know I could trust her? Maybe this was Chloe Palmer all over again, only this time I'd actually caught the warning signs. With Chloe, it came out of the blue, but Annie... she'd already shown she was willing to mix with some pretty questionable sorts.

'Joe?'

'Hm?'

'Are you okay? You've been staring at me with a strange look on your face for about a minute now.'

'Those demons you used to sell your soul to...'

'Yeah? What about them?'

'Are you ever tempted to go back down that well and bargain for more stuff?'

'What? Of course not. You know I wouldn't, I have a daughter to think about now.'

'Right. Of course.'

My heart was hammering against my chest as I tried to decide whether she was in on it or not. In on whatever it was that was happening to me. Maybe she knew about all those dead farm animals, too.

I felt sweat prickling my forehead. Christ, was the room getting smaller? It was. The walls were crowding in, trying to smother me. I grabbed my glass of beer and drank half of it in one go, my brain turning somersaults. Had I fallen for it again? Did I have another Chloe on my hands? Typical me, typical me. Eva was right, I was an idiot.

'Joe, seriously, what's wrong with you? We were having a nice time.'

'Yeah, it really seemed like we were.'

I stood and rummaged for my wallet, pulling out enough to cover the cost of the meal.

'Sorry, no dessert, I've got to go.'

'Joe?'

'Just, a big monster thing to deal with that I forgot about, sorry.'

I headed for the exit, eyes straight ahead, stopping for no one.

8

Yeah. You don't have to say anything. I know I messed that up.

As I approached my flat, moving like I was trudging through treacle, I realised that what I'd experienced was some sort of panic attack. Paranoia had crept in and had its wicked way with me. The hurt I was still feeling from Chloe had sent me off into some creepy fantasy land.

Well, that was me and Annie over with, anyway. Over with before it had even had a chance to begin. There was no way a woman like her was going to put up with her date turning into a sweaty, unstable mess, not to mention running out on her like a panicked animal.

Well done, Joseph.

Well done, Janto the dumb-dumb warlock.

I tossed my keys on the sideboard as I entered my flat. I could hear the TV was still on.

'Hey, fox.'

'What?'

The fox was gone. In his place sat Eva, who looked back at me with a giant bong between her thighs.

'Jesus, Eva. You scared me.'

'Did you just call me a fox?'

'What? No, I did not.'

'Pretty fucking sure you called me a fox.'

I peered around, but it seemed like my furry friend had made himself scarce, a scattering of empty crisp packets the only clue to his having been there.

'Listen, I know I'm hot-to-fucking-trot,' said Eva, 'but if you call me a fox again I'll tear off your balls and make you wear them as earrings. Understand, love?'

'One-hundred percent. Absolutely.'

I flopped onto the couch next to her, utterly demoralised.

'Jesus, what's up with your mush? Realised what a piece of shit you are again? Yeah, that's gotta be rough.'

'No. Well, actually, a bit, yeah.'

Eva huffed at the bong and twirled her hand in my direction, gesturing for me to elaborate.

'Just. Remember Annie?'

'Nope.'

'Sold her soul to a demon.'

'Keep going.'

'Sold her soul to lots and lots of demons.'

'Oh,' said Eva. 'Yeah, no, nothing.'

I sighed and grabbed the bong, taking a huff of my own to try and relax.

'Well, we were on a date and I just messed things up. Properly messed things up. No doubt for good.'

'Jesus. You give up easily, eh? You never used to. That was one of the best and—in the end—worst things about you. You skinny fuck.' She ruffled my hair and grinned, Eva, clearly off her nut, even by her standards.

'I think the whole Chloe thing may have given me some teensy trust issues,' I said.

'Right. And Chloe is?'

'Okay, now you're just messing with me.'

Eva shrugged and grabbed the bong back. 'I've had my own

dating fuck ups, you know? Once this girl told me she would meet me at eight and didn't turn up until ten past. I got so pissed off I turned her into a frog.'

'Really?'

'Really. And then I couldn't work out how to turn her back. A dog ate her. Can't help blaming myself for that one.'

Moving right along...

'Annie did nothing wrong and I just got paranoid and had a little breakdown in front of her. Ran out of the place. I'm such an idiot.'

'I agree.'

'Yeah, I got that.'

'A big idiot.'

'Thanks.'

'And a toss-pot. Wanker. Fucking arsehole bastard—'

'I get the idea,' I said.

Eva slumped down further, her hooded eyes fixed on the TV. It was playing an episode of *Quincy*. It was always *Quincy* with her. Or *Columbo*. Or *Diagnosis Murder*.

'What is it with you and these detective shows, anyway?'

'You don't need to talk to me about trust issues, Janto,' she said. 'I used to trust you unthinkingly. Absolutely and completely. With my life. With everyone in the county's life. You broke that.'

'I know.'

'But that wasn't all you broke.'

If I didn't know better, I'd swear Eva's eyes were welling up.

'Eva,' I started, but she leapt to her feet, sending the bong tumbling to the floor and spilling nasty brown water all over my best rug. Well, my only rug.

'Hey, they opened a new vodka place in Workington,' she cried. 'Let's get over there and drink until the world disappears. What d'you say turd-face?'

'Turd-face says okay.' I stood up. 'Let's make morning me hate night me.'

It was as we were leaving the vodka bar at two in the morning, the pair of us looking for a convenient alleyway to vomit into, that I got the call from Detective Myers.

We were needed.

In no fit state to drive, we dialled a taxi rank and headed over to Hobbes Farm crashed across the back seat of a cab.

Detective Myers did not seem at all impressed when we staggered out of the car and swayed her way. 'Well isn't this nice?' she said, wafting a hand in front of her face. 'Christ, how much have you two had?'

'All of it, I think,' I replied.

'Yeah we have!' said Eva, doing a little dance, almost falling over, then pulling a can from her coat pocket and continuing to drink. I swear she must have some sort of magic coat with black holes in its pockets. No matter where she was, there always seemed to be an infinite number of drinks secreted in the thing.

'This is an official investigation,' said Myers. 'This is my job. If you two are fucked, you can get another taxi and get out of here, understand?'

'Understand,' I said, taking a few mouthfuls of the cold night air and trying to centre myself.

'Don't worry, Detective,' said Eva, 'I've never been more focused.'

'I'd be a lot more convinced by that if you weren't crouched in the dirt, urinating.'

'Don't look if you don't like it.'

After Eva was done, we headed into a stable set behind the house to find the latest scene of slaughter. Six horses, dead. Like before, they hadn't been stabbed or bludgeoned over the head, they'd been ripped to pieces. It was as if their bodies had exploded.

'There's no way a normal person is capable of this,' said Myers.

'No shit,' replied Eva.

'Are aliens still off the table?' I asked, trying not to gag at the sights and smells contained within the blood-spattered stables.

'It's some sort of monster, or monsters, right?' said Myers.

'Right,' said Eva. 'Though why do this? What's the point?'

'Maybe it's just a crazy monster without any purpose,' I suggested. 'Monsters can probably just snap, too. Can't they?'

Myers was breathing a little heavy, her face paler than usual.

'Are you okay?' I asked.

'Fine, I'm fine.'

She really didn't look it.

'Do you need to sit down?'

She waved me off, irritated. 'Migraines or something. They come and go. I'm fine.'

Deciding it best not to prod any further, I made my way to the nearest horse corpse and crouched, willing the magic inside the barn to flow into me. I placed my hands on what was left of the poor creature, and commanded the magic to show me the horse's final moments.

'Well?' asked Myers.

I grimaced, willing the magic to work, but just like with the sheep, I was getting nothing. Just a tingle of static that prickled my hands, prickled my mind. I grunted and gave up.

'Okay, this can't be a coincidence. I'm getting nothing again.'

'Which means?' said Myers.

'Which means that something is purposefully hiding from us,' replied Eva, her face set into a grimace.

9

What Eva had said immediately made me think of Annie. Perhaps I wasn't being so paranoid after all. Was she involved in the animal slaughters somehow? Was she playing me for a fool and using magic to cover her tracks? To make it so that I wouldn't see her, recognise her, stop her?

It was all a bit vexing, which is not a word I drop very often.

The first chance I got, I decided to do something creepy that would get me fired if anyone ever saw me doing it.

I went down to the mortuary to touch some dead bodies.

Now, believe me, dead people are not high on my list of fun things to touch. In fact—and I'd like to be crystal clear here—touching dead things doesn't appear on my "Fun Things to Touch" list at all. Silly putty, I like to touch. Same goes for velvet and, on frequent occasions, myself. But not dead people. You can quote me on that.

Still, I had good reason to make this grim room-call. After what happened at the last two crime scenes, I had to find out if there was a connection between the case and my insight magic not working. Or whether I'd just lost a grip on how to do the thing entirely.

I ghosted down the corridor, illuminated by the stuttering strip lights I'd been told to replace three days ago and hadn't got around to. I poked my head around the door jamb to check the way was clear, and was happy to find the room empty. Empty apart from the corpses, anyway. A quick glance over my shoulder to make sure no one was heading in this direction, then I slipped into the mortuary and darted over to the wall of drawers containing the cadavers.

A deep breath or two, then I tugged open a waist-height drawer to reveal the corpse within. It was a man; bloated, bald, his skin the colour of spoiled milk. The toe tag he was wearing would give me his identity, but I had no wish to be on first name terms with the poor sod.

I closed my eyes and willed the magic in the room to swarm me. To wash over me, into me, to soak into my very bones. I sensed it respond to my command, felt the warmth of it as it became part of me. It was intoxicating. The more I did it, the more adept I became at controlling the magic around me, the more of a high I seemed to get off it. My pleasure receptors tingled, my senses sharpened, the certainty of my control grew stronger.

'Show me,' I whispered as I placed my palms on the cold flesh of the dead man's shoulder.

It happened instantly.

I wasn't me anymore.

I was inside this man looking out.

His final moments had become my reality; a virtual reality I had no control over. I was along for the ride, for the experience. There was no way of interfering with the events I saw. This was a recording of a man's final minutes. I was seeing the past, that's all, and there's no altering the past, no matter how much I might like to. And believe me, knowing my past, if I could, I really, definitely would.

The view flared suddenly, bright lights blooming, crowding

my vision. I fell to one side, then I was on the floor, reaching a hand to my chest, to my arm, as the colour drained from what I was seeing, static crowding in around the edges as the picture dilated down, down, down.

I jerked back, pulling my hands away from the man.

A heart attack. I'd just experienced his last seconds alive as his heart betrayed him and sputtered to a stop.

I looked down at him. He could only have been in his late forties. A life half-lived.

A noise from outside the room caught my attention. I slid the dead man back into his drawer and scampered out of the room before my luck gave out.

I sat on a wall in the car park after my shift and lit a cigarette. Terrible habit, I know, but I never said I was perfect.

I wondered some more about the perpetrator of the cattle murders. I knew for sure now that the lack of insight I was getting when I touched the dead animals was related to the crimes somehow. The man in the mortuary had given up his death to me the moment my skin touched his. So that was that. Theory confirmed. The animal killer was blocking me. But blocking me specifically, or anyone who had my ability? Were there other people with the power to see the dead's last moments? Eva couldn't do it, but others must be able to, surely? I certainly hoped so, because if that wasn't the case, whoever was behind the killings knew me—knew what I could do—and that meant I might very well be in their firing line.

Come off it Joseph, when aren't you in danger these days?

'Hey.'

I almost fell off the wall as Annie stepped suddenly into view.

'Oh, hi. Hey, it's you.'

'It is me, yeah.'

Well, wasn't this a coincidence?

Or was it?

She sat down beside me. 'You really messed up that first date, hey?'

'Yeah, sorry, I suppose I did.'

'Want to tell me why? Because I thought we were having a pretty nice time, then you came back from having a wazz like you'd seen a ghost.'

'There's no point lying to you,' I said, 'I'm working on a bit of a weird case.'

'I thought as much.'

Oh, did you now?

'Yes, and I got this sudden, strange insight.'

'While you were having a pee?'

'Yes. Well, no, after that. While I was washing my hands.'

'It's good to know you wash. Some men don't.'

'I'm not *some men*, Annie.'

'No, I worked that out for myself.'

She smiled, and Christ alive if I didn't feel a few butterflies break loose in my stomach.

'You can take me for a drink now if you like,' she said. 'To make up for it.'

What was this now? Did I trust her? I didn't *not* trust her? Really, I had no reason to think she was involved in any of this cattle-killing mess. What was my evidence beyond *The last girl I fancied was insane and friends with monsters*?

But still, better to be safe than sorry.

'Sounds good,' I replied. 'I know a nice little pub in Keswick.'

Mickey Finn's was the local Uncanny pub. A pub where magical creatures of all stripes came together to drink in peace, away from 'normal' people. It was a safe place to knock back a pint, too, as it was protected by a magic-dampening bubble that stopped the worst, most life-threatening magic from being used within its walls. Given that I was currently unreasonably suspicious of the woman I fancied, I thought taking her there was a smart option.

Of course, she could have offed me on the thirty-minute drive over there, but that only occurred to me as we parked up. I'm not always the sharpest knife in the drawer, it's true.

'I don't understand,' she said as I pointed to what, to her, appeared to be a brick wall.

'Mickey Finn's is located down a blind alley,' I explained.

'A what now?'

'A sort of secret passage. The world's full of them. It keeps certain places hidden from prying eyes. Especially from the prying eyes of non-magical sorts.'

'Like me.'

'Exactly. Muggles.'

She grinned.

'Take my hand,' I said, offering it to her and waggling my fingers. I wasn't sure how to perform the spell that allowed someone to see the entrance to the blind alley, but I assumed I could lead someone through it physically. Either that or I was about to walk Annie into a brick wall.

'Okay,' she said. 'I'm trusting you.'

I felt a little guilt peck at me as she said that. 'And in we go.'

You'll be pleased to hear that I didn't walk Annie face-first into a rock-solid magic facade.

A few minutes later, I was placing a glass of wine in front of Annie and sipping at my pint, the two of us tucked away on a corner table. Now we were inside the pub's magic dampening bubble, I could relax. The guilt did not relax, though. The chances of Annie being another Chloe Palmer were astronomical, completely unreal, and yet the piss-poor way I was treating her was very, very real.

'So, this is where all the wizards hang out, is it?' asked Annie, peering around the old-fashioned pub.

'Yup, this is the place. Wizards, vampires, ghosts, trolls.'

'Trolls?'

'And not the annoying internet kind. I mean, I assume. I suppose they could be both.'

As Annie snorted, I decided I was going to risk it. I wasn't going to let my own stupidity ruin a good thing. I was going to get past this insanity and give myself a shot at romantic happiness, and she would never have to know about my twisted, unwarranted suspicions.

'So,' she said, 'want to tell me the truth about why you acted like a giant arse at the restaurant?'

Well, balls.

'It was nothing,' I said. 'Not really.'

'I can tell you're lying to me, Joe.'

'No, you can't. I mean… no I'm not…?'

Annie arched an eyebrow.

'Okay. It's not my fault. Or yours. Okay, it is partly mine.'

'This is about your ex, isn't it?'

She was perceptive. And had a hell of a memory on her. I think maybe those were two of the things she sold her soul for.

'Yes.'

'I'm not evil, Joe.'

'I never thought you were, honest. Not for a second!'

Annie said nothing.

'Okay, for a little bit, I did. Tiny, tiny bit. Possibly. There might be a small chance of it. Sorry.'

'Oi, Janto!'

I turned to see a wall of a man strolling towards me. He had a head the size of a barrel, fists like bowling balls, and he did not look at all happy to see me.

'Janto, you vicious piece of shit.'

'And hello to you...?'

'I heard you were back. Didn't believe it. Couldn't. But here you are, after everything you did, just sitting there.'

I stood slowly, hands held up in surrender. I sensed that this wasn't an old friend about to offer me a handshake and a round of beer. I'm quite perceptive in that way.

'I'm not sure what it is I did in the past to annoy you,' I said, 'but I'm a very different man now.'

'So it's true,' said the giant man, grimacing, the veins on his temple bulging, fit to burst. 'You don't have your memory, don't have your powers.'

'I have *some* powers.'

'He can make a little ball of fire appear,' said Annie, trying to help me out.

The giant man laughed long and hard. It was a touch demoralising.

'You ruined my life, Janto. And now, I'm going to ruin yours. Permanently. By killing you dead.'

'Right. Shit.'

The man pulled a large knife from his belt and licked his lips. I tried to make fire appear in my hand. I failed to make fire appear in my hand. Stupid magic-dampening bubble!

Oh, I'll take Annie to Mickey Finn's, I'll feel safe there.

Great idea, Joe. Another winner.

'Joe, be careful' said Annie.

'Don't worry,' I replied. 'I've got this.'

'You know how to stop him?'

'No,' I admitted, 'it just seemed like the thing to say.'

'Here I come, warlock!' bellowed the giant.

'Joe, you've got to...' then Annie paused, looking past the giant advancing man, confused. 'Is that a fox with an axe?'

And yes, praise be to every god that man ever created, it was.

'All hail the saviour!' said the fox, axe aloft, and for once, I was very, very happy to hear it.

10

The drive home was not an entirely comfortable one.

The fox had dispatched the enormous man before he could swing his knife once. The little beast really is quite a vision to see in action. A beast with a battle-axe. It wasn't the first time my furry little friend had pulled my arse out of the fire, either. He was like my personal, bushy-tailed, snack-loving, guardian angel.

'So,' said Annie, having sat beside me in silence for most of the drive. 'I like your foxy friend.'

'Thanks. Well, he's not a friend exactly. Or maybe he is now. I suppose he is. Point is, I'm sorry.'

'What is it you're sorry for?'

'I think everything. I think sorry for everything just about covers it.'

'Why did that huge man want to kill you?'

'I've lived a... questionable life. I've done bad things. Very bad things.'

'Are you dangerous, Joe?'

'No!' I replied, then said it again but with less volume. 'I've mentioned that I'm a warlock; one of three trusted with looking after Cumbria and saving it from bad things. Apparently, somewhere down the line, I became one of those bad things. But I'm not bad now, and I don't even remember the old me. You can trust who I am now. Honest, guv.'

'I can trust you?'

'Yes, one-hundred percent. Absolutely.'

'But you can't trust me?'

That certainly slid the knife in. It was well deserved, though.

'I'm sorry,' I said.

'Yeah. You don't make a great early impression.'

'I've heard that from more people than I'd care to admit.'

Annie smiled, then rubbed my arm, sending my stomach all swirly again.

It was late by the time I got back to my flat.

'Hey, fox, are you here? Just wanted to say thanks again.'

I poked my head into each of the limited number of rooms my flat contained, but it seemed like I was alone. I sloughed off my coat, grabbed a beer from the fridge, and flopped down on the couch.

I was convinced now that Annie wasn't the evil animal killer who was clouding my vision. I mean, I was a good eighty-five percent sure. Eighty-seven percent, even. But the blocking of my insight magic still felt as though it may have been a measure designed to stop me specifically, so the spectre of it being someone who knew me, or was at least aware of what I could do, hung over me like a bad smell.

My mind was whirring, so I flicked on the TV, hoping to quieten it down so I could be tucked up in bed as soon as possible.

Of course, there was a knock at the door.

'Balls.'

I stood unhappily and waited a few seconds, hoping that the mystery knocker would realise they had the wrong door and bugger off.

There followed another, more urgent knock.

'Okay, okay, I'm coming.' I paused at the door. 'Who is it?'

'Paul. Paul Travers,' came a voice from the other side.

Paul Travers. The sweat-browed man who'd, briefly, wanted to hire me, and then legged it.

'Can this wait, Paul? It's a bit late.'

'Please. I need to tell you things, need to tell you now, before... before...'

I heard a pained grunt as his words trailed off.

'Paul?'

I threw the door open, worried he was having some sort of attack, or perhaps even *being* attacked. Paul Travers was on his knees, bent over, hands gripping his stomach.

'Bloody hell, come on.'

I helped him up and guided him inside. His knees were jelly, so I had to take almost his entire weight. Depositing him on the couch, I darted to the sink and poured him a glass of cold water. He accepted with trembling hands, getting more of the liquid on his clothes than down his throat.

'I'm not going to lie, Paul, you don't look great.'

That was an understatement. His skin had a yellow hue to it now, his eyes bulged from their sockets, and he was positively drenched in sweat.

'I need to tell someone.'

It looked to me like the only thing he needed was a hospital.

'Okay, how about you tell me as we drive on over to Carlisle A&E, eh? That sound good?'

I tried to lever him up and towards the door, but showing surprising sudden fortitude, he pulled himself free of my grip and staggered back until the wall stopped his journey.

'No! I need to tell you! You need to know before it's too late!'

'Too late for who? For me?'

'No. Yes. Maybe. Too late, too late.' He screamed and doubled over, gripping his stomach.

'Paul, what are you on? Have you taken something?'

He looked up, a strange grin on his face. An insane grin. 'Me? It's not me. Not me at all. Not just me. It's Joan Smith. And Fred Collier. And Mary Pekar. And on, and on, and on. One by one, it was all of them. An infection spreading all over the village. All over Combe. I think I'm the only one left.'

Combe Village. I knew of it: a tiny little place, right on the southern edge of the Lake District.

'People are sick?' I said. 'Have you not, I don't know, called in a doctor?'

Paul stood and leaned his head back against the wall, that strange grin that I did not care for still stretched across his face.

'Not sick. No one is sick, Mr Lake. Do I look sick?'

'Yes. Obviously. Really, really sick.'

His eyes bugged out further still and his jaw yammered silently as though he were trying to stop himself from speaking.

'Paul, I really think we should—'

'When… when Mr Many Mouths… when…'

He began to giggle in a way that made my skin crawl.

'When he comes to… when…'

'Paul, you came to me for my help because something strange was going on in your village, so tell me, what is it, what's wrong?'

'When Mr Many Mouths comes to town, the town becomes Mr Many Mouths.'

'Yeah, that doesn't really help.'

'Mr Many Mouths, Many Mouths, Many Mouths!'

And then something surprising happened. Paul Travers' face began to change. His head twitched back and forth at inhuman speed as he screamed. His head bulged and crunched and shifted until his face was gone, and in its place was a multitude of large, yammering mouths. Toothless, gummy, horrors.

And they all said the same thing.

'When Mr Many Mouths comes to town, the town becomes Mr Many Mouths.'

11

I'd seen more than my fair share of terrifying sights by this point, but the thing I saw before me now—the thing that Paul Travers had morphed into—that really took the biscuit. He was like something from a nightmare. Something that gave me that deep fear, that deep dread, way down in the very core of my being. And he was in my home. It's a wonder I didn't piss my pants.

Okay, full disclosure, a drop or two did squeeze out.

'Paul are you... okay...?

Yes, the question may have been a mite redundant.

'Mr Many Mouths, Mr Many Mouths Mr Many Mouths,' Paul babbled from his, well, many mouths.

The multiple maws all jabbered and chattered at once, each dripping with saliva.

At this point, the most obvious move would have been to bolt out of the door, jump behind the wheel of the Uncanny Wagon, and get the hell out of there. Unfortunately, as I reached for the door handle, I found something yanking me back. That "something" was a tongue, which had shot out of one of Paul Travers' icky mouths and wrapped itself around my wrist.

'Fox?' I cried. 'If you're around, now would be a really good time for you to start swinging that axe about!'

I tried to pry the horrible, wet thing off of me, only to find a second tongue hurtling towards me and seizing my other wrist.

'Paul! I'm not quite sure what's going on here, but surely we can talk about it?'

The answer to that question proved to be a resounding "no" as a third tongue shot from another mouth and wrapped itself around my throat, tightening its grip and cutting off my air supply.

All in all, I'd say I was in a bit of a tight spot.

Trying not to pass out as more tongues hurtled towards me, I focused on seeing the magic that filled my flat. Meanwhile, whatever it was that Paul Travers had changed into made its way slowly towards me.

'Mr Many Mouths, Mr Many, Many, Many Mouths.'

Then I saw it: saw the waves of brilliant colours swirling and swooshing about the room. I closed my eyes and willed it into me.

The tongue around my neck coiled tight, turning my windpipe into a pinhole. I could feel my lungs burning, my vision blurring at the fringes.

'When Mr Many Mouths, comes to town, the town becomes Mr Many Mouths.'

He was just a few feet away from me. It was now or never. Either he'd step closer and do something horrible to me, or I'd pass out and die.

As my lungs screamed for air, I tried to make my hands ignite with flames. A desperate last gasp. The problem was, my brain was going fuzzy and I couldn't quite concentrate on the command. This resulted in something unexpected and, actually, better. My hands didn't ignite. My fists didn't erupt into flames. Instead, my entire body began to blaze.

I heard every mouth Paul Travers had screech in pain, then

I was launched across the room, flung away as every tongue that he'd used to hold me caught light.

I landed heavily on the other side of the breakfast counter, gasping for air. I peered over the edge of the countertop to see Paul thrashing around the room, scorched and in pain, his blackened tongues retracting back into their wet mouths.

'Sorry, Paul. Looks like you're going to be lisping for a while.'

He turned his attention back to me, so I threw a toaster at him. It glanced off his head and sent him reeling. Seizing the moment, I raced for the door, only for another tongue to wrap around my ankle and tug me back, sending me whirling through the air and crashing into the TV.

I staggered up and looked down at the smashed television set. No more *Frasier* for this poor sap. Paul straightened up and his many mouths giggled.

'You can do what you like to me,' I spat, 'but how dare you break my TV!'

Paul screamed as he charged my way, but this time I was able to fight back without the distraction of being throttled. I didn't panic, didn't listen to the part of my brain yelling, *'Run, Joseph, you're gonna die!'* Instead, I concentrated on the magic in the room and focused it into a laser point.

He was so close now that I could feel the breath of his many mouths. This was the moment. Feet planted, I pushed forward with my hands and allowed the magic to punch through them. Paul's mouths gave a small note of surprise as he was lifted from his feet and hurled through the air, through the front window, and out into the street.

'Yes!' I said, giving myself a high-five.

I had him out of my house, but I couldn't just let him get away. Don't get me wrong, I wanted to—I still have a healthy amount of coward in me—but stopping monsters is my job. My very much unpaid job. So, after a rueful swear word or two, I made my fists ignite with red-hot flame and ran out of the front door in pursuit.

I half expected to find Paul running right back at me, eager to carry on the battle, but as I burst into the street, I found him sprinting in the opposite direction, tongues trailing in the road behind him.

'Where do you think you're going?' I shouted, feeling macho for perhaps the first time in my life.

I threw my hand forward, sending a ball of fire in his direction. He failed to heed the warning shot, though, so I gave chase.

I managed to keep him in view for the first quarter-mile or so, but then a combination of Paul apparently being some sort of jogging machine, and me having all the stamina of a sixty-year-old asthmatic left me outpaced and bent over, coughing and wheezing. Soon, Paul Travers and his weird multi-mouthed head had disappeared from view completely.

So that was certainly quite the thing. Paul was apparently some kind of monster, but was he the same monster that was responsible for the animal slaughters? It seemed a likely connection. Perhaps Paul Travers was Cumbria's own Jekyll and Hyde.

After a sit-down and a smoke, I made my way home, only to almost unleash another ball of fire and set my flat alight as an intruder appeared from behind the breakfast counter.

'Hi,' said the fox, waving hello with his battle-axe.

'Christ, I almost barbecued you,' I said, sinking into the couch and looking glumly at my broken TV set. I'd only had it a year; just long enough for it to be out of warranty. I'd even splashed out on a brand new one rather than my usual habit of only buying second-hand and, if possible, third-hand goods.

'What has happened?' asked the fox. 'Another battle? Did the large man from the public house track you to your home?'

'Yes to the first question, no to the second. I don't suppose you know if the Red Woman was behind this?'

'The Red Woman does not want you hurt, nor does she feel the need to push you anymore. You know that already, she told you so herself.'

'And I'm just supposed to believe her, am I? And you too, for that matter.'

'As the Red Woman has said, you will soon want to sit on your throne without her having to threaten, trick, or beg.'

Fat chance of that. 'By the way, where were you? I called for you and you didn't appear. I could have used a helping hand... well, paw at least.'

The fox straightened and growled in displeasure. 'I am not at your beck and call, Magic Eater. I am my own fox, and I come and go as I please.'

'Right. Sorry.'

'I serve nobody. Not anymore. I will not.'

'I said I'm sorry.'

'Sorry about what?' said Eva, swaying in the doorway.

I let out a little cry of surprise which I styled out and turned into a high-pitched, 'Hello'.

'I said, what are you sorry about?' repeated Eva.

I looked around, but the fox had made himself scarce. Eva began looking around the flat too, eyes lidded with suspicion.

'No one!' I assured her. 'Just me. And myself. And I.'

'I heard you talking to someone,' said Eva, her voice low and serious. 'Why do I feel more and more like you're keeping shit from me?'

'No shit, no shit,' I said, my voice still a little too high to sound convincing.

'You know what'll happen if I find out you've been messing around with any of that Dark Lakes bollocks again, don't you?'

I nodded, and don't mind telling you, I felt both a little scared and a little ashamed. I didn't like keeping my dalliances with the Lakes and its inhabitants from her, but I also feared what her reaction would be if she found out. But what did it matter anyway? I wasn't the old me, I wasn't about to go to the bad side, I wasn't going to become that monster again. If only I could make her believe that. If only I could convince her to trust me.

Detective Myers stepped in, breaking the silence.

'Hey! Detective Maya Myers! There you are! And what a lovely jacket that is you're sporting. How are the migraines?'

'Break in?' she asked, ignoring the question and looking around at the broken window and the knackered TV.

'Not quite. I invited a man in and he turned into a monster. And I do not mean that figuratively.'

'What kind of a monster?' asked Eva.

'Not sure what you'd call it. Basically his head sort of bubbled and bulged and them he was covered in mouths.'

'Well, that's... odd,' said Myers.

'I agree. It is odd, isn't it?' I replied. 'And then all of these tongues shot out of him. I almost died, but then I was very heroic and, some might say, macho, then I threw it out and chased it away.'

'I'm going to put you in for a medal for bravery,' said Myers.

'Really?'

'No.'

'Right. Of course not. I was just joining in with the joke, so... joke's on you.'

Myers arched an eyebrow.

'So, monster spotted,' I said, 'and we're looking for a monster. I say we have a suspect.'

'Yeah, could be,' said Eva. 'If so, it was busted before it dropped in on you.'

'Another attack?' I asked.

'Another attack,' Myers confirmed.

Eva headed for the door and gestured for us to do the same.

'Wait, I can't leave,' I said. 'My window's broken. Anyone could get in.'

Eva clicked her fingers. 'There you go.'

And the window was fixed, good as new.

'Wow. How did you do that?'

'I'm magic, idiot. I used magic.'

'Makes sense. What about the TV?'

'Sorry, magic's used up.'

'That's not a thing, is it?'

She shrugged and stepped out into the street.

'Eva!' I sagged as I looked at the remains of my poor television set.

'Myers, you don't have a spare TV at your place, do you?'

Myers walked out.

12

Whatever was behind the recent spate of animal slaughters, it wasn't slowing down.

I followed Myers' car to a farmhouse inhabited by Mr and Mrs Madden and their two young children, then parked up and jogged to catch up with Myers and Eva. Eva had decided to share the detective's car for the journey there. She was being notably standoffish, even more so than usual. It was obvious that our relationship was on somewhat rocky terrain. I knew Eva had her reasons—very, very good reasons—for treating me so poorly, but surely at some point, the bullying had to stop?

This time there were two different crime scenes. The first was a barn located around the opposite side of the farmhouse. We were told that the barn used to contain thirty pigs, but now contained about a hundred pig chunks. But that's not where we were headed. Because this time the killer had stepped up his game...

Forensic officers wearing protective white onesies were gathered around scene-of-crime floodlights, carefully collecting and logging evidence. Myers made sure we had the go-ahead to enter the farmhouse, and then in we went.

There were three dead bodies in total.

Mr Madden was the first to be found. His body was distributed in seven or eight pieces around the kitchen, his intestines pulled from his torso and draped across the dining table. The other two bodies were upstairs. The kids; Ally, six years old; and Toby, about to see his fourth birthday. Both now torn to bits and tossed around their bedrooms. I decided to take Myers' word on that, I had no wish to see the ripped-apart bodies of two young children. I already had enough nightmare fuel in the tank from the last few months.

Mrs Madden had been the one to stumble across the scene, arriving home from a local play with her mum. I was happy to hear that she'd already she'd been taken elsewhere. I didn't want to see her eyes. The eyes of a mother who'd discovered that her life had been so brutally blown apart.

I knew it would be pointless, but I tried my insight magic again, touching something that used to be part of Mr Madden. Just like with the sheep at the first crime scene, and the horses at the second, Mr Madden refused to give up his secrets. I moved from limb, to torso, to another limb, but it was useless.

'Oh Jesus, here come the bloody *X-Files*,' barked Detective Martins, Myers' less-than-friendly partner, as he stepped into the kitchen.

I quickly stood up from one of the piles of meat that used to be Mr Madden.

'You knew I was bringing them in on this,' said Myers.

'Dead sheep, fine, but this is people,' Martins replied. 'This is *kids*.'

'I've figured it out,' said Eva.

'Figured out what?' asked Martins.

'You're ashamed because you secretly like to visit a dungeon where a big lad called Carl uses sandpaper on your balls, so acting like a twat helps you release the tension.'

'I'm not gay,' said Martins, practically snarling.

'Martins, step out for a couple of minutes,' said Myers.

'The mother's down the station. She's broken. And you bring in these... these frauds?'

'You're just going to have to trust me on this, Martins.'

He looked at us, then leaned in closer to Myers. 'First thing tomorrow, I'm asking for a new partner. You got that?'

'As is your right, Detective,' she replied.

Martins threw a dirty look my way, then headed out.

'Give my best to Carl,' Eva said with a wave, but Martins didn't look back.

'Okay, time to get serious,' said Myers.

'Always am,' replied Eva. 'Especially when it looks like I'm not.'

'Whoever is behind this—Joe's monster perhaps—is escalating things,' said Myers. 'Three attacks in the space of a week, and now it's attacking people, too. I see no reason for this bastard to slow down, let alone stop, so that means it's up to us. This is clearly beyond what the police can handle.'

'Oh yeah,' said Eva, 'this is for us all right. This stinks of us.' She plucked a severed hand out of the sink and gave it a sniff.

'That is, at the very least, a bit disrespectful,' I said, nose wrinkling.

'I wish I gave a fuck,' replied Eva, 'but alas, I have no fucks to give. Literally, none. Tis a tragic story, but true.'

'Okay, well...' Myers faltered and staggered to the side.

'Myers? Are you okay?' I asked.

She shook her head, trying to clear it. 'I'm... it's...'

Her knees giving way as she leaned on the blood-splattered table for support.

'Whoa, let me help,' I said, scampering forward to help her into a chair.

'It's okay, I'm fine,' said Myers, shrugging me off.

'Sure?'

'I told you, I'm fine!'

That was the last thing she said before her eyes rolled back into her skull and she crumpled to the floor, unconscious.

It seemed like I was becoming something of a fixture at Carlisle Hospital. Even when I wasn't working a shift, I was there. A few weeks ago, I was visiting Annie, and now here I was again, sat at Myers' bedside. She was unconscious, still. The doctors had run various tests over the last few hours, but so far, all they knew for sure was that she wasn't conscious. Not the most enlightening of discoveries, really.

She'd been filed away in a private room while the doctors tried to figure out what was happening.

I reached out and placed my hand over hers. 'Detective Myers? Maya, can you hear me?'

I pulled in the magic of the room and attempted to use it to reach her, to speak to her unconscious mind, to wake her up, even. Of course, I had no idea how to do any of that, or if it was even possible, and so I failed miserably.

The doctors said not to worry, that she was stable, that she was, to all intents and purposes, "Fine". I looked at the deathly-still Myers, her breathing barely perceptible, and decided I was going to worry as much as I wanted. People don't just lapse into unconsciousness for no reason.

I couldn't help but feel a little suspicion itch at me. That perhaps this was connected to the murders somehow. Could whatever had happened at Madden's Farm have somehow affected her? As I thought that, I recalled the other times I'd seen her affected, the times I'd heard her complain about her head. They'd all been at crime scenes.

There was a clear chain there. Three crime scenes, three strange turns. Perhaps something about the crime scenes, something in the air, had reacted badly with her. If an Uncanny thing was behind it—if it was whatever Paul Travers turned into—perhaps some trace of it had affected Myers, but no one else. Like how most of us could munch down peanuts all day long, but for others, doing so would be a death sentence.

That could be something, yes? I wasn't sure quite what, but it was possible. It felt significant anyway.

Or maybe Myers, in a completely unconnected way, was just suffering from a spate of ordinary migraines. One of the two. Something that was very clear to me, though, was that this new life of mine was dangerous. People got hurt, people died. Detective Sam Samm, Chloe, and now even the unflappable Detective Maya Myers had been laid low.

I thought about Annie and our burgeoning romance—about her being a mother to a little girl—and found myself starting to worry.

'D'you know the vending machine in this place doesn't have any alcohol?' said Eva, entering the room and flopping on the foot of Myers' bed with a bounce.

'Hospitals don't tend to have an extensive stock of inebriating beverages,' I replied.

'I know, right? I mean, what fucking century is this? Get with the times! I don't know, maybe there's a suggestion box around here...'

We sat in silence for a few moments, the only sound, the *beep-beep-beep* of Myers' heart monitor.

'I've been thinking things over,' I said.

'Haven't I warned you about trying to use that lump between your ears? It's not meant for anything more complicated than remembering your names how to tie your laces.'

'It's about Myers and the murders.'

'You've been thinking there might be a connection between the crime scenes and PC Plod's current condition.'

'Well, yes,' I admitted.

'Wow, consider me blown away by your Sherlock Holmes-level insight that I in no way put together several hours ago.'

'You don't have to be an arse about it.'

'I think we both know that's not true,' Eva replied. 'Come on then, they fucked with one of ours, let's get to work.' She stood and patted Myers' foot. 'Don't be a dick and die while we're gone, eh?'

'Where are we going?'

'Your transforming man, he told you where he's from, right?'

I thought back. 'Oh, oh! Combe Village!'

'Give that monkey a lemon.'

'That's not a saying.'

Eva ignored me and headed for the door. As I followed, I glanced back at Myers, still and silent, and hoped.

13

The beautiful scenery of the Lake District rolled past the window as I steered the Uncanny Wagon towards Combe.

As I gazed at the hills, at the blanket of fields stretching out in all directions, I wondered how anyone could confine themselves to a big city. To those closed-off, smog-filled, man-made places, disconnected from the natural world. Living elbow-to-elbow with millions of people, and yet somehow more isolated because of it. Okay, perhaps the people around here could be a little on the, uh, let's be generous and say "old-fashioned" side, but one breath of the crisp, clean air and you know this is exactly where you belong. That this is the way human beings are meant to live.

And yet, the majesty of the landscape was lost on Eva, who I could see in the rearview, stretched out across the back seats as usual, eyes closed.

'Are you awake?' I asked.

'Nope. Very much asleep.'

'There's a woman,' I said. 'A woman that's interested in me. Romantically.'

'Sounds like a nutcase to me. I'd steer clear if I were you.'

'Hilarious. It's just... I'm worried.'

Eva sighed and sat up, pulling out her tobacco tin and rolling herself a smoke. 'Okay, I sense you're not going to allow me to relax in solitude back here, so get on with it.'

'You are so caring, has anyone ever told you that?'

'No, but one man did once describe me as, *"That fuck who tore off my balls and dropped them down a well,"* so maybe watch your mouth.'

'Okay. Well, I was telling you about her the other day, remember?'

'Absolutely. Chloe.'

'No! That was...' I sighed and felt as though I might get a headache at any second, 'she's called Annie.'

'Oh right, yup.'

'We may or may not find ourselves in a boy-girl relationship at some point, complete with naked times.'

'Oh, Christ, just the idea of you naked...'

'Cheers. Anyway, I was sat looking at Myers back there, and thinking about the kind of world we move in, and, well... Annie has a daughter. A little girl.'

'And you're wondering if it's too dangerous to involve them in your life. If there's any way to keep them safe, because you don't want to be the cause of any pain, or be the reason they find themselves being torn to pieces by some bastard with giant teeth.'

'Yes, basically. I mean, is it even worth me trying to have a relationship, or am I just being selfish?'

Eva snapped her fingers and the end of her fag ignited. I'd seen her do it maybe a thousand times by now, and it still impressed me.

'Well, I've got good news, turd.'

I sat up straighter, a smile on my face. 'What? What is it?'

'There is no way to make sure they're safe, because they won't be safe, and the best thing you can do is stay the hell away from romantic entanglements and get used to a monastic life of self-abuse.'

'How is that good news?' I cried.

'It's not good news for you, but it is for the female population.'

I grumped and fantasised about tossing a little fireball into the back seat. 'You know, I do possess human feelings?'

'Yeah, that's what makes it so much fun,' she replied, then stretched out again, a smug look on her face as I zipped my lips and concentrated on finding my way to Combe.

The village Paul Travers lived in was a simple affair; really more of a hamlet than a village, in fact, though it did feature a small church at its centre.

I parked up and we stepped out to survey the sleepy-looking place. We were presented with a village green surrounded by a gaggle of old buildings. Little, detached homes with neatly ordered front gardens. Combe was the sort of place that hadn't seen any redevelopments since the Seventies, not that the few residents who lived there minded. It was a place where time stood still. A place whose inhabitants were keen to keep out as much of the modern world as possible.

'Are you sensing anything?' I asked Eva.

'Oh yeah, I'm sensing something.'

'Really? What is it?'

'That I'm dangerously close to sobering up,' she replied, pulling out a bottle of vodka and taking a hefty slug. 'Jesus, close one.'

'Detective Myers is in the hospital, in case you've forgotten.'

'I don't sense anything, okay? It's a picture-perfect little shit-hovel, home to a gaggle of people losing the battle against gravity and Father Time. That's all I'm getting so far.'

An elderly woman shuffled past us, smiling. 'Another beautiful day,' she said.

'Case in fucking point,' said Eva.

I smiled at the old woman, who seemed not to have heard Eva. 'Hey, could you tell me which house a Mr Paul Travers lives at?'

'Who?'

'Paul Travers. He's a friend of mine but I, uh, forgot where he lives.'

'Very convincing,' whispered Eva, giving me a withering thumbs-up. 'Truly, Oscar-worthy.'

'Let me have a think,' said the old woman, rubbing at her wispy chin. 'Paul Travers, you say?'

'Yep, that's the guy.'

'No. I'm afraid the name doesn't ring a bell.'

'Oh. Really?'

'Though I am getting on a bit.'

'Really,' said Eva, 'you don't look a day over should-be-dead.'

'I do have trouble remembering names. Oh...' she said, waving over another local, a short, bald gentleman with a pug nose.

'Hello there, Dot,' he said, patting his stomach.

'Arthur, these two are after a... who was it again, dear?'

'Paul Travers. Apparently, he lives here in Combe.'

'Does he now?' replied the man. 'First I've heard of him, and I've been here close to forty years.'

'You've both been very, very, massively helpful,' said Eva.

'Cheerio,' said the old woman, and the two of them wandered off.

'Well, that's odd,' I said. 'He definitely said he was from Combe. What reason would he have to lie?'

'He wasn't lying,' said Eva.

'What? How do you know?'

'Because those two were. I could practically taste it. Something very weird is going on in this place.'

I flashed back to when Paul Travers visited my flat and tried to kill me. Something he said before he changed trickled back into my consciousness. 'All of them!' I clapped my hands.

'What?' said Eva.

I levered Eva around so our backs were facing Dot and Arthur, who'd turned to look at us again.

'Paul; when he came to see me, he was babbling, but he did say the whole place was part of it.'

'A conspiracy?'

'I nodded. 'Could be, right?'

'Ooh, I like that. Paranoia. Trust no one. *Body Snatchers*. The original version, or the 70s one, the other ones, not so much. Definitely not the Nicole Kidman one. Nothing against her, but that film really shit the bed.'

'A cult?' I asked.

'It definitely has cult vibes. Potential animal and people sacrifice and everything.'

'Seems a bit samey,' I replied. 'We only took down that undead cult a month ago. And by "we", I mean "me", with that brilliant plan I put together and executed all by myself.'

'You do the right thing *once* and look at how big your head gets.'

'I'm just saying, I did pretty good there.'

Eva dithered. 'Yeah. You did. Idiot.'

I was basking in the half-compliment I'd managed to drag, kicking and screaming, out of Eva, when a front door opening caught my eye. Not so much the door as the person opening it and stepping out of the house.

'Wait a minute, that's him. That's Paul Travers!'

Eva squinted at him. 'I thought you said his whole head was covered in mouths?'

'He must've changed back. Come on!'

We scooted over, intercepting Mr Travers as he stepped beyond his front gate.

'Paul!' I said, because it was his name.

He looked up, startled, clearly having caught up in his own thoughts. 'Yes?'

'Paul, it's me.'

'Is it?' he replied, edging away.

'Are you a monster?' asked Eva, taking a more direct route. 'Only this guy says you're a monster, so if you are one you'd better own up or God will be angry.'

'I'm sorry, what are you talking about?'

'Paul, it's me, Joseph Lake. You sought me out, twice. And then you tried to kill me.'

'You're mad,' he said, his eyes darting around nervously.

'If you're secretly a monster, blink three times,' Eva tried.

'I never sought you out, never met you, and I have no idea who either of you are.'

One of Paul's neighbours opened their door: a man in his fifties with a big, bushy moustache. He stepped out and began to shuffle our way.

'You know that talk we had when we first arrived?' asked Eva.

'Yeah.'

'Well, I'm getting a really weird vibe now.'

'Yeah, I think I'm picking up on that, too.'

'Look,' said Paul, 'I don't know what this is all about, but I do not know you.'

'Paul', I said, 'it's okay, something's clearly wrong. I'm not angry you attacked me, if that's what you're thinking.'

'You're a pair of raving lunatics!'

'Yes,' agreed the neighbour, stood behind his gate, looking over at us. 'They must be mad.'

'Quite, quite mad,' said Dot and Arthur, who'd completed their circuit of the village green and were passing us once again.

'You came to my flat,' I said. 'You know you—'

Eva grabbed me by the shoulder. 'Whoa there, drunky,' she said, pulling me back and laughing. 'Sorry about him; had a little too much of the old voddy,' she said waggling her half-empty bottle.

'I'm not drunk,' I insisted, 'something strange is going on here.'

Eva pulled me away, smiling at the Combe residents. 'Ignore this fella, he has issues. We're having an intervention this weekend. You can all come, I'll email out invites.' Eva turned me around and guided me back to the Uncanny Wagon. 'Just shut up and keep walking like everything's okay.'

'What are you doing?'

'Something very, very bad is happening in Combe, and your friend Paul Travers back there is right. The whole place is in on it. Him and all his robot neighbours.'

'Robots?'

'Metaphorical robots.'

'Oh. Aw. So why are we heading off with our tails between our legs?'

'Because we don't want them to see us coming. We need to come back at night and do some sneaking around, see if we can shake out what we're dealing with here.'

I got behind the wheel of the Uncanny Wagon and took a quick glance back in the direction we'd hustled from. Paul and his three neighbours were stood, stock still, eyes boring into us.

What Paul Travers had said when he came to my flat was right. Something was wrong. Something was wrong with that whole place.

14

We had a few hours before nightfall, so I decided what better way to spend the time than by doing something horrible, awkward, and entirely unpleasant?

Eva's crushing pep talk earlier had only solidified my own thoughts regarding me and Annie, or romantic situations generally. Maybe one day I'd be able to explore girl-boy stuff, but right now it was just too dangerous. I couldn't guarantee I'd still be alive from one day to the next, so what good was it pulling someone else into my world of monsters and horror?

No, this was the right thing to do. Even if it broke my heart to do it.

I was the eye of a tornado, and I needed to protect Annie and her daughter from the chaos swirling around me. Harsh, but on the bright side, I was used to being single, alone, and wading through a world of frustrated, empty longing. Same shit, different day for good ol' Mr Lake.

'Hey, Joe!' chirped Annie, waving as I approached.

I waved back and even managed a smile, but felt my insides clench as I realised she wasn't alone. She'd said she was feeding the ducks by Mulgrave Pond when I called, and I'd said I'd drop by. It hadn't crossed my mind to ask if she was feeding the ducks alone, because of course she wouldn't be. People don't generally feed ducks on their own unless they're a bit old and dotty. They take their children. And so this was where I met Mille for the first time.

Millie had a riot of thick blonde curls, a hundred-watt smile, and was rocking blue dungarees with an elephant stitched on the front. She was enthusiastically launching fists full of bread chunks towards the eager ducks, who flapped to get away from the shards of stale bread tossed towards their heads, before turning back to gobble them up as they bobbed around on the pond's surface. Mille was obviously adorable, and seeing her only strengthened my resolve. Someone so young, so innocent, definitely had no place in my world, not even on the periphery of it.

'Hi,' I replied, feeling awkward.

Annie leaned in smiling and kissed me on the cheek. Damn, damn, and double damn. My knees quivered and I felt a sudden hollow thud in my stomach as I realised I'd never actually get to kiss Annie properly. And she had the sort of mouth I'd very much like to have mushed my own against.

'Millie, come here. This is Mummy's friend, Joe.'

Millie came waddling over, mittened hand clutching her half-full bread bag.

'I'm feeding ducks,' she proclaimed proudly.

'That's great,' I said. 'The poor things are terrible at shopping. Send them to the supermarket and they'll come back with toilet paper and shoe polish, and not a crumb of food.'

Millie wrinkled her nose and tilted her head, clearly confused at my poor attempt at humour. 'You're silly.' She hoisted her bag. 'This is duck bread.'

She turned, apparently done with the conversation, and made her way back to the birds.

'I think she likes you,' said Annie.

'Well, we both like ducks, so we have that in common.'

Annie laughed and I felt like a bastard.

'I'm glad you called,' she said. 'I wanted you to meet Millie before, you know, things go anywhere with us.'

'Oh? Things are going somewhere?'

She slipped her hand into mine. 'I was hoping so.'

Bugger and balls and also bums. I should have gotten it over with right there and then. Torn off the plaster and had it all over and done with. It was for her own good. For her daughter's, too. I wasn't being horrible, I was protecting them. I was being the good guy!

So, of course, I crumbled and listened to the cowardly part of me instead. 'Me too,' I said, smiling on the outside but calling myself a variety of colourful names on the inside.

We spent the next hour together. Me, a lovely woman I was pretending I had a future with, and her awesome little daughter. We walked around and around the pond, named all the ducks, and described the workings of their duck society. Their relationships, politics, double-crosses, scandals. Oh, you wouldn't believe the number of juicy scandals in duck world. At one point, I even found Millie holding my hand as we strolled.

I really am a rotten bastard at times.

I waved goodbye, with promises to call and set up a date ASAP, then drove away, furious at myself.

It had been a lovely, normal hour or so. An hour that—even as I ignored the part of my brain trying to shame me for dragging things out—had made me feel ordinary. For that hour I wasn't the Magic Eater, I was a man on the cusp of a wonderful new relationship, someone who might become a father figure to a cool little girl. But it was make-believe and it was cruel. All I'd done was shift the bad news a little further down the road. But there it was, sat there still, not even far enough ahead to be out of view. And by spending an hour playing family man, meeting Annie's daughter and pretending like we had a future, I'd only made the oncoming bombshell all the more destructive.

Or perhaps I was inflating things out of proportion. It's possible. We'd barely begun anything, really. It's just as possible that Annie would be disappointed, but shrug it off and move on.

churned this around in my head, driving without really paying attention to where I was headed. I took country road after country road, green fields and dry stone walls whipping past, half-seen. It was muscle memory, taking me back to the same place I often found myself when I was at a low ebb.

Derwentwater Lake.

The place I was found ten years previously.

I killed the Uncanny Wagon's engine, then got out and trudged towards the water, flopping heavily on the grass. I launched a stone in the water's direction and watched it land with a deep splash and disappear from view.

'Balls.'

I lay back on the grass, hands behind my head, and looked up at the sky. It was still light, but I could already see the moon.

'Swim down.'

I sat bolt upright as the words floated over me.

'Hello? Lyna, Melodia?'

'Swim down, Janto.'

I pushed myself up and walked towards the lake's edge, the water lapping gently at the toes of my boots.

'Swim down.'

The air hazed in the distance as I looked out over Derwentwater, and there, indistinct and stood impossibly on the surface of the water, I found two figures.

My dead witches.

'Swim down, Janto.'

'Can you perhaps, elaborate a wee bit?' I asked.

'Swim down.'

'I'll take that as a no then.'

For a mad moment, I considered stripping off and jumping into the lake. Swimming over to the dead phantoms to try and talk to them properly. But then I felt my hand being yanked, and I looked down to see a furry paw tugging at me. I sat up sharply, eyes blinking, realising I'd fallen fast asleep, flat out on the grass.

'Fox?'

'You were talking in your sleep, Magic Eater.'

I peered past the fox and out across the lake, but there was no sign of the witches, hazy or otherwise. Just water, and past that, the hills and mountains of Cumbria.

'Does something trouble you?' asked the fox.

'Oh, you know how it is. Women.'

'Ah,' he replied, sadly. 'I know of such sorrows.'

The fox had lost his own partner, he'd told me that. What had happened to him is exactly what I feared would happen to me. I'd fall for someone, they'd fall for me, and then life would stick the knife in.

'I think I might have to be alone forever,' I said. 'An eternal bachelor boy.'

'It is not so terrible,' replied the fox, sitting down beside me and resting his axe across his little legs.

'Isn't it?'

He looked to the ground. 'I lied to make you feel better. It is very bad. Very awful and tragic and also heartbreaking.'

I patted the fox's Roman helmet, then the two of us sat in silence, looking out over the calm waters. For a few moments, I could pretend we were the only two around for miles. Just me and a talking fox. No romantic woes, no monsters, and no people in mortal peril.

Until the serenity was interrupted by the ringing of my phone.

'Big Marge, to what do I owe this rare call?'

'It's about your detective friend.'

I straightened up, turning suddenly serious. 'Detective Myers? What's wrong?'

15

I ran so fast into the hospital's reception area that the automatic doors didn't have time to fully open, forcing me to wriggle through them sideways and almost careen into an old man being pushed along in a wheelchair.

'Slow down, Joe,' said Big Marge from the reception desk.

'Is she okay? Is she talking?

'Oh, she's done more than that. She's fucked off.'

'What? Do you mean she's really angry or she's gone?'

'She was awake when I called you, but then she went and checked herself out. Doctors tried to stop her, but she shoved them out of the way and just walked out.'

'Did she say where she was going?'

'Nope. She wasn't in the mood for conversation, she was in the mood for getting the hell out of this building.'

I dashed from the hospital and made my way to the Uncanny Wagon, dialling Myers' number as I went.

'This is Detective Myers. I'm not available. Leave a message.'

Her voicemail was certainly on-brand.

'Hey, Myers. What's with the walkabout, you silly goose? Call me back.'

I didn't like the idea of Myers wandering around in her condition. Whatever that condition was. Yes, she was a kick-arse police officer who could tie me in knots, but she'd been unconscious for hours and laid up in a hospital bed. Who knew what might happen to her while she was out there?

I tried the police station she worked out of, but as far as they knew, she was still at the hospital.

I decided to drop by her home and see if she'd found her way back. I pulled up in front; it was your standard terraced house, a three-up two-down. The sort of place that had sprung up in a lot of northern towns about a hundred years ago, built to house factory workers. No front garden, just a step and a front door. When I arrived, it looked as though I might have gotten lucky. The front door was slightly ajar.

'Hey, Myers, you in there?' I tapped at the door with my knuckles and it swung open with a creepy creak.

There was no reply from inside.

'Myers, it's Joe, are you in?'

Still nothing.

Worry nibbled at me. Perhaps Myers had managed to stumble home, only to collapse the moment she got in, and was lying unconscious on the hallway floor, bleeding from the brain.

Now was no time for caution or following rules, so I stepped across the threshold and trespassed on a police officer's home.

'Myers?'

No sign of her on the bare wooden boards of the corridor. That was a good sign. I poked my head into the downstairs rooms, the living room and kitchen, but there was no sign of her there, either. I looked out on to the small back yard area, just a narrow rectangle with paving slabs rather than grass, but spied only a ginger cat, stalking something invisible to my eyes.

There was a photo stuck to the front of the fridge. It was Myers, smiling hugely, arm around a man whose smile was equally as large. I'd never seen her looking so happy. I wondered who the man was; her dead ex-partner from London, the man whose death at the claws of some monster had led to her being transferred here, away from the city she'd called home her whole life? Or perhaps a brother she never mentioned, or an ex-boyfriend. I realised I didn't know that much about Myers' personal life, despite the fact we'd shared so much time together recently. She wasn't exactly the sort of person who delved into personal matters without good reason.

I made my way upstairs. I tried the two bedrooms first. They were, like the rest of the house, extremely neat, minimal, and ordered. Detective Myers ran a tight ship. I looked to see if there were any more photos displayed in her room, more evidence of a personal life I knew nothing about, but there were no pictures to be seen.

Finally, the bathroom, which is where my imagination decided to place a potential, shower-dwelling monster. I stepped into the room, its white tiles gleaming, and eyed the shower curtain suspiciously.

'If there's a monster behind there, I'm warning you, I taste terrible.'

I reached out and the world seemed to hold its breath...

...and then my phone's ringtone screamed out, eliciting a similarly high-pitched noise out of me and almost bringing about my death by heart attack.

Myers' name flashed up on the phone's screen.

'Detective?'

'Hi.'

'Thank God,' I sighed, 'you scared me, running off like that.'

'I didn't run off,' she replied. 'I just discharged myself.'

'Right. You don't think it might have been wiser to at least stay in overnight? For observation and things of that nature?'

'No, I just... I woke and I needed to get out. Can't stand hospitals. I don't like laying around when there's work to do.'

'Okay, but you did fall mysteriously unconscious for quite a few hours.'

'And now I'm conscious.'

'It's just, I have this flimsy but perhaps accurate theory that what happened is linked to the crime scenes. Like it tainted the air and it affected you for some reason.'

'Why would it just affect me?'

'Well, I dunno, that's the million-dollar question, isn't it? Promise you'll just rest up? At home? I'll get Eva to give you some sort of magical once-over after we get back from snooping on monsters in Combe.'

I heard a heavy sigh on the other end of the line.

'Please? Pretty please?'

'Fine. I'll rest this once, but you two aren't cutting me out of the investigation.'

'Scout's honour,' I replied.

'Okay. I expect to see you at my house in a few hours.'

I glanced around but thought it best not to mention where I currently was.

'Absolutely.'

'Okay. I'll see you later.'

I hung up and sighed with relief. She'd been a pig-headed swine about spending a few extra hours under a doctor's care, but at least she was okay.

I checked behind the shower curtain, just to be safe, then headed downstairs, pausing halfway as I saw a figure framed in the doorway.

'What are you doing here?' asked Detective Martins, forcing the words through clenched teeth.

'I know it may appear like I'm trespassing, Detective, but I'm actually not. Honest.'

'Where is Detective Myers?'

'Not sure, but she's okay.'

'How do you know that?'

'I just spoke to her on the phone. She's being stubborn about her hospital stay, but she sounds fine.'

Martins seemed to sag a little. Was that relief?

'I'm sure she'll be touched to know you care, Detective Martins.'

He stepped towards me, jabbing a finger in my direction. 'She might be annoying, but she's a good copper, and she's my partner. We might not see eye-to-eye ninety percent of the time, but that doesn't alter the facts.'

I nodded, finding myself slightly warming to this total shit. 'She does engender trust and loyalty for someone so stand-offish, doesn't she?'

'Yeah. And she's too good for this place. I'll never understand why she asked for a transfer up here.'

I thought about correcting Detective Martins; telling him that Myers had been forcibly moved up here after the murder of her partner by an Uncanny monster caused her to have a bit of a breakdown. But Martins didn't strike me as the sort of person who enjoyed being corrected.

In any case, night was creeping in, and I had a date to keep with Eva.

16

I parked the Uncanny Wagon a few hundred metres before the turn that funnelled drivers into Combe.

'I told you,' said Eva, after I'd finished filling her in about Myers absconding from the hospital, 'they need to offer a decent selection of alcoholic drinks in that place.'

'I'll bring it up when I put in for a new mop.'

Keeping low, we skirted a tall hedgerow, crouching as the first building hoved into view.

'What's the plan of attack here, exactly?' I asked.

'I'm not really a plan in advance sort of woman.'

'This is shocking news. Behold my face of shockedness.'

I winced as Eva's finger jabbed me in the ribs.

'I was thinking we'd wander around, maybe break into a house or two, poke around a bit, and see if we can find some clues that tell us what's going on with this place, and why the twats have been dropping in on farms and talking out the inhabitants.'

We shuffled forward, reaching the edge of Combe's village green. There was no street lighting, and no glows from behind the residents' closed curtains. Everyone had gone to bed. Combe was slumbering, and the dark was all that was left.

'Okay, which house should we try?'

Eva licked her finger and held it in the air, then spun and pointed at Paul Travers' home. 'Might as well start there.'

We began hustling across the green toward the house.

'What happens if we're caught?' I asked. 'This may come as a surprise, but I have little, and by little I mean no experience of breaking and entering a person's home while they sleep upstairs.'

'Don't worry, I've done this a million times.'

'Bit worrying, but keep going.'

'We'll be in and out like ghosts,' said Eva. 'No one will even realise we've been here. Trust me, love, I've got this.'

And that's when the lights in every house turned on and we froze like escaped prisoners bathed in a giant spotlight.

'Bugger,' said Eva.

The front door to each house opened, and the occupants stepped out in unison.

'I'll take your bugger and raise you a bollocks,' I said.

Eva straightened up, somehow regaining her nonchalant composure as I pirouetted in little, panicked circles, doing my best to keep all the residents of Combe in view at the same time.

'Hey, freaky, possessed people of Combe,' said Eva, giving them all a hearty wave. 'Me and this lanky twat have you rumbled.'

The residents said nothing, their faces hidden by the bright glow from their homes backlighting them. Which was more than a little unnerving.

'The silent treatment's wasted on us,' said Eva, pulling out her tobacco tin and retrieving a pre-rolled smoke from inside. She lit it with a click of her fingers and popped it between her lips. 'I'm Eva Familiar, and that's Janto the warlock. Maybe you've heard of us; or whoever's in control of you has.'

'There's someone in control?' I said.

'There's always someone in control. An original piece of

shit who enslaved this backwards lot. Am I right? Stay ominously silent if I am.'

The residents of Combe stayed ominously silent.

'Told you.'

'That could be a coincidence,' I said.

'We represent the Cumbrian Coven,' said Eva. 'We don't like what you've got going on here, and if you don't bugger off, me and him are going to fuck you the fuck up. Understand?'

No reply, no movement.

Eva turned to me. 'Okay, I've had enough of the silent treatment.'

To be fair, I preferred it infinitely to what happened next.

As one, the villagers spoke: 'When Mr Many Mouths comes to town, the town becomes Mr Many Mouths.'

'Fuck's that supposed to mean?' inquired Eva.

'I think it means we should maybe consider a hasty retreat,' I suggested.

'Eva Familiar doesn't run; not unless the shop's about to shut and I've drunk the last of the lager.'

'The town becomes Mr Many Mouths,' the residents of Combe repeated, and then they began to scream and thrash as their heads bulged and quivered and cracked.

'That is not pretty,' said Eva, flicking the ash off the end of her ciggie.

The residents fell silent again and straightened up, stepping away from their homes, down their garden paths, and out of their gates towards us. Each of them, like Paul Travers when he visited my flat, sported heads covered in multiple, jabbering mouths.

'Jesus, imagine the amount of lipstick the women get through,' said Eva, taking another drag on her cigarette.

We backed away as the people of Combe stalked across the green towards us. Eva raised her hand and a ball of fire appeared, ready to be unleashed.

'No!' I said.

'You're right, let's just sit here and wait for them to kiss us to death.'

'They're not monsters.'

'Well, they sure as fuck ain't beauty queens.'

'You said someone is controlling them, so this is against their will. If you kill them, you're not killing monsters, you're killing people who need our help.'

Eva raised an eyebrow, then turned to look at the nightmare folk that were approaching us with no doubt ill intentions.

'Shit, you're right,' said Eva. 'Second time today. That really pisses me off.'

We stood back-to-back, watching as the residents of Combe slowly moved towards us. Truth be told, I didn't see a way out of this that didn't involve Eva physically assaulting at least some of them.

'You two, over here!' said a voice, yelling out from the side. I recognised the voice;

it was Detective Maya Myers.

Yes, that was quite an unexpected appearance.

'That is quite an unexpected appearance,' said Eva.

See, told you.

Myers was stood by the open door to the church, waving frantically.

'Come on.' I grabbed Eva by the wrist and yanked her away, towards the only gap in the constricting circle, directly towards the entrance of the small church where Myers waved us in. We dashed inside, and I laid my back against the door and it slammed shut, the noise reverberating around the nave.

I peered into the gloom of the church and pulled the building's magic into me, causing my hand to ignite. We stepped deeper into the church, our feet scraping the stone floor. I thought about the last time I'd been in a place like this. The appearing/disappearing cathedral where I'd had a nice chat with a skeleton and the Red Woman. She said something was happening, something was coming, and that it would cause me to finally fulfil my stupid destiny. And now here I was, in another house of the holy, quite possibly about to meet some sort of Uncanny monster with the power to enslave a whole village. Coincidence? Christ, I really hoped so.

As we crept forward I was happy to discover that the stained glass windows of this place pictured more standard religious fare than the Dark Lakes cathedral. No skeleton, either. Always a bonus in any building.

'So, Detective,' said Eva, 'wanna fill us in on what you're doing here?'

'Joe told me what you two were up to.'

'Yes,' I said, 'but Joe also said to go home, rest up, and wait for us.'

'This is my case, and I'm not being shoved behind a desk.'

'You really are a reckless, stubborn sod,' said Eva. 'And I mean that as a compliment.'

A heavy bang on the church doors made us all jump.

'Sounds like the natives are getting restless,' said Eva.

'Those things outside, that's what you described attacking you, right?' asked Myers.

'Yep. Looks like it's the whole place that's affected, not just Paul Travers. Something very, very weird is happening in Combe.'

'What exactly?' asked Myers. 'What's happening?'

'I am happening,' came a booming voice from behind us. I turned to see a hulking figure just about visible in the shadows.

'Have you been hiding back there listening in this whole time?' asked Eva. 'Not cool.'

'All will be me,' said the thing, and oh, it was most definitely a thing. Even though it was still mostly shrouded by gloom, the creature talking to us twitched and quivered and didn't have the shape of a person at all.

'So what are you?' asked Eva. 'Another turned resident? Or are we talking with the boss man at last?'

The church doors burst open and the monstrous residents

stepped inside, tongues flicking in and out of their multiple, gummy mouths.

'Enough of this drama,' said Eva. She raised both hands, clicking her fingers and igniting the many candles dotted around the place.

To be honest, I really wish she hadn't, because what she revealed was, at best, a puke-inducing nightmare of epic proportions.

'Jesus,' said Eva. 'You are one ugly motherfucker.'

And no one would argue with her.

'I am Mr Many Mouths,' said the thing from one of the numerous mouths that covered not only the giant lump of pummelled, grey flesh that passed for its head but the entire extent of its damp, slug-like body. Tongues darted from each mouth, lapping at the moisture oozing from its own flesh.

'You look like something that Jabba the Hutt shat out,' said Eva.

Again, who could argue?

'Your words mean nothing, Familiar,' replied Mr Many Mouths.

'What's your deal then?' asked Eva. 'You're from the Dark Lakes, aren't you?'

I glanced a little uneasily at her as she mentioned that place, but her eyes were fixed on the creature. Was this connected to the Red Woman? Was this the thing she mentioned that would push me towards the throne after all? Because right now it was doing nothing to sell me on the idea.

'You might as well fill us in,' said Eva, leaning against a pew and rolling a fresh smoke. 'I mean, I assume you're going to kill us, or turn us, so now's the time for a little gloating.'

The creature laughed—a laugh multiplied by its many mouths—and the transformed residents crowded within the church entrance joined in, too. The noise echoed horribly around the church's stone interior. It fair put the willies up me, I don't mind telling you.

'I am Mr Many Mouths. When I come to town, the whole town becomes Mr Many Mouths.'

'Yeah, yeah, heard it. But this can't be it, right? Not this little, shitty nothing of a place.'

'All will become Mr Many Mouths. *All.* I will remove the people. I will remove the birds. The dogs, too. Then the cats. The ants. The fish. The germs. It will take time, but I don't mind putting in the hours. I will work. And I will work. And eventually, there will only be me. Me and me and me and silence and nothing and then I will stop and look upon the very fine thing that I have done and I will smile with every mouth I have.'

'Shit,' said Eva. 'It's good to have a goal, keeps a person motivated… trouble is, we're here now, and we're going to kick your arse. Assuming you have an arse, that is. Maybe you're all arse, you definitely look it, but I'm not an expert of monster biology.'

'Wait,' I said, 'there's something I don't understand.'

'I for one cannot believe this unexpected news,' said Eva.

'Why kill the animals?' I asked. 'You say all will become you, but those animals didn't. That man and his kids didn't. Why kill them?'

'Actually, yeah, good point, love. Well? Answer the twat. Why'd you kill 'em?'

'I have killed no one,' said Mr Many Mouths.

'Come again?' replied Eva.

'I do not kill. I replace. I become.'

I looked to Eva, who was looking back at me and, for once, seemingly caught off guard. If Mr Many Mouths hadn't been behind the deaths, then who?

There was, unfortunately, no time for further interrogation or contemplation, as without a word being spoken, without a command relayed, the residents suddenly surged forward and took hold of us.

'One of you two, do something!' cried Myers.

'Can I set them all on fire now, idiot?' asked Eva.

'Can't you do some other trick?'

'I don't do *tricks*. I'm not David fucking Copperfield, pretending to walk through the Great Wall of China or some shit. I'm the real deal.'

'Could you walk through the Great Wall of China, though?' I asked.

Eva grimaced but didn't answer.

'I am Mr Many Mouths,' said the creature.

'He really likes saying his own name, doesn't he?' said Myers.

'When Mr Many Mouths comes to town—'

'—the town becomes Mr Many Mouths?' I suggested. 'Yep, got it.'

The creature opened its mouths wide, screaming, tongues bursting for us. Such a sight causes an involuntary reaction; specifically, we each opened our mouths in surprise.

This proved to be a bad thing.

Because as our mouths popped open, the creature's tongues found their entrances, and forced their way past our lips, our teeth, and wormed their way down our throats.

I thrashed, disgusted, terrified, trying to clench my teeth, to bite down on the tongue that had invaded my body, but it was no good. It was like trying to chew through a tractor tyre. I could bite all I liked, but it wasn't going to make a difference.

I was consumed with panic, a mindless horror as a foreign body did what it wanted with me and I couldn't even scream in pain or fury or fear. Instead, I gagged and choked and wondered when I would pass out. Wondered if I'd actually wake up again when I did.

It was turning me into one of them. I could feel myself becoming part of it. I could start to sense the whole gestalt being, the numerous voices, but all the same voice at the same time.

Many Mouths.

Many Mouths.

We all become Mr Many Mouths.

I was about to be submerged at any moment, and there was nothing I could do about it. I struggled to draw the magic towards me, but I couldn't think, couldn't focus. The black was edging in on me, the voices becoming louder, sharper, all-consuming.

I was done.

It was over.

The village would become Mr Many Mouths.

The world would become Mr Many Mouths.

I felt a hand slip into mine. My head twitched to the left and I saw Myers looking at me, but her eyes, they were strange. Wrong. They weren't hers. I saw no panic or fear in those eyes. I saw only a cold, calm certainty.

And then something washed over me. Myers clenched my hand harder, and all the fear, the panic, was gone like ingrained dirt blasted away under a pressure washer.

I was stood in the same place. Still restrained by unyielding hands with that disgusting, snake-like tongue shoved down my throat. But I was okay. Because I wasn't just daft old Joseph anymore.

I was a warlock.

I was Janto of the Cumbrian Coven, and I had power over the magic that this world swam in. These things shouldn't be attacking me, they should be cowering in fear, because *I was fear*.

I closed my eyes and demanded the magic did as I asked. There was a noise like a sonic boom, and then I had no hands restraining me, no tongue down my throat, no creature trying to claim my consciousness as its own.

I heard myself scream and I pulled my hand free of Myers' as I fell to my knees on the stone floor of the church. I coughed and spat and tried to stop my body from trembling.

'Well, shit on my face,' said Eva, 'you must've been paying more attention to the training than I thought.'

I opened my eyes to see her looking down at me. She didn't seem happy, though. Not exactly. More curious. Like she couldn't believe what I'd done.

And what exactly had I done? I looked behind me to see the inhabitants of Combe now back to their normal appearance, all laid out on the floor, none of them moving. 'Shit. Are they dead?'

Eva crouched by one prone figure who I recognised from earlier, Arthur, and checked his pulse. 'No. You just knocked the fuckers out.'

I pushed myself shakily back up to my feet, trying to ignore the disgusting taste in my mouth.

'Here,' said Eva, passing me a bottle from her pocket.

I gratefully unscrewed the cap and drank, the vodka burning away the foul taste, or at least replacing it with a new one. I turned to pass it on to Myers, but she wasn't paying the rest of us any attention. She was stepping slowly towards the creature, towards Mr Many Mouths. Like the people of Combe that it had been controlling, the thing seemed to have been knocked unconscious by whatever power had exploded out of me.

'Detective? You'll want to drink some of this,' I said waggling the bottle in her direction.

But she didn't reply, and she didn't look back.

'Hey, Detective,' said Eva, 'I know that thing looks knocked out, but you might wanna stay a little back from it. We've all seen horror films. Fuckers like that love a good back-from-the-dead jump scare.'

But Myers didn't stop.

'Hey, I'm not joking,' said Eva moving to pull her back.

Myers swept her arm back and Eva flew through the air. I stared at Eva in astonishment as she landed in a heap across the other side of the pews.

Myers hadn't even touched her.

No.

She did that with magic.

17

I ran to Eva and helped her to her feet.

'Eva, that was magic.'

'I know.'

'Detective Myers just used magic on you.'

'I know.'

'But she can't do magic.'

'If you make me say "I know" one more time, I swear to god I'm going to punch you in the neck.'

The detective stood over the prone bulk of Mr Many Mouths.

'Myers, what are you doing?' I asked, but it's like she was in a trance, her face pale.

The stone floor began to tremble, dust rising with the vibration. I could see the magic in the air begin to swirl and snarl. I wasn't having to force myself to see it, it was just there, visible.

And it was all flowing towards Myers.

She raised her hands above her head and the magic struck them like lightning rods.

'Yep, this feels like something really bad is going to happen,' said Eva.

'Like what?' I asked, unable to take my eyes off Myers.

And then something bad happened.

Myers sprang through the air and onto the unconscious Mr Many Mouths. Her hands dug into its flesh—no, *melted* through the flesh—until she was up to her wrists in it, head thrown back in rapture. She was draining something from the creature. An essence? A life force?

'Oh no. Oh no, no, no,' said Eva.

'What? What is she doing?'

'Stand back,' she commanded, and ran towards Myers, her hands igniting.

'Eva, no!'

She thrust out her hands and flames arced from her and went roaring towards Myers. I staggered back, unable to believe what I was seeing. But then yet another surprising thing happened. The flames didn't touch Myers, nor Mr Many Mouths. It's like there was a bubble around the two, and the flames just bounced right off.

'We've gotta stop her,' cried Eva.

'What is it she's even doing?'

Dark smoke trails were pouring from the body of Mr Many Mouths and flooding directly into Myers, who bucked and writhed in ecstasy.

'She's draining him,' replied Eva.

'Of magic?'

'Yes, but not just magic. Of its essence. Of its very *particular* essence.'

She was talking about the Dark Lakes.

'Why is she doing that?' I asked.

'Does it look like I have all the answers, idiot? I'm seeing this for the first time, just like you!'

A fair point.

'So what? What can we do?'

As it turned out, there was nothing to be done, and no time to do it.

Myers screamed and ripped her hands apart, sending the

shredded body of Mr Many Mouths flying around the church. Many Mouths was no longer a threat; he now lay spread around the church in football-sized chunks. Just like all the farm animals. Just like Mr Madden and his young children.

Eva stepped in beside me, her face dripping with gore.

'You've got something on your face,' I said.

She snorted.

I turned back to Myers, who was now unconscious, curled up on the ground and wearing an unnerving smile.

'She's had a big meal,' said Eva. 'Let's get her before nap time's over.'

We cleaned the church up as best we could and then left the residents to it. They'd wake up at some point and wonder why they all decided to take a slumber party in the local parish, then wander off to their homes, and hopefully, never mention it again.

We laid Myers out on a bed back at the coven. Actually, we went a step further than that; we strapped her down, ankles and wrists, and added a further restraint across her torso, just in case.

Eva entered the room, a drink in her hand, and a grimmer-than-usual look on her face.

'Any ideas?' I asked.

'Yup.'

'Go on.'

'I think jockeys should be made to race with a horse on their back to see how they like it.'

'That's fascinating,' I sighed, 'but not terribly useful in this current situation.'

Eva threw up her hands. 'Isn't it obvious, idiot? Myers is possessed.'

'Possessed like... *The Exorcist*?'

'Dunno. Could be a demon, yeah. Could be a lot of different things. Whatever it is, it was feeding on the essence of all those dead animals.'

'And Mr Madden and his two children.'

'Yeah. But she didn't attack any of the other farmers, which means maybe she couldn't. Maybe whatever was inside her was trying to grow in strength, bit by bit, and the Madden guy and his kids were the first time it was strong enough to take down people.'

'Oh, at the first crime scene, she mentioned how things had been scaling up. From single animals at first, to the barn full we saw.'

'Right.'

'And then it got strong enough to do that to Mr Many Mouths.'

Eva nodded and prodded at Myers with the toe of her boot. The detective rocked back and forth, but didn't wake, didn't make a sound.

'What I don't understand is, why whatever's inside her would suddenly be so brazen,' I said. 'The other attacks were done in secret; this time she did it right in front of us.'

'Yeah. I have a not great theory about that.'

'Awesome, I love foreboding-sounding theories that will forever haunt my dreams.'

'It's like I said back at the church, she was draining a kind of energy that could only be part of something from the Dark Lakes.'

I shifted uncomfortably.

'Couldn't hold itself back. It wanted that Dark Lakes hook-up, and it didn't care about hiding anymore, because, after that meal, it wouldn't need to hide. It wasn't going to let the opportunity slip away for that kind of meal, so it took her over right in front of us. Grabbed hold of the wheel and shoved Myers into the back seat.'

I thought back to the church, to when I thought I was

about to be taken over, a tongue down my throat. And then Myers had taken my hand and I'd done something impossible. I'd felt... in control. I had complete mastery of the magic that surrounded me. I felt like a giant. I could make it do anything I wanted it to. And what I'd wanted it to do was attack, and attack it did, bursting from me in a powerful, concussive wave.

A cough erupted from Myers and her eyes snapped open, causing me to almost fall off my chair in surprise.

'Myers? Is that you?'

She pulled at the restraints, trying to sit up and failing. 'What happened, where am I?'

'Myers, it's okay, you're okay,' I said.

'The same can't be said for the mouthy twat back at the church,' said Eva. 'You turned that ugly fucker into meat confetti.'

'I don't remember. I don't remember. I woke in the church and then... I don't remember!' She panicked, writhing in the bed, pulling against the restraints. 'Why am I tied down? What are you doing to me?'

'They're a safety precaution,' said Eva.

'To protect me from what?' she replied.

'No,' I said, 'they're to protect *us* from *you*.'

Myers looked at me in utter, silent bewilderment. 'What are you talking about? Untie me. That's an order!'

'You can't order shit,' said Eva.

'I am an officer of the law and you will release me!'

'No can do, sexy,' said Eva. 'Besides, if anyone's in trouble with the old bill, it's you.'

Myers looked to me. She was starting to regain her composure, or at least, she was pretending she had. 'Joe, what is this mad cow talking about?'

'The animals,' I said. 'The sheep, the horses, the pigs.'

'What about them?'

'We think that was you.'

Myers let that sink in for a moment. 'What the fuck are you talking about?'

'You're possessed,' said Eva, reaching over to rap her knuckles against the top of Myers' head. 'Oi, whoever's hiding in there, you might as well come out and say hello. You already gave the game away back at the church, so there's no point playing shy.'

'Joe, please,' said Myers.

'Eva's telling the truth. It's you. Well, something that's inside of you. It killed those animals. It killed Mr Madden and his children.'

'No...'

I frowned and nodded.

'I... I couldn't.'

'Well, you did,' said Eva.

'I'd know if I had. Surely, I'd know?'

'Technically, it wasn't you,' said Eva, 'but they did die at your hands.'

'Oh, Christ. No. You're lying. You have to be.'

'I think that's why you were feeling off at the crime scenes,' said Eva. 'Why you passed out at the Madden place. You unconsciously recognised the places, the scenes you were walking through. Conscious and unconscious mind and memory fighting over what you were seeing. Short circuit. Down you go.'

There wasn't a lot I could say to make her feel better. She'd just found out that she had the blood of children on her hands. Maybe she hadn't meant to do it, maybe she hadn't had any control or awareness at all, but the last thing those kids had seen had been her face.

'I'm bored now,' said Eva, shoving the bed with the sole of her boot. 'Whoever it is hiding inside of you like a cowardly little fuck better come out right now, or I'm going to stop playing nice.'

'It's me, it's just me,' pleaded Myers.

'Right, fuck this,' said Eva, her fingertips glowing white-hot. 'Either you come out and say hello, or I'm going to shove my hand in there and pull you out.' She raised her fist and it began to blur.

'Can you really do that?' I asked.

'Done it before. I'll reach in and drag the fucker out.'

Myers' head snapped back and she began to shake, to convulse. I instinctively ran to her, tried to hold her still.

'We need to force something between her teeth,' I said.

'Get back, idiot,' ordered Eva.

'She might bite her tongue off!'

Eva yanked me away. 'I said, get back!'

Now it wasn't just Myers convulsing, it was the whole bed, its legs bouncing and thumping against the floor.

'What's happening?' I asked.

'I think Myers' guest is making an appearance at last.'

The shaking stopped. All was quiet. I leaned closer to the bed, wanting to reach out and take her hand. Then Myers' eyes opened and she turned to me, smiling. But it wasn't her smile, and her eyes didn't look like her eyes. They looked like they had back at the church when she'd taken my hand in hers.

'So, you finally decided to come out of the closet, eh?' said Eva, lighting a smoke. 'You know I'm still getting you out of there. Whether you choose the easy way or the hard way, that's up to you. But I'm giving you the chance to walk out yourself because I'm a fucking sweetheart.'

Myers chuckled.

'Did I say something funny, fuck face?'

'Spit from my mouth,' growled Myers, her voice strange and deep.

Eva's eyes widened.

'What did you say?' she asked.

'It's already too late, Eva. It's done.'

The cigarette tumbled from Eva's fingers and she stepped back. 'No...' she said, her voice a whisper.

'What's happening, Eva?' I said. I'd never seen her look like that before, and it terrified me right through to my bones.

'Dirt from the ground, spit from my mouth,' said Myers, said the thing *inside* Myers.

'It can't be,' said Eva.

'Can't be what, Eva? Talk to me!'

'Say my name, familiar.'

Eva shook her head.

'Say it. Call me by my name.'

Eva's fists were clenched to her chest, her face drained of colour.

'Say. My. Name.'

Eva's lips trembled, but no sound came from between them.

And then she said it. Then she called the thing by its name.

'Janto.'

18

Unpredictability is Eva's default, but I still found myself taken aback by what she did next. She didn't throw obscenities, or conjure a wall of flame, or even pull out a can of absurdly strong lager.

No.

She left.

'Eva!'

She didn't pause, didn't reply, she just said the name, turned around, and walked out.

The name.

To be more precise, *my* name. My real name.

I should have left, too. Should have got the hell out of that room as quickly as I knew how. But my name had been spoken and I needed to know why. I thought again about when Myers had held my hand back at the church. How I'd suddenly felt more complete. How I'd been in total control of the magic that surrounded me.

'Is that really you? Or, well, *me*, I suppose?'

'You aren't me,' she said. 'I'm Janto of the Cumbrian Coven, you're just what was left behind after the real me was scraped out and tossed aside. After they tried to exterminate me.'

If she, or he, was telling the truth, I suppose that explained why I couldn't remember any of my past before I woke up naked next to Derwentwater. I hadn't just forgotten, it had literally been removed from me. I'd been split in two, and everything I was now was the bits of me that weren't somehow wrong. That weren't attracted by the lure of that unholy Dark Lakes throne.

'So, we were... I was, I mean, split in two?'

'But you kept the body. What they did, what *she* did, it was supposed to kill us. Instead, it did this.'

'So you possessed Myers just to get close to me?'

'Oh, I've been inside of her since long before you ever met. For years, after what happened, after we were torn apart. I drifted, barely sentient, more an idea than a reality. But bit by bit, I forced myself back into being. They underestimated me. The sort of power I possess. My iron will. You cannot simply scrub me from existence. I am Janto of the Cumbrian Coven, destined to walk across this small world as the Magic Eater.'

The old me was a bit of a big-head, that much was clear.

'But why Myers?' I asked. 'What did she do to deserve this?'

'I needed a body. I couldn't just drift in and out of this plane of existence, not if I wanted to come back. To *really* come back. You have no idea what it takes to carry on existing in this state, blown around by the Uncanny winds. Slipping between planes of existence. But I persevered. I refused to fade. And then I met Detective Maya Myers, radiating fury, pain, strength, crouched by the body of her murdered partner. She was a beacon, shining bright, guiding me to her. So I homed in. I homed in and I took her.'

I thought about what Detective Martins had said when he found me at Myers' home.

'She *did* ask for a transfer up here,' I said. 'She wasn't pushed here to get her out of the way. *You* made her come here.'

Janto chuckled. 'It seems as though not all of the intelligence was knocked out of you.'

I was trying not to focus too much on the strange notion that I was, essentially, having a conversation with myself. But this was all very bloody weird. 'You've made my friend do horrible things,' I said.

'Necessary things. I needed to feed. And I did. On fear. On the possibility of a life cut short. On flesh and blood and sinew. Each new death made me stronger. Made me more *real.* And Eva was correct, that meal from the Dark Lakes, I could not let that pass me by. Could not wait. But I was still not strong enough to tackle the creature head-on.'

'So you took my hand,' I said. 'That's why you did that, why I felt like I did for those few moments.'

'For a few heartbeats, we had access to our full potential. Access to enough magic to take the creature down, ready to eat. And now, I am ready to reclaim what's mine. To take the throne that was promised me.'

Janto sat upright, the bonds that had held Myers' body in place melting away, turned to water. I darted for the door, only for it to slam shut in front of me.

'Where are you going, Joe?' asked Janto.

I twisted the handle desperately, yanking at the door, but it stayed stubbornly shut.

'I think I left a hob on,' I said. 'Safety first.'

'Look what she made of us. A chattering fool.'

'But we still have lovely hair.'

I gasped as I was yanked from my feet and sent flying across the room as if attached to a giant elastic band. I crashed against the wall and slammed heavily to the floor.

'You're not going anywhere,' said Janto, climbing from the bed, hands glowing with arcane power.

'You don't really want to hurt me,' I said, 'we're not the self-destructive type.'

'I'm not going to hurt you, Joe.'

'Great, thanks.'

'I'm just going to take my body back. For good.'

'Right. Not so great.'

'A decade of drifting, of barely existing. I've been so patient. I had to grow. Had to gather the power to reclaim you without Eva pulling me back out. And now, thanks to that feast from the Dark Lakes, I am ready.'

Janto reached out to me, and I scrabbled backwards until my shoulders met the wall.

'Don't be scared. This is good. Look what she did, that lowly bitch familiar. Look at what she did to us. Look how we've had to hide inside a lowly human body.'

'But what'll happen to me? To Joseph Lake?'

'There is no Joseph Lake. You made him up. There will only be me.'

'If it's all the same to you then, I don't think I really want you back in here. I've not heard the most pleasant of stories.'

I stood slowly, pulling the magic that swam around the coven into me.

Janto smiled, amused. 'You really think you can take me on, Joe? You can barely create a little ball of fire. You're pathetic. She made you pathetic.'

'That's good, because hurting you hurts my friend, and she'll get really pissed off if I ruin that leather jacket of hers.'

Janto smiled. 'Then what are you doing?'

'This, you dick.'

I grunted and swept my hands across him, managing to pull enough power into me to shove Janto out of my path. I didn't pause. I sprinted for the still-locked door, conjuring a fireball that I tossed in its direction. The fire smashed through the door, sending wooden splinters firing, and out I went.

I ran from Myers, from Janto, from the Coven, leapt behind the wheel of the Uncanny Wagon, and got the mother-shitting hell away from there.

19

I drove fast, my heart going like the clappers, my eyes on the rearview more than the road ahead. I expected to see Myers, to see Janto, surging after me to reclaim his body.

I drove aimlessly, not knowing where to turn. I tried phoning Eva but wasn't surprised when she didn't answer. I kept replaying that look she had in her eyes when she realised who it was that had taken over Myers. The look in her eyes when the detective said my real name.

The Red Woman had told me that something was coming, that she didn't have to trick me into taking my throne, that I would be taking it soon enough without her assistance. And now the part of me that wanted that throne was back, and wanted his body back, too. Wanted to be complete again.

The Red Woman may not have known what it was she was sensing, what was causing ripples to spread across the lake, but she had felt Janto's return.

My return.

I had no doubt that when I was complete, when Janto got his body back, I would walk into the Dark Lakes and fulfil my destiny. I'd take the throne that sat on top of the blood-red hill.

I'd become the Magic Eater. I'd lead an army of the dead into this world.

It was all a bit grim, really, and yet, I couldn't see any way around it. Especially not with my so-called familiar playing hide and seek. No Eva, no Myers for backup, just me against me. And there was only going to be one victor in that tussle.

I needed to hole up somewhere for a while and try to think, try to bolt together something that looked vaguely like a plan. But where could I go? Janto knew all of the places I might head to, and those he didn't, Myers did. I couldn't go home, couldn't go to the hospital, couldn't go to the coven. I needed somewhere that felt safe. Someplace I wouldn't have to look over my shoulder for a little bit.

And then the answer popped into my head. It was obvious where I had to go. I made a not entirely safe three-point turn in the middle of the road, drawing a chorus of enraged car horns, and I headed to the pub.

Mickey Finn's.

Of course.

The Keswick pub secreted down a blind alley that served the area's Uncanny types. The place stood within a magic-dampening bubble, so if Janto did steer Myers' body there in the hope of carrying on our fight, I would at least be standing on a more level playing field.

Sure, he could just beat the crap out of me physically instead of magically and then drag me outside, away from the effects of the bubble, but this was the best option on offer, so I parked up, legged it down the blind alley, and breathed a sigh of relief as I stepped inside and pressed my back against the door.

I headed for the bar, glancing around the place to make sure Janto wasn't already there, waiting to get the drop on me.

'Your fox friend is barred,' said Grunt, the giant barman.

'Oh? Why?'

'He hit one of my best customers with an axe.'

'Fair enough,' I said. 'Could I get a pint, please?'

Grunt went about pulling the required. 'She's been waiting for you over there,' he said, as he slid the glass over to me.

'What? Who? Myers?' I whirled to find a figure slumped across a table in a corner booth.

It was Eva. Great minds and all that.

I paid, picked up my glass, then walked across the pub to sit on the free side of the booth.

'Look at this,' I said. 'Disaster strikes and we both head straight for the pub.'

Eva sat up, almost knocking over the many empty pots littering the table. She'd clearly made herself busy since running out on me.

'Is it still you?' she asked. I didn't like the fact that she didn't put "idiot" at the end of her sentence. It made me feel uncomfortable.

'I'm afraid so. Just Joseph Lake in here,' I said, tapping my noggin.

Eva reached over and took my drink, gulping it down in one.

'Could have used your assistance back there, though.'

Eva slammed the glass down and lunged across the table, grabbing me by the shirt and yanking me forward.

'You have no idea!' she roared. 'You have no fucking idea!' Her eyes practically burned holes through me.

'You know my shirt collar is digging into me a little.'

Eva hissed and pushed me away. 'Oi, Grunt, another round for me,' she said waving her hand.

'Maybe you've had enough?' I suggested.

'Never. Never enough... not since then.'

'Since when?'

Her eyes momentarily met mine then darted away. It seemed to me like she looked, well, ashamed.

Grunt arrived with a pint and a bottle of whiskey with one glass. Eva pushed the glass away and drank straight from the bottle.

'Okay, what's going on?' I asked.

Eva laughed.

'No, I want to know. What's up with you? Myers is taken by the dark side, and you just run away?'

'You wouldn't understand.'

'She's our friend, Eva. It doesn't matter who's controlling her. She's our friend.'

'It matters when it's him.'

She lifted the bottle to her lips again, but I reached across the table and pulled it out of her hands.

'Give me that back,' she demanded.

'We need to come up with a plan.'

'Give me. That. Back.'

I poured the contents on the floor. 'Since when were you the coward out of the two of us?' I said.

Before I knew what was happening, I was on the floor and I could taste blood in my mouth. I pressed a hand to my jaw and looked up in shock as Eva slid out of the booth and stood over me.

'You just hit me...' I said.

'Yeah, and now I'm going to kick you.'

Eva took a step and kicked me in the ribs. I rolled on to my back, gasping for air.

'The things you made me do. Look what you did to me. Look what you made of me!'

Another boot to the side. I cried out in pain and scrambled backwards until I met the bar. I think I heard Grunt say something about taking it outside, but he wasn't going to step in. No one in this place would risk getting in Eva's way.

'Eva, stop. Stop, please. It's me, it's Joseph!'

'You made me do it. I didn't have a choice. You made me!'

I held my hands up, ready for another kick, another punch. 'Eva! Eva, please, it wasn't me. Whatever he made you do, whatever Janto did to you, it wasn't me.'

She lunged at me, pulling me to my feet by my coat collar, fist raised. I closed my eyes, helpless, ready to feel her knuckles make mush of my cheek, but the punch never came. I opened my eyes. Eva was crying; great, fat tears rolling down her cheeks. I think that hurt more than the kick in the ribs.

She let me go and slumped on a barstool. Tentatively, I took a seat beside her.

'I never told you the truth,' she said. 'Not all of it, anyway. Why should I?'

I didn't say anything, I just waited for her to tell me in her own time.

'It was Lyna who first noticed something was wrong with Janto. She told me even before she told Melodia. He was always the darker of the witches. Always the one who had to be tempered. Had to be stopped from going too far. Too fucking brutal. But he was one of them. One of the trio. Fuck, he was one of the people that gave me life in the first place, and I loved... I loved him with every part of me, just like I loved the others.'

I'd never heard Eva talk like this. So clear and direct, so honest. Was this what she was like before the coven fell?

'Lyna suspected something was up and had me keep an eye on him. It was me who saw him talk to the Red Woman, though it wasn't the first time he'd spoken to her, as it turned out. Lyna and Melodia, they thought they could pull him back from the brink. He made them believe they could. But he was lying. He was just biding his time until he was ready to take them out.'

'And they destroyed themselves trying to kill him,' I said. 'Trying to kill me.'

And yet, in the end, they hadn't killed him at all. They'd given their lives, and it hadn't mattered one bit.

'No,' said Eva. 'They didn't destroy themselves. Not exactly.'

'What?'

She looked me directly in the eyes. 'I killed them.'

The whole pub seemed to tilt like the world was drunk and was trying to throw me to the ground.

'I don't... I don't understand. I attacked them, and they killed themselves trying to kill me. That's what happened, that's what you said happened. And then I woke up next to Derwentwater.'

Eva shook her head.

'They tried. They thought they could. It was two against one, but they'd waited too long. They tried to help him, to believe his lies, long enough for him to gain enough power from the Dark Lakes that he was a match for them both. No, more than a match. But Melodia... she was always one for a back-up plan. She knew if they failed that the Magic Eater would walk the Earth. So she handed me a spell. A sort of doomsday scenario spell that she and Lyna created. They fought inside the coven. Janto, he had them on their knees. They were done. So I did what I had to do. What they told me to do. I detonated the spell. I saw his face the moment before the thing unleashed. The confusion. Betrayal. I killed the witches of the Cumbrian Coven. All three died because I made it happen. And it turns out it was for nothing. I killed my creators for nothing.'

And there it was.

The whole thing at last.

I hadn't killed my fellow witches at all. Not exactly. A spell they created had done the damage, and it was Eva who had cast it. I didn't know how to feel about that. It didn't make any difference to what I'd been back then. I was still the witch gone bad, ready to become a beast. I still caused it all.

'Eva...'

'Forget it.'

She stood and straightened her tatty coat, drying her eyes with her sleeve.

'You should have told me,' I said. 'Why did you carry that on your own?'

Eva didn't answer, she just walked away. I knew without asking that she didn't want me to follow.

'But what about him?' I called after her. 'What about Janto?'

'I'm leaving the lakes. For good this time. Fuck trying to be a hero. It doesn't suit me. It never did.'

Eva grabbed a bottle from another patron's hand.

And then she was gone.

20

I slumped back into the booth I'd recently been punched out of and helped myself to the pint Eva had abandoned. Eva leaving perfectly good alcohol behind; now I knew things were serious. I chuckled to myself but I didn't feel jolly at all.

Oh, was I ever royally screwed.

Eva was gone and what did that leave? Just me. The weak half of a witch with only a smidge more magical ability than a Las Vegas stage magician. Actually, that was overselling myself; I had no idea how to do card tricks, let alone the sawing a woman in half bit.

Despite my current, bad situation, all I could think about was Eva. About how she'd carried around that secret for so long. That she'd been forced to kill her own creators. They told her to, but I don't suppose that made the aftermath any easier to swallow.

Eva was a drunk, a drug addict, a don't-give-a-fuck mess. That's what my turning to the Dark Lakes had done to her. No wonder she warned me that if she ever saw me near that place, she'd kill me. It's incredible she ever came back to Cumbria at all, really. Ever told me what I was, let alone started to train me.

For ten years, she stayed away, but something in her, something she couldn't numb with denial or drink, had pulled her back to this place, and back to me. I don't think I could have done what she did. And I don't think if I had that I could ever have come back, or ever trust again.

I winced and held my ribs, hoping that Eva's boot hadn't cracked one. So what now? That was the question. If I really was on my own, I needed to try and formulate some plan of attack that made a virtue of my limited knowledge, skills, and magical abilities. I mulled this as I sipped at my pint, and I came up with nothing. Actually, nothing would have been a start.

My phone rang and I pulled it out of my coat, hoping against hope that I'd see Eva's name. I'd answer and she'd tell me, *'Fuck it, let's get our friend back, even if it kills us.'* But it wasn't Eva's name I saw, it was Annie's.

I considered ignoring it, but hey, I seemed to be on a run as far as horrible events went, so why not tell Annie that I was calling time on our barely-even-a-relationship, and what's more, it was all for her own good. I couldn't allow this to drag on any longer, not with all that was happening.

I sighed and hit answer. 'Hey.'

'Hey, Joe? Are you okay?'

'Sorry. Sorry. Just, this has turned into a real shit of a day.'

'Well, maybe it's just about to get better again,' she said, playfully.

'I don't think so.'

I could hear Millie chattering in the background, and I knew I was doing the right thing. I was bad news. Look at what had happened to Myers, look at what I'd done to Eva. Being with me meant putting yourself at risk, and I couldn't do that to Annie, let alone a child.

'Joe, what's wrong? What's happened?'

'Too much to get into, and none of it pleasant.'

'You can tell me. I've had my own share of the bizarre, remember. I'm here for you.'

I savoured that for a moment. I was as isolated as I could remember. Myers possessed, Eva walking out, holed up in a pub waiting for the bad guy to turn up; the bad guy was me.

'I'm sorry but I have to do this, Annie.'

'Have to do what?'

There was a muffled bang at her end of the call.

'What was that?' I asked.

'I think something hit the door.'

Another muffled bang.

'Let me just check what's going on,' she said.

And then a thought crept into me that turned my blood cold.

'Annie? Annie, listen to me.'

Another bang.

'Hey, who is that?' said Annie.

'Annie, get away from the door!'

All I could do was listen. Listen as the door to Annie's house crashed open. Listen as Annie screamed.

The call ended.

It was, of course, far too late to do anything by the time I pulled up outside Annie's home, leapt out of the Uncanny Wagon and sprinted to the front door of her house. I saw the splintered wood around the broken lock, then shoved the door open and went inside.

Should I have called the police on my way over? Maybe. But then what use have that been? It would already have been over by the time they got there, and if Myers had been there, if Janto had been there, no officer who entered would have walked out again.

'Annie?'

I hadn't heard Janto during the call, but I knew. He wanted me, so he searched Myers' mind and found a weak link. He could have come directly to me, but it seemed like the old me liked playing games. And now exactly what I'd feared might happen if I became romantically involved with someone had happened.

There was blood on the wall in the entrance hall. I reached out and trailed my fingers through it, the red smearing against the cream of the wallpaper. The skeleton in the cathedral; it said it had seen death in my future.

'My death?'

'That would be telling. But it's there. Clear as night. Tragedy. A fall is coming. A fall that stings and shocks.'

Maybe this is what the skeleton saw. Maybe this was the death to sting and shock. A woman I liked, and her innocent child. Dead because of me.

Toys littered the floor, evidence of the innocent caught up in my horror. Each room I went into, I expected to find a body. I wondered which I would find first, adult or child. But I only found one body in Annie's house, and it was neither of the bodies I was expecting.

It was a cat.

The animal was laid out on the tiles of the kitchen floor, it's intestines yanked out of a tear in its belly. Why do this? What was the point?

I reached out and touched the dead cat, drawing the house's magic into me. I wanted to *see*. This time the insight magic wasn't blocked. Now the killer wanted me to see. Had no reason to hide his identity from me anymore.

The world as I saw it was torn away, then I was looking through something else's eyes: the dead cat's. Witnessing its final moments. I was low to the ground, brushing through the grass in the back garden. I was hunting. My every instinct was trained on the mouse that was trying to evade me, but then a new sound caught my attention. Prey forgotten, I padded to the back door, pushing my way into the kitchen through the cat flap.

'Please, don't hurt her!'

Annie's voice. Desperate, anguished, terrified.

I could see her now, backed into a corner, placing her body between the intruder and her daughter. Millie clung to her mum's leg. Did she even know what was going on? What would happen next?

Annie clutched a kitchen knife in her shaking hands, ready to defend her daughter, but she'd no idea what she was up against.

'Get away!'

She lashed out with the knife, swinging it in an arc. It wasn't an offensive move, she wasn't trying to stab or slice anyone, she was warning the intruder to keep at a distance. But this intruder didn't need to get close to hurt her.

The knife spun out of Annie's hand as though attached to a wire, and flipped handle over point until it embedded itself in the floor, causing the cat to hiss and recoil.

'Well, now who is this little one?' It was Myers' voice.

She crouched into view as I, the cat, backed up under a table. The sound of feet. I saw Annie gather up Millie and race for the door, trying to slip away while Janto's attention was fixed on the cat.

'Stop,' said Janto, without taking his eyes off the animal.

Annie came to a sudden halt as though the floor was made of glue. 'Let us go, please!'

'Back against the wall.'

Millie wailed in Annie's arms as they were thrown through the air and pinned against the kitchen wall next to Millie's brightly-coloured stick drawings.

Myers' hands reached out towards the hissing cat. 'Stop that.'

No more hissing from the cat. Now more swinging claws. The moggy was lifted into the air and aimed at the same wall that Annie and her daughter were stuck to, then all three were fixed there like bugs to flypaper.

'Look at who I dropped in on, Joe,' said Janto, using the cat's eyes like a camera, recording the scene. Because of course he knew I'd come here, knew I'd see the dead cat and use my insight magic. So why not record a little message for me?

He swung the cat close to their faces, moving it back and forth and laughing at their distress. Enjoying their fear.

'Look at what you've made me do, Joe. And people think I'm the worst part of you. I mean, the poor woman has a young child, for God's sake.'

'Joe isn't here,' screamed Annie. 'You're a lunatic!'

'That's not very nice,' replied Myers. The view blurred, and then her smiling face filled my vision. 'I know this must be a difficult time for you, Joe, but imagine what it's been like for me for the last ten years. All I want is what's mine. All I want is to be complete again. To be whole. Why is that so wrong? Why would you want to fight that? Are you telling me you're happy with your small life, your weak grasp on the Uncanny? A menial day job cleaning up after others? Mopping up their puke. We're high-born. We're a god. The throne is ours, Joe. Our army awaits.' Myers grinned again. 'I'll be in touch.'

I heard the cat scream.

And the vision cut to black.

21

Janto left no clue as to where he might have taken them, but at least I had a little hope to cling to. The only corpse inside Annie's house belonged to a cat, so maybe, just maybe, he hadn't killed them yet. Wanted to keep them alive, as bait. They would wriggle on his hook, and I'd have no choice but to swim towards them with my mouth wide open.

I barged past someone as I staggered, ashen-faced, from Annie's house, and made my way to the car.

'Hey, watch it!' said the woman, but I didn't reply, didn't apologise. I was walking through a muffled world as I fumbled with my car keys and climbed behind the wheel.

What now?

Where would I go?

It seemed like Janto wasn't going to bother chasing after me. He wanted me to come to him now, wanted to be in control, and I wasn't about to disappoint him, not while Annie and Millie were in danger, scared out of their minds. I had no choice now but to face the inevitable. The danger they were in was my fault. My fault twice over, in fact.

Whatever happened next, I wouldn't die. Not as such. Janto would become whole again. I would walk away, still breathing, still alive, but this me would die. The me I'd been for the last ten years.

Goodbye, daft Joseph Lake. Hello, Janto the Warlock. Hello, Magic Eater.

Any part that I thought of as me would be swamped by the bad stuff. Pushed aside by all the thoughts and desires that had once ruled me to such a degree that Eva had been forced to kill all three of her creators. But Eva was gone now. I was all that was left, and I couldn't just let my bad half kill Annie and Millie.

So in you come, Mr Lake.

Your time is well and truly up.

I had no idea where to look beside the coven, so that's where I looked.

As I watched the countryside roll past the driver's window, I felt my heart ache. When Janto joined with me, when I became whole again, this would all be gone. I'd walk across the land and watch it burn. Burn by my hand. I wouldn't feel its loss, wouldn't weep for a world destroyed, I'd look upon my deeds and think that they were righteous.

I parked up and entered the blind alley, the secret pocket in reality down which the Cumbrian Coven hunkered. Safe from the eyes of any hill-walkers or tourists. I pulled the surrounding magic into me as I carefully edged my way forward. My hands became twin suns, burning furiously, ready to make a last stand, no matter how pointless. I may be an idiot, I may be a recovering coward, but I wasn't going to welcome the end with open arms. I'd do my best to fight against the coming of the dark.

The coven door was open, so I slid through, careful not to

nudge it and have a creaking hinge broadcast my approach. Once inside, I tried to reach out with whatever magically attuned senses I had. Tried to get a feel for where Janto might be.

I got nothing.

I walked forward, my hands lighting the way. I peered at the charcoal patches that spread like waves across the coven's walls. I noticed them the very first time Eva had brought me here; the fire damage all over the inside of the building. I had so much to come to grips with back then that it had seemed like the least of my concerns at the time, and soon enough, I stopped noticing them altogether.

This time I saw the scorch marks and a thought clicked into place. This was more than just wear and tear. This was damage from the big fight. It must have been. The three witches had faced off here, ten years ago, inside their own coven. This was where Lyna and Melodia had realised they had no choice but to put an end to me. To kill Janto. The same place Eva realised she was going to have to do something that would change who she was forever.

I quietly moved from room to room, but I needn't have acted so cautiously. No one was home. The flames around my hands puttered out, and I sank into the broken old couch. My foot nudged something, and I looked down to see an open can of lager on the floor. I lifted and shook it; there was still about a third of the liquid inside. I put it to my lips and drank the warm, flat contents.

I awoke curled up on the couch, several hours later.

I left the coven and got in my car, looking at my phone to see if Janto had contacted me. There were no missed calls. No messages.

I didn't know where else to look for Annie and Millie, so I

drove back to Keswick, back to my flat. I sat on my couch and rubbed at my tightly shut eyes, trying to push away the stress-induced headache that was sure to arrive at any moment.

What had my life become?

Just a few months ago, I was Joseph Lake, a bumbling guy who had once woken up next to a body of water without knowing who he was. A curiosity. A lovable rascal with a menial day job and a side-gig investigating the paranormal. A hapless fool with a crush on his best friend who was wildly out of his league. I'd have given just about anything to get back to that. Even just for a little while.

But this had always been coming. It may have taken a decade, but sooner or later I was going to find myself right where I was, whether I wanted any part of it or not. The Dark Lakes wanted me, Janto wanted me. I was screwed right from the start.

There was a knock at the door.

My heart thumped so hard against my chest that I was sure whoever was outside must have been able to hear it.

Was he here? Had Janto decided to come and get me after all? I edged toward the door, wishing it had one of those peep-holes so I could see outside. I dropped to my hands and knees and peered through the thin gap beneath the door. I could just about make out a pair of shoes. Men's shoes. Myers always wore boots.

'Mr Lake, I know you're in there, I saw you go in.'

Detective Martins. What the crap did he want this time?

'This isn't really a good time, Detective,' I said, getting back to my feet.

'Is that right?'

'I had a bastard of a shift at the hospital and I've been rewarded with a headache that I'd really like to sleep through.'

'Open the door or I'll kick it in.'

I opened the door.

Detective Martins was grinning in a way I didn't like.

'Hello, Detective Martins. What can I do for you?'

'Well, Mr Lake, you can accompany me down to the fucking station.'

Of course. Why wouldn't I get arrested at this point?

22

Martins shoved me into the back of his car with more vigour than was strictly required, mashing my face against the rear passenger window.

'Ow,' I said, and really meant it.

I shuffled into a seated position and rubbed ruefully at my cheek. My face had taken a lot of punishment lately.

'You know you haven't read me my rights?' I said as Martins got behind the wheel and turned the key in the ignition.

'That's correct, I didn't.'

I looked at the back of Martins' head, the crown of his thinning brown hair.

'You also didn't tell me what this is all about. As far as I'm aware, I haven't actually done anything that would get me tossed into the back of a police car.'

Martins put his foot down and steered away from my flat.

'Hello? Detective Martins? I'm actually quite busy at the moment. I'm expected somewhere.'

'And where's that?' he replied.

'Not exactly sure about that just yet,' I said, 'but it needs to happen soon, and the person I'm meeting won't be happy if I keep them waiting.'

We drove on, leaving Keswick behind. I assumed that we were heading towards Carlisle, towards the station that Martins and Myers worked out of.

'You were seen,' said Martins.

'Okay. Seen where, exactly?'

'Fleeing a crime scene.'

'What? I haven't fled any...' I stumbled to a stop as I realised what he was getting at.

'There it is,' said Martins, his small, suspicious eyes on me in the rearview.

'I haven't done anything to Annie, or her daughter.'

'Or their cat, I suppose?'

'Right. Yes. I didn't tear their cat's guts out, you have my word on that.'

Martins snorted. 'Forgive me if I don't put a lot of trust in your word, you fucking weirdo.'

'No need for the name-calling.'

I slumped against the door as Martins took a hard left, leaving the road that would take us to Carlisle. 'Where are we going?' I asked.

'We're going to have a chat before things get more official,' he replied.

'Right.'

Oh, dear.

Another few minutes of driving in silence, then we turned into a dirt track and came to a stop by an abandoned stone building. Years ago it had probably been used as storage by farmers, or as a place to rest for people walking through the lakes. A place they could stop overnight and sleep safe from the elements. Now it was just a stone shell without a roof in the middle of nowhere, and there was nothing safe about it.

Martins killed the engine and exited the car, opening the door closest to me and pulling me out.

'What is this?' I asked.

'Told you, I want a word. Come on.'

He shoved me towards the stone shack.

'This isn't the Seventies. Police can't just take a suspect off the grid and beat a confession out of them.'

'Get in there,' he snarled.

The shack smelled bad. It was my guess that quite a lot of local wildlife had come to this place to die. Martins pushed me down on a bench fixed to the wall, jarring my elbow.

'Okay, that's enough,' I protested. 'If you do anything to me, I'll make sure you're fired.'

'I'm not going to do anything to you.'

'Forgive me if I don't take your word for that.'

Martins stood over me, legs astride. 'Where did you take them?'

'Where did I take who?'

'The woman and her daughter.'

'I didn't take them anywhere!'

Of course, that wasn't entirely true, but it wasn't *this* part of me that did it. *This* part of me was innocent.

'So, you're saying you had nothing to do with their disappearance?'

'No!'

'Nothing to do with the blood we found, or the butchered family pet?'

'Of course not.'

'There's blood on your hands.'

I looked down to see dried blood on my fingertips. Blood from where I touched the smear of it on the wall. Blood from when I touched the dead cat.

'Okay, I know this looks iffy. And me running out of her house and not going straight to the police doesn't look great either.'

'I'm glad we agree on something, finally.'

'But I had nothing to do with it. I've been trying to find them.'

'Right. And have you been trying to find Detective Myers,

too? Because no one can find her, either, though you claimed to have spoken to her.'

'Yes, I'm looking for her, too.'

'I might not be Sherlock Holmes, Mr Lake, but there seems to be one thing that connects our missing persons; a thing they all have in common. You.'

I sighed. Martins' small mind was clearly made up.

'And now you're caught fleeing the scene red-handed,' he said. 'Literally.'

'I don't have time for this,' I shot back, standing.

'Easy, now.' Martins said as he reached under his jacket and rested his hand on the extendable baton hanging from his belt.

'Please, let me go.'

'No.'

'If you don't let me go, Annie is dead. Millie is dead. And Detective Myers? I imagine she'll end up dead, too.'

'Is that a threat?'

'No, it's just a fact.'

'I knew from the start you were a wrong 'un, Lake. You may have wriggled out of that business with Chloe Palmer, but I knew you stunk to high heaven. And now here we are.'

I didn't have time for any more chit-chat, and I couldn't let him take me in.

'Okay,' I said, 'I'm going to tell you the truth.'

'About time. Tell me where you've put them, Lake. Are they locked up in a basement somewhere?'

'I don't have them. A powerful warlock has all three. He's possessed your partner, and kidnapped Annie and her daughter as bait to make sure I come running.'

Martins didn't look best pleased with this explanation. 'You're really off your rocker, aren't you?'

'I only wish I were, because then I'd be the only one in danger.'

'What's a warlock?'

'A male witch. Which, actually, is also what I am.'

Martins looked as though he was going to hit me, then he began to laugh. And I mean really howl, almost bending double.

'It's true,' I insisted. 'Magic is real. Monsters are real. And you should be thankful that people like me exist because, without us, this whole place would be a living hell.'

Martins straightened up and wiped a tear from his eye. 'Okay, that's it, you can play the nutter card all you like, but I'm taking you in.'

I took a step back, ready. 'I'm not going with you.'

Martins looked at me as though I were a dog that had just started saying people words. 'Suit yourself, I don't mind doing this the hard way, you sicko.' Martins pulled out his baton and flicked his wrist so it extended to its full length.

'Here we go, then,' I said.

I focused, and the magic in the air flickered into view. Great rolling waves of every colour imaginable, and some outside of the known spectrum. I drew it into me, felt it fill me, then I lifted my right fist and it burst into flames.

Martins stopped so suddenly he almost fell over. 'How... how are you doing that?'

'I told you. I'm a witch.'

Martins wavered, looking at the fire on my hand, over to my face, then back again.

'Let me go, Detective,' I said.

But Martins wasn't going to be scared off so easily. He grimaced and charged. I punched forward, the fire roaring from my hand and firing towards Martins as a warning shot, causing him to instinctively dive out of the way. He landed in the dirt, but tucked straight into a roll, coming to a stop on his knee, still brandishing the baton. He might be a nasty piece of work, but I couldn't help but be impressed.

I didn't have time to see what else he was capable of, though. As he came at me again—the dumb, fearless oaf—I swept my arm across and he was flung through the air and sent crashing against a wall, his baton spilling out of his hand. I ran to him as he lay dazed on the floor, and reached into his pocket, yanking out his keys.

'Fucker,' he said, slurring, his meaty hand gripping my wrist and pulling me back as I tried to escape.

'I'm sorry about this, Detective.'

'Sorry about what?'

The wrist he was holding in his vice of a hand erupted with flame, and he let me go with a scream. I clambered up and bolted for the door, waggling the keys over my head.

'Thanks. I'll try and give it back in one piece.'

I leapt behind the wheel of the car, slotted the key home, started the engine, and stomped on the accelerator. The car's rear end kicked out, wheels spinning, then it lurched away. Before I turned off the dirt path and back into a main road, I glimpsed Detective Martins staggering out of the stone shack, pursuing on foot.

So, to add to my list of pressing concerns, I could now add 'Fugitive from Justice' to my rap sheet. Today was just getting better and better.

23

I had to assume Martins would radio this in and have every officer in the county hunting me down, so driving back to my flat was out of the question. All in all, a terrible situation had just gotten a whole lot worse. So, that was good.

I'd also revealed to Martins that I was a witch, and performed a bit of magic, which kind of went against the Cumbrian Coven code. On the bright side, I'd probably never have to see him again seeing as—chances were—I'd shortly be taken over by my bad side and murder everyone.

There's always a silver lining.

Out of options, I headed for the coven. I'd just have to hunker down there until Janto came calling. As things turned out, I was called upon much sooner than that. My phone buzzed, and I pulled it from my pocket. Annie's name looked back at me.

'Hello? Annie? Are you okay?'

'She said to tell you to come now,' said Annie, her voice cracked.

'Are you hurt?'

'I'm... no, not too badly.'

'Where are you?'

There were some muffled noises as the phone was passed to someone else.

'Hello, Joe.'

It was Myers' voice.

'Don't hurt them,' I begged. 'Please.'

'I'll do my very best not to do my very worst.'

'Where?' I asked.

'The last place we were whole.'

'I don't—' but the call cut off.

Okay, okay, Annie was alive and mostly fine, and I had to assume Millie was, too. But where were they? The place we were last whole? What did he mean? The coven?

And then it clicked.

It was obvious.

It was the first place I saw when I became Joseph Lake.

I yanked the steering wheel, tires screeching, as I pulled a U-turn and steered the car towards Derwentwater.

I abandoned Martins' car half a mile from the lake and went the rest of the distance on foot. This way I wasn't announcing my arrival quite so loudly. Perhaps I'd even take Janto by surprise. A part of me still believed that I actually had a chance of rescuing Annie and Millie, and that all three of us would survive Janto. It's good to lie to yourself on a daily basis, I find. Healthy.

Derwentwater was where I was torn in two. Where the worst of me was ripped out of my body and cast asunder. Where it should have then broken apart and washed away like a sandcastle against the lapping tide, only Janto was too stubborn for that.

I took out my phone as I walked and called Eva. Maybe

she'd pick up. Maybe she'd come and help me save them. The call went straight to voicemail.

'Oh. Hi. Hello. It's the idiot talking. Just on my way to my ultimate doom, so thought I'd give you a quick bell. You probably won't even listen to this, but I'm going to talk for a while anyway and say what I want to say. So here I go. What you did —what Janto made you do—it wasn't your fault. You have nothing to be ashamed of. You did what you had to as a member of the Cumbrian Coven. You did what Lyna and Melodia wanted you to do. Recent revelations suggest it was all a bit pointless in the end, but… sorry… that was stupid. Like I said at the start, it's the idiot talking. The idiot who's more than likely about to die. Janto's going to claim me back and I'm going to disappear. And I'm scared. Really, really scared.'

I realised my cheek was wet and wiped it dry with the sleeve of my coat.

'I just wanted to say, it was very nice to know you, Eva. Even when you were hitting me with a stick. Okay, I suppose I should go now. This is Joseph Lake, saying goodbye. Goodbye.'

I ended the call and stood staring at the phone for a while. 'Okay then.'

I put the phone away and carried on walking. A few minutes later, I saw Derwentwater. I pressed against a tree, stealing glances at my surroundings, looking for signs of movement. I drew the local magic towards me, ready to ignite my hands should the need arise. As if they'd have any effect on Janto. Besides, he was inside Myers, so what was I going to do? Kill her to get him out? To save myself?

No.

I wasn't going to be responsible for that, so I let the magic drift away. There was nothing I could do but hand myself over and hope for the best. I stepped out from the cover and walked towards Derwentwater, whistling a jaunty tune as I went. I'd be damned if I was going to let him see me trembling.

The three of them were waiting on a bench. Annie flinched

when she saw me. She almost looked guilty, like I should blame her for what was about to happen.

'Hey there, Annie. And is that Millie the duck-feeder I see with you?'

Millie looked up at her mum, then smiled and waved at me. 'No ducks here,' she said, pointing at the lake.

'No ducks?' I said. 'Rubbish lake, that.'

'Here we all are then,' said Janto.

'Here we are. Nice day for it.'

'You don't remember what happened here, do you?' he asked.

'Nope,' I replied. 'Annie, are you okay?' I could see she had marks on her face. Cuts. They weren't bleeding, but they still looked painful.

'We made it this far,' said Janto, 'to this lake. We couldn't hold it together after what they did, so out I went and here you stayed, a wretched husk of my true self.'

'Yes, but my hair is always on point. You can't deny that.'

Janto smiled with Myers' mouth.

'You don't need to worry, now,' I said to Annie. 'This person is going to let you both go. Isn't that right, Janto?'

He shrugged. 'It makes no difference to me. One way or the other, they're fucked.'

Millie gasped and pointed. 'She said a bad word!'

Janto laughed and ruffled her hair. 'Oh, I'm going to do a lot more than that.'

'Get over here,' I said, gesturing for Annie and Millie to come forward.

Annie glanced to Janto, then lifted her daughter into her arms and walked over to me. 'I knew you'd come,' she said.

'Of course. I'm the man who put his soul in peril after only meeting you a couple of times.'

She smiled, but it didn't reach her eyes. 'So what happens now?'

'Now you take your daughter home.'

'No, I mean, what happens to you?'

'Oh, I'll be okay. He doesn't want me dead. Not exactly.'

'*He*?'

'This is Detective Maya Myers, but her body has been taken over by an evil part of me that wants to reclaim himself. It's complicated.'

'When isn't it?'

'Good point.'

Annie reached over, placing her hand to my cheek, her thumb rubbing back and forth. 'You're being brave to hide the truth from me.'

'I'm that transparent, am I?' I replied.

'Totally.'

Annie leaned forward and pressed her lips briefly to mine. 'Thank you for being brave, you idiot.'

'My pleasure.'

'And you're right, you know.'

'I am?'

'Yeah, your hair is really next-level.'

I handed Annie some keys. 'There's a car half a mile that way,' I said, pointing in the direction I'd come from. 'It belongs to a Detective Martins. Go home. Be safe.'

Annie looked at the keys in her hand, then over to Janto, who was skimming stones along the surface of the lake.

'Beat her. Him. Whoever. Just beat them.'

I wanted to reply with something encouraging, but my mouth refused.

'Come on, pickle,' she told Millie.

I watched the pair of them walk away, Millie smiling and waving at me until she turned out of sight.

'It's pointless letting them go, you know,' Janto told me as I joined him at the water's edge.

'You think so?'

'You made them think they're safe. They're not. No one is. Not now that we're about to be complete. We'll become the

Magic Eater and none of them will be safe ever again. Not even little girls who feed breadcrumbs to ducks.'

I picked up a smooth pebble and whipped it across the water, achieving a disappointing three skips.

'Maybe not. But for now, they are. For now, they're safe. That's all that matters.'

'I thought you might try and fight,' said Janto.

'You're in my friend's body,' I replied. 'Fighting you would mean hurting her.'

'How very noble of you.'

'Besides, you'd only kick my skinny arse.'

Janto laughed. 'So where's Eva? I thought she might come charging out at me. Always been a hot-head, that one. It's one of the things I like most about her.'

'She's gone,' I sighed. 'Why did you do it, Janto? Why did *we* do it?'

'Hm? You mean turn against our own coven?'

'Lyna and Melodia; they were our family.'

'Oh, closer than that. We three were one.'

'So why turn away? Why betray them and everything we were supposed to stand for?'

Janto crouched and began sifting through the stones. 'We've been alive a long time, Joe. I'm not sure anyone should live as long as we have. I began to search—really search—for the meaning of it all, and you know what I found?'

I shook my head as Janto stood, pebble in hand.

'Nothing. Just an endless expanse of indifferent nothingness. Life is empty. Worthless. Meaningless. Every life, from start to finish, is pointless. Existence is a joke, and I don't like the laughter being at my expense.'

Janto threw the pebble and I watched it skip four, five, six times.

'That was a good one,' he said.

'I think you're wrong.'

'Oh?'

'Life isn't nothing. It's everything. I look at that little girl of Annie's, so full of hope and possibility, and I see all the reason existence needs.'

Janto arched Myers' eyebrow. 'I suppose we're going to have to agree to disagree on that one.'

'So, how do we look?'

Janto turned and straightened out a crease in my jacket. 'We look ready to take our next step.'

I took a look around, surveying the horizon, and breathed in one last crisp, clean gulp of Cumbrian air while I was still me. Still Joseph Lake. Still, the daft man that did his best.

'It really is beautiful, this place,' I said, looking at the water, the mountains, the wonderful enormity of it all.

'More beautiful soon,' replied Janto.

'Okay then,' I said. 'Get on with it.'

Myers' eyes turned white as her hands gripped my face.

I was whole again.

And Joseph Lake was gone.

24

Actually, not quite.

After Janto left Myers' body and moved back into his own, I thought I'd be gone; that the two parts of me would meld together and become whole. I'd be Janto the warlock again, swamped and assimilated by the old me. A man destined to become the Magic Eater.

That's what I thought.

And that's what should have happened.

But instead, I, Joseph Lake, kept going. Kept thinking my thoughts and feeling my feelings, and didn't for one moment believe that turning into a giant monster with flames for skin and striding across the world bringing about pain, misery, and death was a nifty way to spend my twilight years.

Joseph Lake lived.

It was pitch black. Or I was blind. One of the two.

I tried to stand but wasn't sure if I was even sitting. Then I realised I wasn't even sure I had legs or feet to stand on.

Maybe I was nothing. Just thoughts. Alone with my thoughts for eternity. Bit grim.

'Swim down.'

The voice was distant. Maybe I just imagined it, so I

decided to imagine other things: things like having legs and walking and not being in the dark anymore. I concentrated on the idea of legs. Of motion. Of light. Concentrated like a motherflipper. And soon enough, the dark began to be, well, less dark.

'Here I go. Walky walk walk.'

Then there was too much light, and I screamed and shielded my eyes. As it turned out, I now had eyes and hands to shield them with.

How had this happened? Me still being aware? Joseph Lake, not Janto?

I was floating above a grimy alley, looking down at a woman crouched over a body. I recognised the woman. It was Detective Maya Myers. She was telling the man curled up at her feet that it was going to be okay. That help was coming. He just had to hang in there. But I could see what she was pretending not to: that the man had long since stopped hanging on.

Was this Myers' partner? The one she saw murdered in London? Was I seeing what Janto had been drawn to? The point he latched on to her and began to take control?

'Janto, come to us.'

It was the voice again. I knew the voice, because it belonged to family. It belonged to Lyna, one of the witches of the Cumbrian Coven.

'Janto,' said the other witch, Melodia, 'we need to talk.'

'My name isn't Janto. I'm not him. I'm not even nearly him. My name is Joseph Lake. I mop floors and mess with monsters, and I absolutely do not want to murder the entire planet, thank you very much.'

The world below me rushed past, streaking, sights and colours blurring. I could feel the wind in my hair, feel it vibrating my organs as I travelled at inhuman speed. I was dragged north. Dragged home.

I was in the Cumbrian Coven. I looked down and was

relieved to see that I had a body. Legs, torso, elbows, the whole shebang.

'Hello?'

There were two women sat by the fire.

'Welcome home, Joseph Lake,' said Lyna, smiling.

'What are you two, then?' I asked. 'Ghosts or memories?'

'Both, most likely,' replied Melodia.

'Well, thanks for not clearing that up.'

I looked around the coven's common room. It looked neater, more homely, than the room I was familiar with. No scorch marks on the walls, no battered, crack den-rejected couch.

'So, would either of you like to tell me what's going on?'

'You haven't been lost within Janto,' said Lyna.

'Instead, you are trapped inside yourself.'

'Oh. Sort of a good news/bad news deal,' I said.

'You may not have been assimilated into the whole, but Janto's consciousness is too big, too noisy, too powerful.'

'So I've been pushed aside, instead. Kicked into the attic, out of harm's way.'

'Exactly. And Eva calls you an idiot...' said Melodia.

'In her defence, I do a lot of idiotic things.'

'At first, you were what was left behind, but over time you became someone entirely new,' said Lyna.

'You became Joseph Lake. And as Joseph Lake was never part of the whole, never truly part of Janto, how could you become part of him now?'

'So, what you're saying is, I have a powerful, electric, alluring personality and I ain't no mo-fo's bitch?'

The two witches just looked at me.

'See,' I said, 'Eva really does have a point.'

I dragged an empty chair over and joined the witches by the fire. 'It's the three of us huddled inside the back room of Janto's mind from now on then, is it?'

'No,' said Lyna.

'No?'

'No,' repeated Melodia, 'because you're getting out.'

'Am I?'

'Unless you'd like to see the world stomped below the Magic Eater's cloven hoof?'

'Well, no. Ideally not.'

'Then you need to get out,' said Melodia, 'and you need to fight,'

'Win the battle for your own mind, Joseph.'

'That all sounds terrific. Just two teensy problems. One, I have no idea how to push him out, and two, even if I did, he'd just beat the shit out of me and climb back in. Otherwise, I'm fully on board with this little gambit.'

The witches stood and held hands.

'You just need to remember what we told you,' said Lyna.

'As for the rest? You're Joseph Lake. Last remaining witch of the Cumbrian Coven. You'll find a way,' said Melodia.

'Or you'll die trying,' added Lyna.

And then the two witches vanished.

'Good pep talk, ladies. I'm brim-full of confidence now. Yes, this is sarcasm.'

I blinked and I was no longer in the coven. I was outside. I recognised where I was. Bloody Derwentwater. It's always bloody Derwentwater.

I turned in a little circle as the wind whipped at the tails of my long coat. 'So, what now, exactly?'

I walked towards the water's edge and started to skip stones again. Maybe this wouldn't be so bad. I was alive... in a way. I had a world inside my own mind to explore. I was safe. I could just stay here, and maybe I'd be okay.

I sat with that idea for a little while as I threw stones at the water, watching them hop along the lake's surface. Of course, I knew there was no way I could actually do that. Hide in here and forget about whatever Janto was doing out in the real world. I pictured Millie, waving at me, a big grin on her face. I was Joseph Lake of the Cumbrian Coven. I may be an idiot, I may be ill-equipped to save anyone, I may have a weaker grasp of magic than a First-Year at Hogwarts, but there was no way I was going to let Millie, or any child, die without at least staging an entirely futile final stand.

I just had to remember what the witches told me. That's what Lyna had said. And I was pretty sure I knew what she meant.

I shrugged off my coat and yanked my boots from my feet, then I waded into Derwentwater, shivering as the cold water crept higher and higher up my body.

Swim down.

I took three breaths, and on the fourth, I held it and ducked beneath the surface. I kicked my legs and swept out my arms, driving down, down down.

Swim down, Janto.

I'm not Janto. I'm Joseph. Janto isn't me at all.

At all.

The world was turning black, but I kept on swimming. Kept on driving down and down, lungs burning, screaming, demanding I take a breath. Can a consciousness trapped within the walls of another's mind actually suffocate? Did I even need to breathe? Whatever passed as my lungs here seemed to think so.

Swim down.

How much longer could I go? Surely I'd hit bottom, hit dirt and rocks, and then what? My thoughts began to fuzz, but my body kept on kicking. I kept Millie in my mind's eye, smiling and waving, throwing breadcrumbs to the ducks.

And I swam down, down, down.

But it was no good.

I could feel myself breaking apart.

What passed for my body, my limbs, my bones, it was all coming loose.

Becoming a sandcastle against the tide.

Not a person.

Only the idea of a person.

Swim down.

I'd tried, but it was for nothing. A fruitless last stand, after all. I closed my eyes and wondered what would happen next.

What happened next, was that I felt a small hand inside mine. A small, furry hand.

My eyes opened and I saw a figure stood on the lake bed, reaching up to me and pulling me down.

Hello, fox.

Hello, saviour.

25

Things went a bit wibbly-wobbly at that point. I know that's not exactly the clearest of descriptions, narratively speaking, but it's the best I have.

I was underwater, looking down at the fox as his paw gripped my hand and he pulled me to him, and then it's as if there were an explosion and a rush of sights, smells, and sounds. Everything seemed to twist in on itself, over and over, until reality folded and stretched and spiralled. And then everything stopped and I let loose a bowel-shaking, high-pitched scream.

Once I was done with that, I caught my breath and pushed myself upright on trembling legs. The grass beneath my feet was blood-red, and smeared crimson on my trousers, on my boots. The sky above me roared with furious flames.

I was in the Dark Lakes. But was I in the *Dark Lakes*-Dark Lakes, or was I in a version of the Dark Lakes inside my own mind?

'Hi,' said the fox.

I spun to see the little guy, Roman helmet on his head, axe gripped in his paws.

'Is this...?' I pointed around me wildly, at the red grass, at the fiery sky, at the distant mounds of bones. 'Is this real? Am I here, or in here?' I tapped at my head.

'You are in the Dark Lakes. You have pushed out the other one.'

'I have?'

The fox nodded. 'I helped.'

'How did you do that, exactly?'

'My whole purpose for the last decade has been to find you. To know where you are.'

'Yes, but I was inside my own brain. I was just thoughts and a personality kicking around some grey matter.'

The fox shrugged. 'I am brave and clever and resourceful, and I can find you wherever you might be.'

I tried to reply. Then I tried to say thank you. Then I gave up, picked him up, and hugged him.

'I'm not sure this is proper,' said the fox.

'Thank you for coming to get me.'

'You're welcome.'

'I told you, didn't I?' said the Red Woman.

I turned to see her leaning against the throne. My throne. A throne fashioned from human skulls.

The Red Woman went on. 'I told you something was happening, something that would bring you back here to take your throne and become the Magic Eater.'

'Well, tough luck,' I said, 'because I just beat the twat who wanted that.'

The Red Woman laughed. 'No, I don't think so.'

I didn't like the sound of that. 'What are you talking about?'

'Perhaps put me down now,' suggested the fox, who I was still holding in my arms.

'Right, yep, sorry.' I crouched down, placing him back on the red grass.

'You think because you pushed your dark side out that it's all over?' asked the Red Woman. 'You underestimate yourself.'

I looked to the fox. 'She's lying, isn't she? It's done, right?'

'No. The Red Woman does not lie.'

The Red Woman straightened up and walked towards me, her eyes dreamy, seductive. 'You pushed poor Janto out, but that's all you did. He'll be reclaiming what's rightfully his, and soon.'

That seemed like my cue to get a very long way away from the creepy hill with the blood-red grass.

'In fact,' said Detective Myers, stepping into view as she reached the hill's summit, 'that'll be happening very soon.'

Janto had somehow reclaimed Myers' body and followed me here. So this had probably all been nothing but a pointless, momentary delay. Smashing.

'Janto,' said the Red Woman, cupping Myers' face in her hands and pressing her lips against hers. 'So good to have the real you back in the Dark Lakes.'

'I told you I'd take the throne,' replied Janto. 'That I would fulfil my destiny and lead an army of the dead from the Dark Lakes; become the beast, the Magic Eater, with you as my bride.'

'Sir,' said the fox, tugging at my sleeve, 'perhaps it is time to run? I can do my best to aid you.'

'Thanks,' I said, 'but what's the point? Wherever I go, he'll find me. Sooner or later I'll end up back on this hill.'

'You're not wrong,' said Janto. 'I have to say, you surprised me with your strength of will. I thought we would become one again. I wasn't expecting you to stage a coup inside my brain.'

'I'm not you. Not anymore. Janto the Warlock? That isn't me. I'm Joseph Lake.'

'Not for much longer,' said the Red Woman, resting her head on Myers' shoulder, hands wrapped around her waist.

'Just take the throne if that's what you want!' I cried. 'It's right there; just have a seat!'

'I can't,' replied Janto.

'He cannot claim the throne in any person's body but his own,' said the Red Woman.

'Then you're out of luck,' I said, 'because the moment you jump in me, I'll push you right back out again.'

'No, you won't,' replied Janto.

'And why's that?'

Janto pulled out a large knife and pressed it to his neck; to Myers' neck.

'Don't hurt her!'

The Red Woman stroked the blade, the point pressing against Myers' jugular, hard enough to break the skin and draw a small red bead of blood.

'I won't hurt her, Joseph, I'll fucking kill her. If you refuse me or reject me, she's a dead woman.'

I didn't know what to do, what to say. I watched as the knife was pushed harder, sending a trickle of blood running down Myers' neck.

'Try to refuse me, I'll kill her. Push me out? I'll kill her.'

'What a bind this is, Joseph,' said the Red Woman, bending to lick the blood from Myers' neck.

There must be something I could do. There had to be.

The fox frowned and bowed his head. 'I am sorry that I helped her. I am so sorry.'

I had no moves, no options. I had to agree to save Myers. It may only save her for a short time, but maybe... maybe I would think of something. Maybe, like the witches coming to me, there was another twist to come, and everything would be okay.

You never know.

'Okay,' I said. 'I'll take the throne.'

Janto smiled and removed the knife from Myers' neck. 'This was always where we were meant to end up, Joseph. Our fate. Don't feel bad, you can't prevent fate. No one can.'

And then came the twist.

'Fate never met me, fuck face.'

Eva Familiar appeared over the crest of the hill, a can of strong lager in her hand.

'Eva, I thought...' I started, but I was so shocked, so happy to see her, that I wasn't able to finish.

'Don't get mushy on me, idiot,' she said, but she smiled as she said it.

'I thought you'd gone, Eva,' said Janto. 'Ran away like a scared little child.'

'Only a fool isn't scared sometimes, Janto,' she replied, crouching and running her hand through the blood-red grass. 'Walking through this shit must be murder; having to constantly wash out the stains.'

'Are you going to try and kill me again, Eva?' asked my evil counterpart.

'Thought I'd have another crack at it, yeah,' she replied, standing up and wiping her bloody hand on her coat.

'Last time you had a weapon that Lyna and Melodia conjured for you. This time you have nothing. I don't think this is going to go well for you.'

'Probably not, but fuck it. You're a twat, and twats get slaps.'

'You're not welcome in my world, familiar,' said the Red Woman, stepping towards Eva.

'I go where I want, you skinny, sexy bitch.'

Eva clapped her hands together and thrust out a fist. The Red Woman's eyes bulged in surprise as she was lifted from her feet.

'How dare you!'

'I know, aren't I a total bastard?'

The Red Woman opened her mouth to speak again but was whipped back and away, sailing out over the horizon as though a giant had tossed her in the air and struck her with a bat.

'Well, that's one done with,' said Eva. 'Gives us time to end this whole saga before the bitch finds her way back.' She pulled out her tobacco tin, retrieved a smoke, and popped it between her lips.

Janto strode towards her. 'Very well, Eva, spit from my

mouth; I brought you into this world, and now I will take you from it.'

'Come get me.'

Eva ran at Janto, right fist raised. The hand began to blur, just as it had back at the coven when Myers was strapped to the bed. Her hand ghosted straight into Myers' head, and Eva fell back, pulling something from the detective's body as she did so. Something dark that writhed and shuddered. Was that Janto? Was that what had become of him?

Eva grimaced and shoved the thing inside her belly before collapsing on the red grass, gasping for air.

'Shit,' I said. 'Shitting hell.'

I darted over to Detective Myers, who had crumpled to the ground like a marionette whose strings had been cut. 'Myers? Can you hear me?'

She was unconscious but alive.

'That really fucking hurt.' said Eva, propping herself up on her elbows.

'What did you do?' I asked.

'Told you. I can uproot something that's set up shop inside a person, so I pulled that fucker out of your detective friend and stuck him into me. I can feel him wriggling about in there, and not in a good way.'

She stood and made her way over to the fox, who snarled and brandished his axe. 'I remember you,' she said.

'And I know you,' the fox replied.

'It's okay, Eva,' I said. 'He's my friend.'

The fox grinned.

'Hey, who you choose to mix with is up to you,' said Eva.

'I am a good fox, now,' said the fox.

'So this is what all the fuss is about,' said Eva, walking over to the skull throne. 'Bit tacky.'

'Eva,' I said, 'your nose.'

She sniffed and ran a coat sleeve across her nostrils, wiping away the blood that was dripping from it. 'He's really fighting in there,' she said. 'It won't take him long to get out. You remember those fairies I had in the fridge?'

I nodded.

'I munched down a sewer full of them to power up for this awesome final stand, but even with all that extra juice, he'll bust out in a minute, tops.'

'Why did you come back?' I asked.

'Maybe you're not the only stupid one.'

'Did you listen to my message?'

Eva tried to walk over to me, but she stumbled and fell to one knee.

'Eva!'

'Stay back. It's okay, I have a plan.'

'Okay. That's good. That sounds good.'

'It's a really good plan. A bit of a downer for me personally, though.'

'Why.'

'Kamikaze, bitch,' she said, pulling out a knife and aiming it at her heart.

'Eva, what are you doing?' I cried.

'I need to kill him, Joe, and the only way to do that is to make him physical, then kill the body. Unfortunately, I'm the body. I'm the only one who can hold him long enough to do it.'

'It won't work,' I said. 'He was going to kill Myers while he was inside her. He held a knife to her neck.'

'He was bluffing, love.'

Bluffing. He was stuck and he tricked me.

'Okay then, gotta do this now,' said Eva. 'No time to waste.'

'No, there must be another way!'

She smiled at me and shrugged. 'There isn't. Wish there was.'

I yelled out as Eva tensed and thrust the blade at her heart, but it didn't happen. She struggled and screamed with the effort, but the knife wouldn't enter her.

'Eva?'

'Can't... he's too strong... he's stopping me...'

She was trembling all over, blood pouring from her nose, her ears, even her eyes. 'Die, you fuck!' she screamed, but her body bucked and fought and refused.

'We'll find another way!' I said, dropping to my knees beside her.

What way? Was there another way? I just couldn't lose her. We were family.

'This is the way. This is it, Joe!'

She took my hand in hers and pulled it towards the handle of the knife.

'Push, Joe.'

'No.'

'Push!

She wanted me to kill her.

'Do it, Joe. Do it! Kill him!'

I looked at the knife, Eva's hand gripping mine.

'I can't.'

'You have to. You have to be the hero here, Joe, I've done all I can.'

Eva screamed, her head dropping. She was fighting like a lion. I could only imagine the pain she was going through, and there I was, on my knees, as weak as I'd ever felt.

'I can't hold him!' She was terrified. But not because she was about to die, but because *he* was about to escape. About to burst free and become something unstoppable. The Magic Eater. Hell on Earth.

I leaned forward, both hands on the butt of the knife. I could do this. I had to. I had to kill her. I had to kill Eva. Kill her, kill Janto.

I tried, I screamed, willing myself to do it, but still, the knife didn't move. Didn't thrust into her chest.

'You have to, love.'

Tears blurred my vision. 'I don't want to lose you.'

'I don't matter.'

'You're wrong!'

I felt a hand rest upon my shoulder. 'Saviour, step aside.'

I looked back to see the fox, battle-axe at the ready.

'Do it!' screamed Eva.

The fox looked to me.

'Now! Kill me now!'

'It would be my honour,' said the fox.

He raised his weapon high above his head, and I saw the flames that rolled across the sky reflected on its double-headed blade.

I looked at Eva, and she looked back at me. I knew what was right. It had to be me. Had to be.

'No,' I told the fox. 'I have to do this.'

'Second time's the charm,' said Eva, smiling, blood on her teeth.

I wouldn't defer to the fox to help me out again. To do the dirty work. I'd brought Eva into this world, and if she was going to do the bravest thing imaginable, I should be brave enough to do as she asked.

So I gripped the handle of the knife.

'Let's end this bastard,' she said.

I nodded. 'Together. Together, we win.'

'A pair of bad motherfuckers.'

Eva let go of the handle, spreading her arms wide.

And the blade slid into her heart.

26

Three days passed before I could bring myself to bury Eva.

I sat with her body the whole time, just me and her in the coven, waiting for her to open her eyes at last and call me names. Yell at me to get her a beer out of the fridge, and tell me about the secret trick she'd had up her sleeve all along. The one that allowed her to cheat death.

But she didn't open her eyes.

She didn't call me names.

She didn't stop being dead.

So I dug a hole next to the coven and placed Eva inside. I shovelled dirt on her body and sat a stone on top to mark the spot.

Myers and I pulled chairs outside and sat by the grave. We didn't talk for a long time, just sat and drank, and let the silence wrap around us.

Finally, Myers put down her empty can and stood, walking over to the grave.

'You know, sometimes I still feel like he's in there,' she said, tapping at her head. 'It's like I can feel scars he left behind.'

'He was part of you for a long time,' I said.

'I'll never have the words to thank you properly,' said Myers, as I stood and joined her, looking down at the stone sat atop the freshly-turned soil.

'They're not needed,' I replied.

Myers hugged me, then kissed me once on the lips.

'You're leaving, aren't you?'

She nodded. 'I only came up here because of him. Because of Janto. I don't belong here. I want to go home.'

Go home. Back to London. Another one, gone.

I wanted to talk her out of it. Persuade her to stay here, stay with me, carry on fighting the good fight. But I didn't. I just nodded and hugged her again, then watched as she walked away.

So now it was just me.

I crouched and brushed my hand gently over the soil. 'Thanks, Eva. Thanks for everything.'

I looked up. A bird was circling above. Its feathers were black, its wings huge.

'I'll never believe you're really gone. Really dead. You're too much of a hard-nosed bastard to let something as ordinary as death take you.' I brushed away the tear that was rolling down my cheek, then sipped at my drink. 'You know, you always bought really disgusting beer.'

The chill night air brushed my skin as I stood and I hugged myself, shivering.

It was time to become the witch I should have been. I'd study the books, I'd practice all the hours available to me, and I'd make her proud. I'd keep people safe. Because I'm not Janto the Magic Eater, I'm Joseph Lake of the Cumbrian Coven, guardian of the Lake District.

A small figure stepped in beside me, axe in one hand, a bundle of possessions in the other. He took off his helmet and looked down at Eva's grave.

'I don't want to be in the Dark Lakes anymore,' he said, 'and I don't think the Red Woman wants me there, either.'

I nodded and ruffled the fur atop his head.

Maybe I wouldn't be entirely alone after all.

'Come along, fox,' I said.

He smiled up at me with his sharp little teeth, and we walked into the coven together.

LEAVE A REVIEW

Reviews are gold to indie authors, so if you've enjoyed this collection, please consider visiting the site you bought it to rate and review.

MORE STORIES SET IN THE UNCANNY KINGDOM

The Spectral Detective Series

Spectral Detective

Corpse Reviver

Twice Damned

Necessary Evil

The London Coven Series

Familiar Magic

Nightmare Realm

Deadly Portent

The Branded Series

Sanctified

Turned

Bloodline

The Hexed Detective Series

Hexed Detective

Fatal Moon

Night Terrors

The Uncanny Ink Series
Bad Soul
Bad Blood
Bad Justice
Bad Intention
Bad Thoughts
Bad Memories

The Myth Management Series
Myth Management

BECOME AN INSIDER